SPAC
MOUNTAIN

DISNEY COMICS PROUDLY PRESENTS

SPACE MOUNTAIN

Based on an idea by MICHAEL SIGLAIN

Inspired by WALT DISNEY'S TOMORROWLAND ATTRACTIONS

Story by MICHAEL SIGLAIN, BRYAN Q. MILLER,

and KELLEY JONES

Written by BRYAN Q. MILLER

Pencils and Inks by KELLEY JONES

Letters by ROB LEIGH

Colors by HI-FI DESIGN

Cover by KELLEY JONES and BRIAN MILLER

SPECIAL THANKS TO WALT DISNEY IMAGINEERING

DISNEY PRESS

NEW YORK • LOS ANGELES

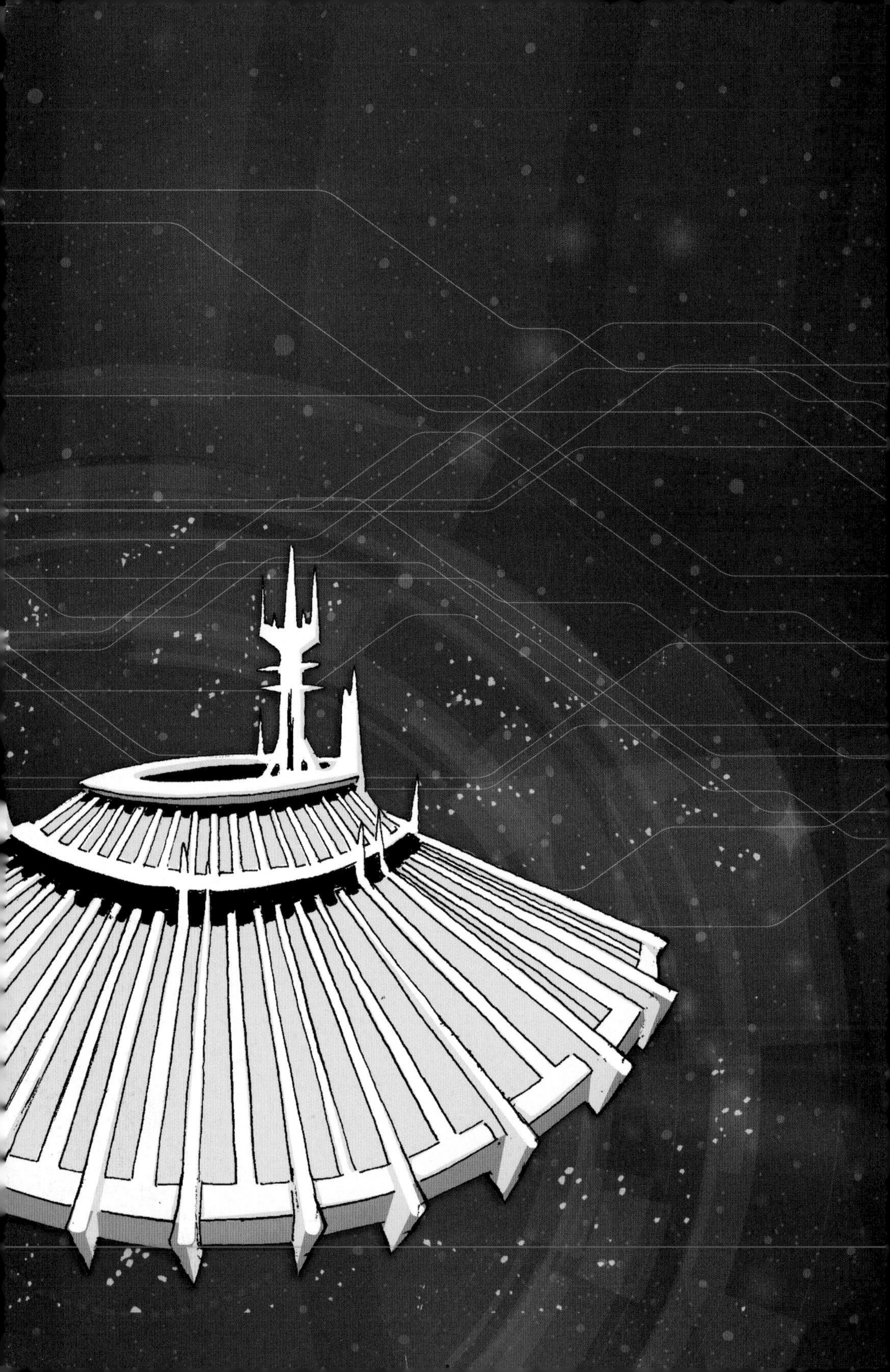

Disney Comics

SPACE MOUNTAIN

*In memory of Leslie Nielsen, Ralph McQuarrie, Ray Bradbury, Neil Armstrong,
Stuart Freeborn, and Ray Harryhausen, all of whom passed during the making
of this book, all of whom influenced the people who made this book.
(Look 'em up if you don't know 'em. . . . You'll be thankful you did!)*

𝒟𝒾𝓈𝓃𝑒𝔂 PRESS

NEW YORK • LOS ANGELES

An Imprint of Disney Book Group

Printed in United States of America

First Edition

978-1-4231-6229-2

For more Disney Press fun, visit www.disneybooks.com

SUSTAINABLE FORESTRY INITIATIVE

Certified Chain of Custody
At Least 20% Certified Forest Content
www.sfiprogram.org
SFI-00993

For Text Only

CONTENTS

CHAPTER ZERO: ONCE UPON A TIME . . . 7

PART ONE: THE LIVING BLUEPRINT
    OF THE FUTURE 21

CHAPTER ONE: TO INFINITY AND BEWARE 23

CHAPTER TWO: TIME-TRAVEL TUTORIALS 37

CHAPTER THREE: TOMORROW IS TODAY 51

PART TWO: THE FUTURE THAT NEVER WAS
    IS FINALLY HERE 65

CHAPTER FOUR: SABOTAGE IN SPACE 67

CHAPTER FIVE: IMPOSSIBLE RESCUE 81

CHAPTER SIX: CHILD'S PLAY 95

PART THREE: BACK TO THE FUTURE 109

CHAPTER SEVEN: SEEMS LIKE OLD TIMES 111

CHAPTER EIGHT: TIME-TUNNEL TRAVELS 125

CHAPTER NINE: TOMORROW ARRIVES TODAY 139

EPILOGUE: PAST IMPERFECT 153

THE ONLY REASON FOR TIME
IS SO THAT EVERYTHING
DOESN'T HAPPEN AT ONCE.
—ALBERT EINSTEIN

CHAPTER ZERO:
ONCE UPON A TIME...

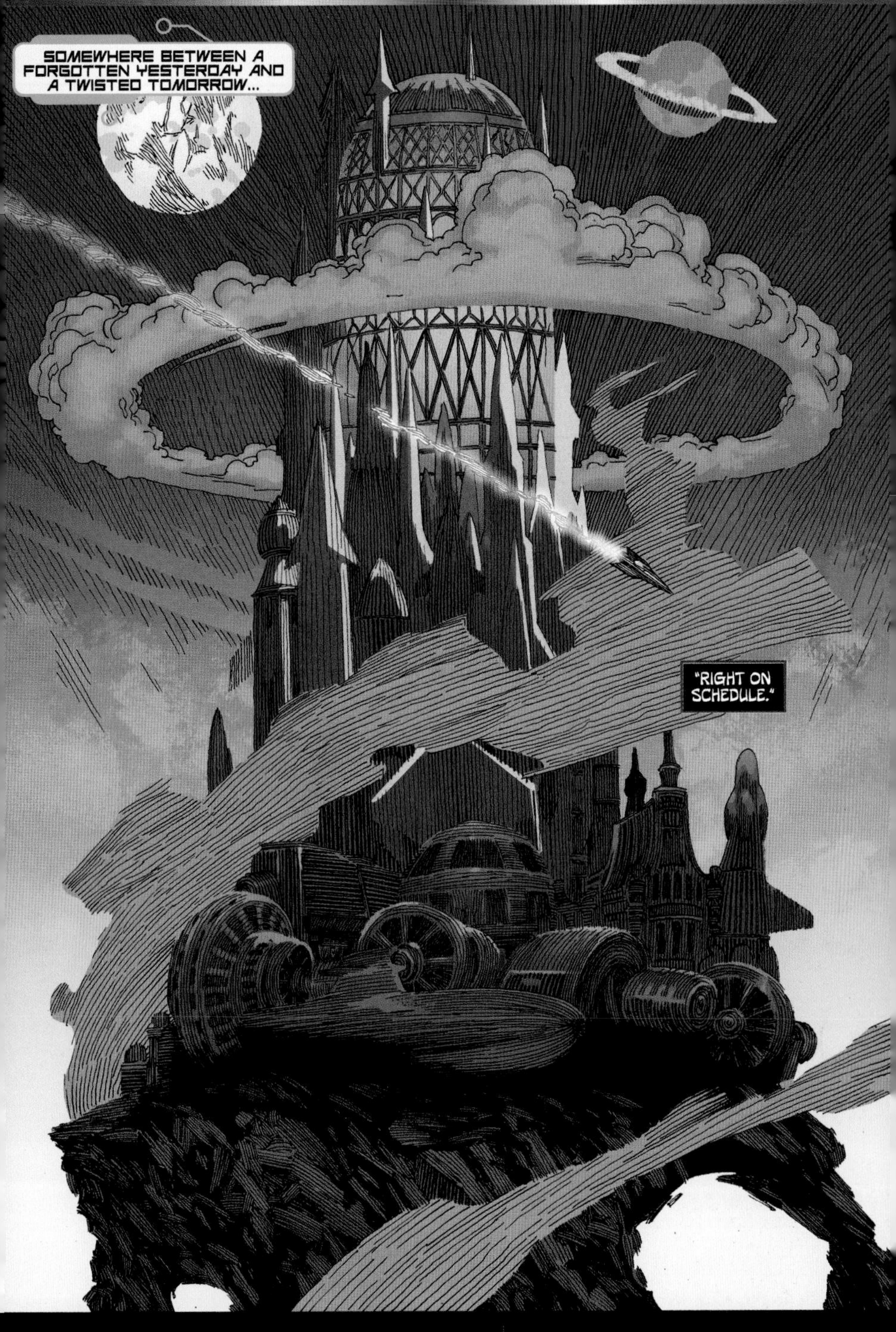
SOMEWHERE BETWEEN A FORGOTTEN YESTERDAY AND A TWISTED TOMORROW...
"RIGHT ON SCHEDULE."

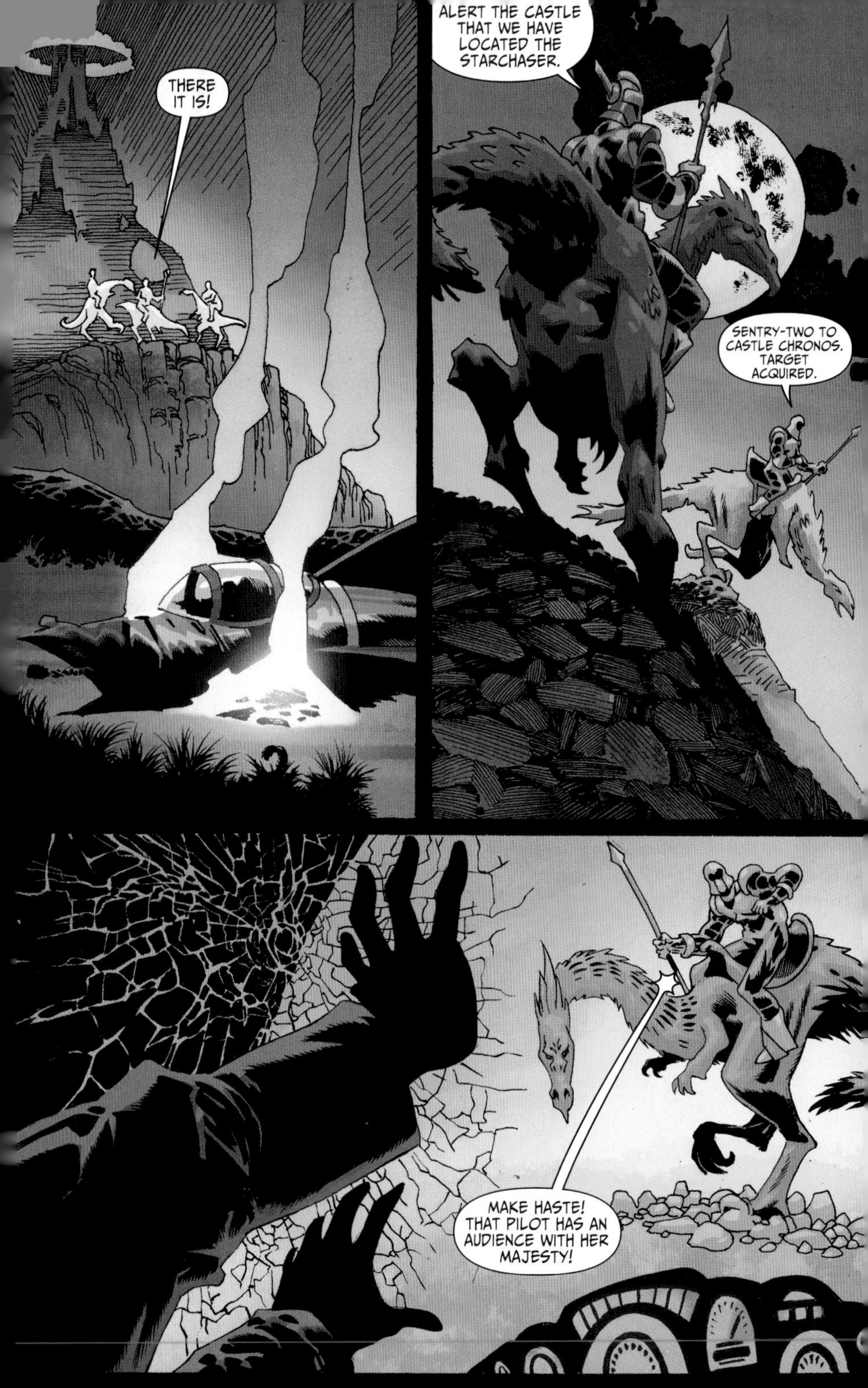
THERE IT IS!
ALERT THE CASTLE THAT WE HAVE LOCATED THE STARCHASER.
SENTRY-TWO TO CASTLE CHRONOS. TARGET ACQUIRED.
MAKE HASTE! THAT PILOT HAS AN AUDIENCE WITH HER MAJESTY!

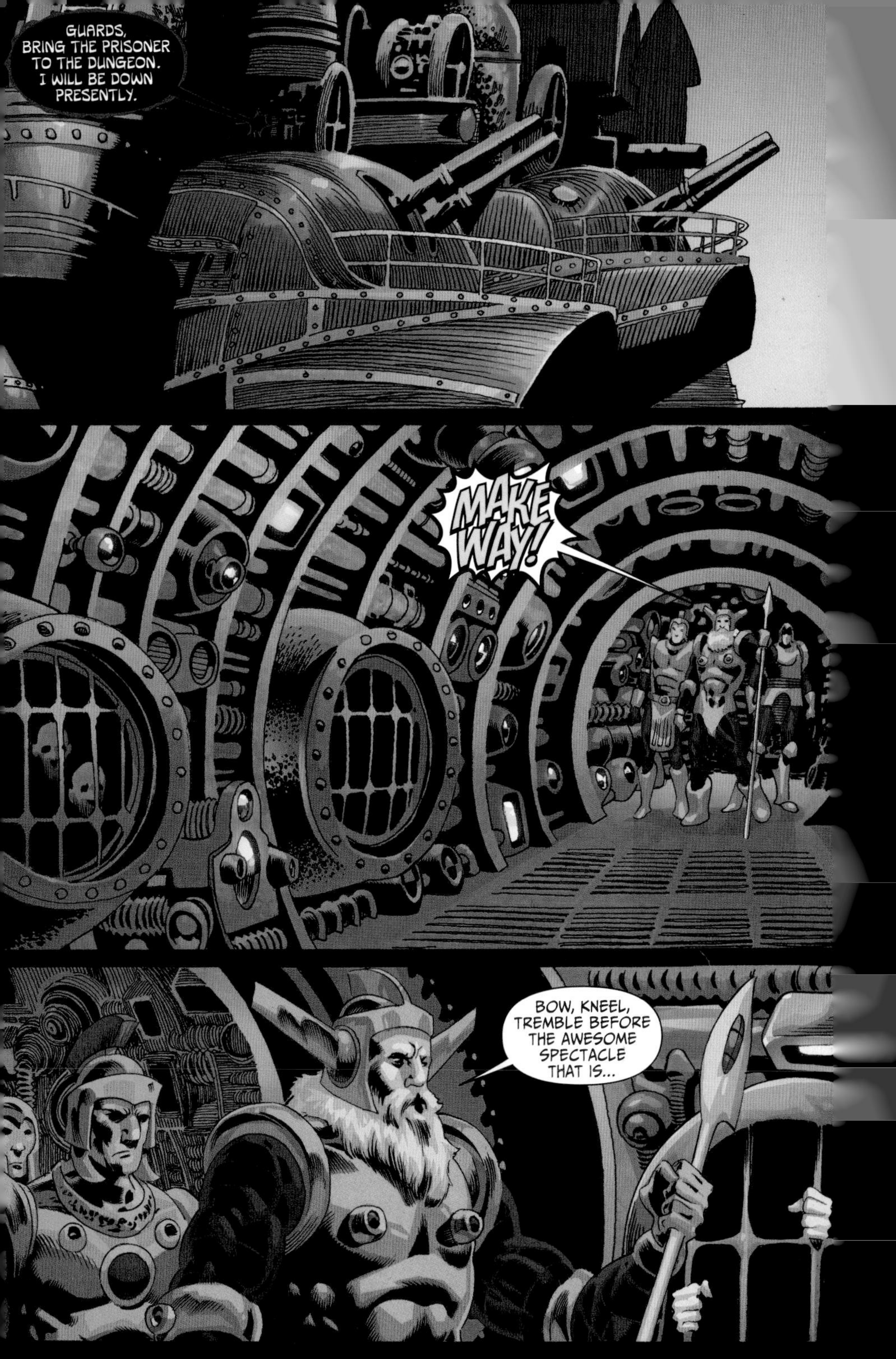
GUARDS, BRING THE PRISONER TO THE DUNGEON. I WILL BE DOWN PRESENTLY.
MAKE WAY!
BOW, KNEEL, TREMBLE BEFORE THE AWESOME SPECTACLE THAT IS...

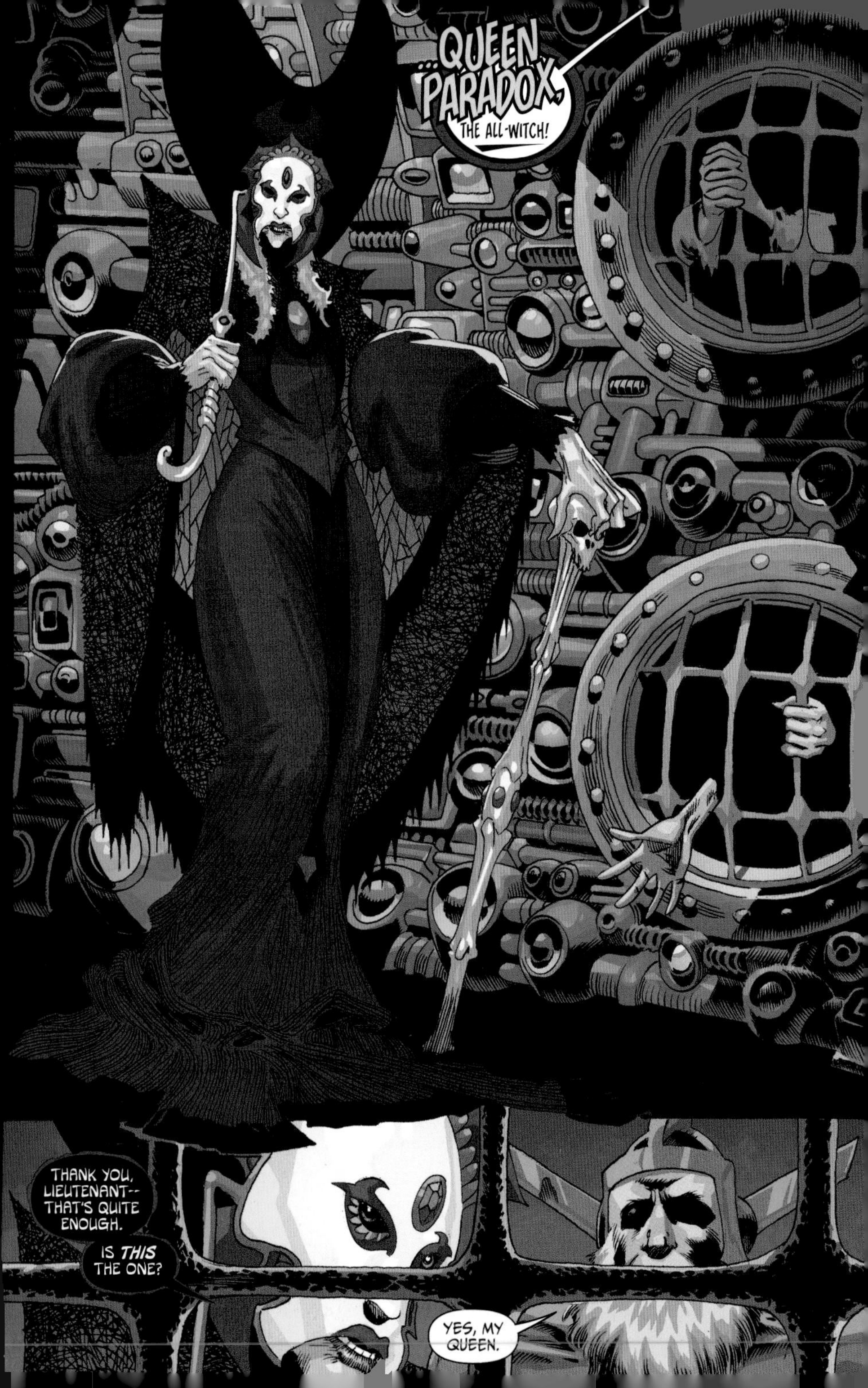
...QUEEN PARADOX, THE ALL-WITCH!
THANK YOU, LIEUTENANT-- THAT'S QUITE ENOUGH.
IS THIS THE ONE?
YES, MY QUEEN.

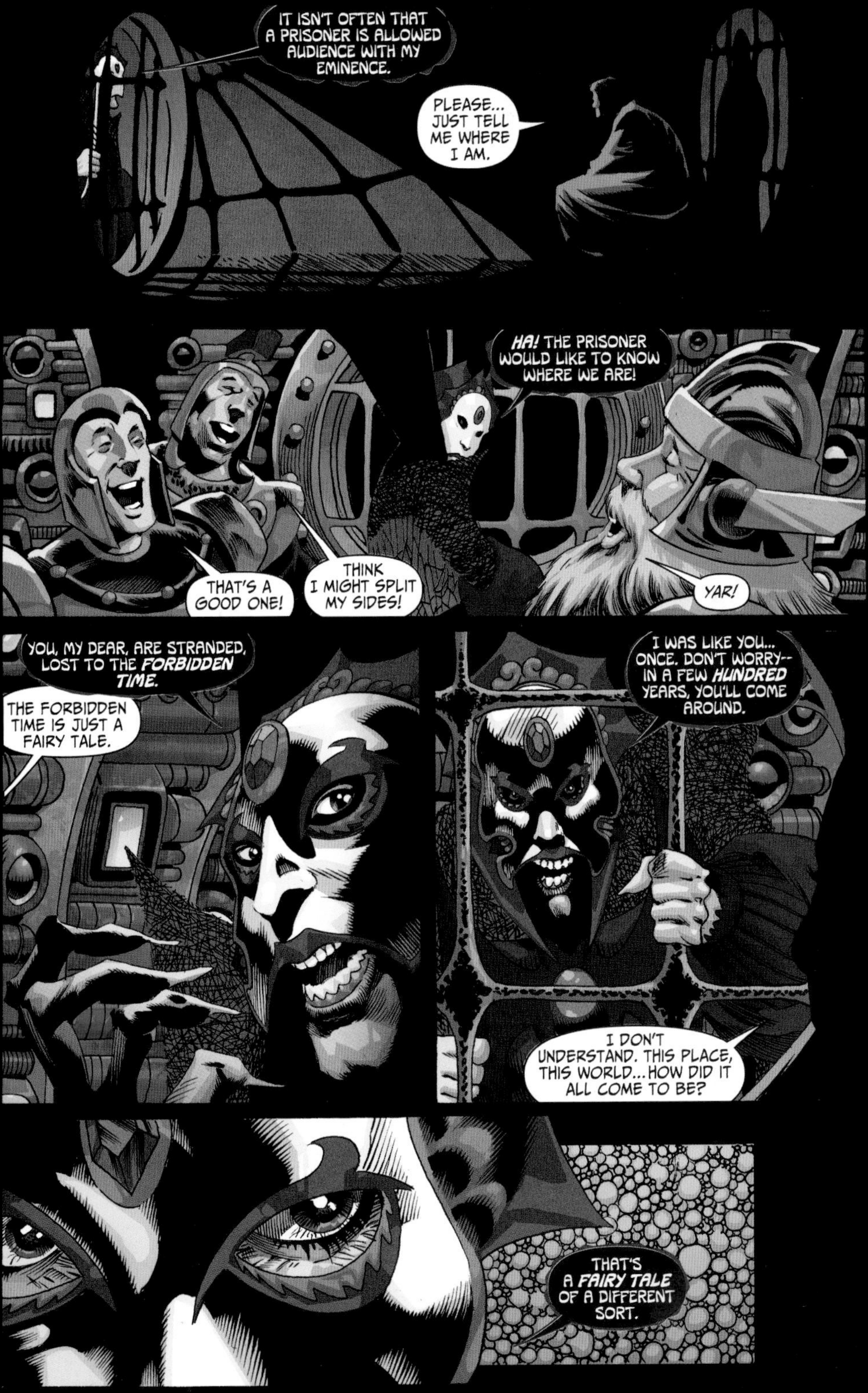
IT ISN'T OFTEN THAT A PRISONER IS ALLOWED AUDIENCE WITH MY EMINENCE.
PLEASE... JUST TELL ME WHERE I AM.
HA! THE PRISONER WOULD LIKE TO KNOW WHERE WE ARE!
THAT'S A GOOD ONE!
THINK I MIGHT SPLIT MY SIDES!
YAR!
YOU, MY DEAR, ARE STRANDED, LOST TO THE FORBIDDEN TIME.
THE FORBIDDEN TIME IS JUST A FAIRY TALE.
I WAS LIKE YOU... ONCE. DON'T WORRY-- IN A FEW HUNDRED YEARS, YOU'LL COME AROUND.
I DON'T UNDERSTAND. THIS PLACE, THIS WORLD... HOW DID IT ALL COME TO BE?
THAT'S A FAIRY TALE OF A DIFFERENT SORT.

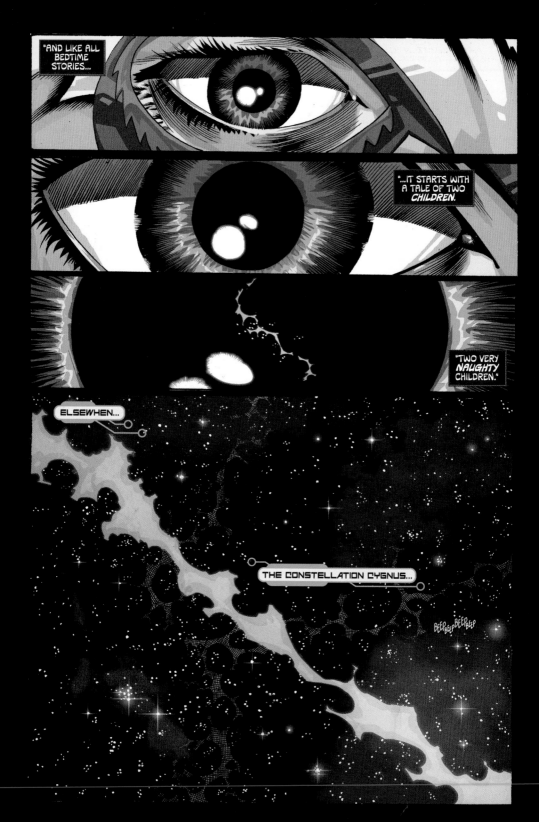

"AND LIKE ALL BEDTIME STORIES...

"...IT STARTS WITH A TALE OF TWO *CHILDREN*.

"TWO VERY *NAUGHTY* CHILDREN."

ELSEWHEN...

THE CONSTELLATION CYGNUS...

BEEP BEEP BEEP BEEP

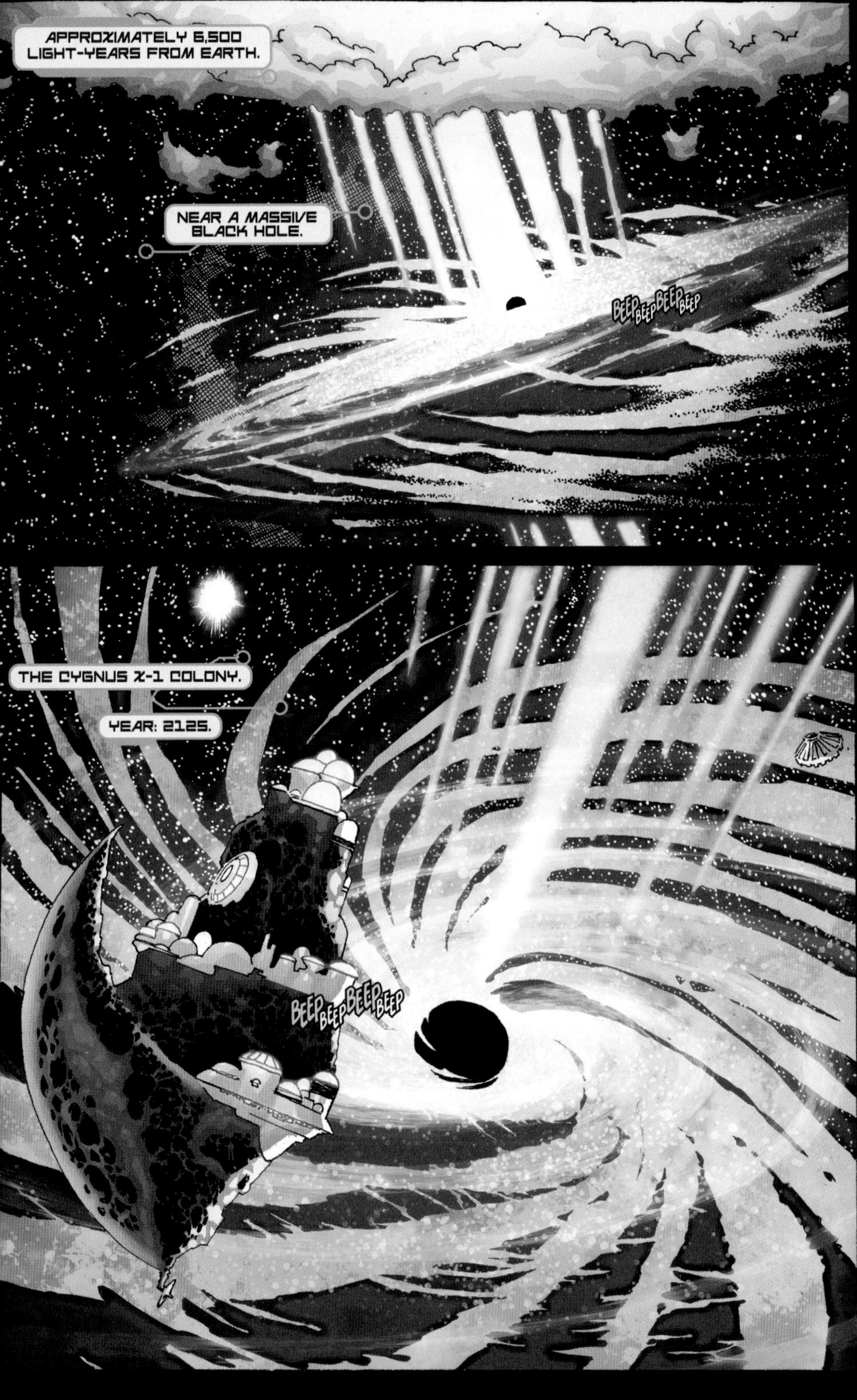
APPROXIMATELY 6,500 LIGHT-YEARS FROM EARTH.
NEAR A MASSIVE BLACK HOLE.
BEEP BEEP BEEP BEEP
THE CYGNUS X-1 COLONY.
YEAR: 2125.
BEEP BEEP BEEP BEEP

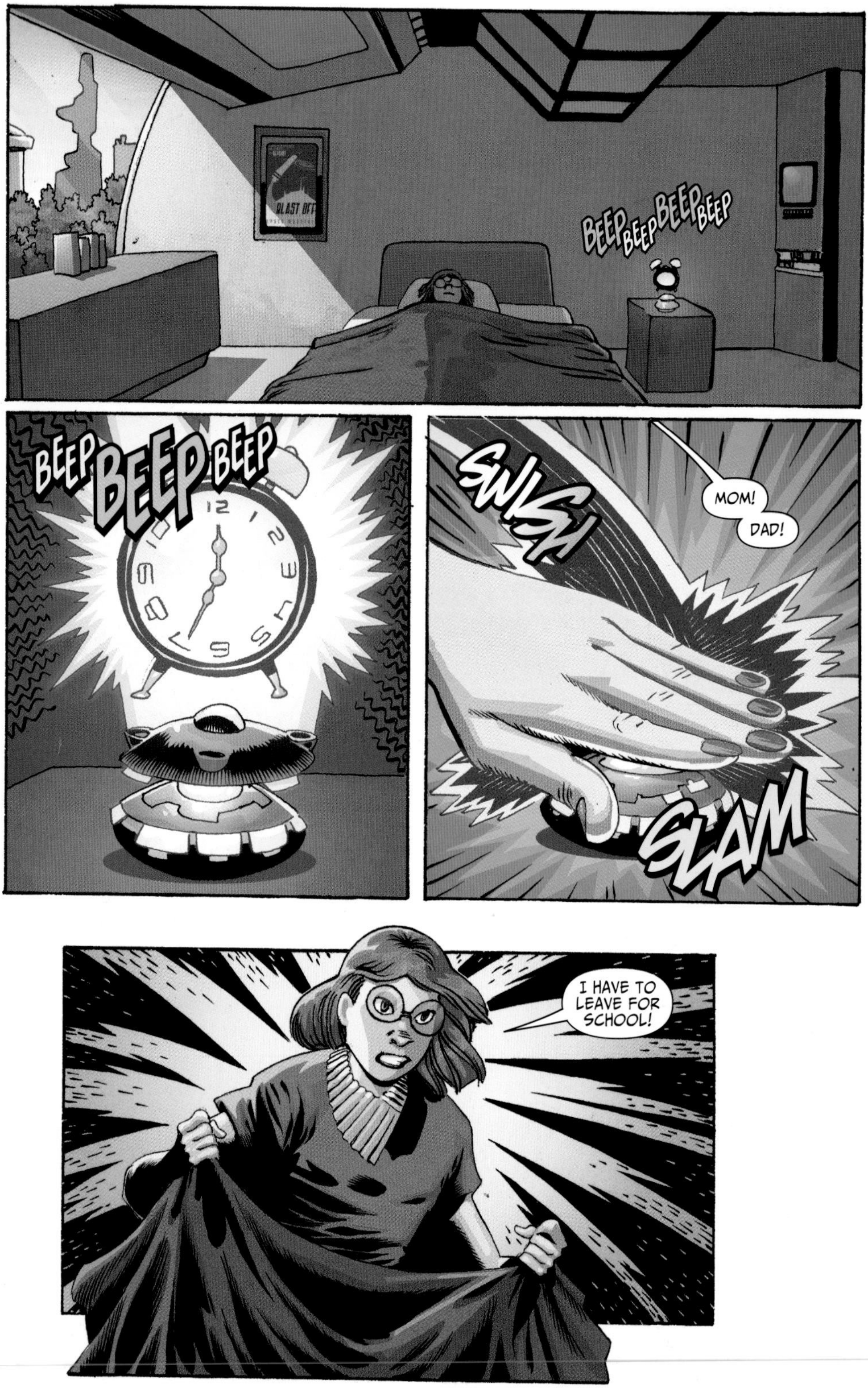
BLAST OFF
BEEP BEEP BEEP BEEP
BEEP BEEP BEEP
SWISH
MOM!
DAD!
SLAM
I HAVE TO LEAVE FOR SCHOOL!

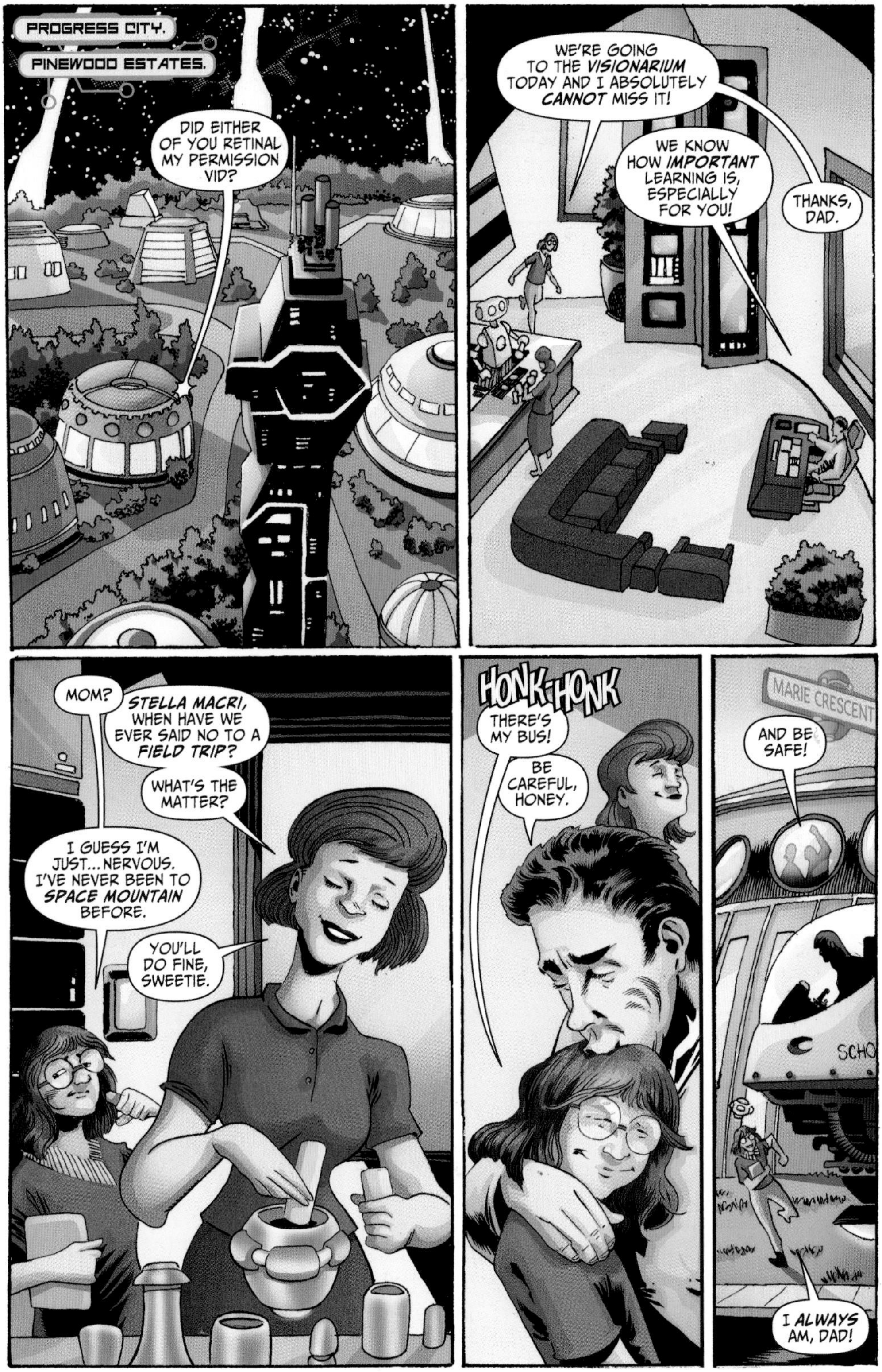
PROGRESS CITY.
PINEWOOD ESTATES.
DID EITHER OF YOU RETINAL MY PERMISSION VID?
WE'RE GOING TO THE *VISIONARIUM* TODAY AND I ABSOLUTELY *CANNOT* MISS IT!
WE KNOW HOW *IMPORTANT* LEARNING IS, ESPECIALLY FOR YOU!
THANKS, DAD.
MOM?
STELLA MACRI, WHEN HAVE WE EVER SAID NO TO A *FIELD TRIP?*
WHAT'S THE MATTER?
I GUESS I'M JUST...NERVOUS. I'VE NEVER BEEN TO *SPACE MOUNTAIN* BEFORE.
YOU'LL DO FINE, SWEETIE.
HONK-HONK
THERE'S MY BUS!
BE CAREFUL, HONEY.
MARIE CRESCENT
AND BE SAFE!
SCHO
I *ALWAYS* AM, DAD!

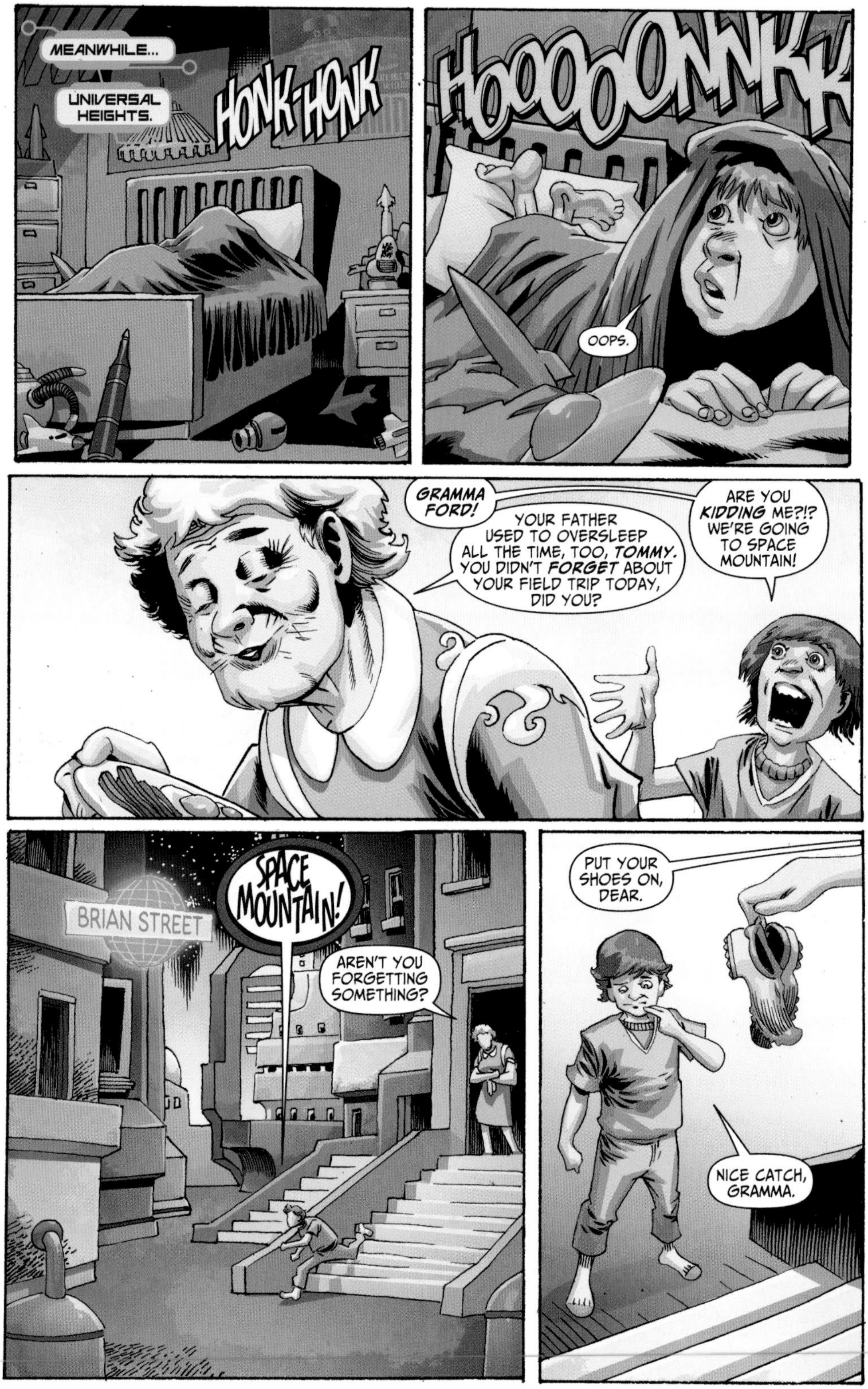
MEANWHILE...
UNIVERSAL HEIGHTS.
HONK-HONK
HOOOOONNKK
OOPS.
GRAMMA FORD!
YOUR FATHER USED TO OVERSLEEP ALL THE TIME, TOO, TOMMY. YOU DIDN'T FORGET ABOUT YOUR FIELD TRIP TODAY, DID YOU?
ARE YOU KIDDING ME?!? WE'RE GOING TO SPACE MOUNTAIN!
BRIAN STREET
SPACE MOUNTAIN!
AREN'T YOU FORGETTING SOMETHING?
PUT YOUR SHOES ON, DEAR.
NICE CATCH, GRAMMA.

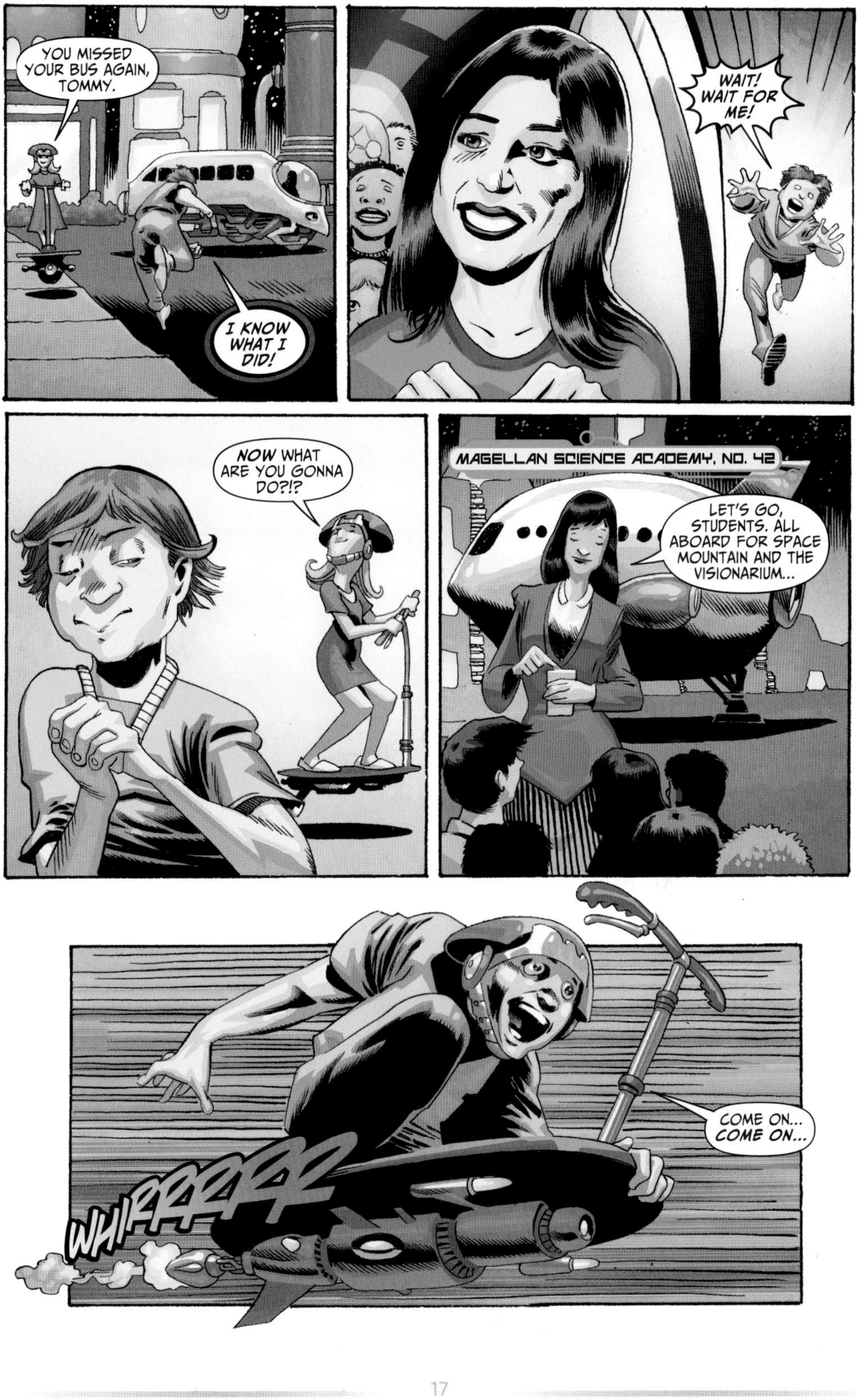
YOU MISSED YOUR BUS AGAIN, TOMMY.
I KNOW WHAT I DID!
WAIT! WAIT FOR ME!
NOW WHAT ARE YOU GONNA DO?!?
MAGELLAN SCIENCE ACADEMY, NO. 42
LET'S GO, STUDENTS. ALL ABOARD FOR SPACE MOUNTAIN AND THE VISIONARIUM...
COME ON... COME ON...
WHIRRRRRR

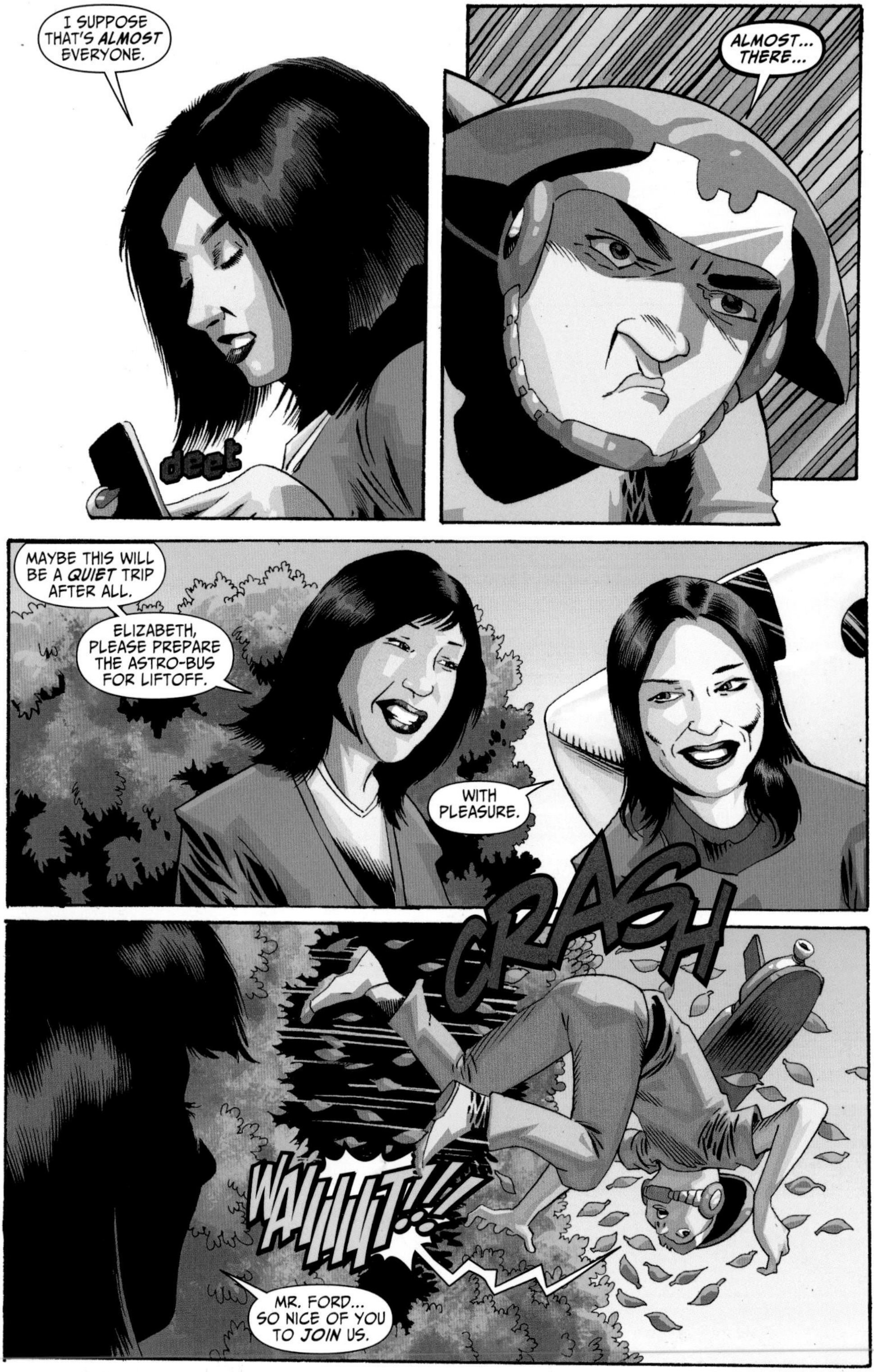

I SUPPOSE THAT'S *ALMOST* EVERYONE.
deet
ALMOST... THERE...
MAYBE THIS WILL BE A *QUIET* TRIP AFTER ALL.
ELIZABETH, PLEASE PREPARE THE ASTRO-BUS FOR LIFTOFF.
WITH PLEASURE.
CRASH
WAIIIIIIT!!!
MR. FORD... SO NICE OF YOU TO *JOIN* US.

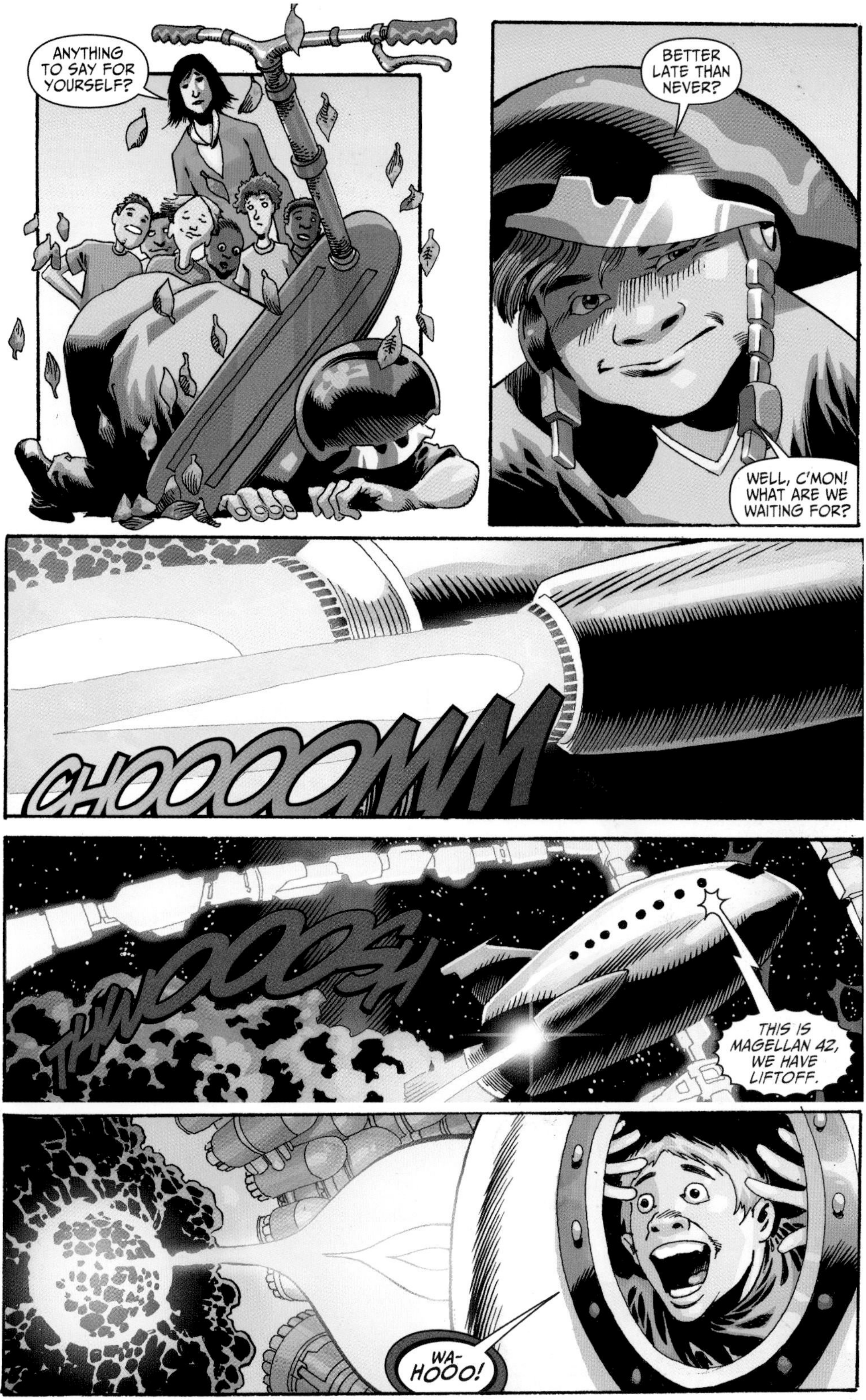
ANYTHING TO SAY FOR YOURSELF?
BETTER LATE THAN NEVER?
WELL, C'MON! WHAT ARE WE WAITING FOR?
CHOOOOMM
THWOOOSH
THIS IS MAGELLAN 42, WE HAVE LIFTOFF.
WA-HOOO!

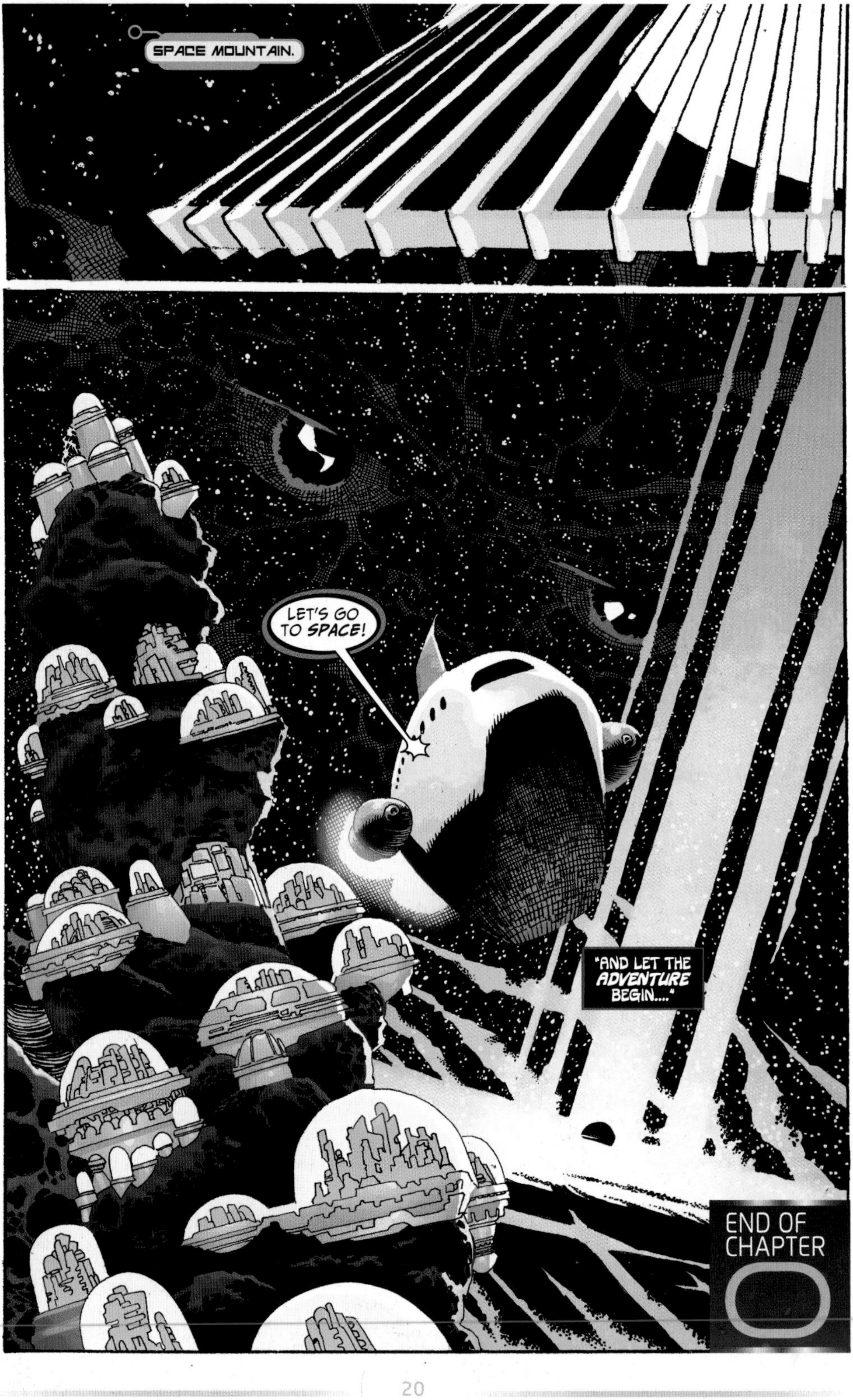
SPACE MOUNTAIN.
LET'S GO TO SPACE!
"AND LET THE ADVENTURE BEGIN...."
END OF CHAPTER 0

PART ONE

THE LIVING BLUEPRINT OF THE FUTURE

THE BEST THING ABOUT THE
FUTURE IS THAT IT COMES ONLY
ONE DAY AT A TIME.
—ABRAHAM LINCOLN

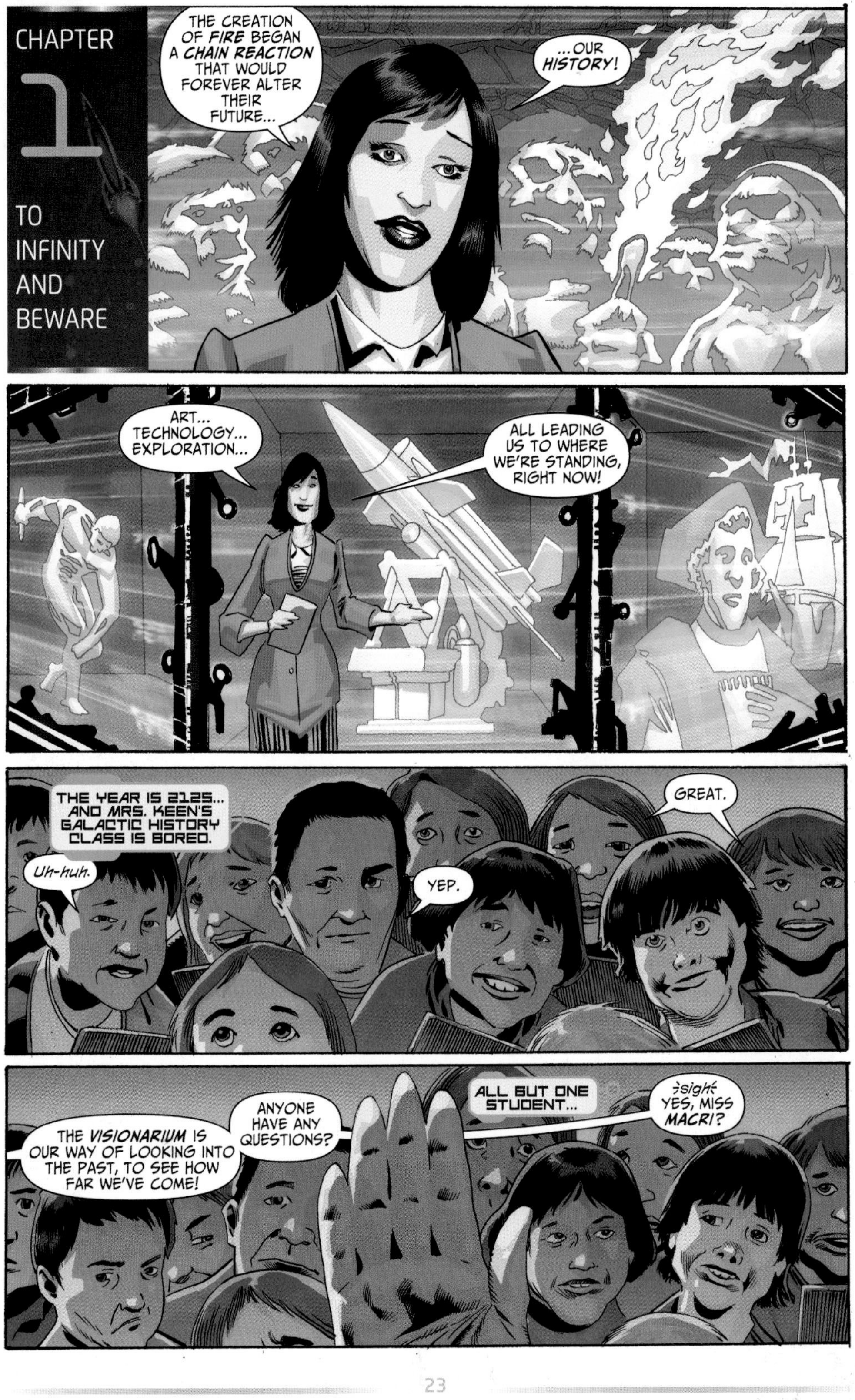
CHAPTER 1
TO INFINITY AND BEWARE
THE CREATION OF FIRE BEGAN A CHAIN REACTION THAT WOULD FOREVER ALTER THEIR FUTURE...
...OUR HISTORY!
ART... TECHNOLOGY... EXPLORATION...
ALL LEADING US TO WHERE WE'RE STANDING, RIGHT NOW!
THE YEAR IS 2125... AND MRS. KEEN'S GALACTIC HISTORY CLASS IS BORED.
GREAT.
Uh-huh.
YEP.
THE VISIONARIUM IS OUR WAY OF LOOKING INTO THE PAST, TO SEE HOW FAR WE'VE COME!
ANYONE HAVE ANY QUESTIONS?
ALL BUT ONE STUDENT...
sigh YES, MISS MACRI?

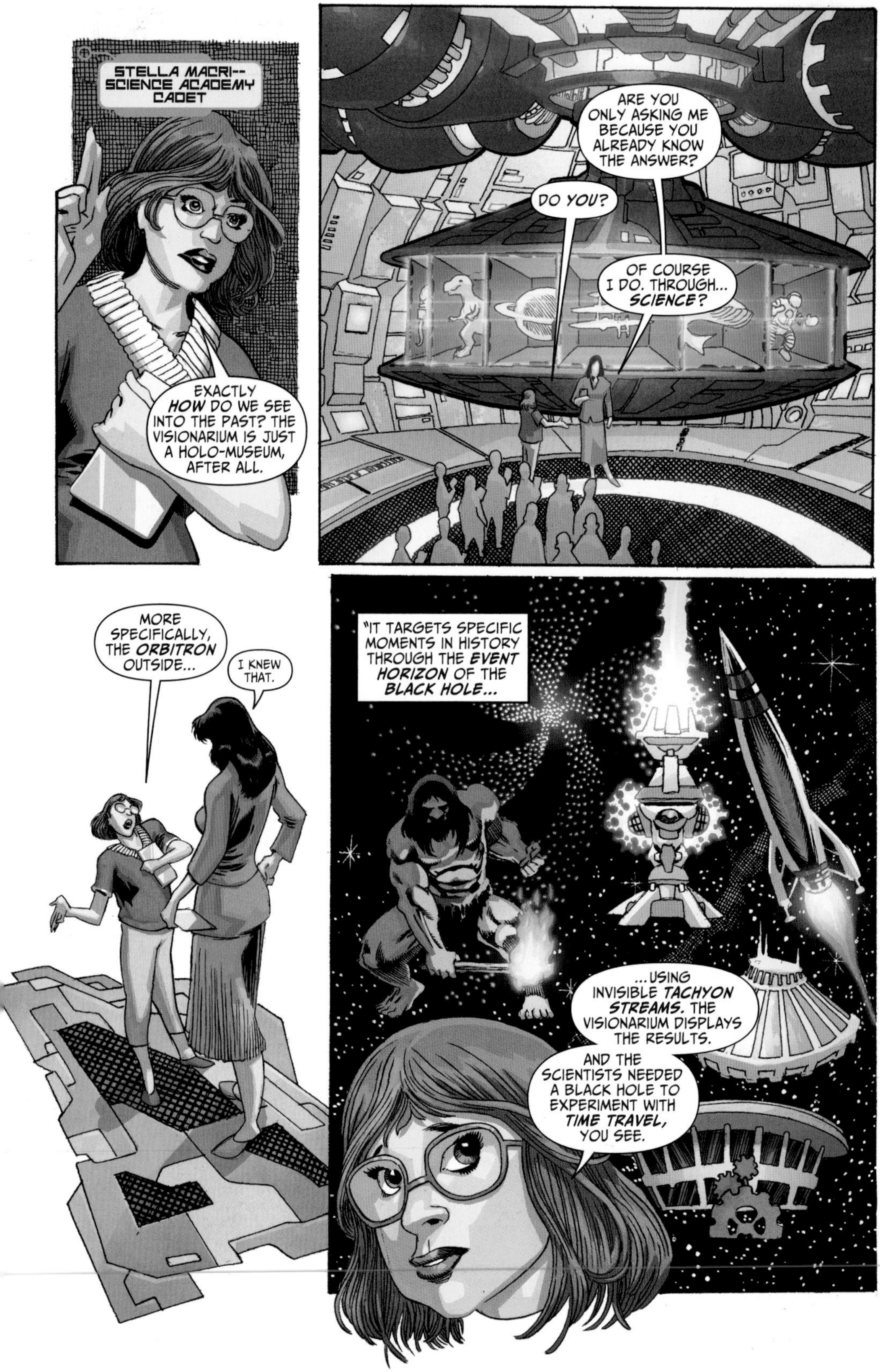
STELLA MACRI-- SCIENCE ACADEMY CADET
EXACTLY HOW DO WE SEE INTO THE PAST? THE VISIONARIUM IS JUST A HOLO-MUSEUM, AFTER ALL.
ARE YOU ONLY ASKING ME BECAUSE YOU ALREADY KNOW THE ANSWER?
DO YOU?
OF COURSE I DO. THROUGH... SCIENCE?
MORE SPECIFICALLY, THE ORBITRON OUTSIDE...
I KNEW THAT.
"IT TARGETS SPECIFIC MOMENTS IN HISTORY THROUGH THE EVENT HORIZON OF THE BLACK HOLE...
...USING INVISIBLE TACHYON STREAMS. THE VISIONARIUM DISPLAYS THE RESULTS.
AND THE SCIENTISTS NEEDED A BLACK HOLE TO EXPERIMENT WITH TIME TRAVEL, YOU SEE.

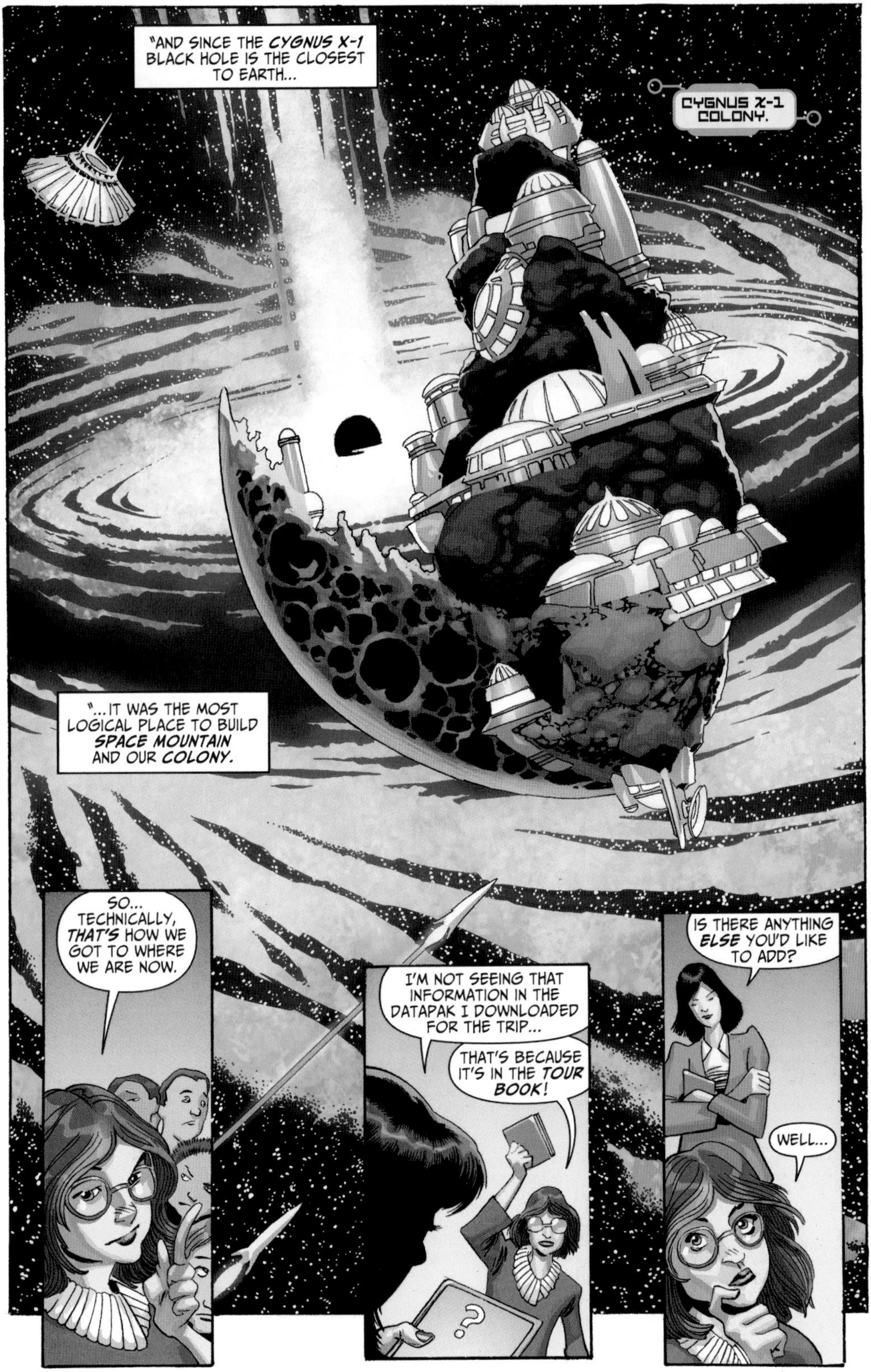
"AND SINCE THE *CYGNUS X-1* BLACK HOLE IS THE CLOSEST TO EARTH...
CYGNUS X-1 COLONY.
"...IT WAS THE MOST LOGICAL PLACE TO BUILD *SPACE MOUNTAIN* AND OUR *COLONY.*
SO... TECHNICALLY, *THAT'S* HOW WE GOT TO WHERE WE ARE NOW.
I'M NOT SEEING THAT INFORMATION IN THE DATAPAK I DOWNLOADED FOR THE TRIP...
THAT'S BECAUSE IT'S IN THE *TOUR BOOK*!
?
IS THERE ANYTHING *ELSE* YOU'D LIKE TO ADD?
WELL...

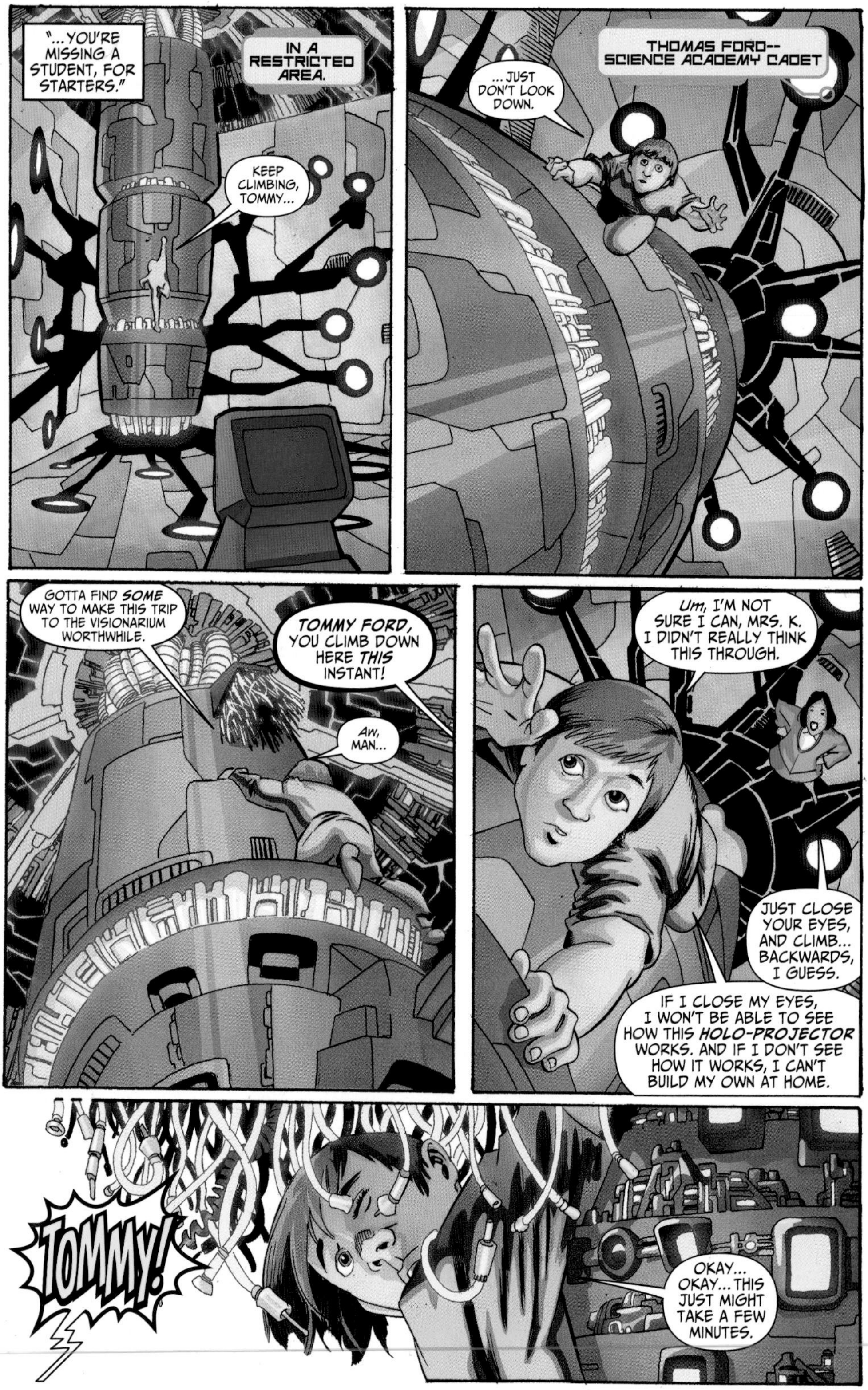
"...YOU'RE MISSING A STUDENT, FOR STARTERS."
IN A RESTRICTED AREA.
KEEP CLIMBING, TOMMY...
THOMAS FORD-- SCIENCE ACADEMY CADET
...JUST DON'T LOOK DOWN.
GOTTA FIND SOME WAY TO MAKE THIS TRIP TO THE VISIONARIUM WORTHWHILE.
TOMMY FORD, YOU CLIMB DOWN HERE THIS INSTANT!
AW, MAN...
UM, I'M NOT SURE I CAN, MRS. K. I DIDN'T REALLY THINK THIS THROUGH.
JUST CLOSE YOUR EYES, AND CLIMB... BACKWARDS, I GUESS.
IF I CLOSE MY EYES, I WON'T BE ABLE TO SEE HOW THIS HOLO-PROJECTOR WORKS. AND IF I DON'T SEE HOW IT WORKS, I CAN'T BUILD MY OWN AT HOME.
TOMMY!
OKAY... OKAY... THIS JUST MIGHT TAKE A FEW MINUTES.

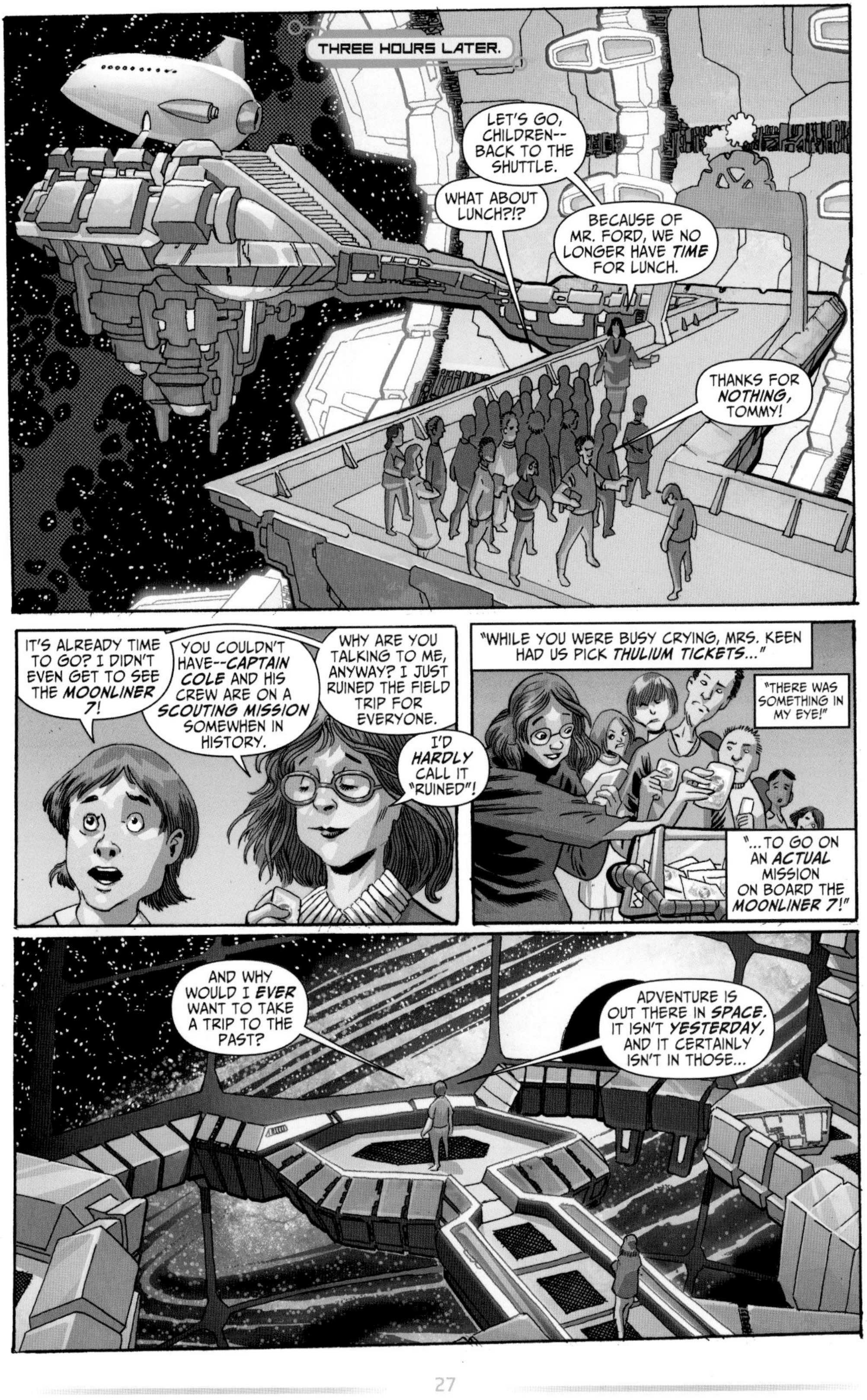
THREE HOURS LATER.
LET'S GO, CHILDREN-- BACK TO THE SHUTTLE.
WHAT ABOUT LUNCH?!?
BECAUSE OF MR. FORD, WE NO LONGER HAVE *TIME* FOR LUNCH.
THANKS FOR *NOTHING*, TOMMY!
IT'S ALREADY TIME TO GO? I DIDN'T EVEN GET TO SEE THE *MOONLINER 7*!
YOU COULDN'T HAVE--*CAPTAIN COLE* AND HIS CREW ARE ON A *SCOUTING MISSION* SOMEWHEN IN HISTORY.
WHY ARE YOU TALKING TO ME, ANYWAY? I JUST RUINED THE FIELD TRIP FOR EVERYONE.
I'D *HARDLY* CALL IT "RUINED"!
"WHILE YOU WERE BUSY CRYING, MRS. KEEN HAD US PICK *THULIUM TICKETS*..."
"THERE WAS SOMETHING IN MY EYE!"
"...TO GO ON AN *ACTUAL* MISSION ON BOARD THE *MOONLINER 7*!"
AND WHY WOULD I *EVER* WANT TO TAKE A TRIP TO THE PAST?
ADVENTURE IS OUT THERE IN *SPACE*. IT ISN'T *YESTERDAY*, AND IT CERTAINLY ISN'T IN THOSE...

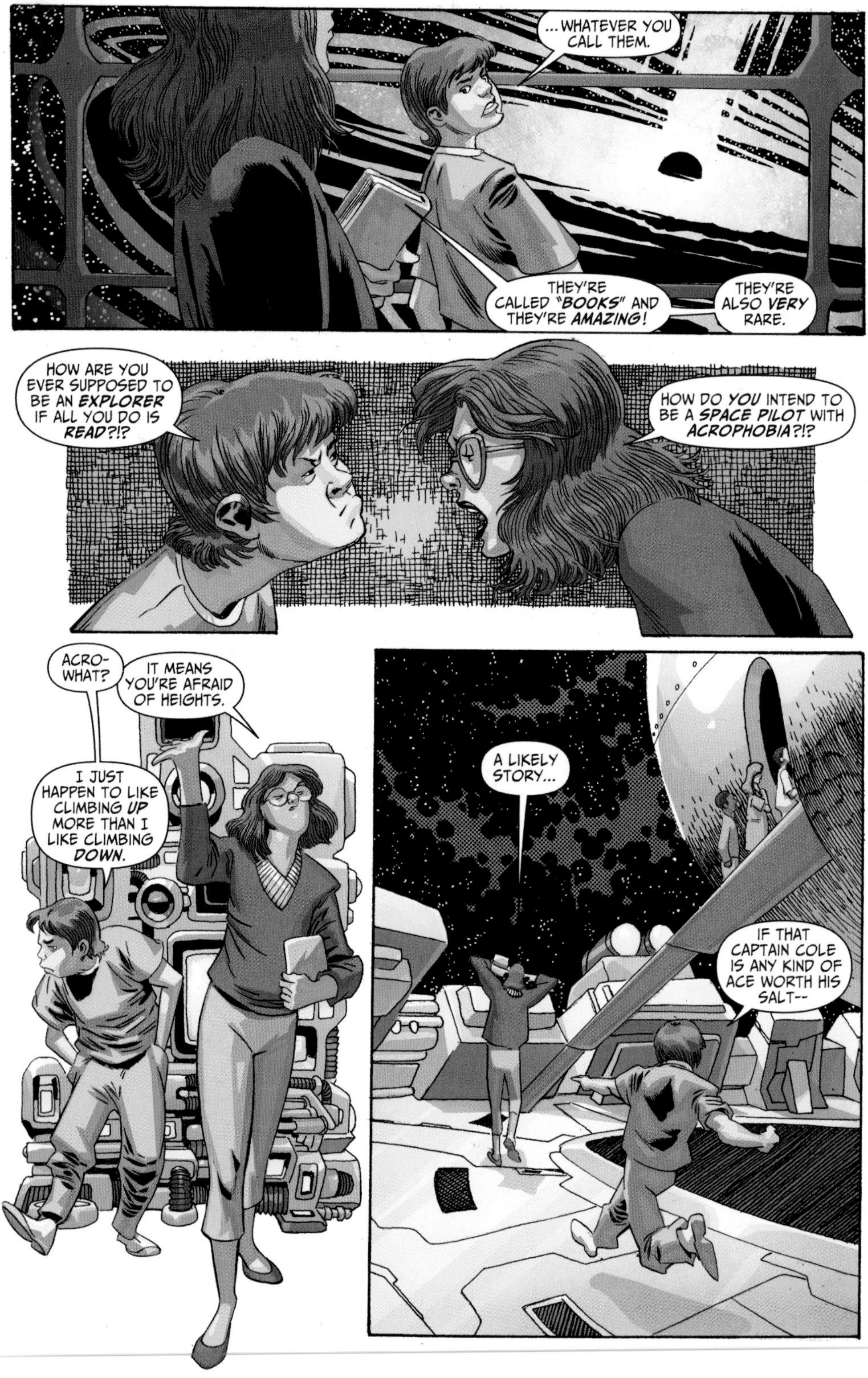
...WHATEVER YOU CALL THEM.
THEY'RE CALLED "BOOKS" AND THEY'RE AMAZING!
THEY'RE ALSO VERY RARE.
HOW ARE YOU EVER SUPPOSED TO BE AN EXPLORER IF ALL YOU DO IS READ?!?
HOW DO YOU INTEND TO BE A SPACE PILOT WITH ACROPHOBIA?!?
ACRO-WHAT?
IT MEANS YOU'RE AFRAID OF HEIGHTS.
I JUST HAPPEN TO LIKE CLIMBING UP MORE THAN I LIKE CLIMBING DOWN.
A LIKELY STORY...
IF THAT CAPTAIN COLE IS ANY KIND OF ACE WORTH HIS SALT--

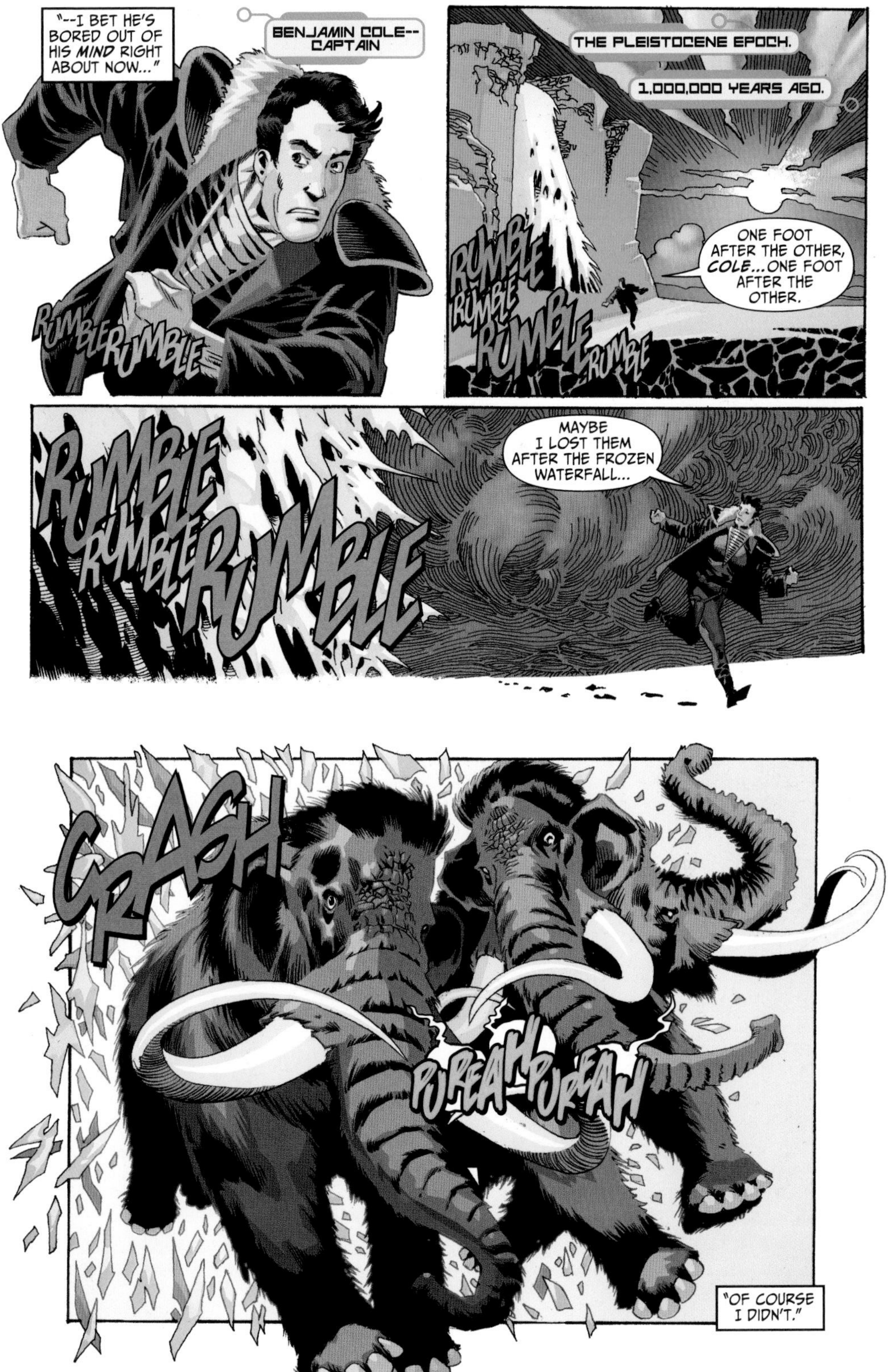
"--I BET HE'S BORED OUT OF HIS *MIND* RIGHT ABOUT NOW..."
BENJAMIN COLE-- CAPTAIN
RUMBLE RUMBLE
THE PLEISTOCENE EPOCH.
1,000,000 YEARS AGO.
ONE FOOT AFTER THE OTHER, *COLE*...ONE FOOT AFTER THE OTHER.
RUMBLE RUMBLE RUMBLE RUMBLE
RUMBLE RUMBLE RUMBLE
MAYBE I LOST THEM AFTER THE FROZEN WATERFALL...
CRASH
PUREAH PUREAH
"OF COURSE I DIDN'T."

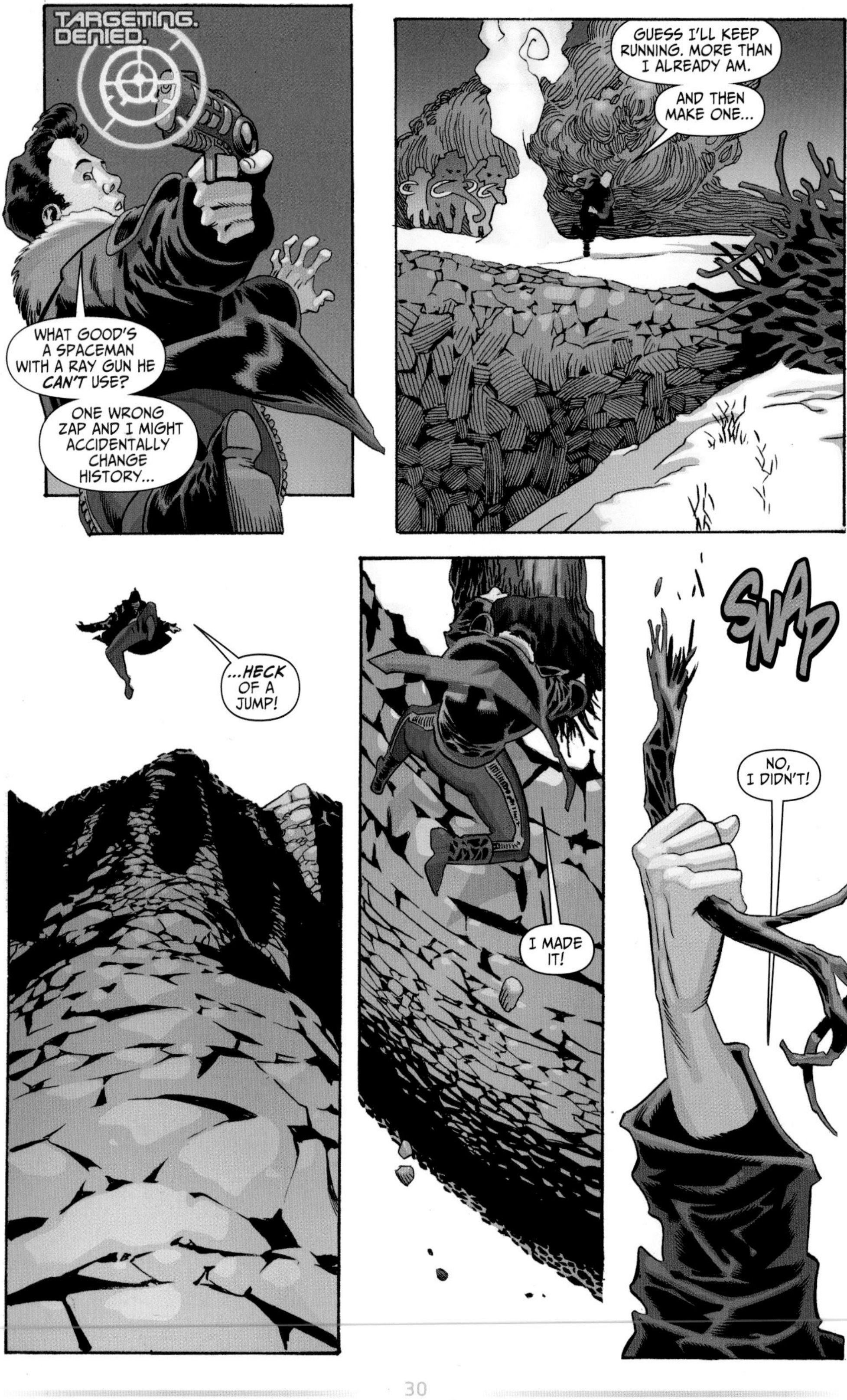
TARGETING. DENIED.
WHAT GOOD'S A SPACEMAN WITH A RAY GUN HE CAN'T USE?
ONE WRONG ZAP AND I MIGHT ACCIDENTALLY CHANGE HISTORY...
GUESS I'LL KEEP RUNNING. MORE THAN I ALREADY AM.
AND THEN MAKE ONE...
...HECK OF A JUMP!
I MADE IT!
SNAP
NO, I DIDN'T!

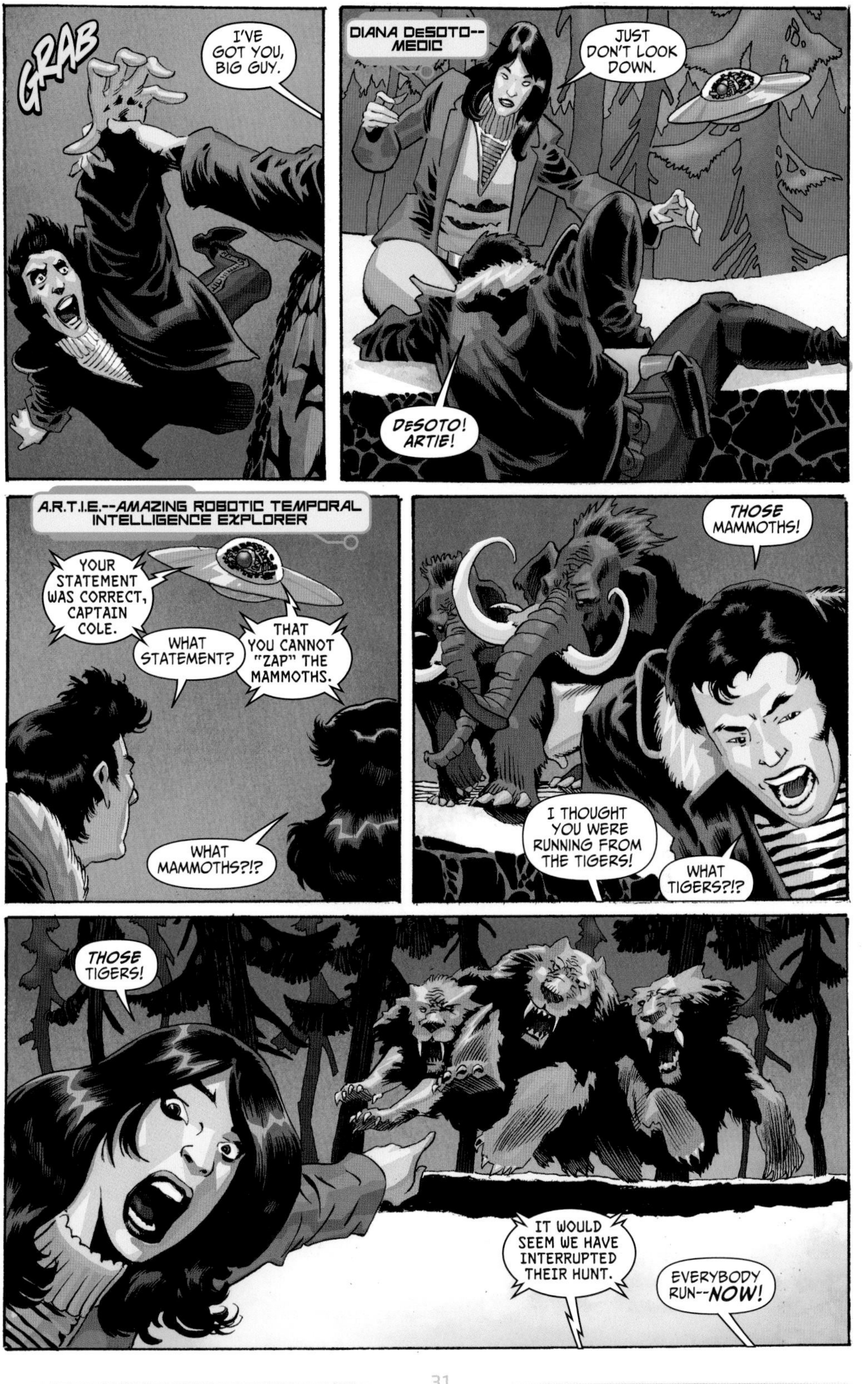
GRAB
I'VE GOT YOU, BIG GUY.
DIANA DESOTO--MEDIC
JUST DON'T LOOK DOWN.
DESOTO! ARTIE!
A.R.T.I.E.--AMAZING ROBOTIC TEMPORAL INTELLIGENCE EXPLORER
YOUR STATEMENT WAS CORRECT, CAPTAIN COLE.
WHAT STATEMENT?
THAT YOU CANNOT "ZAP" THE MAMMOTHS.
WHAT MAMMOTHS?!?
THOSE MAMMOTHS!
I THOUGHT YOU WERE RUNNING FROM THE TIGERS!
WHAT TIGERS?!?
THOSE TIGERS!
IT WOULD SEEM WE HAVE INTERRUPTED THEIR HUNT.
EVERYBODY RUN--NOW!

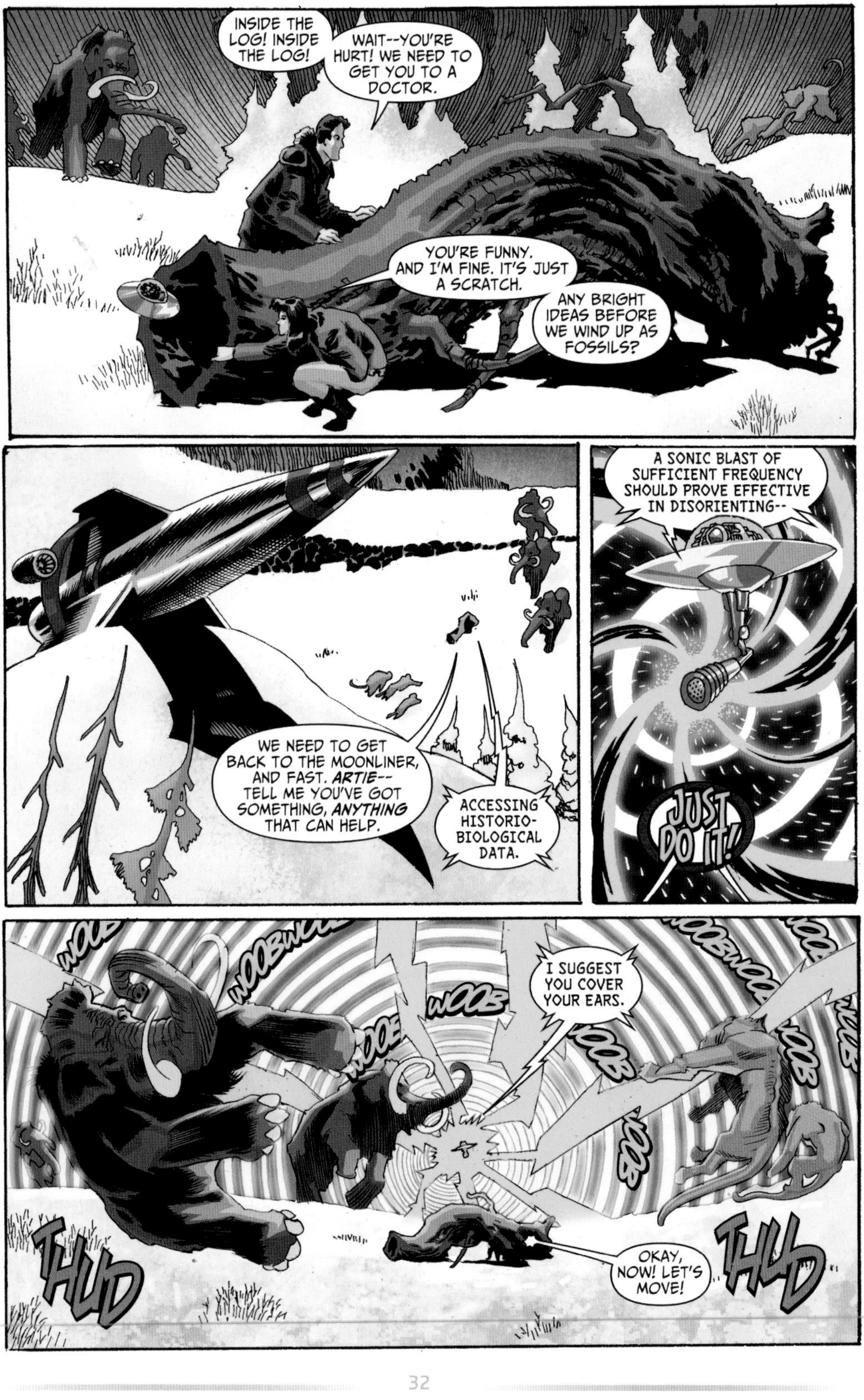

INSIDE THE LOG! INSIDE THE LOG!
WAIT--YOU'RE HURT! WE NEED TO GET YOU TO A DOCTOR.
YOU'RE FUNNY. AND I'M FINE. IT'S JUST A SCRATCH.
ANY BRIGHT IDEAS BEFORE WE WIND UP AS FOSSILS?
WE NEED TO GET BACK TO THE MOONLINER, AND FAST. ARTIE-- TELL ME YOU'VE GOT SOMETHING, ANYTHING THAT CAN HELP.
ACCESSING HISTORIO-BIOLOGICAL DATA.
A SONIC BLAST OF SUFFICIENT FREQUENCY SHOULD PROVE EFFECTIVE IN DISORIENTING--
JUST DO IT!
I SUGGEST YOU COVER YOUR EARS.
WOOB
WOOBWOO
WOOB
WOOB
WOOB
THUD
OKAY, NOW! LET'S MOVE!
THUD

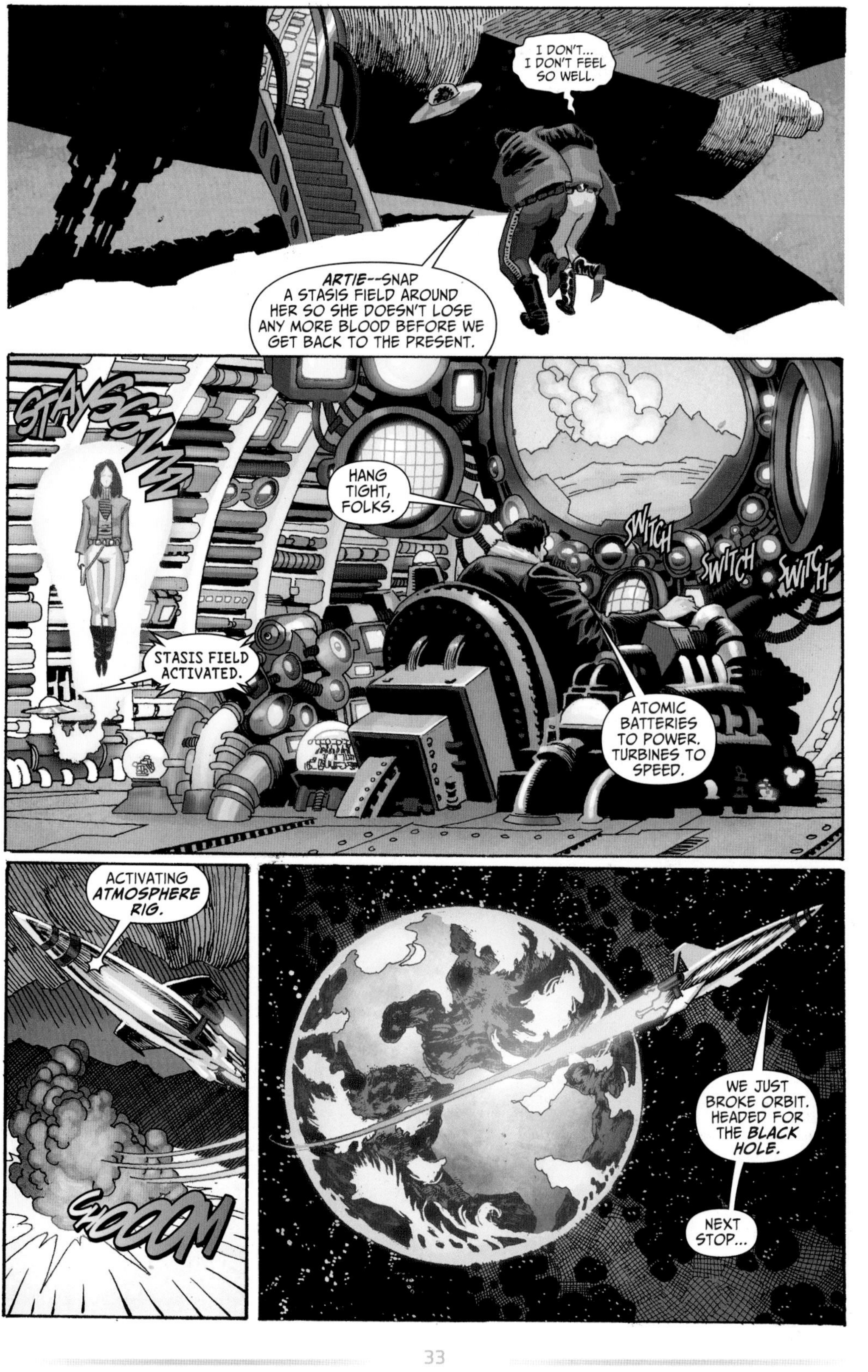
I DON'T... I DON'T FEEL SO WELL.
ARTIE--SNAP A STASIS FIELD AROUND HER SO SHE DOESN'T LOSE ANY MORE BLOOD BEFORE WE GET BACK TO THE PRESENT.
STAYSSSZZZ
HANG TIGHT, FOLKS.
SWITCH
SWITCH
SWITCH
STASIS FIELD ACTIVATED.
ATOMIC BATTERIES TO POWER. TURBINES TO SPEED.
ACTIVATING *ATMOSPHERE RIG.*
SHOOOM
WE JUST BROKE ORBIT. HEADED FOR THE *BLACK HOLE.*
NEXT STOP...

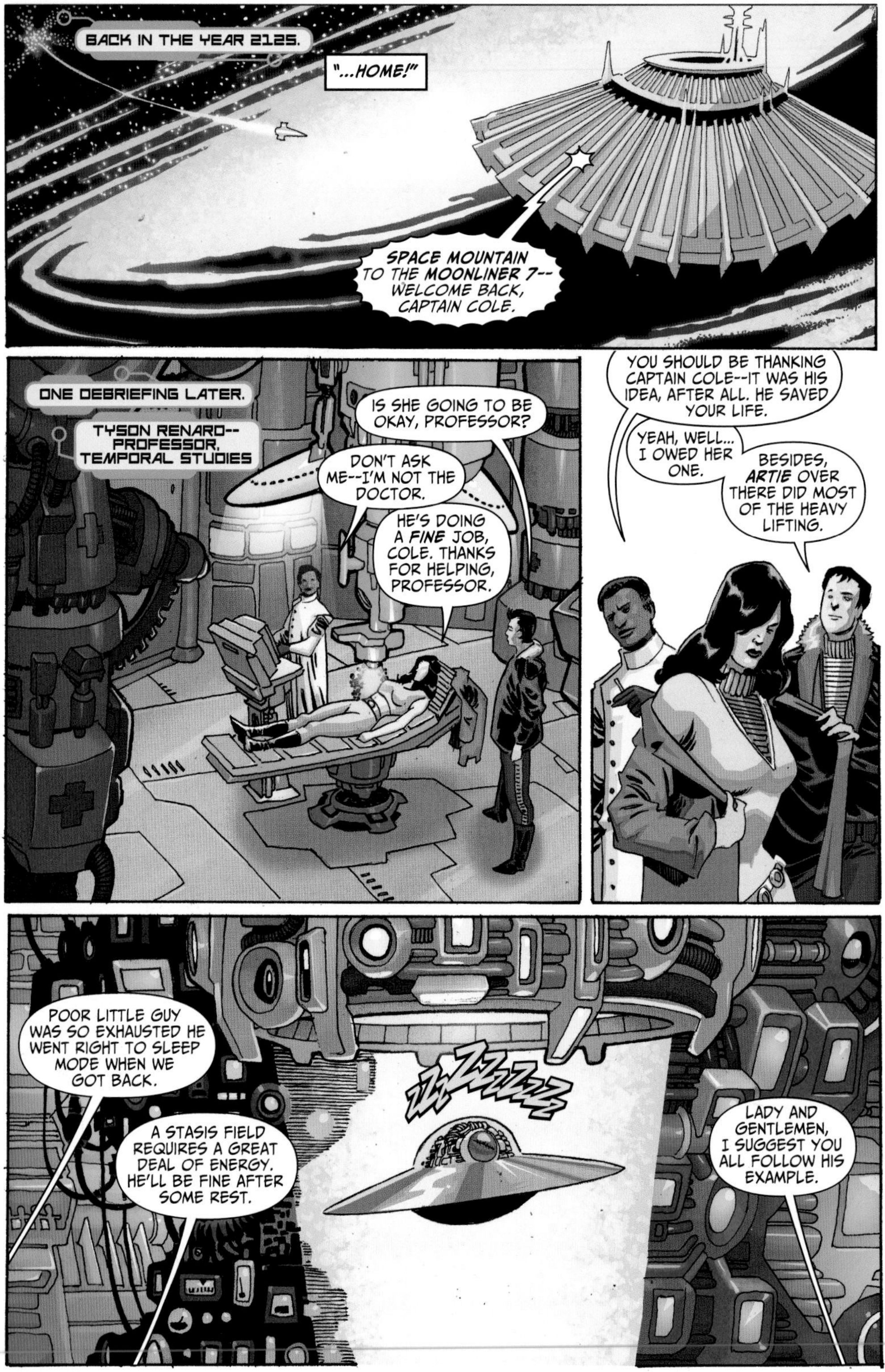
BACK IN THE YEAR 2125.
"...HOME!"
SPACE MOUNTAIN TO THE MOONLINER 7-- WELCOME BACK, CAPTAIN COLE.
ONE DEBRIEFING LATER.
TYSON RENARD-- PROFESSOR, TEMPORAL STUDIES
IS SHE GOING TO BE OKAY, PROFESSOR?
DON'T ASK ME--I'M NOT THE DOCTOR.
HE'S DOING A FINE JOB, COLE. THANKS FOR HELPING, PROFESSOR.
YOU SHOULD BE THANKING CAPTAIN COLE--IT WAS HIS IDEA, AFTER ALL. HE SAVED YOUR LIFE.
YEAH, WELL... I OWED HER ONE.
BESIDES, ARTIE OVER THERE DID MOST OF THE HEAVY LIFTING.
POOR LITTLE GUY WAS SO EXHAUSTED HE WENT RIGHT TO SLEEP MODE WHEN WE GOT BACK.
ZZZZZZZZ
A STASIS FIELD REQUIRES A GREAT DEAL OF ENERGY. HE'LL BE FINE AFTER SOME REST.
LADY AND GENTLEMEN, I SUGGEST YOU ALL FOLLOW HIS EXAMPLE.

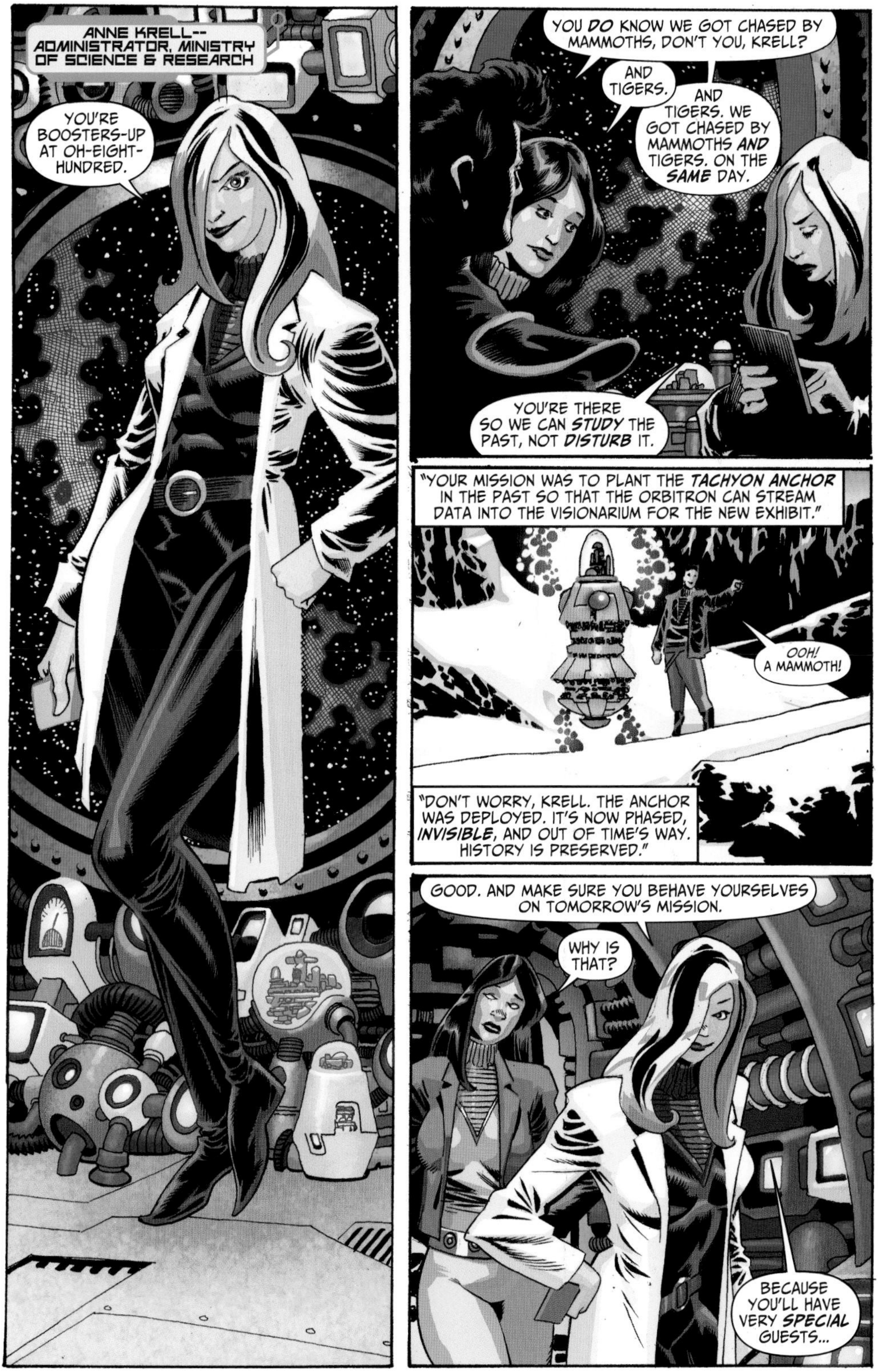
ANNE KRELL-- ADMINISTRATOR, MINISTRY OF SCIENCE & RESEARCH
YOU'RE BOOSTERS-UP AT OH-EIGHT-HUNDRED.
YOU DO KNOW WE GOT CHASED BY MAMMOTHS, DON'T YOU, KRELL?
AND TIGERS.
AND TIGERS. WE GOT CHASED BY MAMMOTHS AND TIGERS. ON THE SAME DAY.
YOU'RE THERE SO WE CAN STUDY THE PAST, NOT DISTURB IT.
"YOUR MISSION WAS TO PLANT THE TACHYON ANCHOR IN THE PAST SO THAT THE ORBITRON CAN STREAM DATA INTO THE VISIONARIUM FOR THE NEW EXHIBIT."
OOH! A MAMMOTH!
"DON'T WORRY, KRELL. THE ANCHOR WAS DEPLOYED. IT'S NOW PHASED, INVISIBLE, AND OUT OF TIME'S WAY. HISTORY IS PRESERVED."
GOOD. AND MAKE SURE YOU BEHAVE YOURSELVES ON TOMORROW'S MISSION.
WHY IS THAT?
BECAUSE YOU'LL HAVE VERY SPECIAL GUESTS...

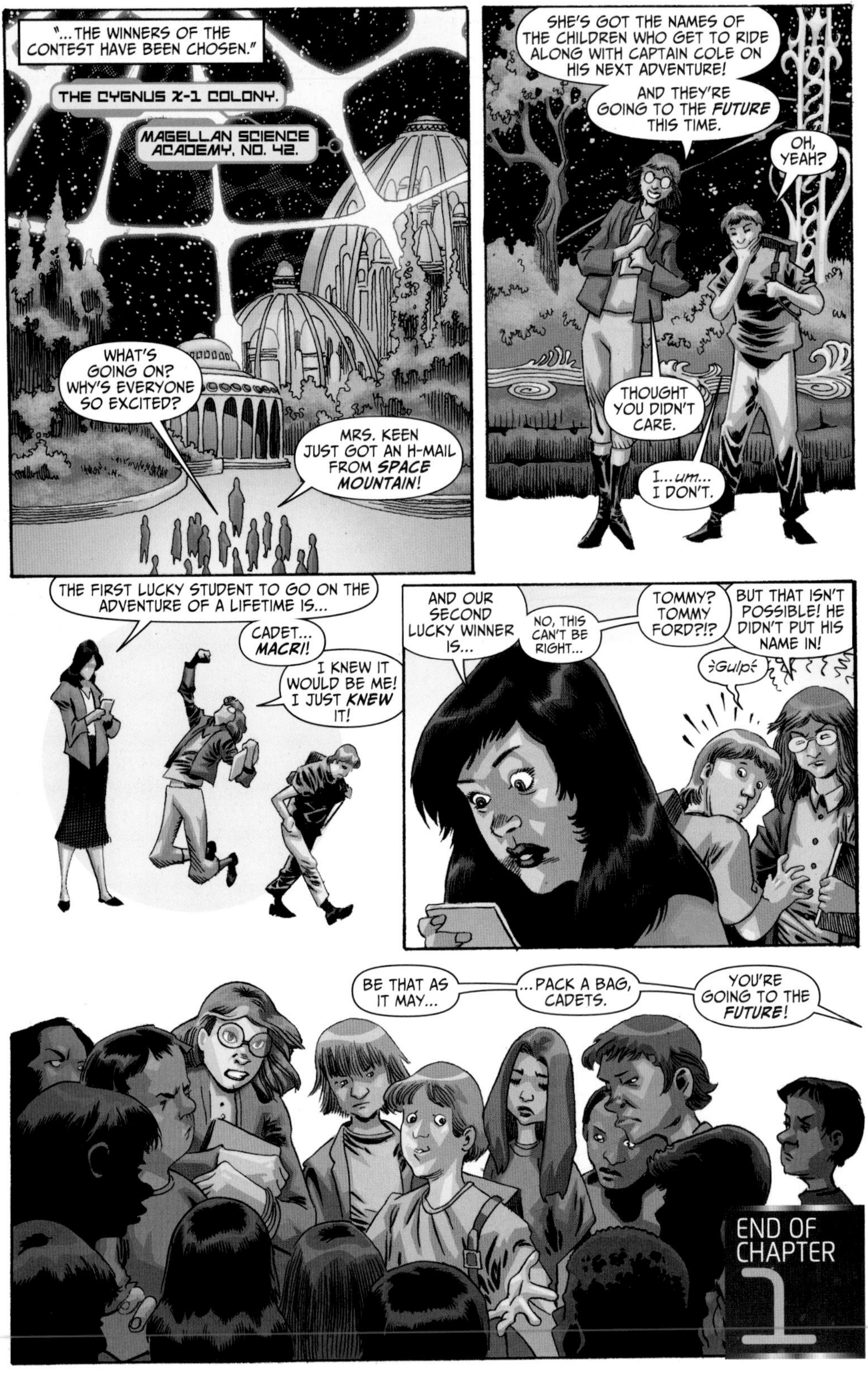
"...THE WINNERS OF THE CONTEST HAVE BEEN CHOSEN."
THE CYGNUS X-1 COLONY.
MAGELLAN SCIENCE ACADEMY, NO. 42.
WHAT'S GOING ON? WHY'S EVERYONE SO EXCITED?
MRS. KEEN JUST GOT AN H-MAIL FROM SPACE MOUNTAIN!
SHE'S GOT THE NAMES OF THE CHILDREN WHO GET TO RIDE ALONG WITH CAPTAIN COLE ON HIS NEXT ADVENTURE!
AND THEY'RE GOING TO THE FUTURE THIS TIME.
OH, YEAH?
THOUGHT YOU DIDN'T CARE.
I...um... I DON'T.
THE FIRST LUCKY STUDENT TO GO ON THE ADVENTURE OF A LIFETIME IS...
CADET... MACRI!
I KNEW IT WOULD BE ME! I JUST KNEW IT!
AND OUR SECOND LUCKY WINNER IS...
NO, THIS CAN'T BE RIGHT...
TOMMY? TOMMY FORD?!?
BUT THAT ISN'T POSSIBLE! HE DIDN'T PUT HIS NAME IN!
Gulp
BE THAT AS IT MAY...
...PACK A BAG, CADETS.
YOU'RE GOING TO THE FUTURE!
END OF CHAPTER 1

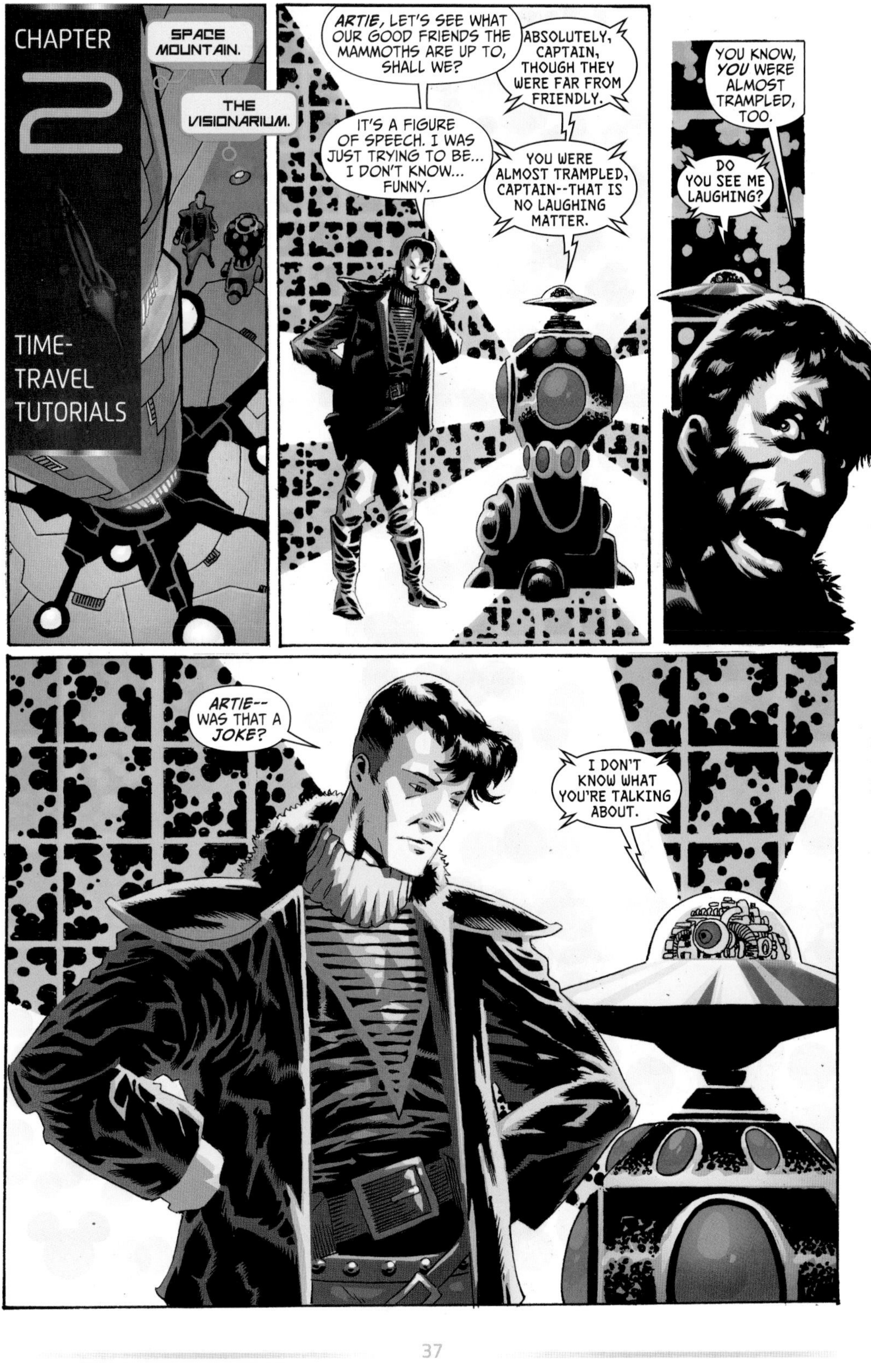
CHAPTER
2
TIME-TRAVEL TUTORIALS
SPACE MOUNTAIN.
THE VISIONARIUM.
ARTIE, LET'S SEE WHAT OUR GOOD FRIENDS THE MAMMOTHS ARE UP TO, SHALL WE?
ABSOLUTELY, CAPTAIN, THOUGH THEY WERE FAR FROM FRIENDLY.
IT'S A FIGURE OF SPEECH. I WAS JUST TRYING TO BE... I DON'T KNOW... FUNNY.
YOU WERE ALMOST TRAMPLED, CAPTAIN--THAT IS NO LAUGHING MATTER.
YOU KNOW, YOU WERE ALMOST TRAMPLED, TOO.
DO YOU SEE ME LAUGHING?
ARTIE--WAS THAT A JOKE?
I DON'T KNOW WHAT YOU'RE TALKING ABOUT.

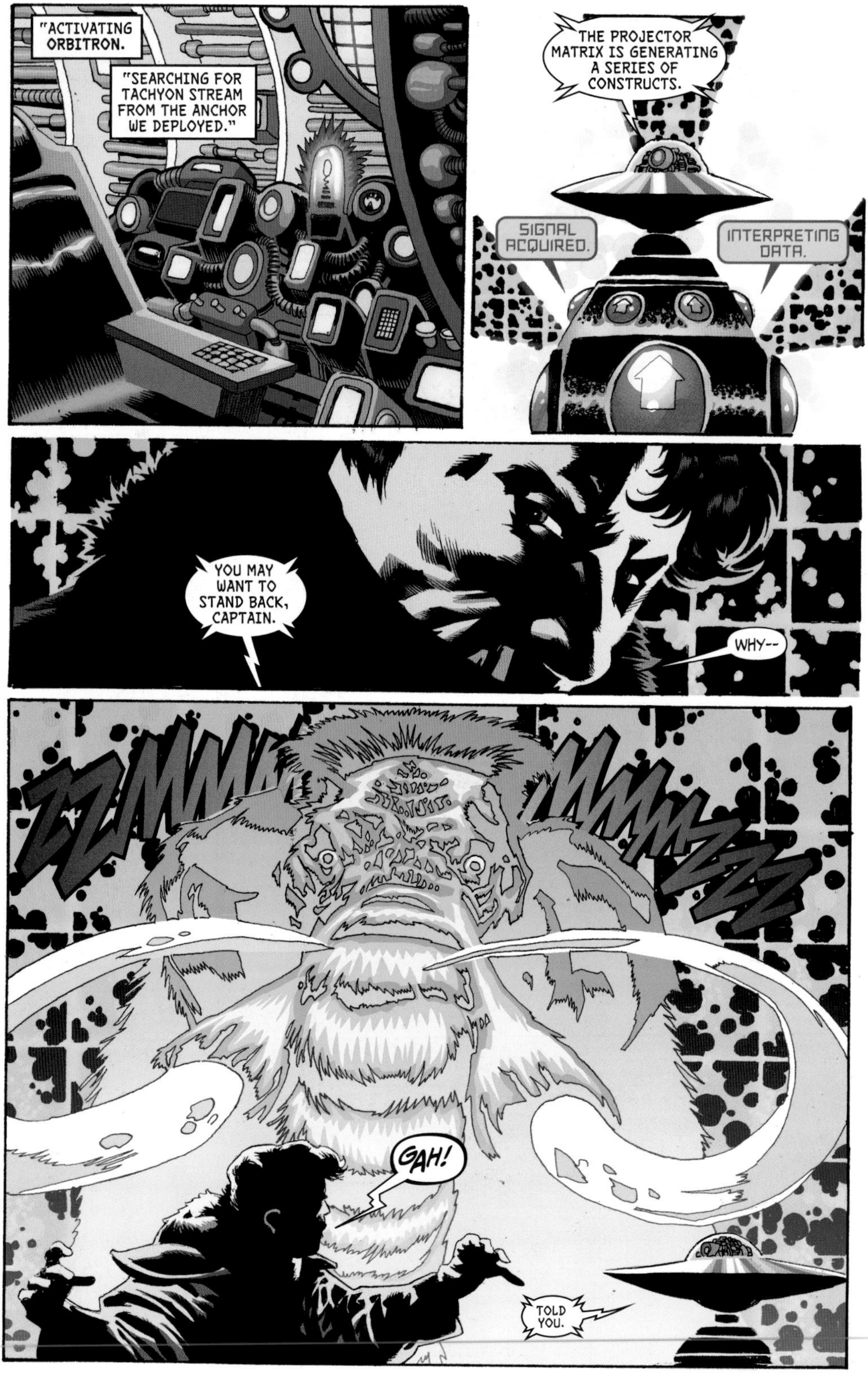
"ACTIVATING ORBITRON.
"SEARCHING FOR TACHYON STREAM FROM THE ANCHOR WE DEPLOYED."
THE PROJECTOR MATRIX IS GENERATING A SERIES OF CONSTRUCTS.
SIGNAL ACQUIRED.
INTERPRETING DATA.
YOU MAY WANT TO STAND BACK, CAPTAIN.
WHY--
ZZMMMMMMMMMMZZZZ
GAH!
TOLD YOU.

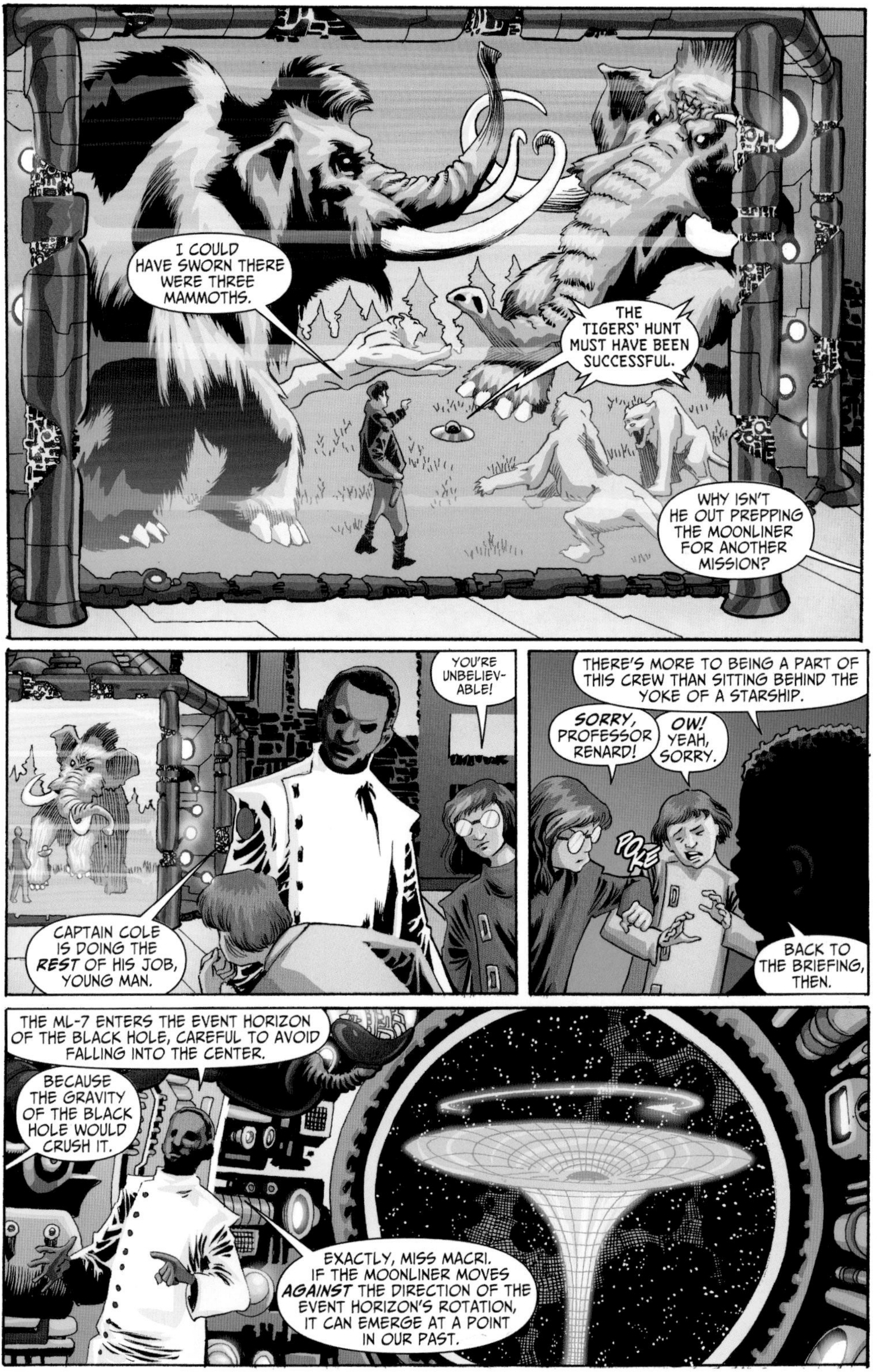
I COULD HAVE SWORN THERE WERE THREE MAMMOTHS.
THE TIGERS' HUNT MUST HAVE BEEN SUCCESSFUL.
WHY ISN'T HE OUT PREPPING THE MOONLINER FOR ANOTHER MISSION?
YOU'RE UNBELIEV-ABLE!
CAPTAIN COLE IS DOING THE REST OF HIS JOB, YOUNG MAN.
THERE'S MORE TO BEING A PART OF THIS CREW THAN SITTING BEHIND THE YOKE OF A STARSHIP.
SORRY, PROFESSOR RENARD!
OW! YEAH, SORRY.
POKE
BACK TO THE BRIEFING, THEN.
THE ML-7 ENTERS THE EVENT HORIZON OF THE BLACK HOLE, CAREFUL TO AVOID FALLING INTO THE CENTER.
BECAUSE THE GRAVITY OF THE BLACK HOLE WOULD CRUSH IT.
EXACTLY, MISS MACRI. IF THE MOONLINER MOVES AGAINST THE DIRECTION OF THE EVENT HORIZON'S ROTATION, IT CAN EMERGE AT A POINT IN OUR PAST.

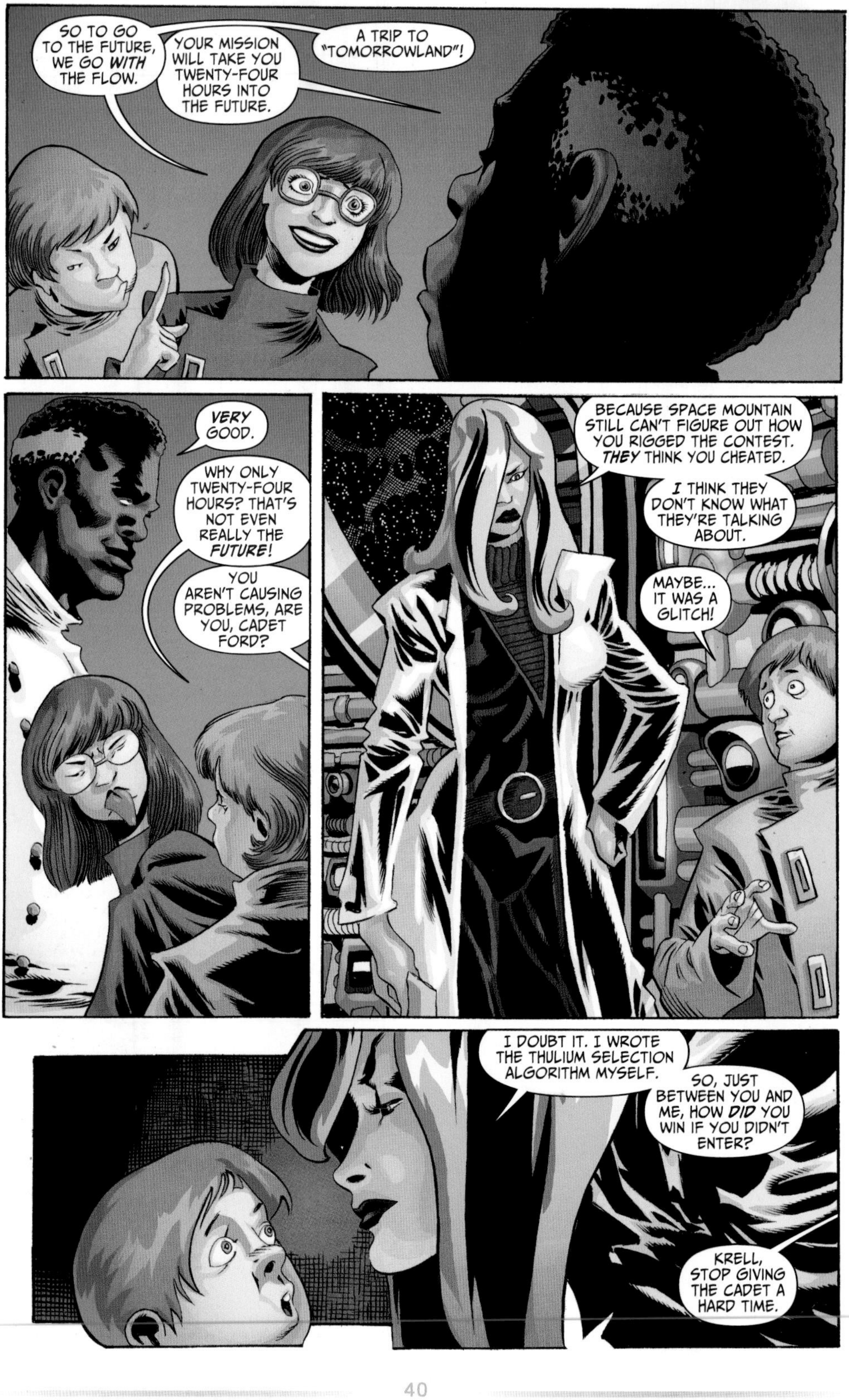
SO TO GO TO THE FUTURE, WE GO WITH THE FLOW.
YOUR MISSION WILL TAKE YOU TWENTY-FOUR HOURS INTO THE FUTURE.
A TRIP TO "TOMORROWLAND"!
VERY GOOD.
WHY ONLY TWENTY-FOUR HOURS? THAT'S NOT EVEN REALLY THE FUTURE!
YOU AREN'T CAUSING PROBLEMS, ARE YOU, CADET FORD?
BECAUSE SPACE MOUNTAIN STILL CAN'T FIGURE OUT HOW YOU RIGGED THE CONTEST. THEY THINK YOU CHEATED.
I THINK THEY DON'T KNOW WHAT THEY'RE TALKING ABOUT.
MAYBE... IT WAS A GLITCH!
I DOUBT IT. I WROTE THE THULIUM SELECTION ALGORITHM MYSELF.
SO, JUST BETWEEN YOU AND ME, HOW DID YOU WIN IF YOU DIDN'T ENTER?
KRELL, STOP GIVING THE CADET A HARD TIME.

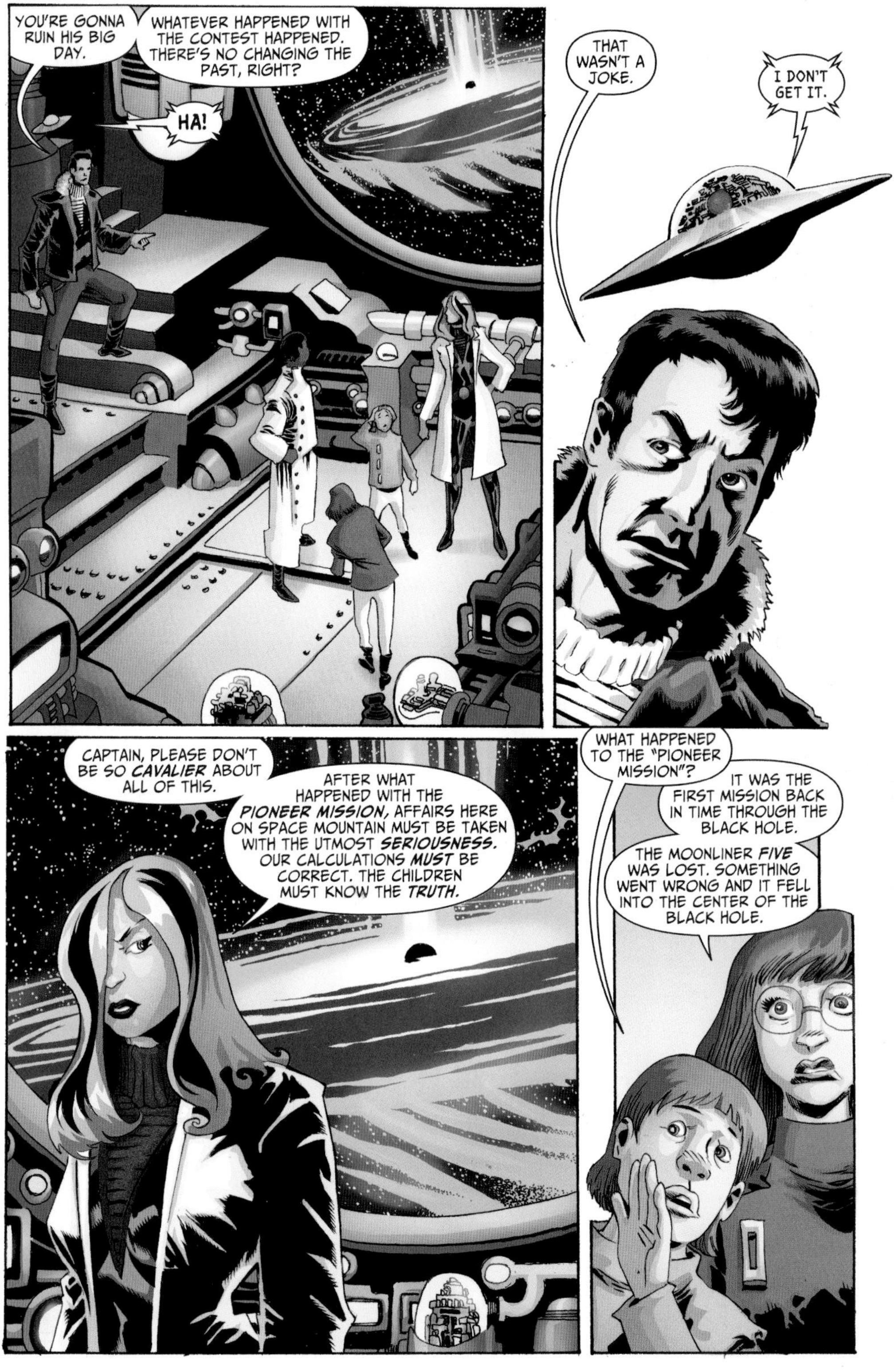
YOU'RE GONNA RUIN HIS BIG DAY.
WHATEVER HAPPENED WITH THE CONTEST HAPPENED. THERE'S NO CHANGING THE PAST, RIGHT?
HA!
THAT WASN'T A JOKE.
I DON'T GET IT.
CAPTAIN, PLEASE DON'T BE SO CAVALIER ABOUT ALL OF THIS.
AFTER WHAT HAPPENED WITH THE PIONEER MISSION, AFFAIRS HERE ON SPACE MOUNTAIN MUST BE TAKEN WITH THE UTMOST SERIOUSNESS. OUR CALCULATIONS MUST BE CORRECT. THE CHILDREN MUST KNOW THE TRUTH.
WHAT HAPPENED TO THE "PIONEER MISSION"?
IT WAS THE FIRST MISSION BACK IN TIME THROUGH THE BLACK HOLE.
THE MOONLINER FIVE WAS LOST. SOMETHING WENT WRONG AND IT FELL INTO THE CENTER OF THE BLACK HOLE.

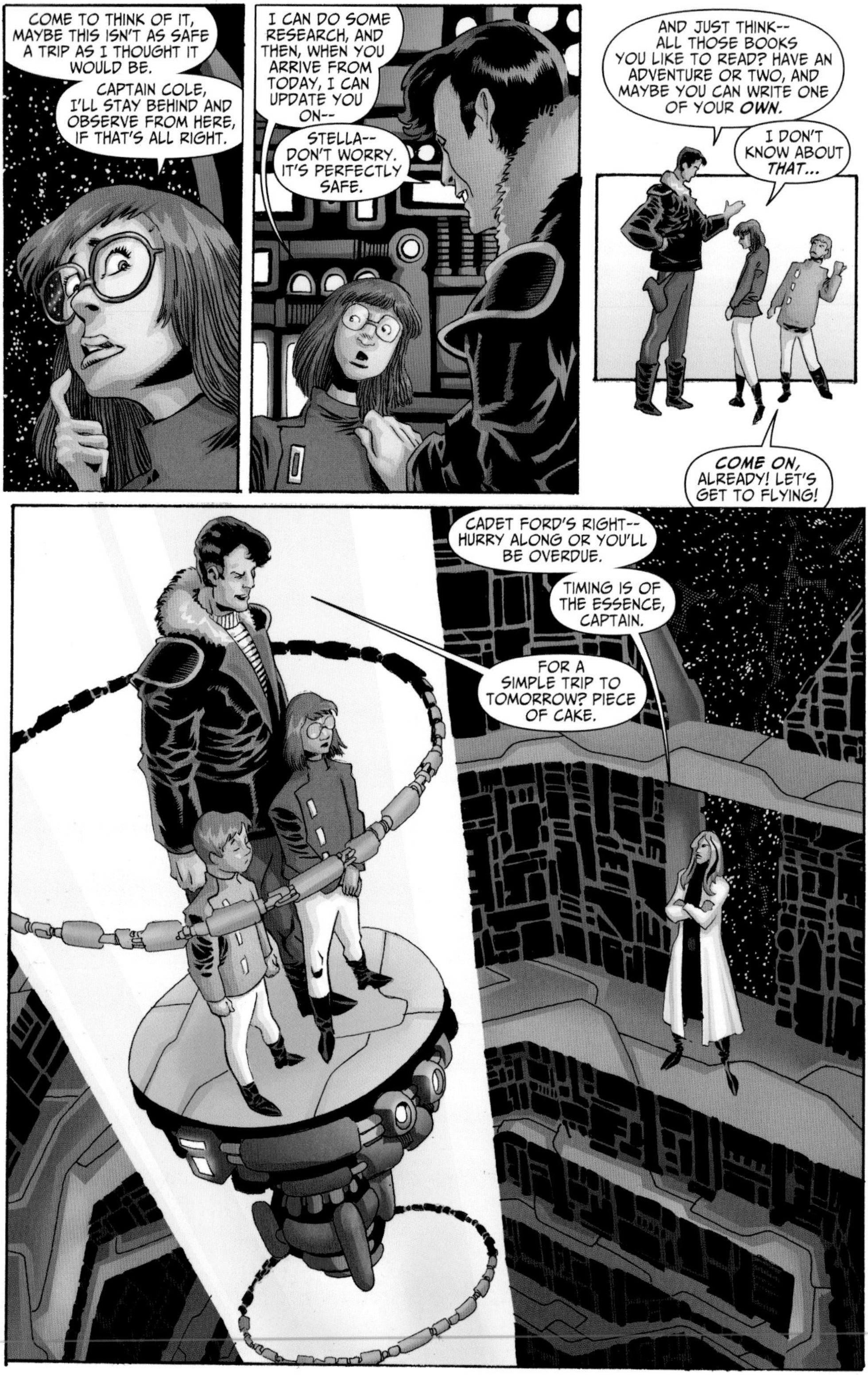
COME TO THINK OF IT, MAYBE THIS ISN'T AS SAFE A TRIP AS I THOUGHT IT WOULD BE.
CAPTAIN COLE, I'LL STAY BEHIND AND OBSERVE FROM HERE, IF THAT'S ALL RIGHT.
I CAN DO SOME RESEARCH, AND THEN, WHEN YOU ARRIVE FROM TODAY, I CAN UPDATE YOU ON--
STELLA-- DON'T WORRY. IT'S PERFECTLY SAFE.
AND JUST THINK-- ALL THOSE BOOKS YOU LIKE TO READ? HAVE AN ADVENTURE OR TWO, AND MAYBE YOU CAN WRITE ONE OF YOUR OWN.
I DON'T KNOW ABOUT THAT...
COME ON, ALREADY! LET'S GET TO FLYING!
CADET FORD'S RIGHT-- HURRY ALONG OR YOU'LL BE OVERDUE.
TIMING IS OF THE ESSENCE, CAPTAIN.
FOR A SIMPLE TRIP TO TOMORROW? PIECE OF CAKE.

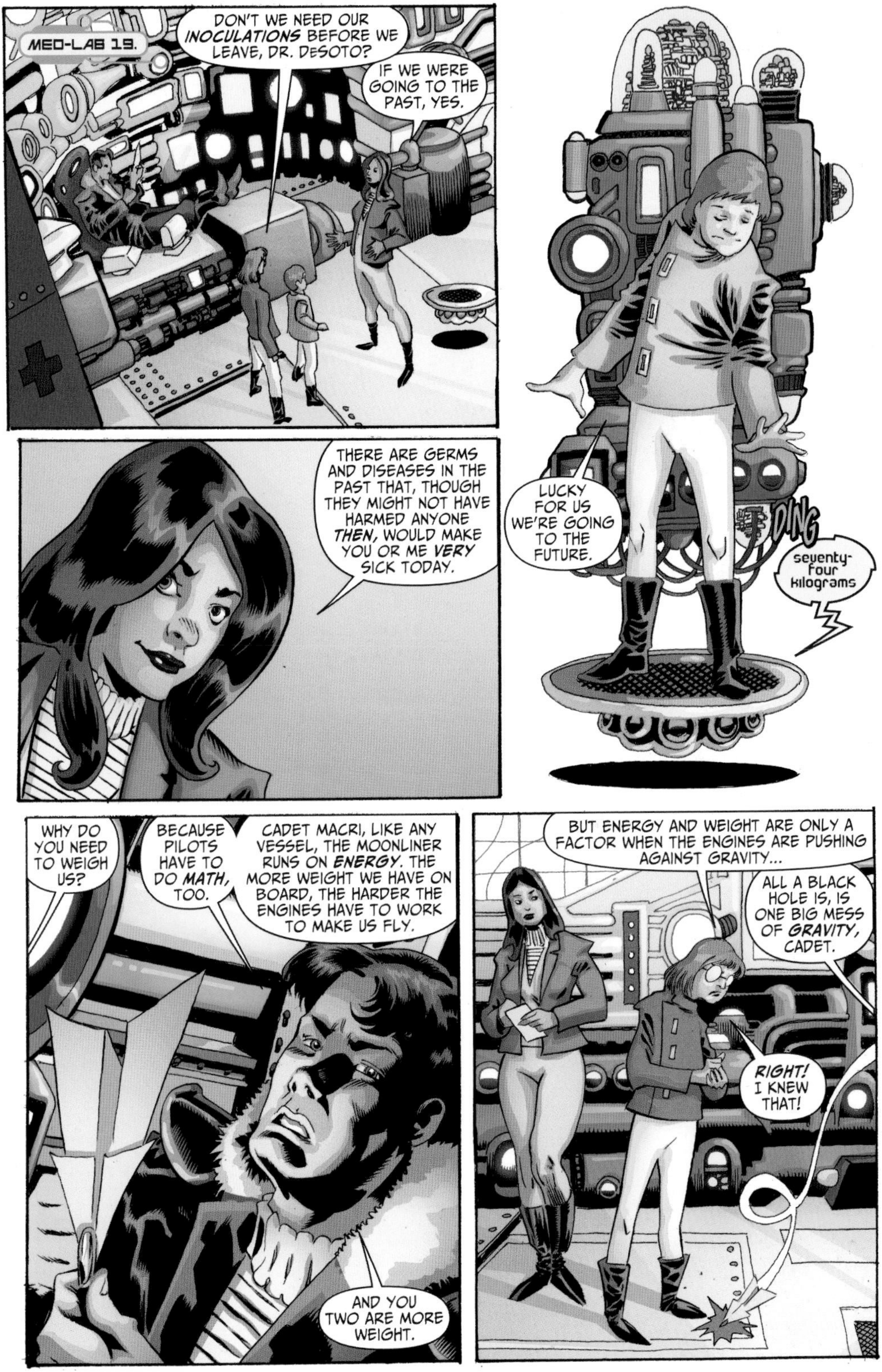
MED-LAB 13.
DON'T WE NEED OUR INOCULATIONS BEFORE WE LEAVE, DR. DeSOTO?
IF WE WERE GOING TO THE PAST, YES.
THERE ARE GERMS AND DISEASES IN THE PAST THAT, THOUGH THEY MIGHT NOT HAVE HARMED ANYONE THEN, WOULD MAKE YOU OR ME VERY SICK TODAY.
LUCKY FOR US WE'RE GOING TO THE FUTURE.
DING
seventy-four kilograms
WHY DO YOU NEED TO WEIGH US?
BECAUSE PILOTS HAVE TO DO MATH, TOO.
CADET MACRI, LIKE ANY VESSEL, THE MOONLINER RUNS ON ENERGY. THE MORE WEIGHT WE HAVE ON BOARD, THE HARDER THE ENGINES HAVE TO WORK TO MAKE US FLY.
AND YOU TWO ARE MORE WEIGHT.
BUT ENERGY AND WEIGHT ARE ONLY A FACTOR WHEN THE ENGINES ARE PUSHING AGAINST GRAVITY...
ALL A BLACK HOLE IS, IS ONE BIG MESS OF GRAVITY, CADET.
RIGHT! I KNEW THAT!

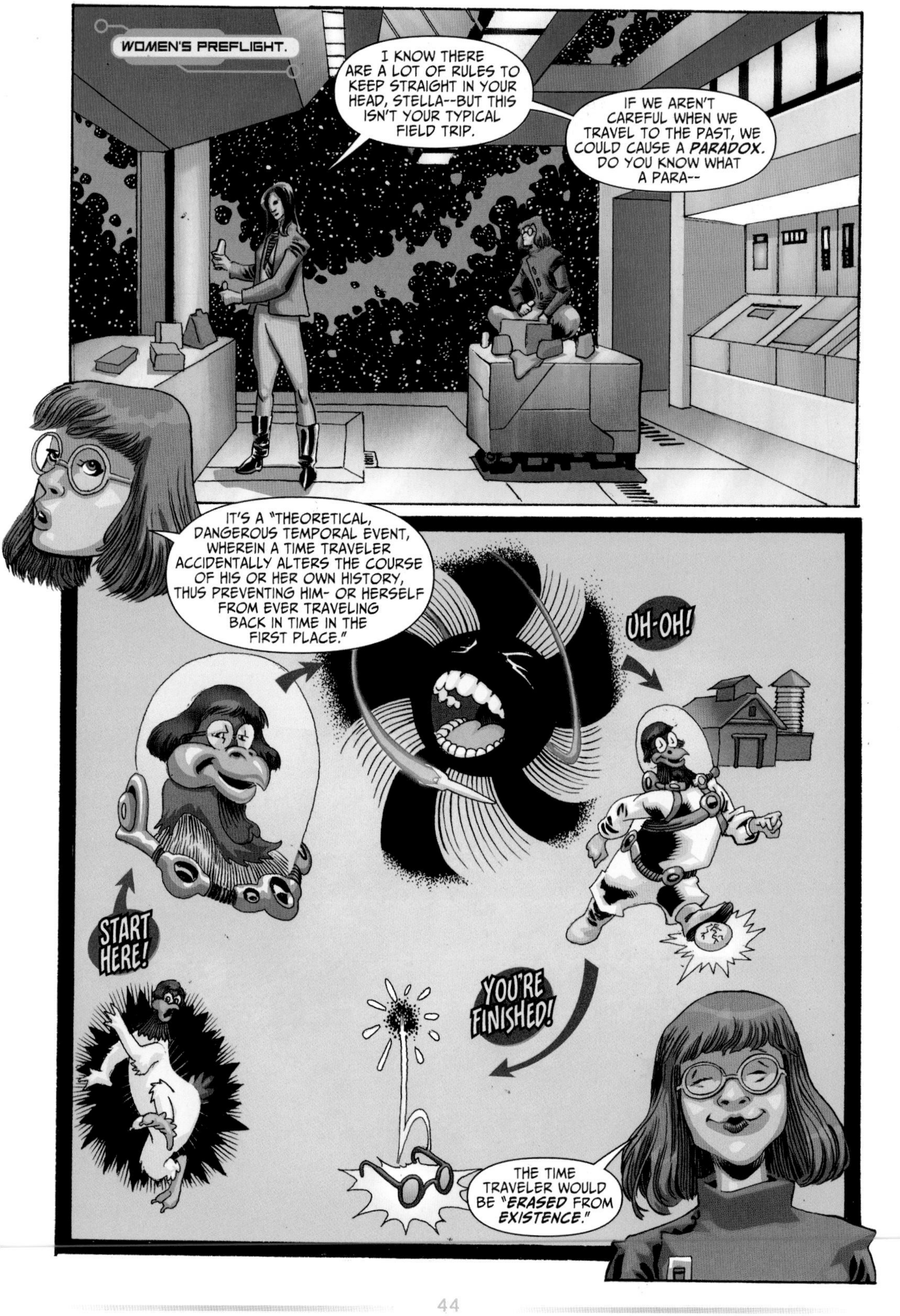
WOMEN'S PREFLIGHT.
I KNOW THERE ARE A LOT OF RULES TO KEEP STRAIGHT IN YOUR HEAD, STELLA--BUT THIS ISN'T YOUR TYPICAL FIELD TRIP.
IF WE AREN'T CAREFUL WHEN WE TRAVEL TO THE PAST, WE COULD CAUSE A *PARADOX.* DO YOU KNOW WHAT A PARA--
IT'S A "THEORETICAL, DANGEROUS TEMPORAL EVENT, WHEREIN A TIME TRAVELER ACCIDENTALLY ALTERS THE COURSE OF HIS OR HER OWN HISTORY, THUS PREVENTING HIM- OR HERSELF FROM EVER TRAVELING BACK IN TIME IN THE FIRST PLACE."
UH-OH!
START HERE!
YOU'RE FINISHED!
THE TIME TRAVELER WOULD BE "***ERASED*** FROM ***EXISTENCE***."

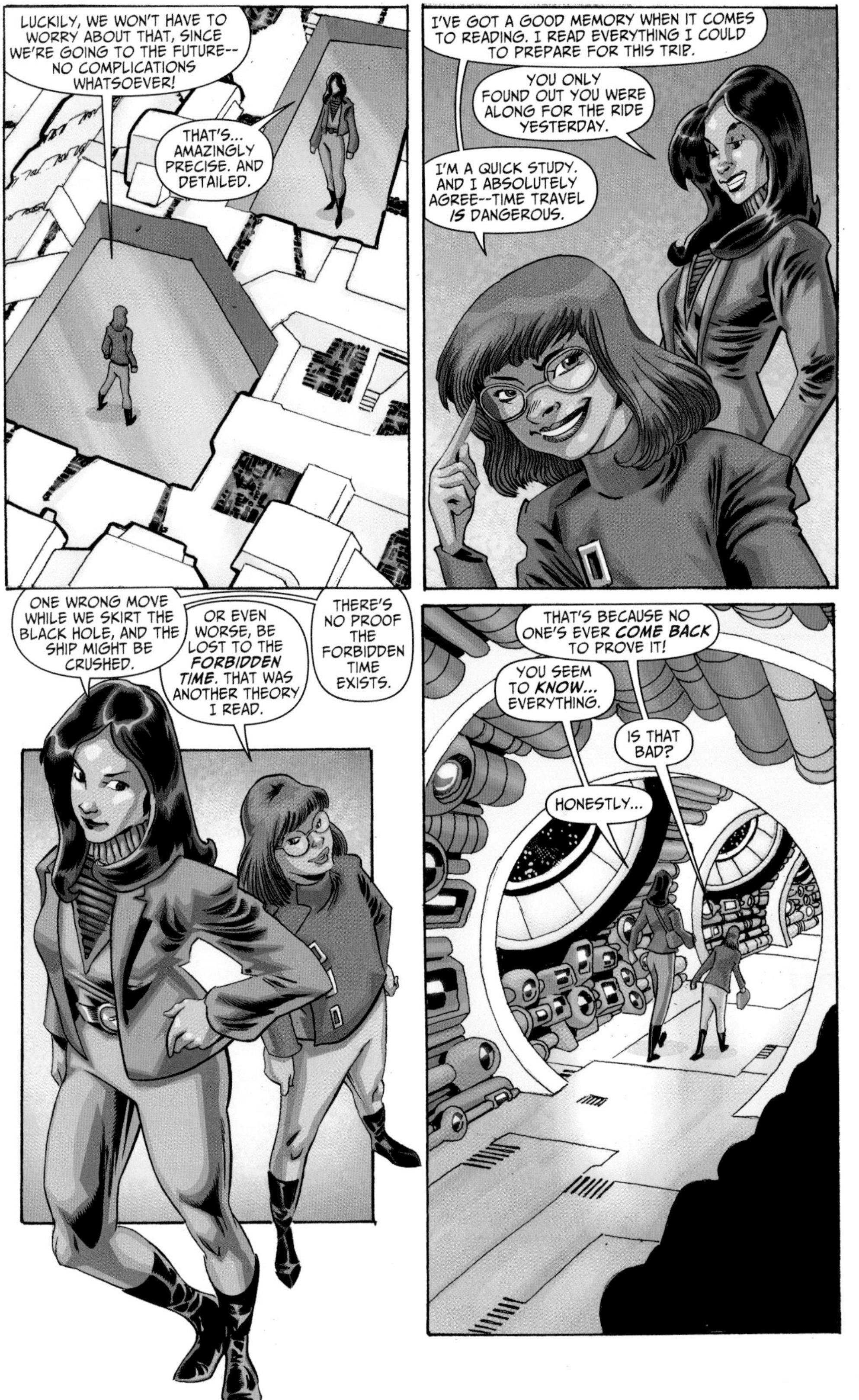
LUCKILY, WE WON'T HAVE TO WORRY ABOUT THAT, SINCE WE'RE GOING TO THE FUTURE-- NO COMPLICATIONS WHATSOEVER!
THAT'S... AMAZINGLY PRECISE. AND DETAILED.
I'VE GOT A GOOD MEMORY WHEN IT COMES TO READING. I READ EVERYTHING I COULD TO PREPARE FOR THIS TRIP.
YOU ONLY FOUND OUT YOU WERE ALONG FOR THE RIDE YESTERDAY.
I'M A QUICK STUDY. AND I ABSOLUTELY AGREE--TIME TRAVEL *IS* DANGEROUS.
ONE WRONG MOVE WHILE WE SKIRT THE BLACK HOLE, AND THE SHIP MIGHT BE CRUSHED.
OR EVEN WORSE, BE LOST TO THE ***FORBIDDEN TIME***. THAT WAS ANOTHER THEORY I READ.
THERE'S NO PROOF THE FORBIDDEN TIME EXISTS.
THAT'S BECAUSE NO ONE'S EVER ***COME BACK*** TO PROVE IT!
YOU SEEM TO ***KNOW...*** EVERYTHING.
IS THAT BAD?
HONESTLY...

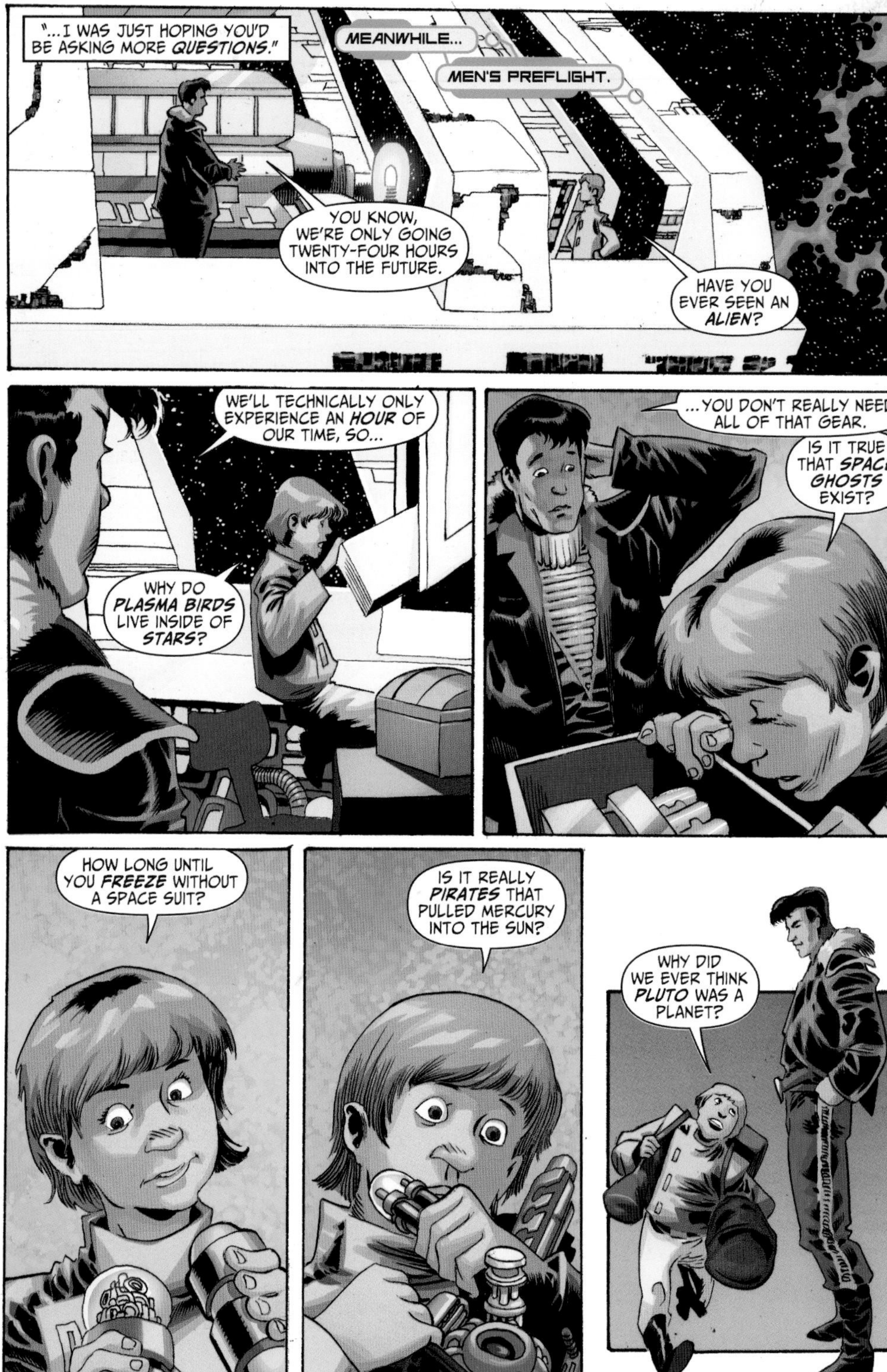
"...I WAS JUST HOPING YOU'D BE ASKING MORE QUESTIONS."
MEANWHILE...
MEN'S PREFLIGHT.
YOU KNOW, WE'RE ONLY GOING TWENTY-FOUR HOURS INTO THE FUTURE.
HAVE YOU EVER SEEN AN ALIEN?
WE'LL TECHNICALLY ONLY EXPERIENCE AN HOUR OF OUR TIME, SO...
WHY DO PLASMA BIRDS LIVE INSIDE OF STARS?
...YOU DON'T REALLY NEED ALL OF THAT GEAR.
IS IT TRUE THAT SPACE GHOSTS EXIST?
HOW LONG UNTIL YOU FREEZE WITHOUT A SPACE SUIT?
IS IT REALLY PIRATES THAT PULLED MERCURY INTO THE SUN?
WHY DID WE EVER THINK PLUTO WAS A PLANET?

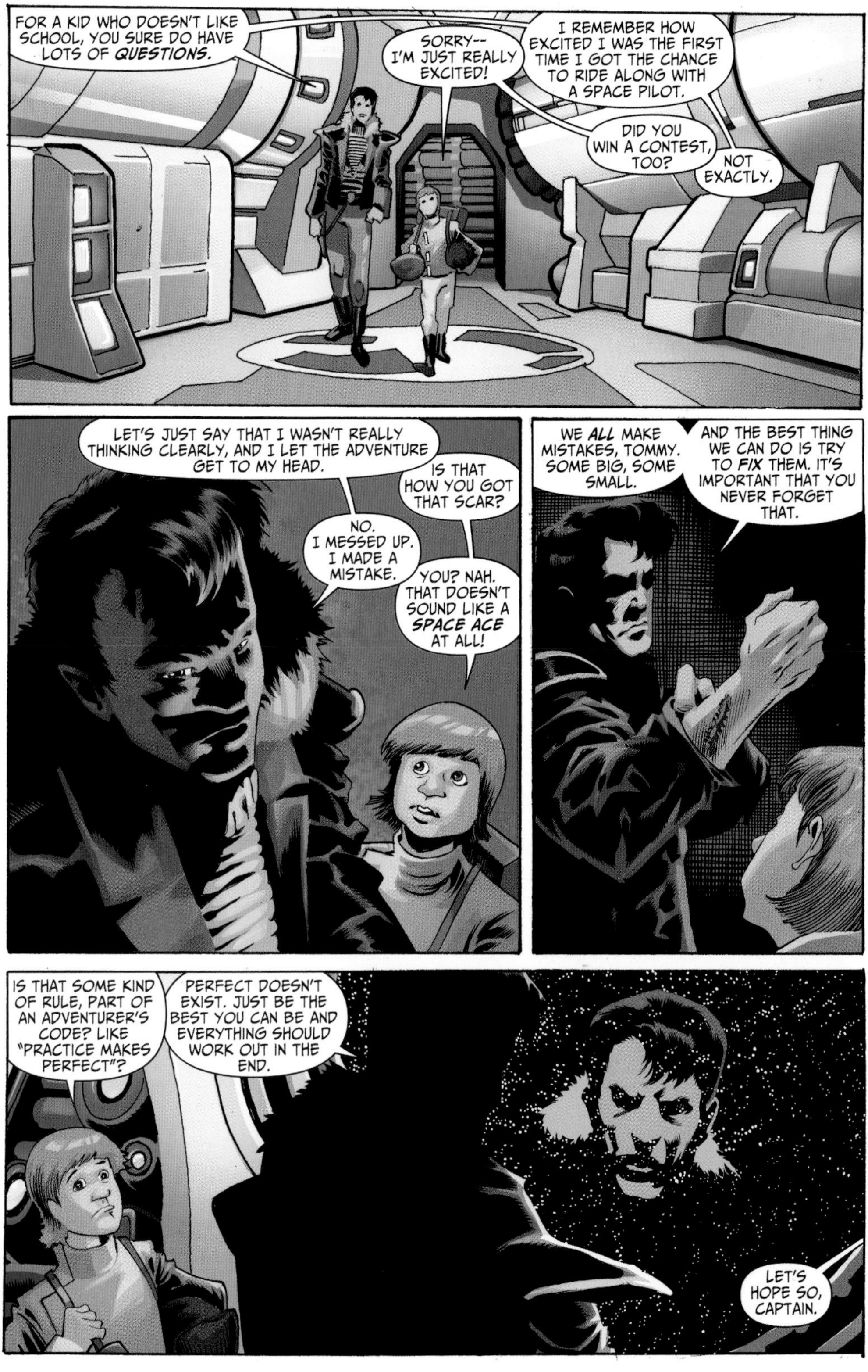
FOR A KID WHO DOESN'T LIKE SCHOOL, YOU SURE DO HAVE LOTS OF QUESTIONS.
SORRY-- I'M JUST REALLY EXCITED!
I REMEMBER HOW EXCITED I WAS THE FIRST TIME I GOT THE CHANCE TO RIDE ALONG WITH A SPACE PILOT.
DID YOU WIN A CONTEST, TOO?
NOT EXACTLY.
LET'S JUST SAY THAT I WASN'T REALLY THINKING CLEARLY, AND I LET THE ADVENTURE GET TO MY HEAD.
IS THAT HOW YOU GOT THAT SCAR?
NO. I MESSED UP. I MADE A MISTAKE.
YOU? NAH. THAT DOESN'T SOUND LIKE A SPACE ACE AT ALL!
WE ALL MAKE MISTAKES, TOMMY. SOME BIG, SOME SMALL.
AND THE BEST THING WE CAN DO IS TRY TO FIX THEM. IT'S IMPORTANT THAT YOU NEVER FORGET THAT.
IS THAT SOME KIND OF RULE, PART OF AN ADVENTURER'S CODE? LIKE "PRACTICE MAKES PERFECT"?
PERFECT DOESN'T EXIST. JUST BE THE BEST YOU CAN BE AND EVERYTHING SHOULD WORK OUT IN THE END.
LET'S HOPE SO, CAPTAIN.

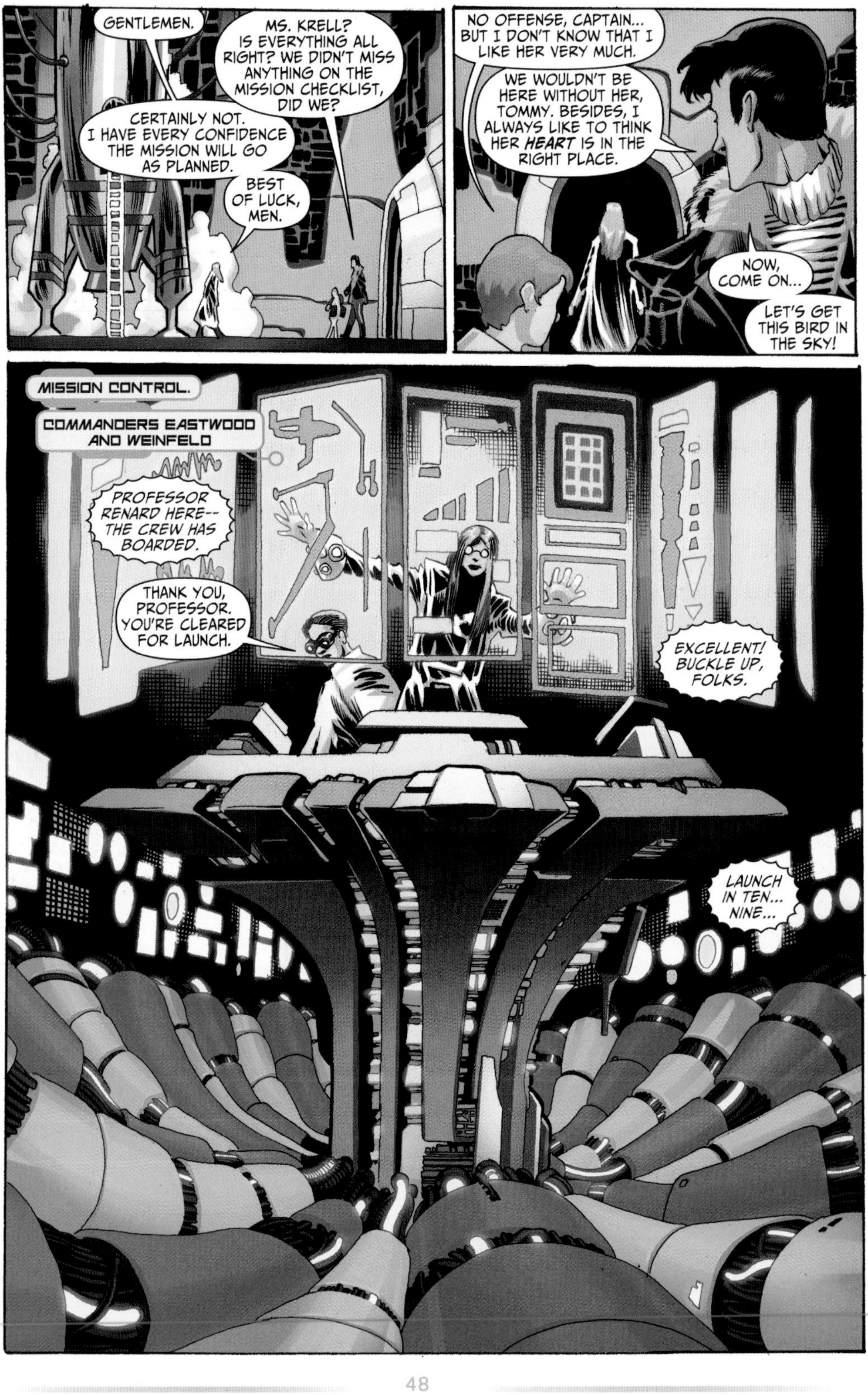
GENTLEMEN.
MS. KRELL? IS EVERYTHING ALL RIGHT? WE DIDN'T MISS ANYTHING ON THE MISSION CHECKLIST, DID WE?
CERTAINLY NOT. I HAVE EVERY CONFIDENCE THE MISSION WILL GO AS PLANNED.
BEST OF LUCK, MEN.
NO OFFENSE, CAPTAIN... BUT I DON'T KNOW THAT I LIKE HER VERY MUCH.
WE WOULDN'T BE HERE WITHOUT HER, TOMMY. BESIDES, I ALWAYS LIKE TO THINK HER HEART IS IN THE RIGHT PLACE.
NOW, COME ON...
LET'S GET THIS BIRD IN THE SKY!
MISSION CONTROL.
COMMANDERS EASTWOOD AND WEINFELD
PROFESSOR RENARD HERE-- THE CREW HAS BOARDED.
THANK YOU, PROFESSOR. YOU'RE CLEARED FOR LAUNCH.
EXCELLENT! BUCKLE UP, FOLKS.
LAUNCH IN TEN... NINE...

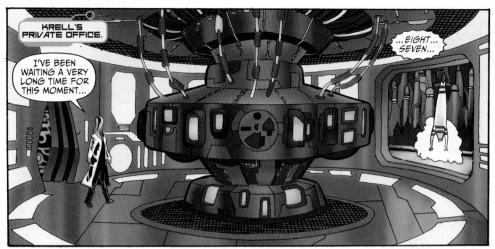

KRELL'S PRIVATE OFFICE.

I'VE BEEN WAITING A VERY LONG TIME FOR THIS MOMENT...

...EIGHT... SEVEN...

...SIX... FIVE...

...FOUR... THREE...

THIS IS SO COOL!

THE MOMENT WHEN EVERYTHING CHANGES...

...TWO...

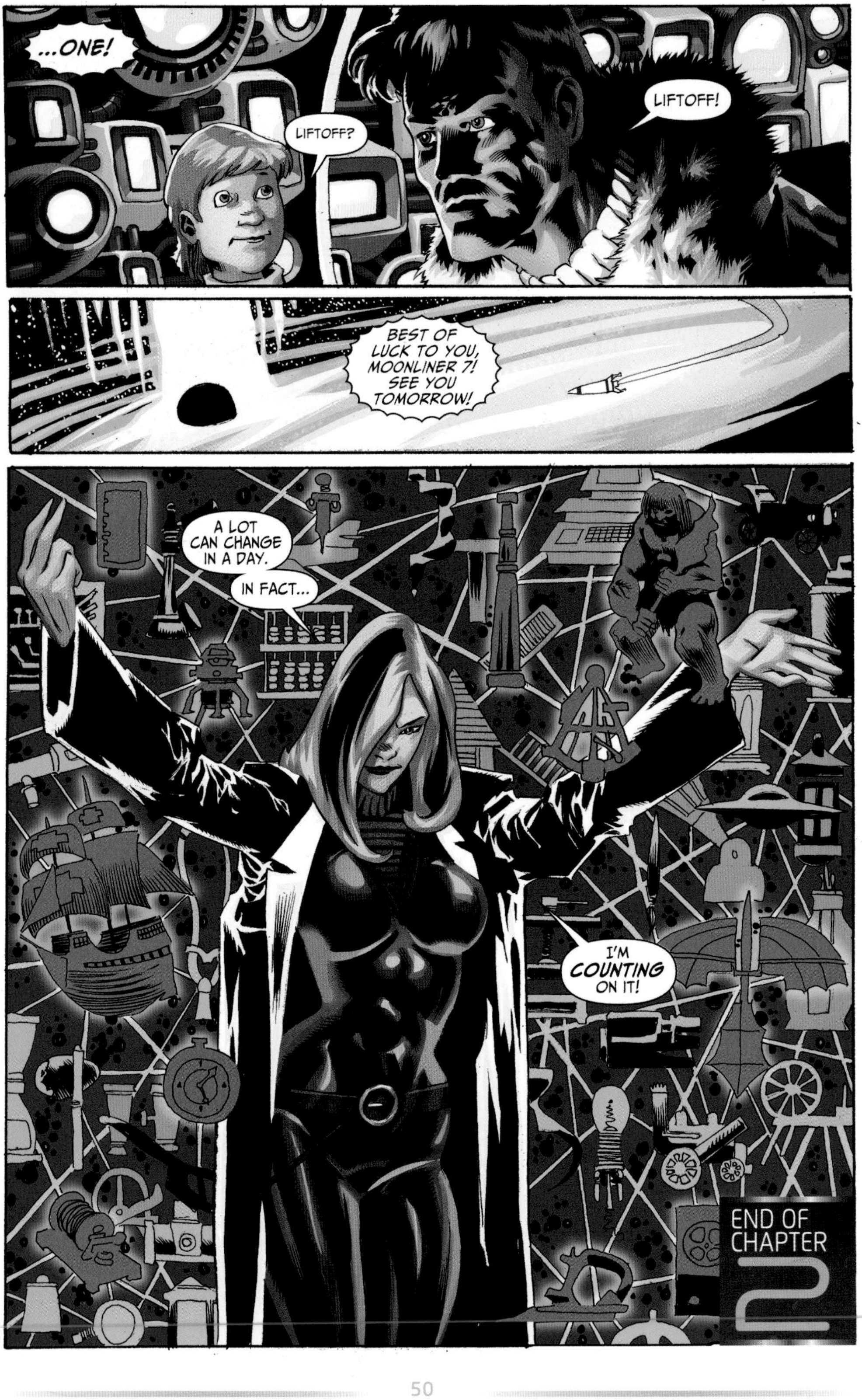
...ONE!
LIFTOFF?
LIFTOFF!
BEST OF LUCK TO YOU, MOONLINER 7! SEE YOU TOMORROW!
A LOT CAN CHANGE IN A DAY.
IN FACT...
I'M COUNTING ON IT!
END OF CHAPTER 2

CHAPTER 3

TOMORROW IS TODAY

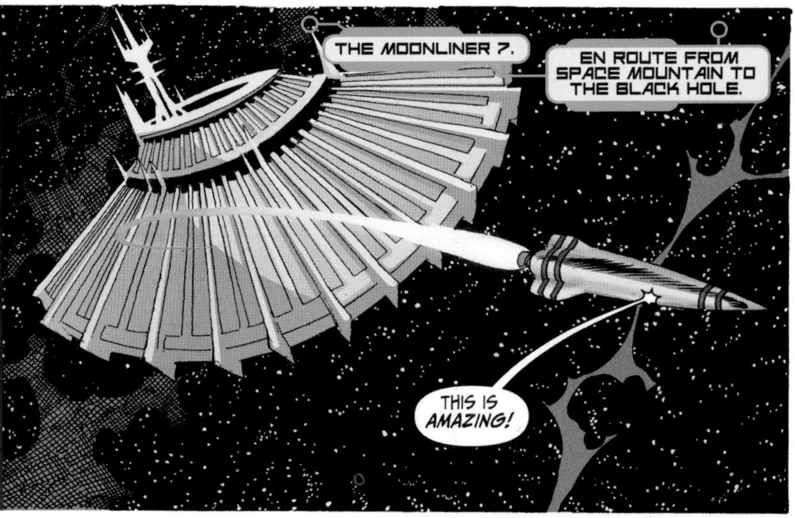

THE MOONLINER 7.
EN ROUTE FROM SPACE MOUNTAIN TO THE BLACK HOLE.
THIS IS *AMAZING!*

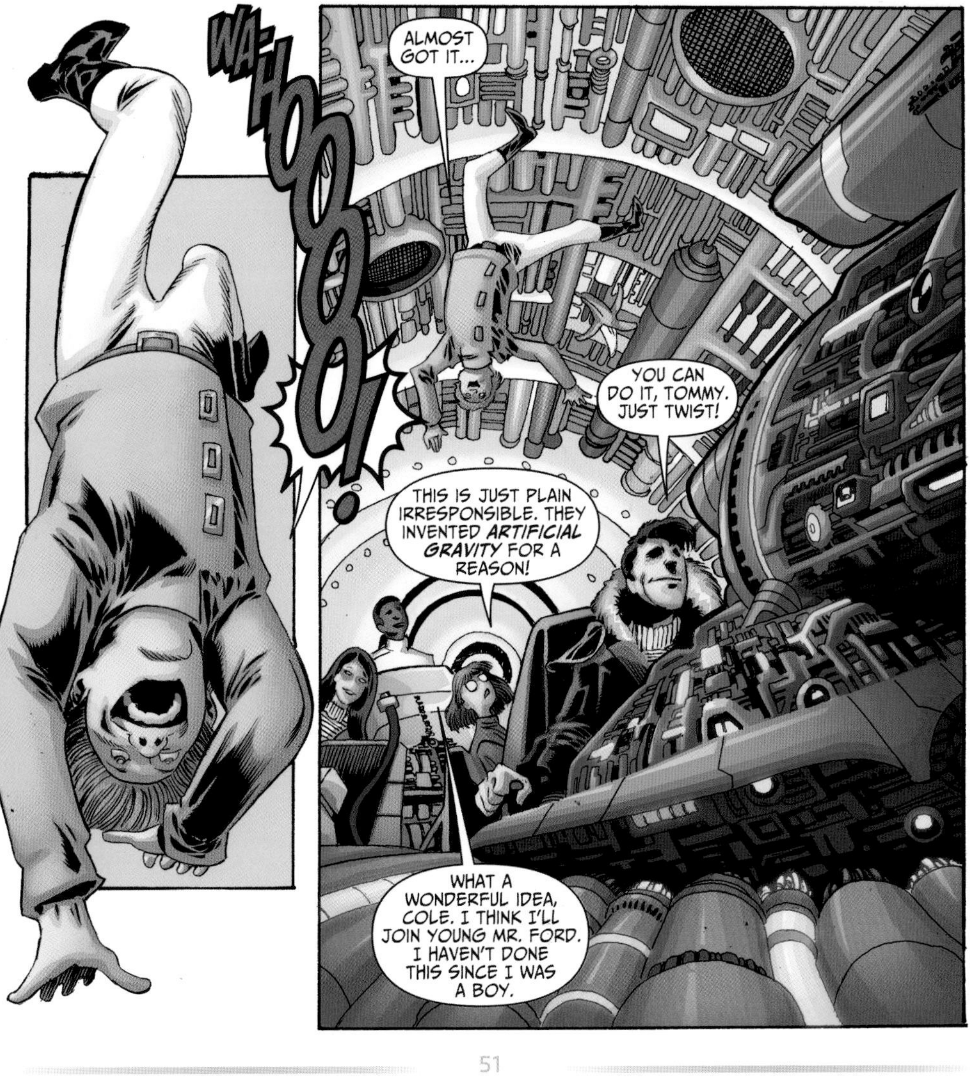

WA-HOOOOO!
ALMOST GOT IT...
YOU CAN DO IT, TOMMY. JUST TWIST!
THIS IS JUST PLAIN IRRESPONSIBLE. THEY INVENTED *ARTIFICIAL GRAVITY* FOR A REASON!
WHAT A WONDERFUL IDEA, COLE. I THINK I'LL JOIN YOUNG MR. FORD. I HAVEN'T DONE THIS SINCE I WAS A BOY.

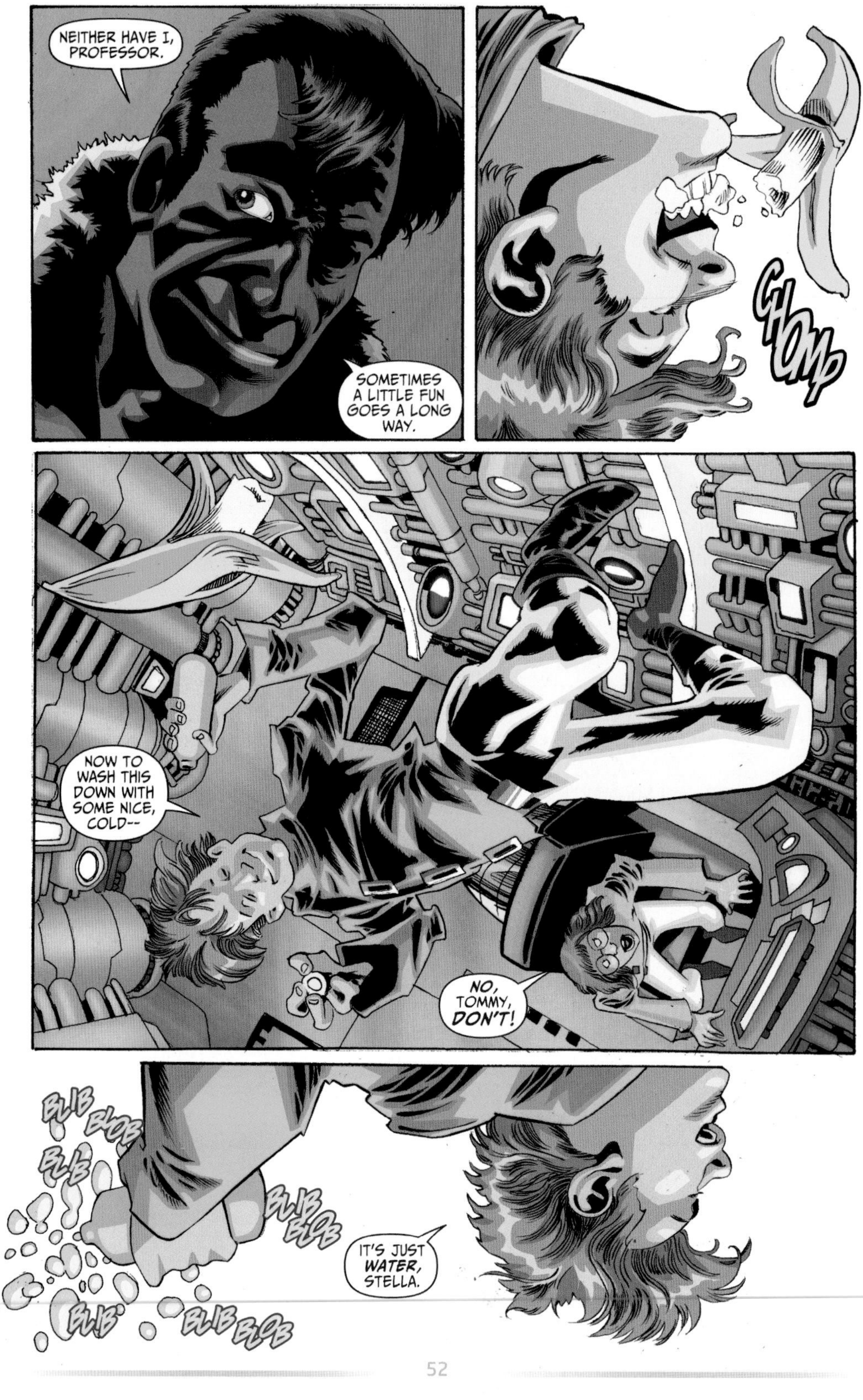
NEITHER HAVE I, PROFESSOR.
SOMETIMES A LITTLE FUN GOES A LONG WAY.
CHOMP
NOW TO WASH THIS DOWN WITH SOME NICE, COLD--
NO, TOMMY, DON'T!
BLIB
BLOB
BLIB
BLIB
BLOB
IT'S JUST WATER, STELLA.
BLIB
BLIB
BLOB

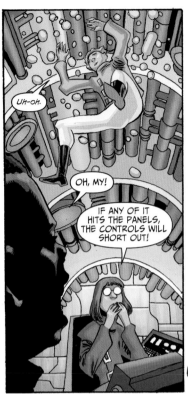

Uh-oh.

OH, MY!

IF ANY OF IT HITS THE PANELS, THE CONTROLS WILL SHORT OUT!

WHY IS IT DOING THAT?

GRAVITY USUALLY HOLDS WATER DOWN. BUT WITHOUT IT, WATER FLOATS UP AND UP AND UP.

SURFACE TENSION CAUSES IT TO STICK TO ITSELF.

ASTRONAUTS OF OLD USED TO HAVE TO DRINK OUT OF POUCHES.

NOW WE JUST KEEP THE GRAVITY ON AND EVERYTHING WORKS JUST LIKE IT DOES BACK ON THE COLONY.

WHAT A MESS!

WE'LL FIGURE OUT *SOME* WAY TO GET IT ALL CLEANED UP.

WAY AHEAD OF YOU, CAPTAIN COLE!

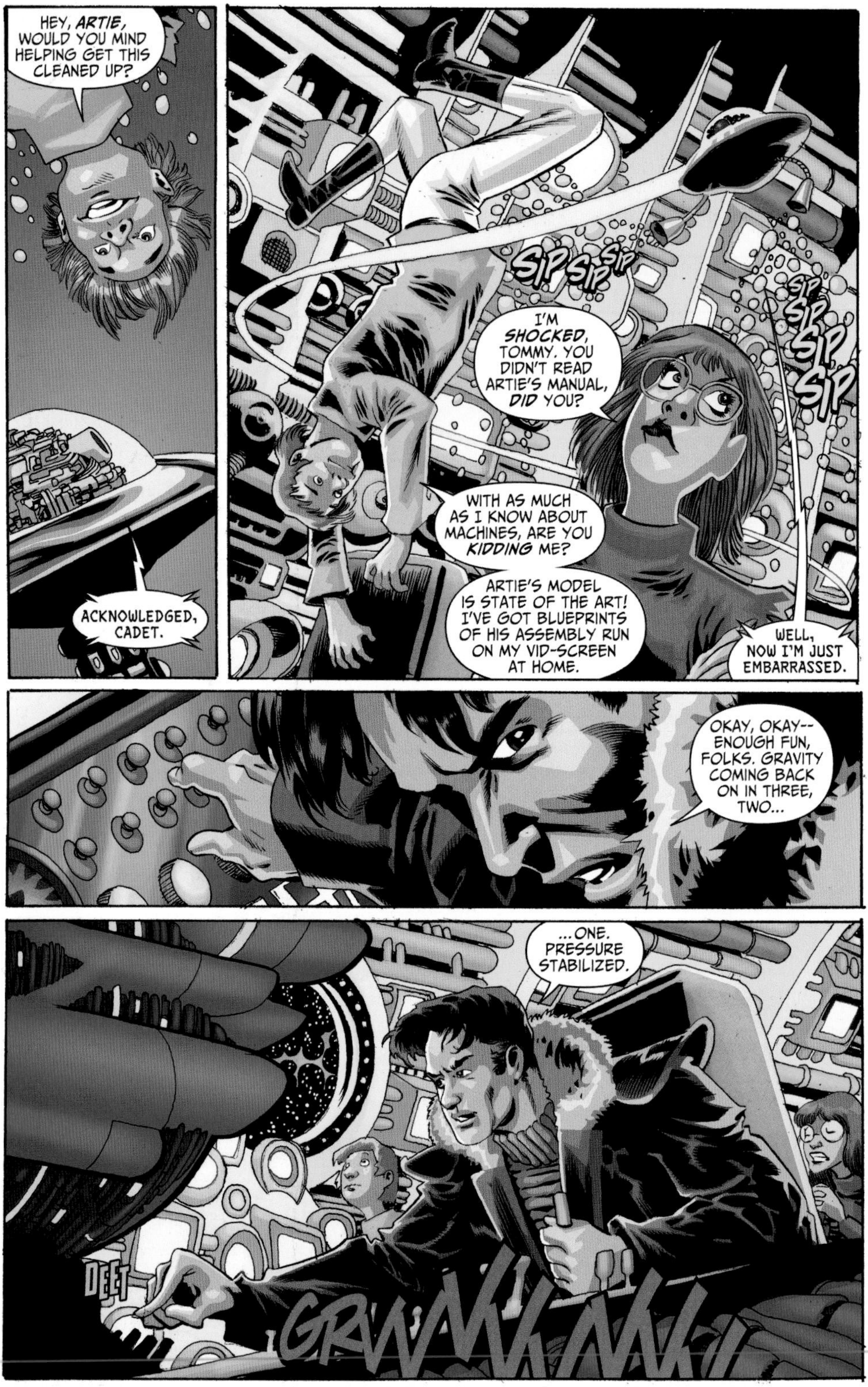
HEY, ARTIE, WOULD YOU MIND HELPING GET THIS CLEANED UP?
ACKNOWLEDGED, CADET.
SIP SIP SIP SIP
SIP SIP SIP SIP
I'M SHOCKED, TOMMY. YOU DIDN'T READ ARTIE'S MANUAL, DID YOU?
WITH AS MUCH AS I KNOW ABOUT MACHINES, ARE YOU KIDDING ME?
ARTIE'S MODEL IS STATE OF THE ART! I'VE GOT BLUEPRINTS OF HIS ASSEMBLY RUN ON MY VID-SCREEN AT HOME.
WELL, NOW I'M JUST EMBARRASSED.
OKAY, OKAY-- ENOUGH FUN, FOLKS. GRAVITY COMING BACK ON IN THREE, TWO...
...ONE. PRESSURE STABILIZED.
DEET
GRWWMMMMM!

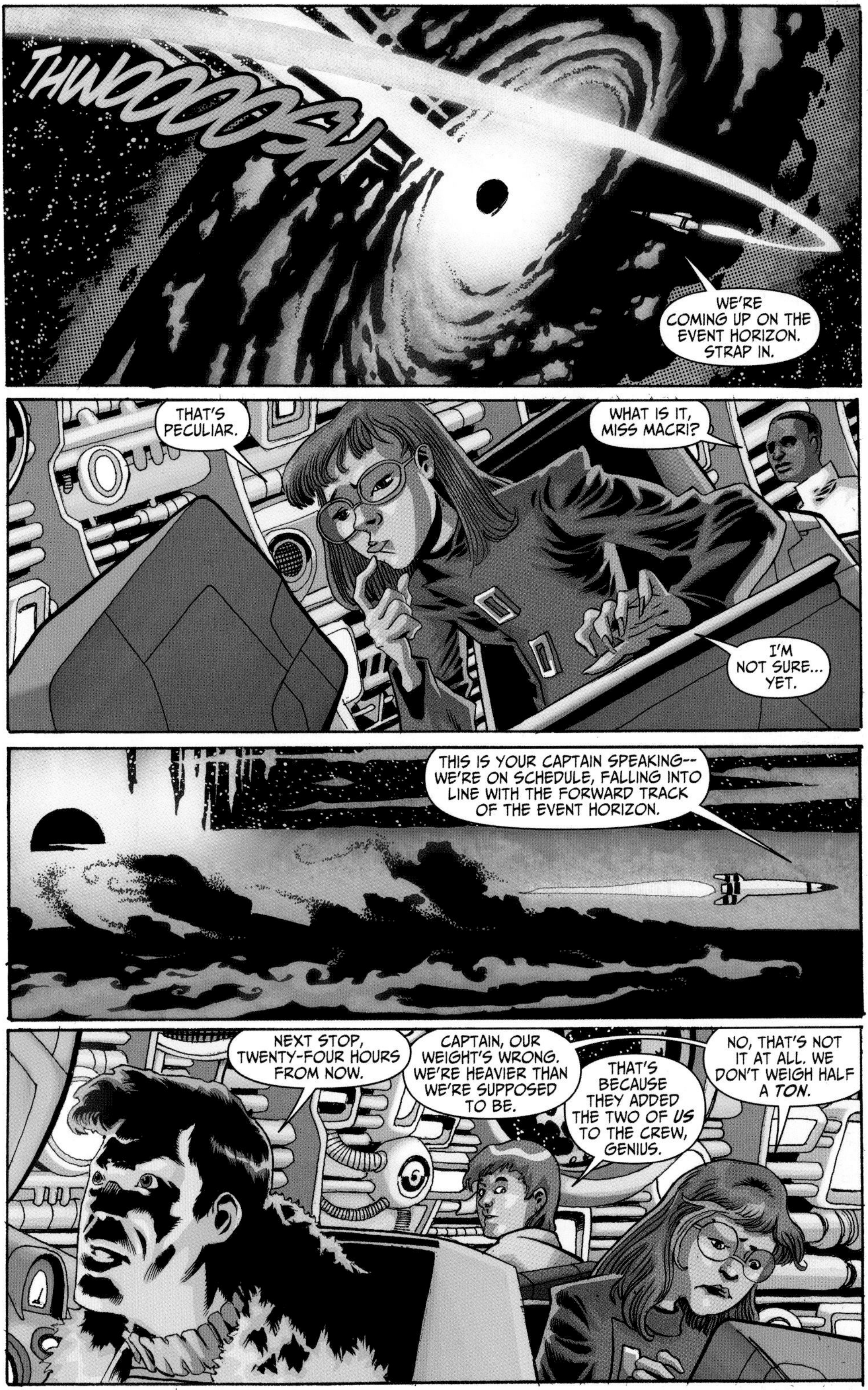
THWOOOOSH
WE'RE COMING UP ON THE EVENT HORIZON. STRAP IN.
THAT'S PECULIAR.
WHAT IS IT, MISS MACRI?
I'M NOT SURE... YET.
THIS IS YOUR CAPTAIN SPEAKING-- WE'RE ON SCHEDULE, FALLING INTO LINE WITH THE FORWARD TRACK OF THE EVENT HORIZON.
NEXT STOP, TWENTY-FOUR HOURS FROM NOW.
CAPTAIN, OUR WEIGHT'S WRONG. WE'RE HEAVIER THAN WE'RE SUPPOSED TO BE.
THAT'S BECAUSE THEY ADDED THE TWO OF *US* TO THE CREW, GENIUS.
NO, THAT'S NOT IT AT ALL. WE DON'T WEIGH HALF A *TON*.

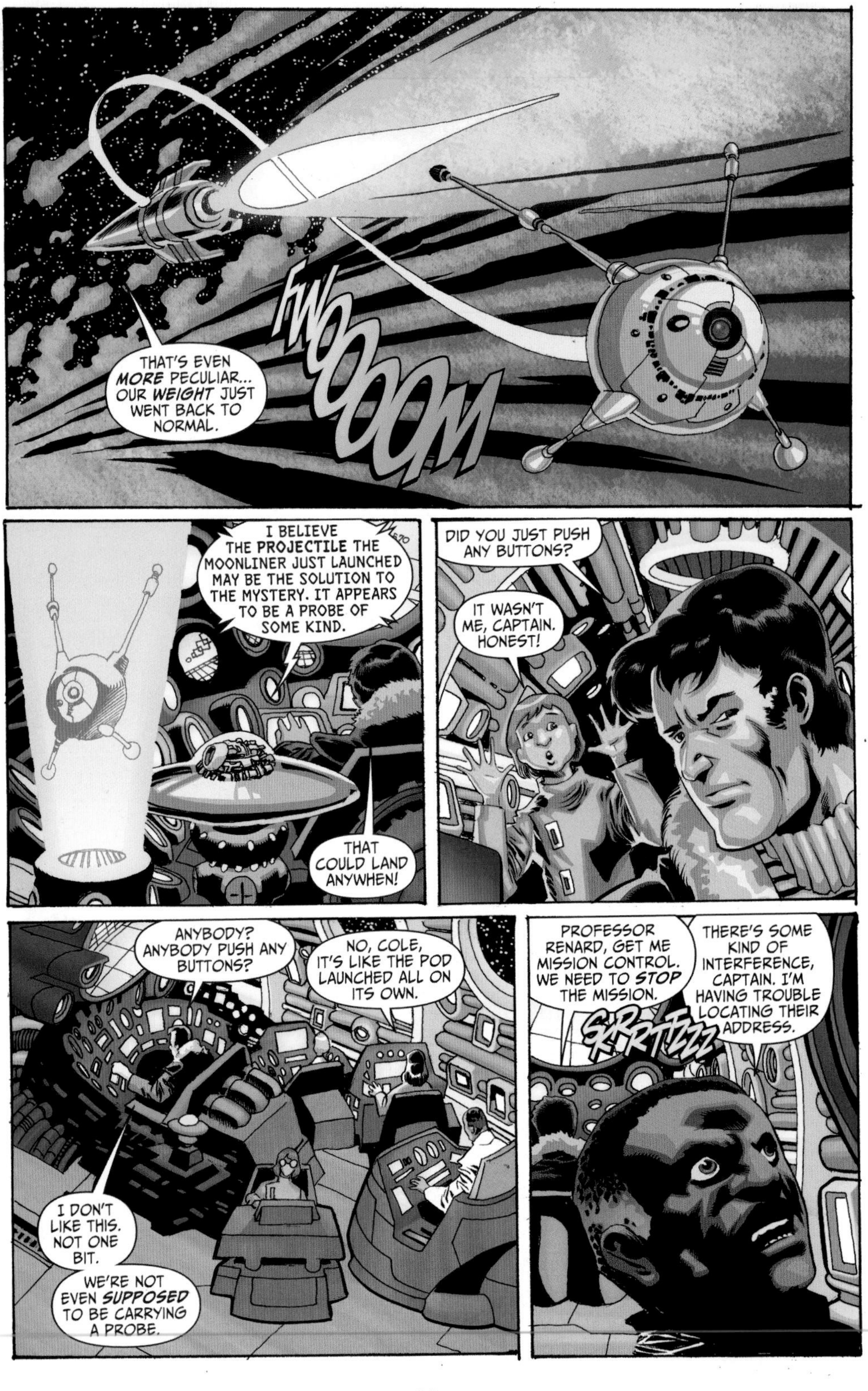

THAT'S EVEN MORE PECULIAR... OUR WEIGHT JUST WENT BACK TO NORMAL.
FWOOOOOM
I BELIEVE THE PROJECTILE THE MOONLINER JUST LAUNCHED MAY BE THE SOLUTION TO THE MYSTERY. IT APPEARS TO BE A PROBE OF SOME KIND.
THAT COULD LAND ANYWHEN!
DID YOU JUST PUSH ANY BUTTONS?
IT WASN'T ME, CAPTAIN. HONEST!
ANYBODY? ANYBODY PUSH ANY BUTTONS?
NO, COLE, IT'S LIKE THE POD LAUNCHED ALL ON ITS OWN.
I DON'T LIKE THIS. NOT ONE BIT.
WE'RE NOT EVEN SUPPOSED TO BE CARRYING A PROBE.
PROFESSOR RENARD, GET ME MISSION CONTROL. WE NEED TO STOP THE MISSION.
SKRRTFZZZ
THERE'S SOME KIND OF INTERFERENCE, CAPTAIN. I'M HAVING TROUBLE LOCATING THEIR ADDRESS.

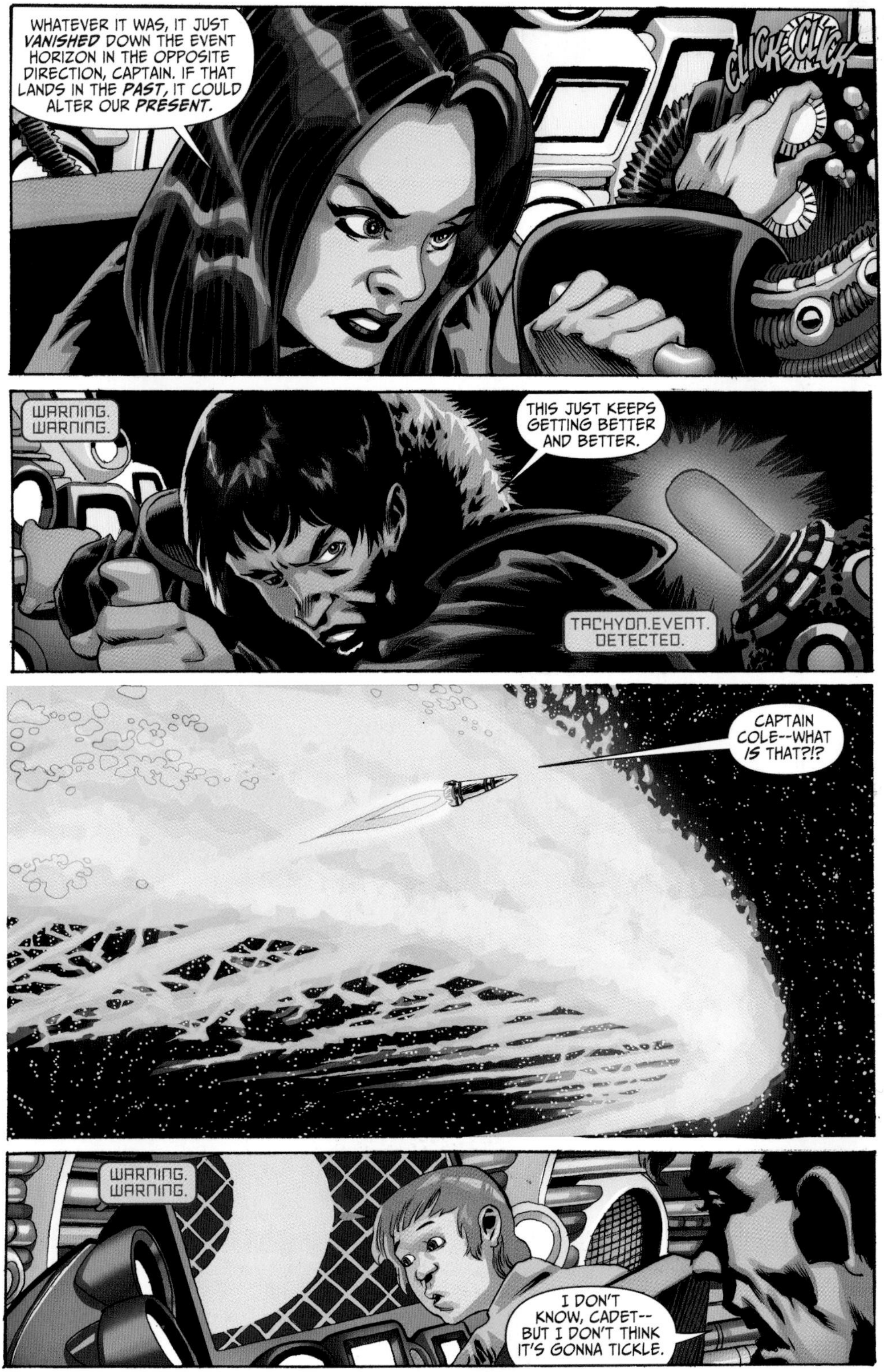
WHATEVER IT WAS, IT JUST *VANISHED* DOWN THE EVENT HORIZON IN THE OPPOSITE DIRECTION, CAPTAIN. IF THAT LANDS IN THE *PAST*, IT COULD ALTER OUR *PRESENT.*
CLICK CLICK
WARNING. WARNING.
THIS JUST KEEPS GETTING BETTER AND BETTER.
TACHYON.EVENT. DETECTED.
CAPTAIN COLE--WHAT *IS* THAT?!?
WARNING. WARNING.
I DON'T KNOW, CADET-- BUT I DON'T THINK IT'S GONNA TICKLE.

WARNING. WARNING.

WE CANNOT OUTRUN IT, CAPTAIN. IMPACT-- IMMINENT.

ALL HANDS--

"--BRACE FOR IMPACT!"

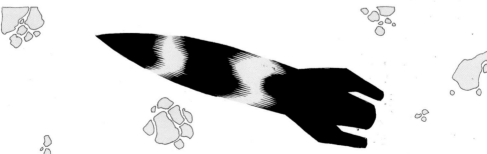

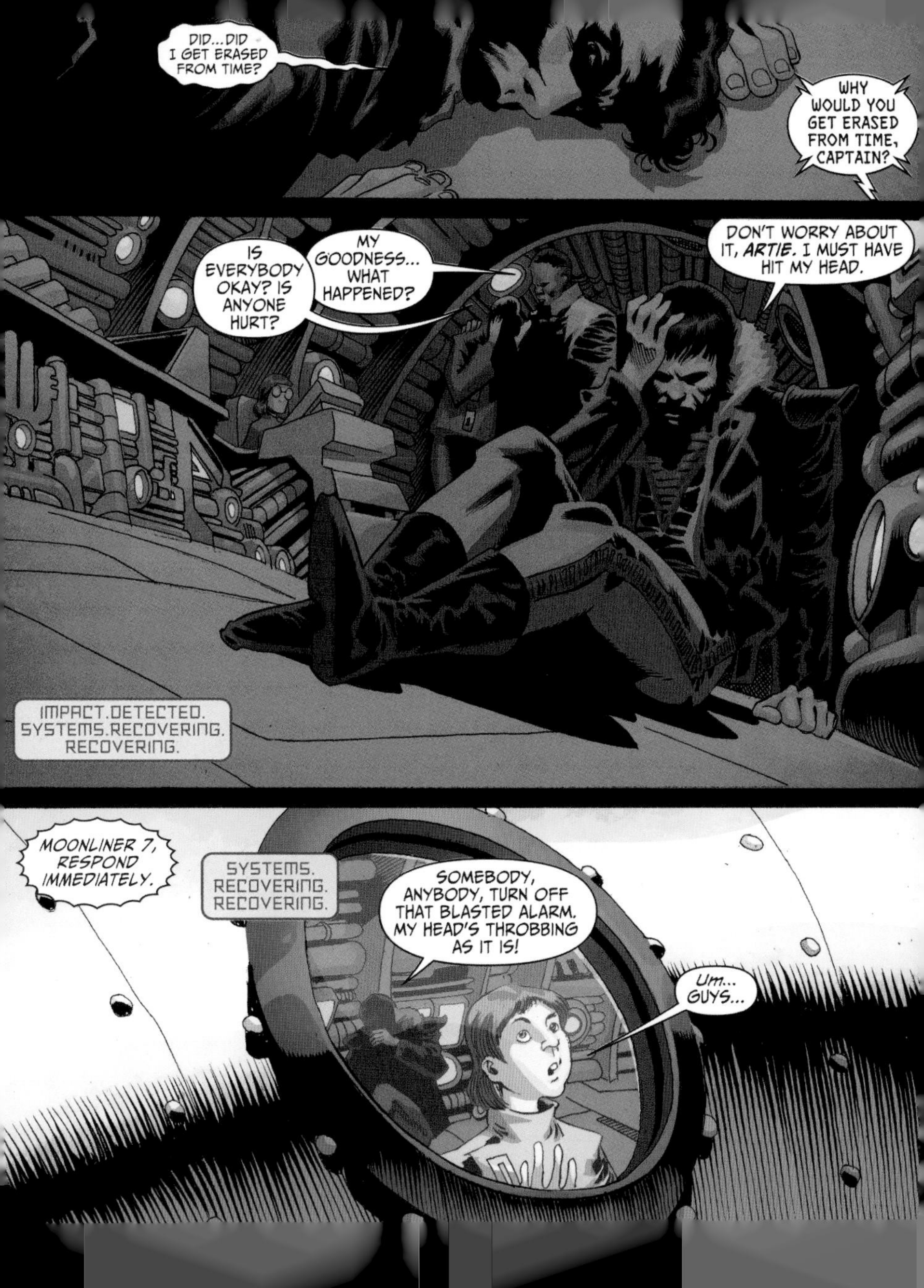
DID...DID I GET ERASED FROM TIME?
WHY WOULD YOU GET ERASED FROM TIME, CAPTAIN?
IS EVERYBODY OKAY? IS ANYONE HURT?
MY GOODNESS... WHAT HAPPENED?
DON'T WORRY ABOUT IT, ARTIE. I MUST HAVE HIT MY HEAD.
IMPACT.DETECTED. SYSTEMS.RECOVERING. RECOVERING.
MOONLINER 7, RESPOND IMMEDIATELY.
SYSTEMS. RECOVERING. RECOVERING.
SOMEBODY, ANYBODY, TURN OFF THAT BLASTED ALARM. MY HEAD'S THROBBING AS IT IS!
Um... GUYS...

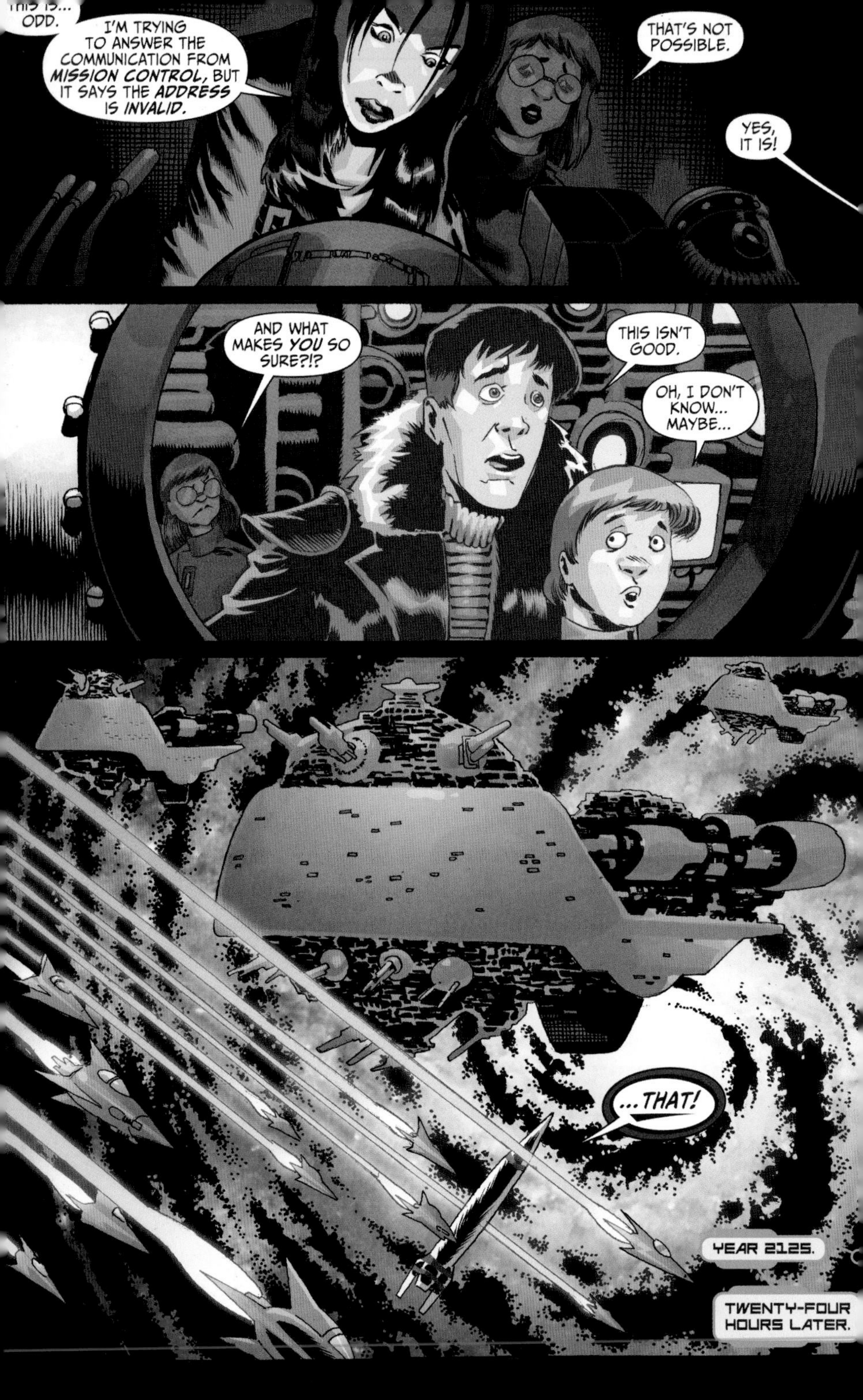
THIS IS... ODD.
I'M TRYING TO ANSWER THE COMMUNICATION FROM MISSION CONTROL, BUT IT SAYS THE ADDRESS IS INVALID.
THAT'S NOT POSSIBLE.
YES, IT IS!
AND WHAT MAKES YOU SO SURE?!?
THIS ISN'T GOOD.
OH, I DON'T KNOW... MAYBE...
...THAT!
YEAR 2125.
TWENTY-FOUR HOURS LATER.

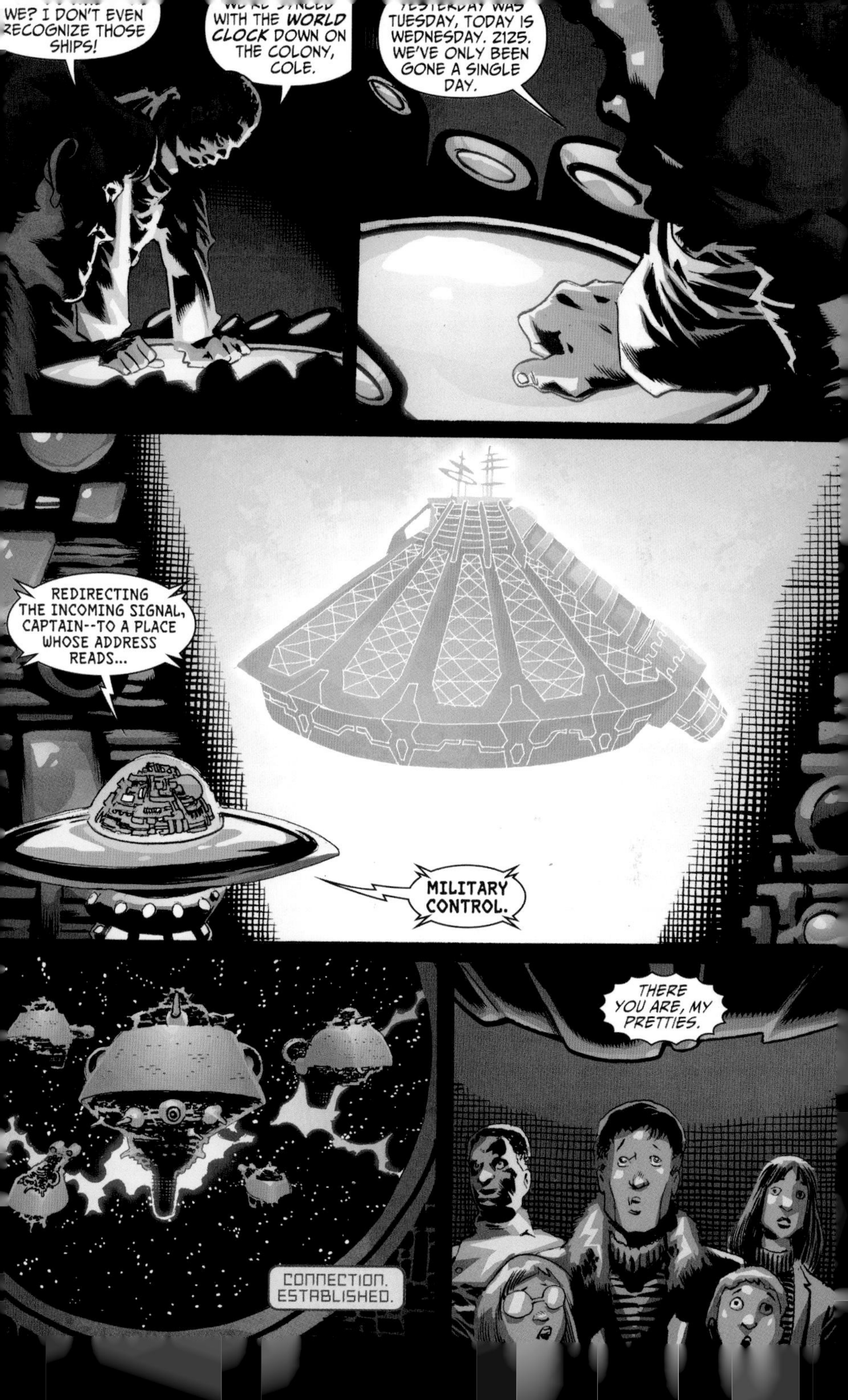
WE? I DON'T EVEN RECOGNIZE THOSE SHIPS!
WITH THE WORLD CLOCK DOWN ON THE COLONY, COLE.
TUESDAY, TODAY IS WEDNESDAY. 2125. WE'VE ONLY BEEN GONE A SINGLE DAY.
REDIRECTING THE INCOMING SIGNAL, CAPTAIN--TO A PLACE WHOSE ADDRESS READS...
MILITARY CONTROL.
CONNECTION. ESTABLISHED.
THERE YOU ARE, MY PRETTIES.

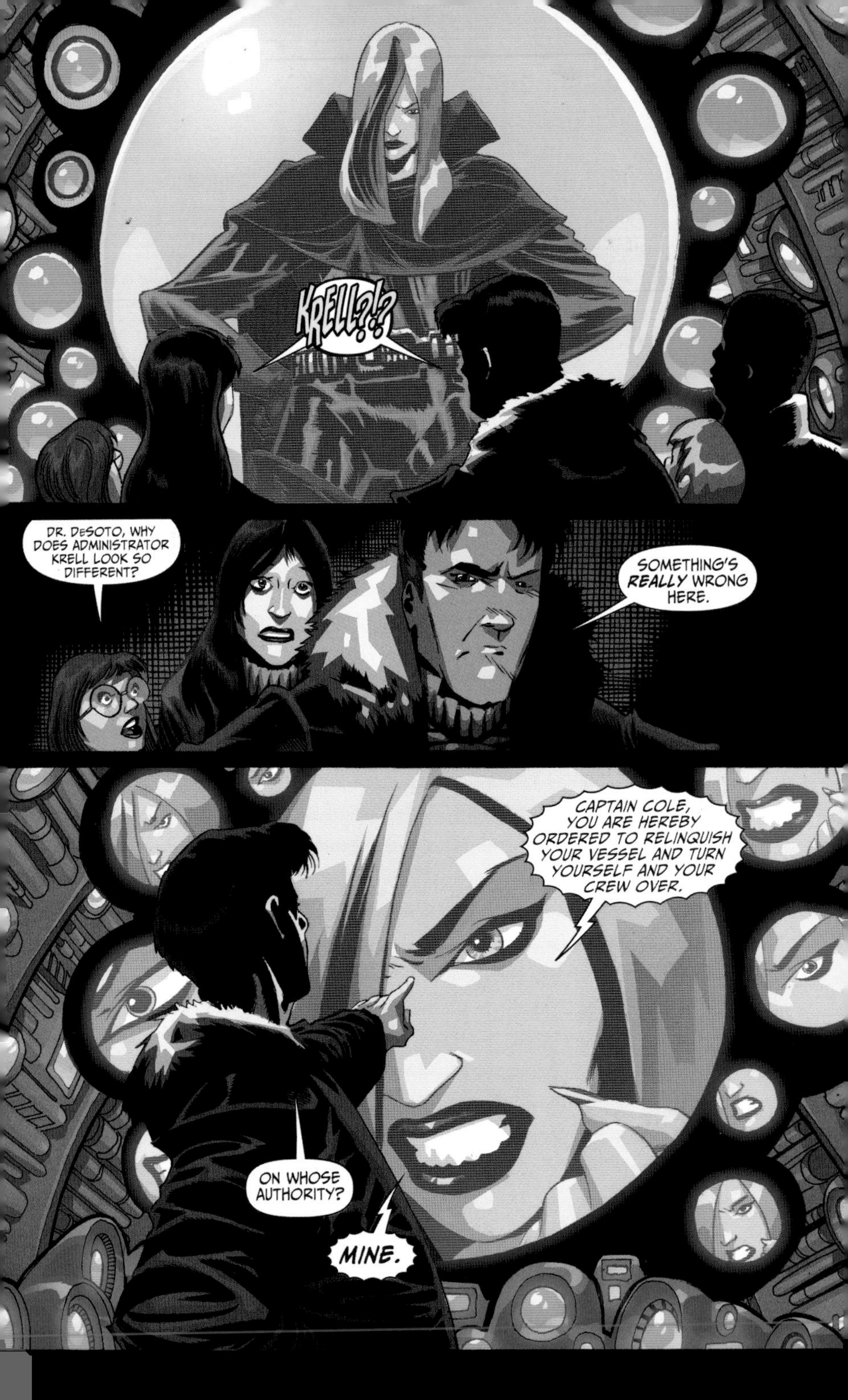
KRELL?!?
DR. DeSOTO, WHY DOES ADMINISTRATOR KRELL LOOK SO DIFFERENT?
SOMETHING'S REALLY WRONG HERE.
CAPTAIN COLE, YOU ARE HEREBY ORDERED TO RELINQUISH YOUR VESSEL AND TURN YOURSELF AND YOUR CREW OVER.
ON WHOSE AUTHORITY?
MINE.

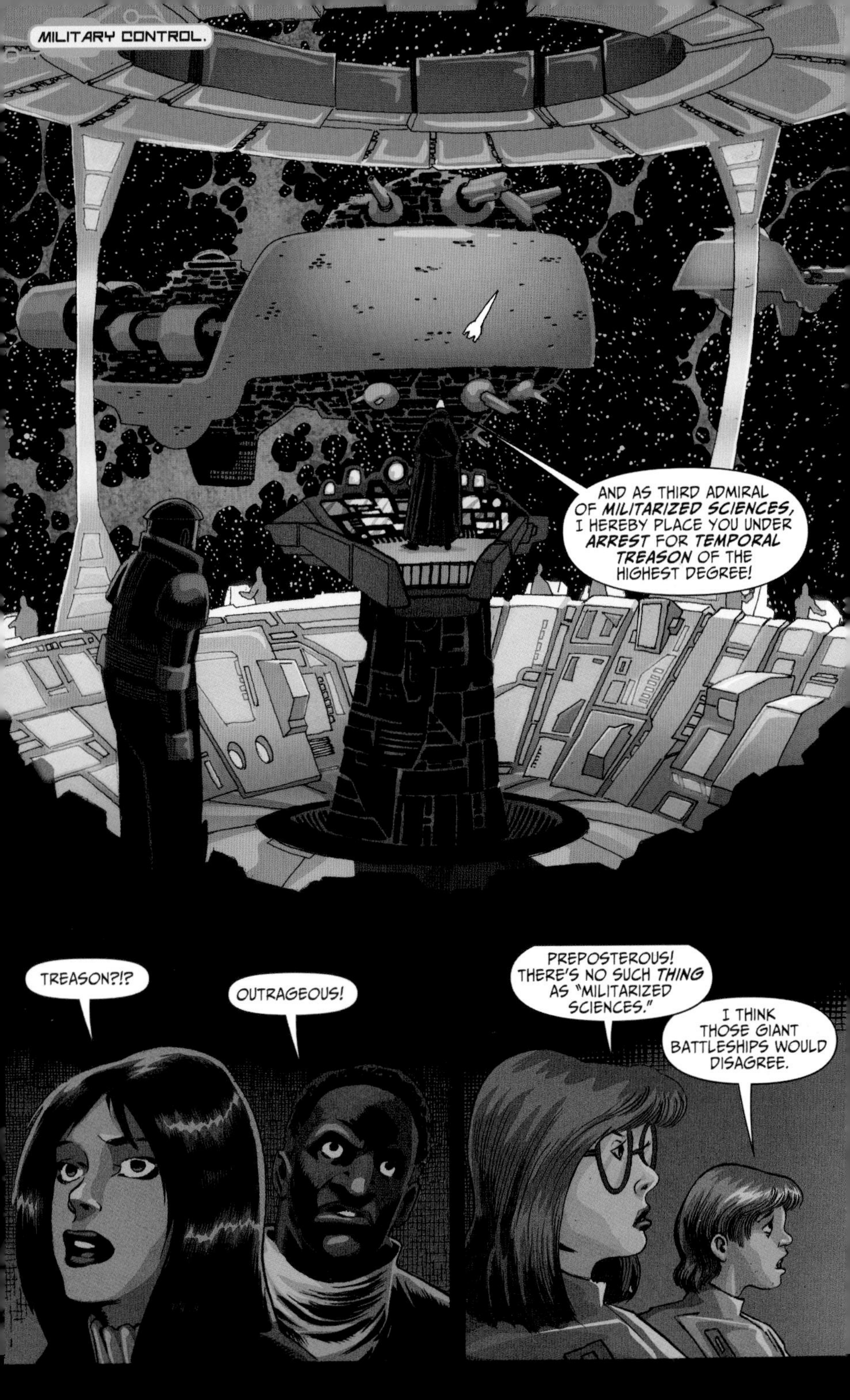

MILITARY CONTROL.
AND AS THIRD ADMIRAL OF *MILITARIZED SCIENCES,* I HEREBY PLACE YOU UNDER *ARREST* FOR *TEMPORAL TREASON* OF THE HIGHEST DEGREE!
TREASON?!?
OUTRAGEOUS!
PREPOSTEROUS! THERE'S NO SUCH *THING* AS "MILITARIZED SCIENCES."
I THINK THOSE GIANT BATTLESHIPS WOULD DISAGREE.

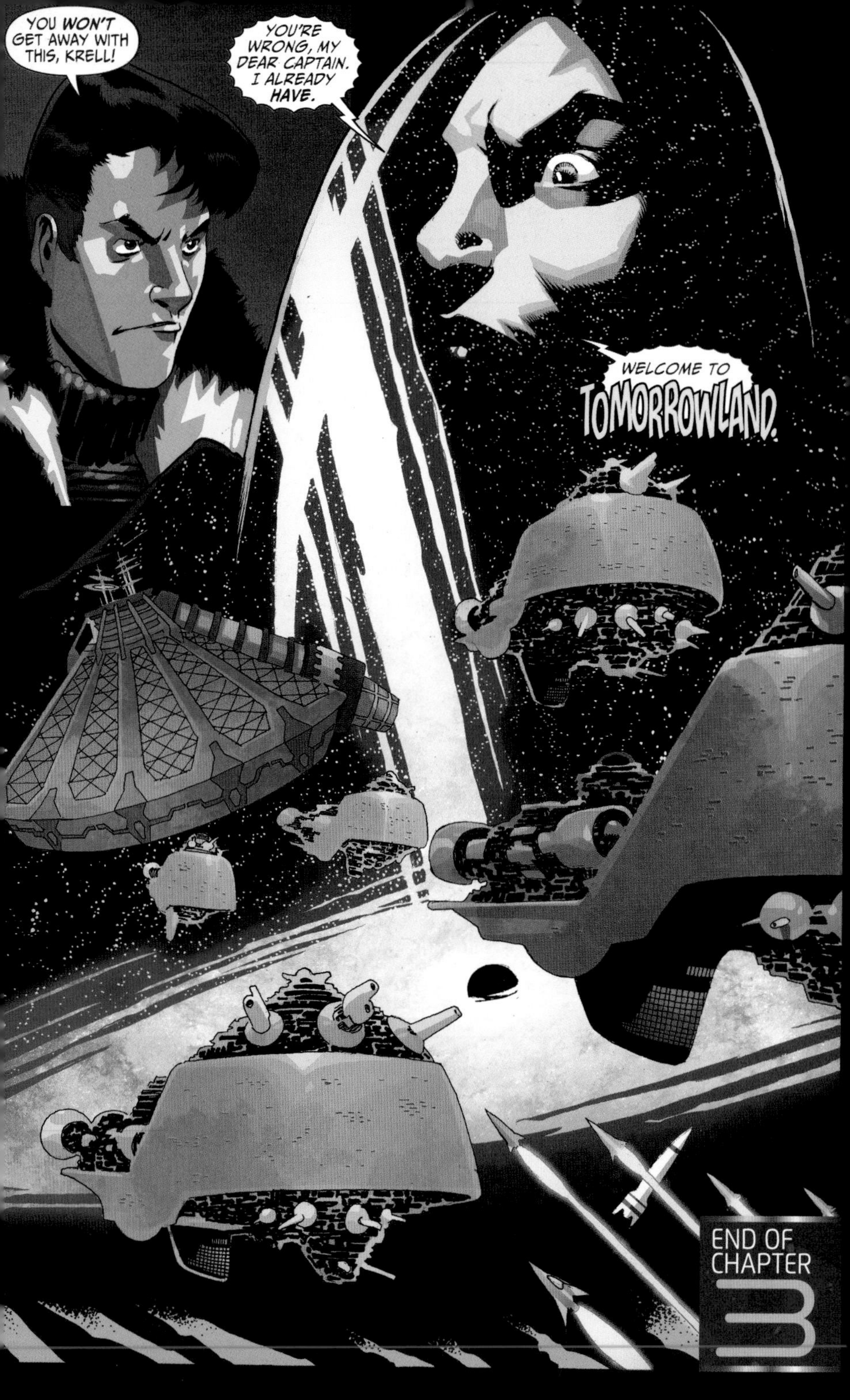

YOU WON'T GET AWAY WITH THIS, KRELL!
YOU'RE WRONG, MY DEAR CAPTAIN. I ALREADY HAVE.
WELCOME TO TOMORROWLAND.
END OF CHAPTER 3

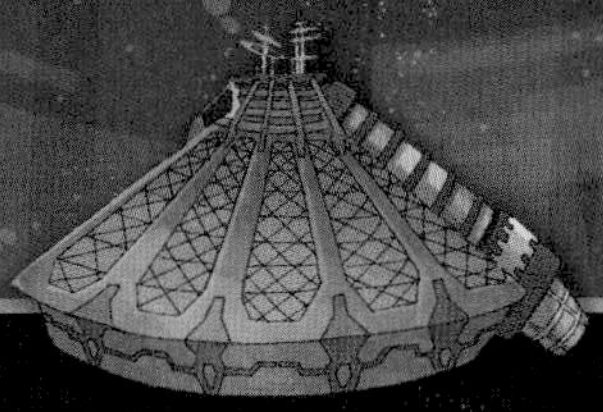

PART TWO

THE FUTURE THAT NEVER WAS
IS FINALLY HERE

THE FUTURE AIN'T
WHAT IT USED TO BE.
—YOGI BERRA

CHAPTER 4

SABOTAGE IN SPACE

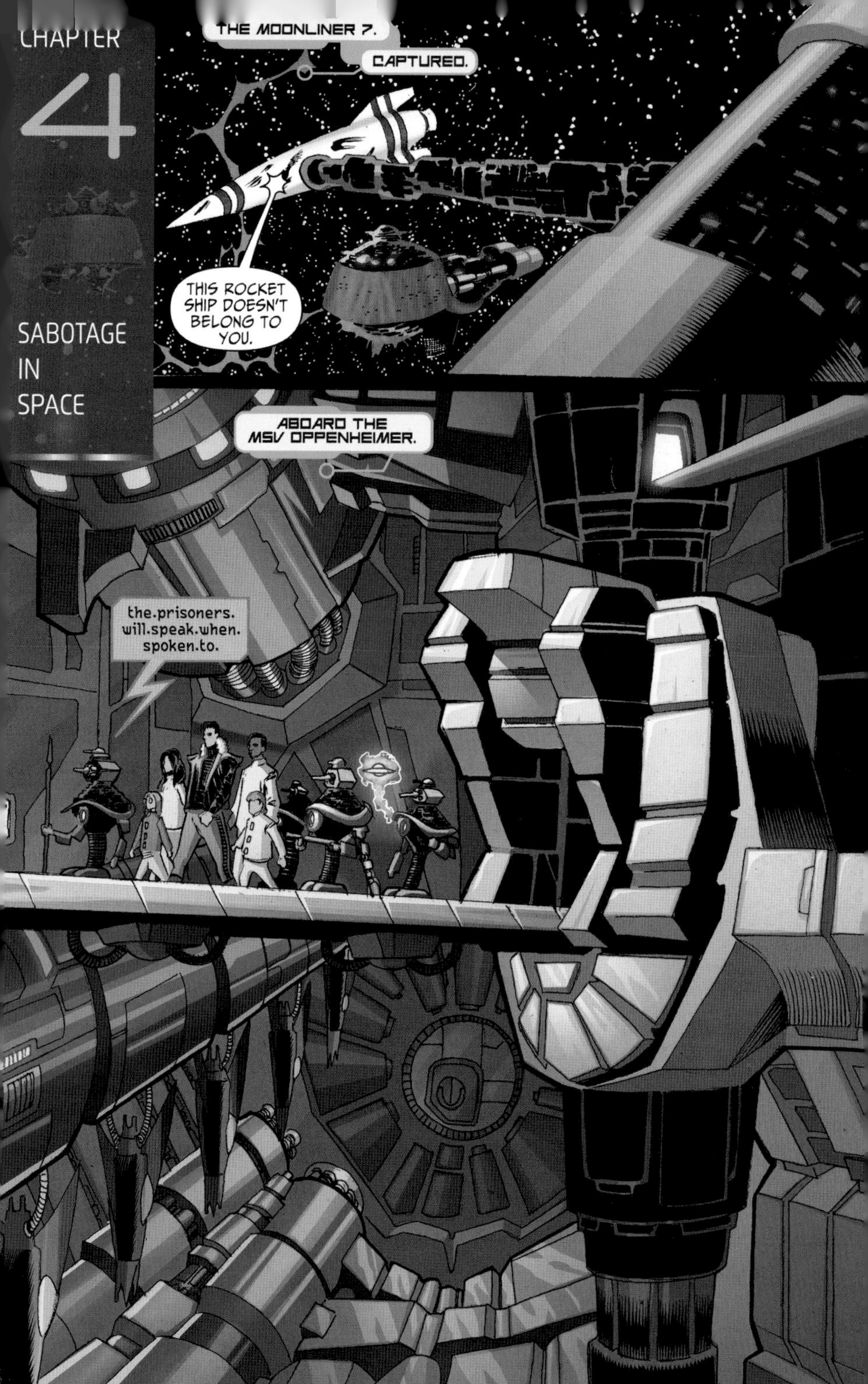

THE MOONLINER 7.
CAPTURED.
THIS ROCKET SHIP DOESN'T BELONG TO YOU.
ABOARD THE MSV OPPENHEIMER.
the.prisoners. will.speak.when. spoken.to.

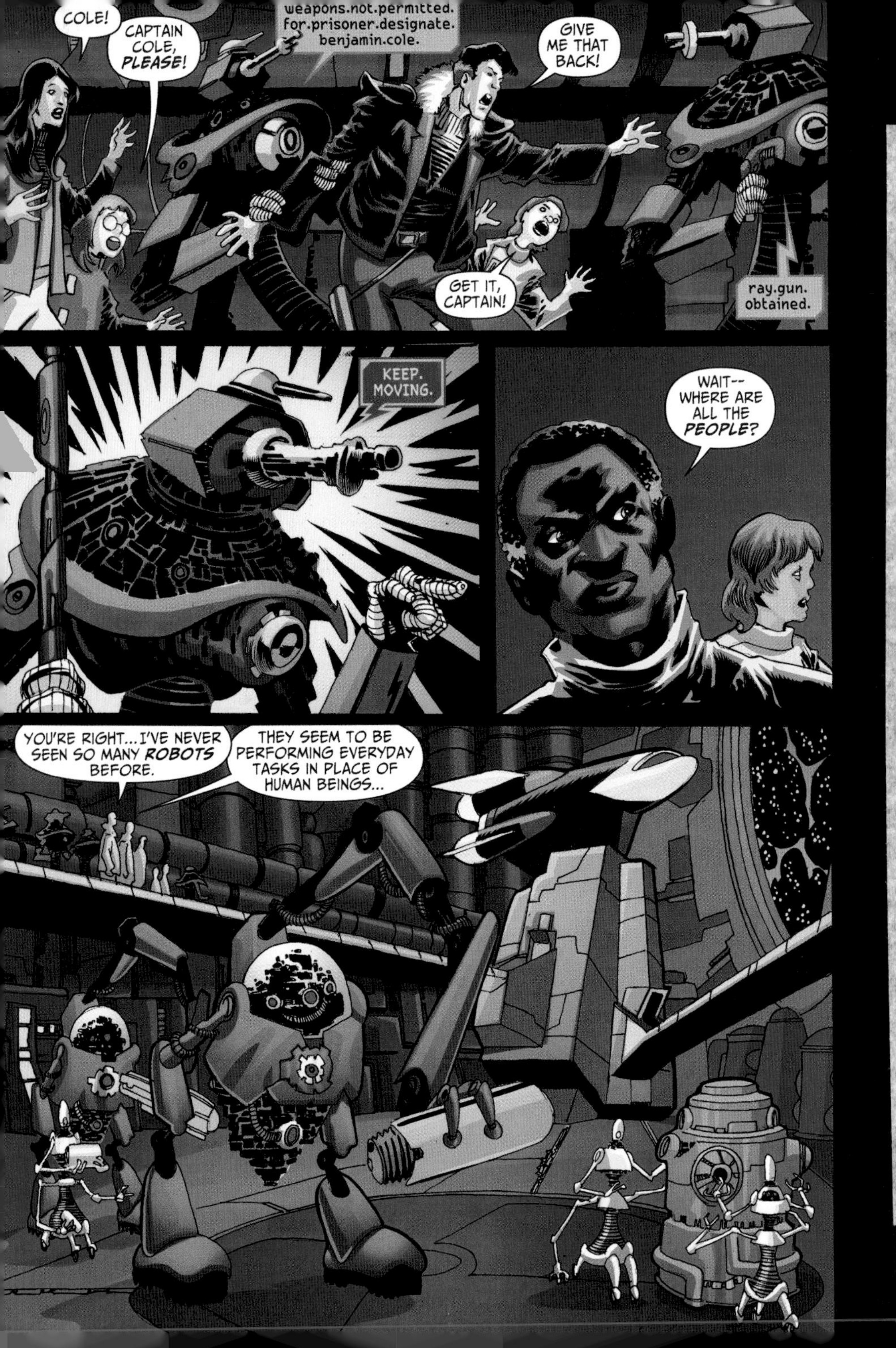
COLE!
CAPTAIN COLE, PLEASE!
weapons.not.permitted. for.prisoner.designate. benjamin.cole.
GIVE ME THAT BACK!
GET IT, CAPTAIN!
ray.gun. obtained.
KEEP. MOVING.
WAIT-- WHERE ARE ALL THE PEOPLE?
YOU'RE RIGHT...I'VE NEVER SEEN SO MANY ROBOTS BEFORE.
THEY SEEM TO BE PERFORMING EVERYDAY TASKS IN PLACE OF HUMAN BEINGS...

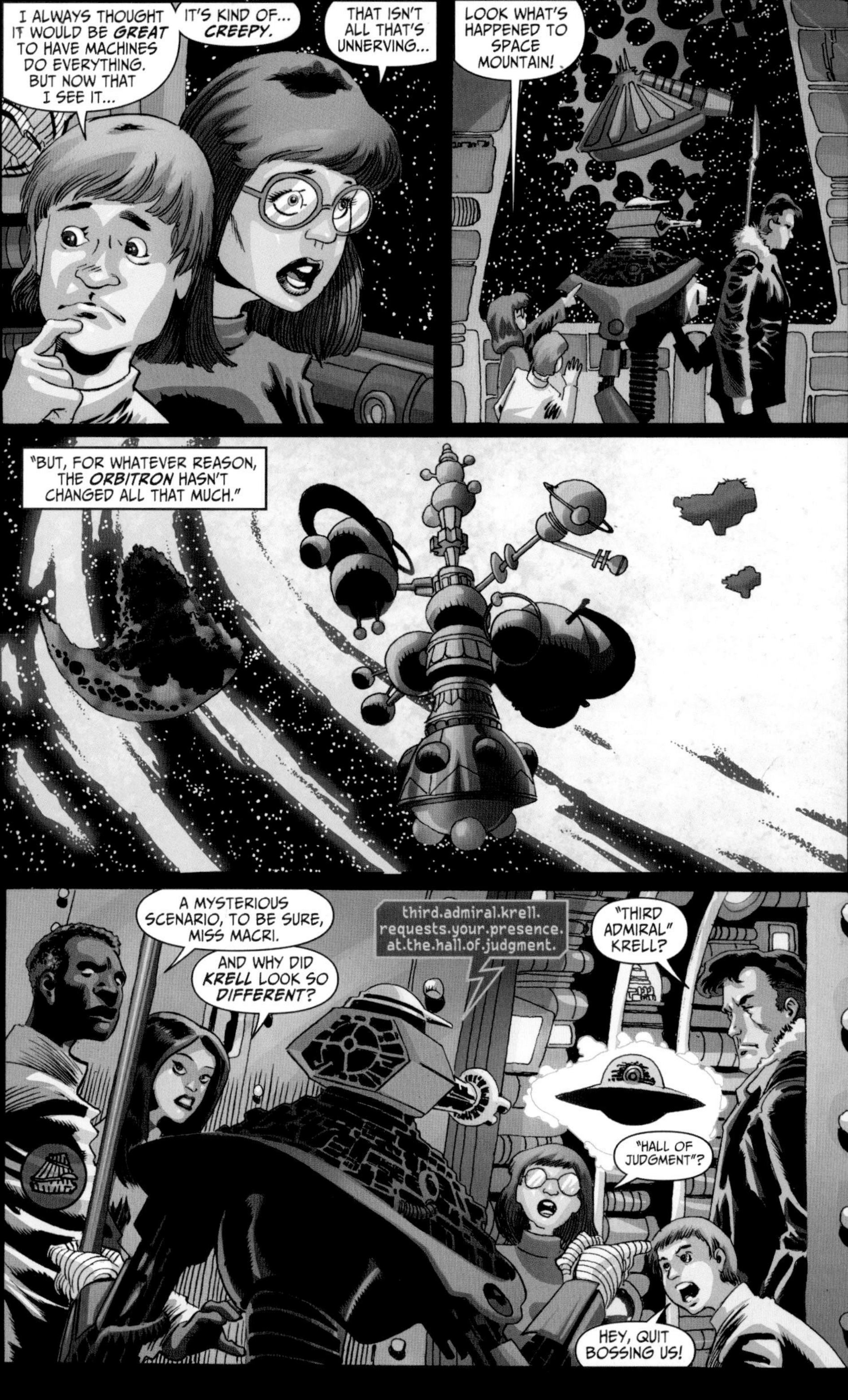
I ALWAYS THOUGHT IT WOULD BE GREAT TO HAVE MACHINES DO EVERYTHING. BUT NOW THAT I SEE IT...
IT'S KIND OF... CREEPY.
THAT ISN'T ALL THAT'S UNNERVING...
LOOK WHAT'S HAPPENED TO SPACE MOUNTAIN!
"BUT, FOR WHATEVER REASON, THE ORBITRON HASN'T CHANGED ALL THAT MUCH."
A MYSTERIOUS SCENARIO, TO BE SURE, MISS MACRI.
AND WHY DID KRELL LOOK SO DIFFERENT?
third.admiral.krell. requests.your.presence. at.the.hall.of.judgment.
"THIRD ADMIRAL" KRELL?
"HALL OF JUDGMENT"?
HEY, QUIT BOSSING US!

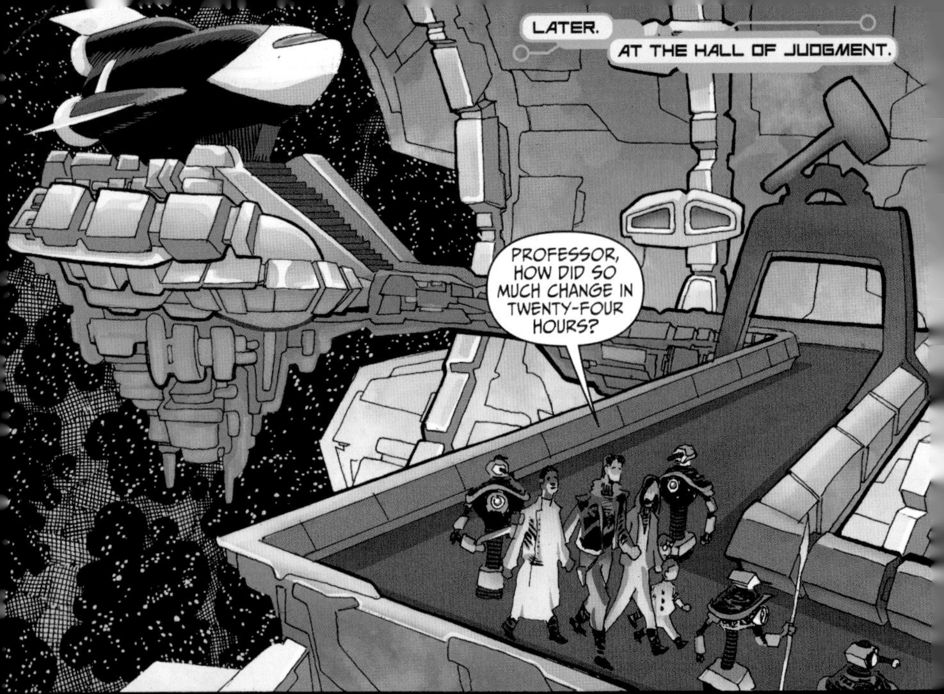
LATER.
AT THE HALL OF JUDGMENT.
PROFESSOR, HOW DID SO MUCH CHANGE IN TWENTY-FOUR HOURS?

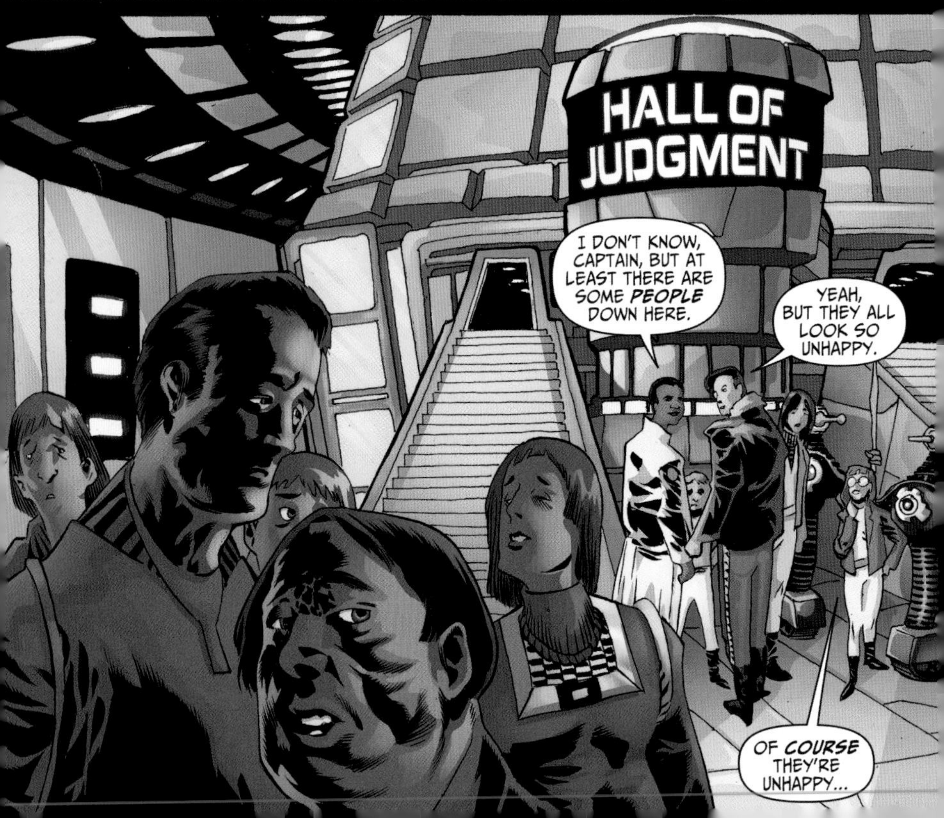
HALL OF JUDGMENT
I DON'T KNOW, CAPTAIN, BUT AT LEAST THERE ARE SOME *PEOPLE* DOWN HERE.
YEAH, BUT THEY ALL LOOK SO UNHAPPY.
OF *COURSE* THEY'RE UNHAPPY...

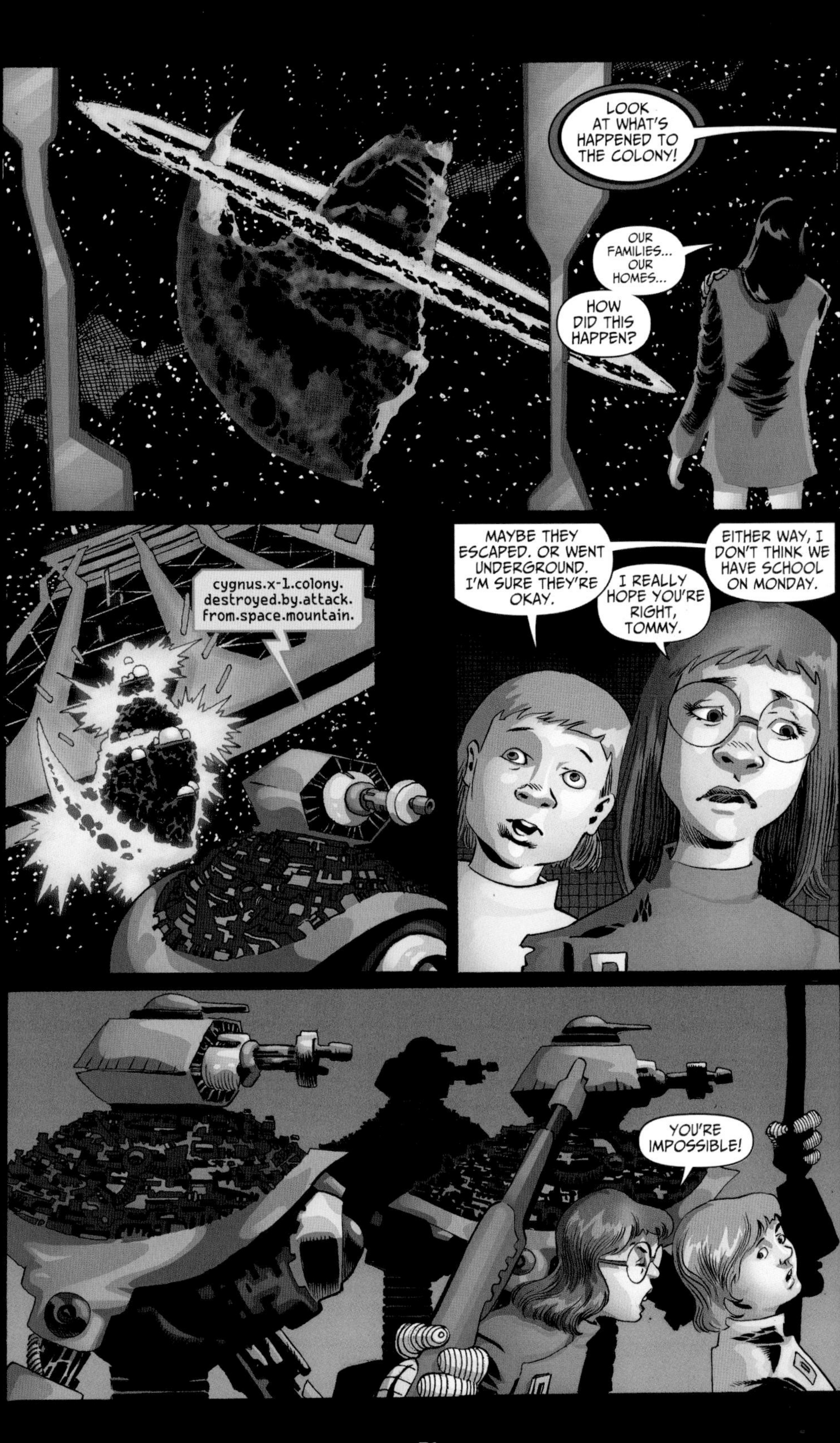
LOOK AT WHAT'S HAPPENED TO THE COLONY!
OUR FAMILIES... OUR HOMES...
HOW DID THIS HAPPEN?
cygnus.x-1.colony. destroyed.by.attack. from.space.mountain.
MAYBE THEY ESCAPED. OR WENT UNDERGROUND. I'M SURE THEY'RE OKAY.
I REALLY HOPE YOU'RE RIGHT, TOMMY.
EITHER WAY, I DON'T THINK WE HAVE SCHOOL ON MONDAY.
YOU'RE IMPOSSIBLE!

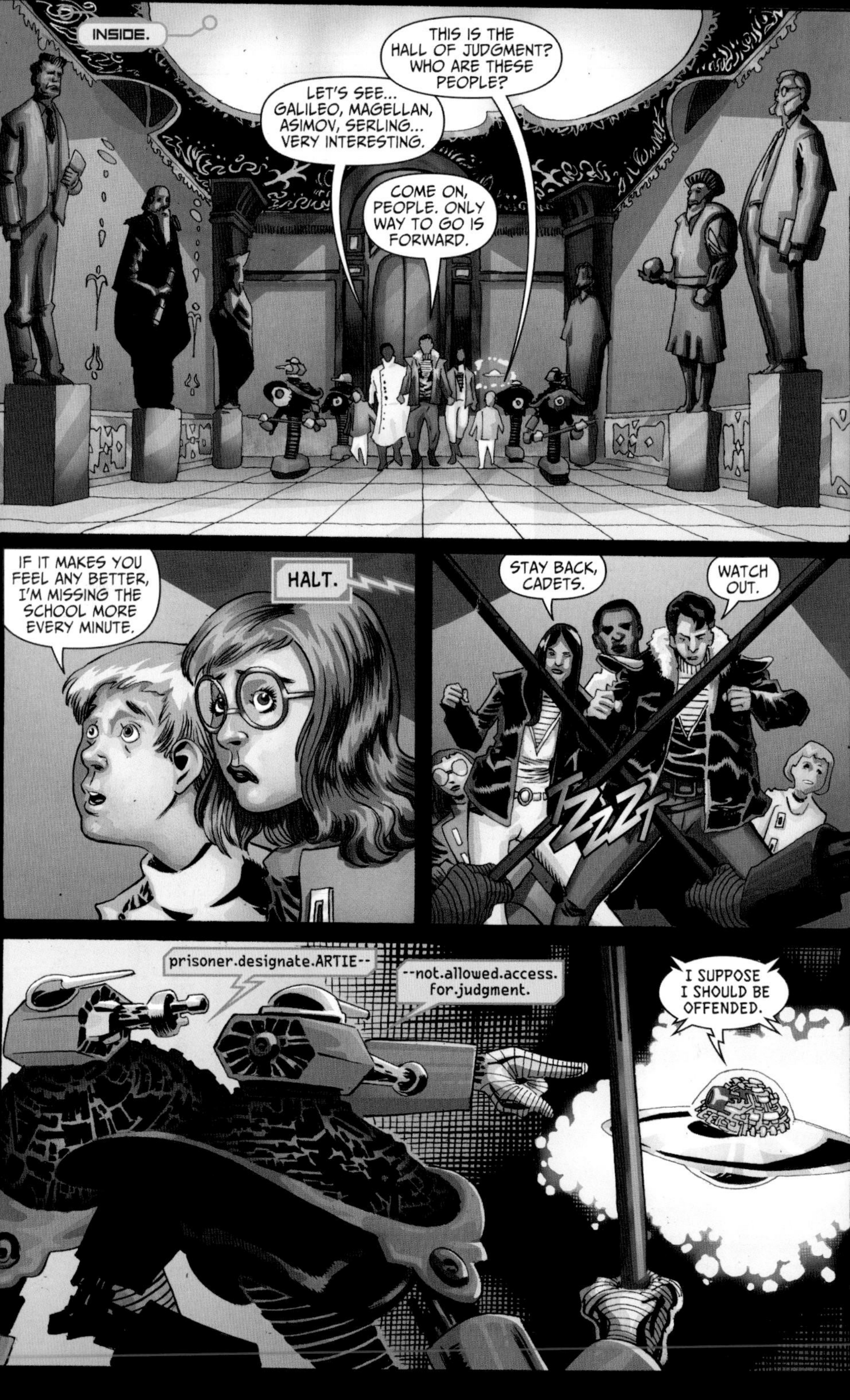
INSIDE.
THIS IS THE HALL OF JUDGMENT? WHO ARE THESE PEOPLE?
LET'S SEE... GALILEO, MAGELLAN, ASIMOV, SERLING... VERY INTERESTING.
COME ON, PEOPLE. ONLY WAY TO GO IS FORWARD.
IF IT MAKES YOU FEEL ANY BETTER, I'M MISSING THE SCHOOL MORE EVERY MINUTE.
HALT.
STAY BACK, CADETS.
WATCH OUT.
TZZZT
prisoner.designate.ARTIE--
--not.allowed.access. for.judgment.
I SUPPOSE I SHOULD BE OFFENDED.

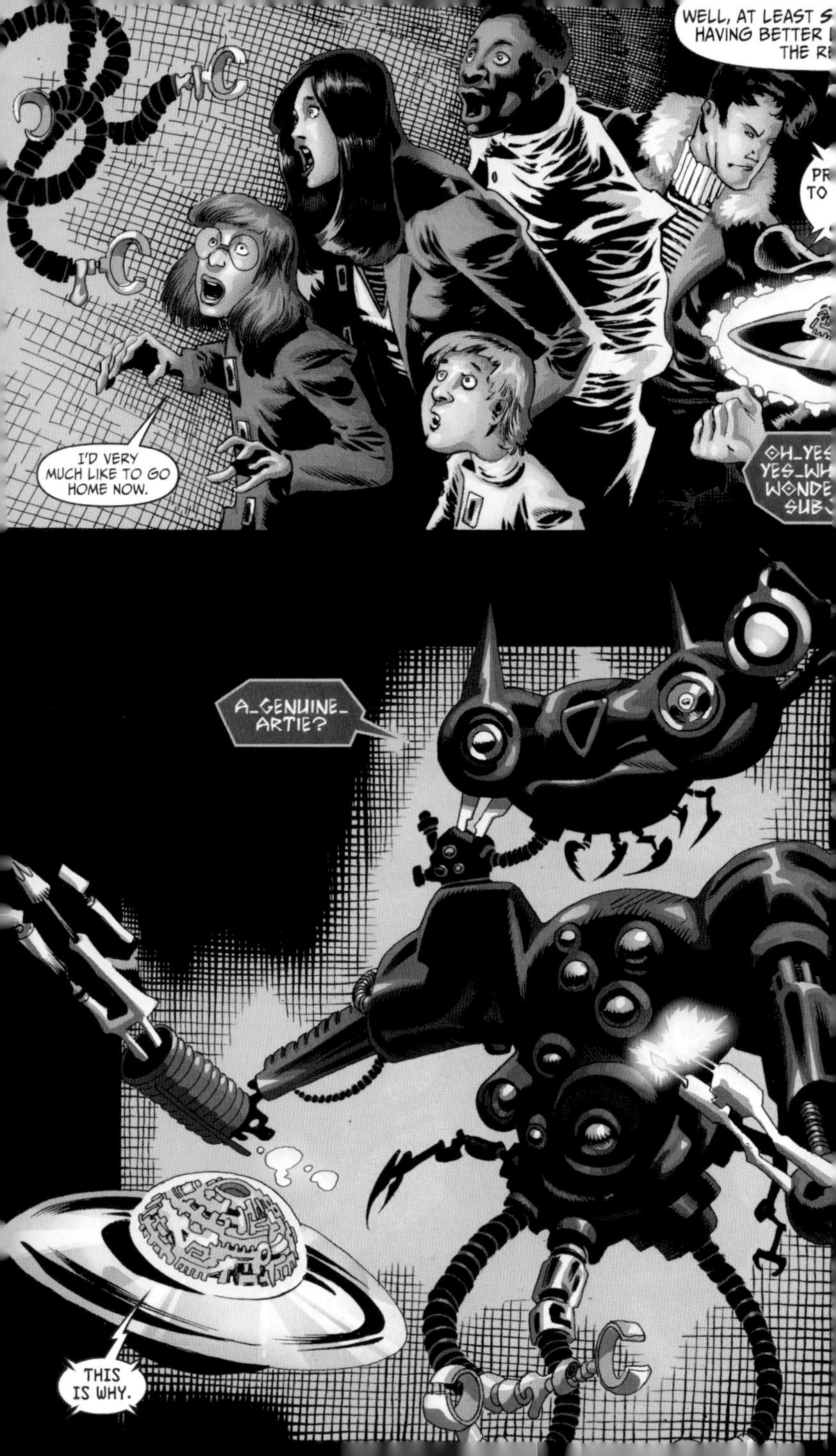
WELL, AT LEAST
HAVING BETTER
THE
I'D VERY MUCH LIKE TO GO HOME NOW.
A_GENUINE_ARTIE?
THIS IS WHY.

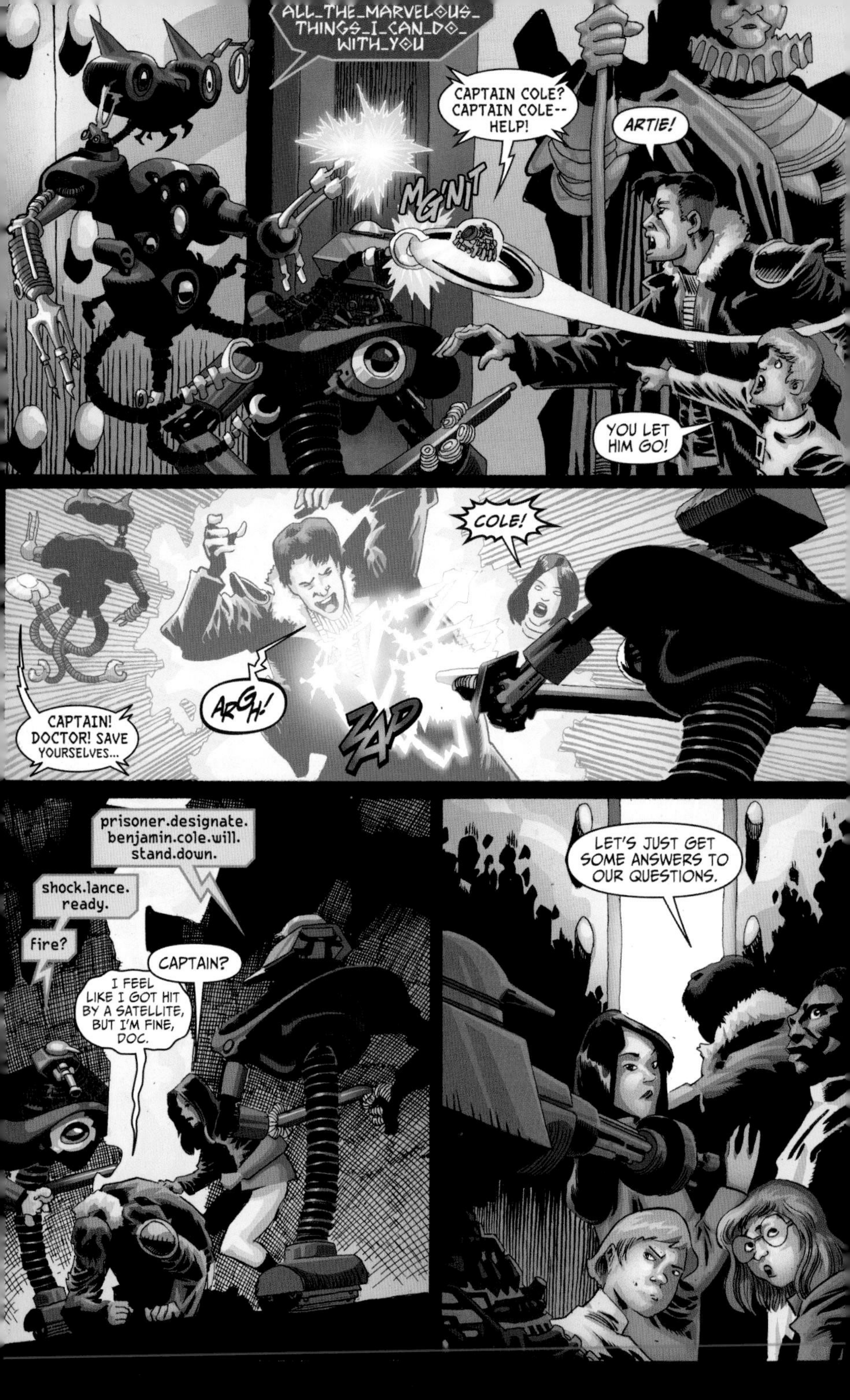
ALL_THE_MARVELOUS_THINGS_I_CAN_DO_WITH_YOU
CAPTAIN COLE? CAPTAIN COLE-- HELP!
ARTIE!
MG'NIT
YOU LET HIM GO!
COLE!
ARGH!
ZAP
CAPTAIN! DOCTOR! SAVE YOURSELVES...
prisoner.designate. benjamin.cole.will. stand.down.
shock.lance. ready.
fire?
CAPTAIN?
I FEEL LIKE I GOT HIT BY A SATELLITE, BUT I'M FINE, DOC.
LET'S JUST GET SOME ANSWERS TO OUR QUESTIONS.

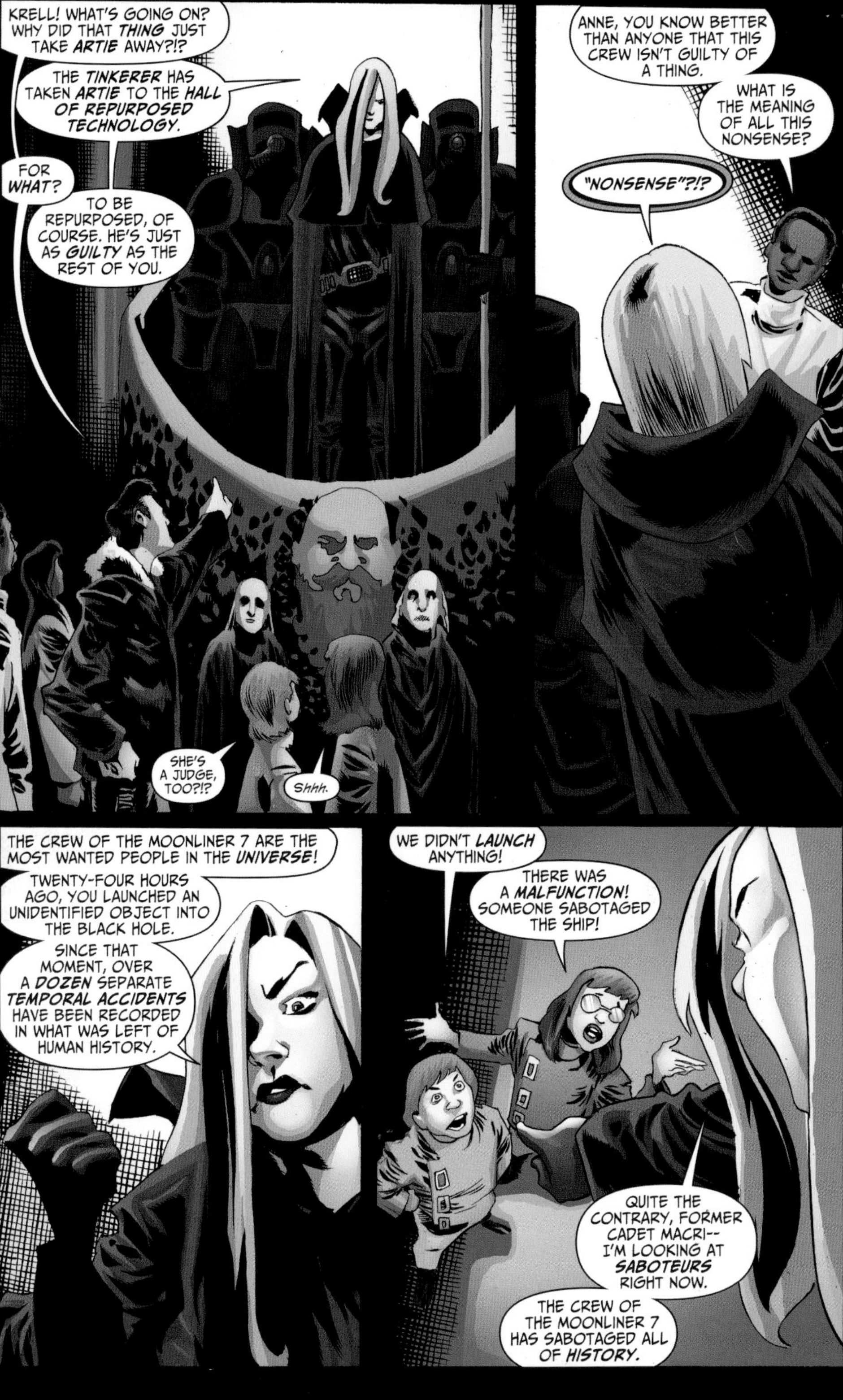
KRELL! WHAT'S GOING ON? WHY DID THAT THING JUST TAKE ARTIE AWAY?!?
THE TINKERER HAS TAKEN ARTIE TO THE HALL OF REPURPOSED TECHNOLOGY.
FOR WHAT?
TO BE REPURPOSED, OF COURSE. HE'S JUST AS GUILTY AS THE REST OF YOU.
SHE'S A JUDGE, TOO?!?
Shhh.
ANNE, YOU KNOW BETTER THAN ANYONE THAT THIS CREW ISN'T GUILTY OF A THING.
WHAT IS THE MEANING OF ALL THIS NONSENSE?
"NONSENSE"?!?
THE CREW OF THE MOONLINER 7 ARE THE MOST WANTED PEOPLE IN THE UNIVERSE!
TWENTY-FOUR HOURS AGO, YOU LAUNCHED AN UNIDENTIFIED OBJECT INTO THE BLACK HOLE.
SINCE THAT MOMENT, OVER A DOZEN SEPARATE TEMPORAL ACCIDENTS HAVE BEEN RECORDED IN WHAT WAS LEFT OF HUMAN HISTORY.
WE DIDN'T LAUNCH ANYTHING!
THERE WAS A MALFUNCTION! SOMEONE SABOTAGED THE SHIP!
QUITE THE CONTRARY, FORMER CADET MACRI-- I'M LOOKING AT SABOTEURS RIGHT NOW.
THE CREW OF THE MOONLINER 7 HAS SABOTAGED ALL OF HISTORY.

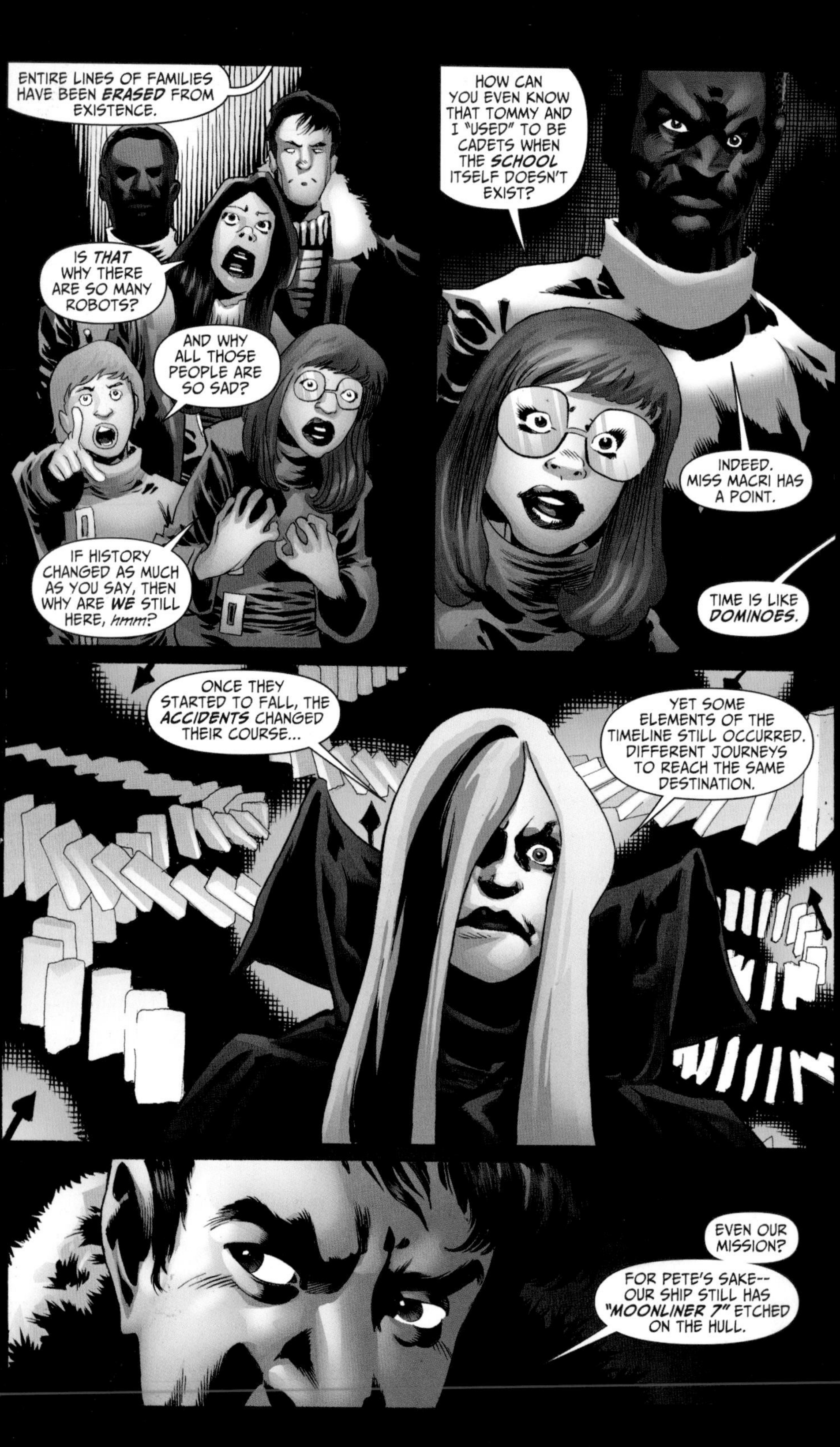

ENTIRE LINES OF FAMILIES HAVE BEEN ERASED FROM EXISTENCE.
IS THAT WHY THERE ARE SO MANY ROBOTS?
AND WHY ALL THOSE PEOPLE ARE SO SAD?
IF HISTORY CHANGED AS MUCH AS YOU SAY, THEN WHY ARE WE STILL HERE, hmm?
HOW CAN YOU EVEN KNOW THAT TOMMY AND I "USED" TO BE CADETS WHEN THE SCHOOL ITSELF DOESN'T EXIST?
INDEED. MISS MACRI HAS A POINT.
TIME IS LIKE DOMINOES.
ONCE THEY STARTED TO FALL, THE ACCIDENTS CHANGED THEIR COURSE...
YET SOME ELEMENTS OF THE TIMELINE STILL OCCURRED. DIFFERENT JOURNEYS TO REACH THE SAME DESTINATION.
EVEN OUR MISSION?
FOR PETE'S SAKE-- OUR SHIP STILL HAS "MOONLINER 7" ETCHED ON THE HULL.

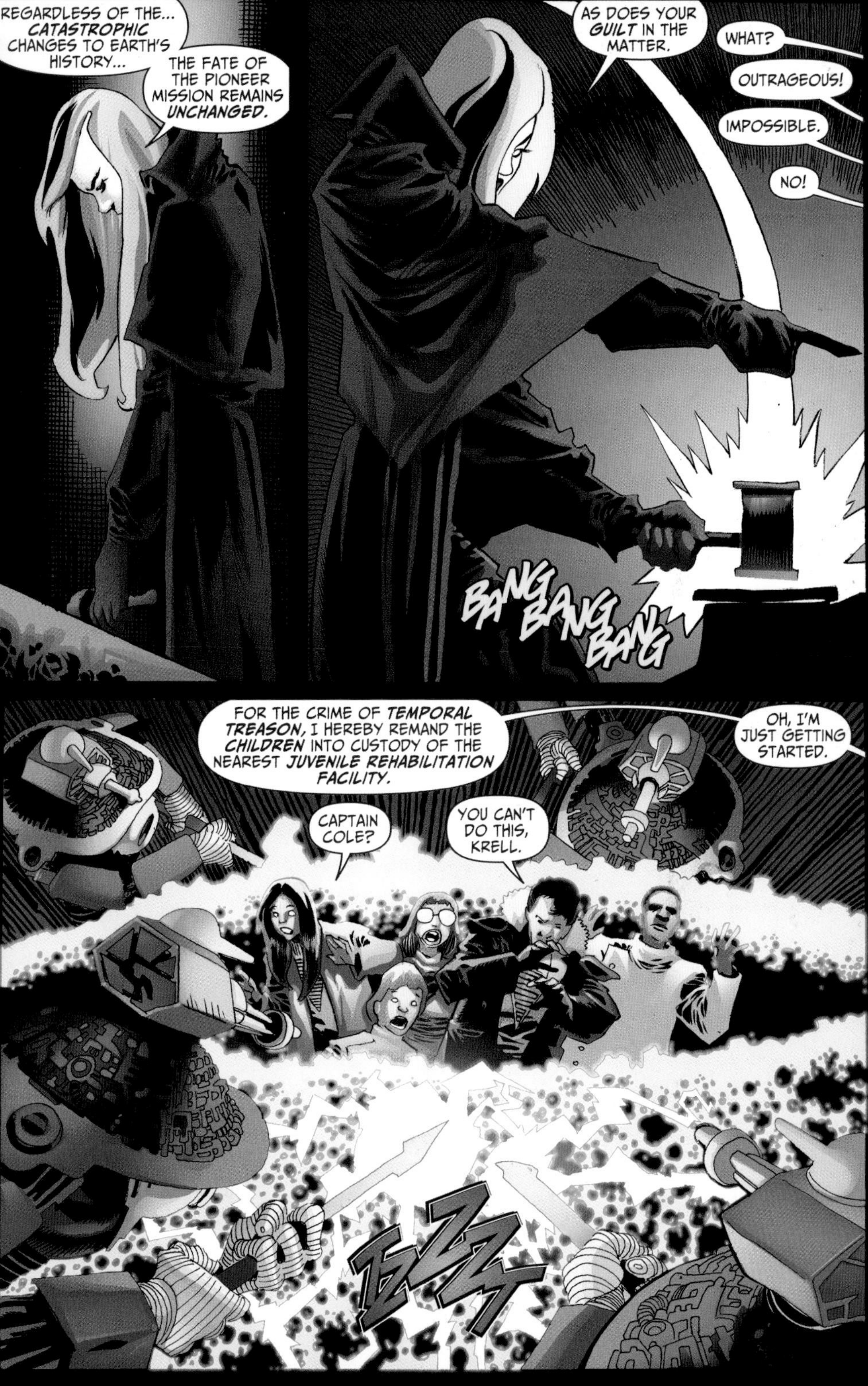

REGARDLESS OF THE... CATASTROPHIC CHANGES TO EARTH'S HISTORY...
THE FATE OF THE PIONEER MISSION REMAINS UNCHANGED.
AS DOES YOUR GUILT IN THE MATTER.
WHAT?
OUTRAGEOUS!
IMPOSSIBLE.
NO!
BANG BANG BANG
FOR THE CRIME OF TEMPORAL TREASON, I HEREBY REMAND THE CHILDREN INTO CUSTODY OF THE NEAREST JUVENILE REHABILITATION FACILITY.
OH, I'M JUST GETTING STARTED.
CAPTAIN COLE?
YOU CAN'T DO THIS, KRELL.
ZZZM

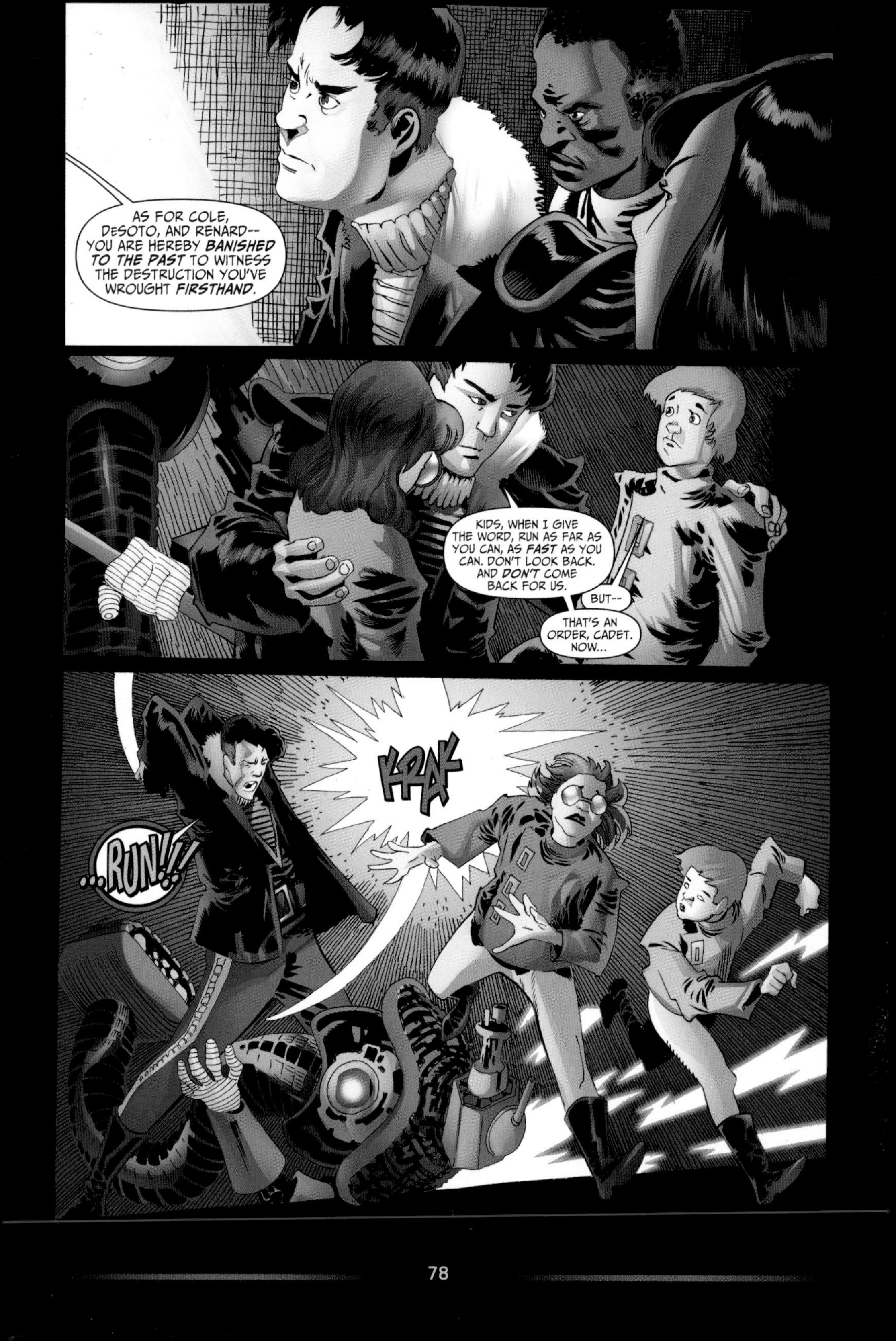
AS FOR COLE, DESOTO, AND RENARD-- YOU ARE HEREBY BANISHED TO THE PAST TO WITNESS THE DESTRUCTION YOU'VE WROUGHT FIRSTHAND.
KIDS, WHEN I GIVE THE WORD, RUN AS FAR AS YOU CAN, AS FAST AS YOU CAN. DON'T LOOK BACK. AND DON'T COME BACK FOR US.
BUT--
THAT'S AN ORDER, CADET. NOW...
KRAK
...RUN!!!

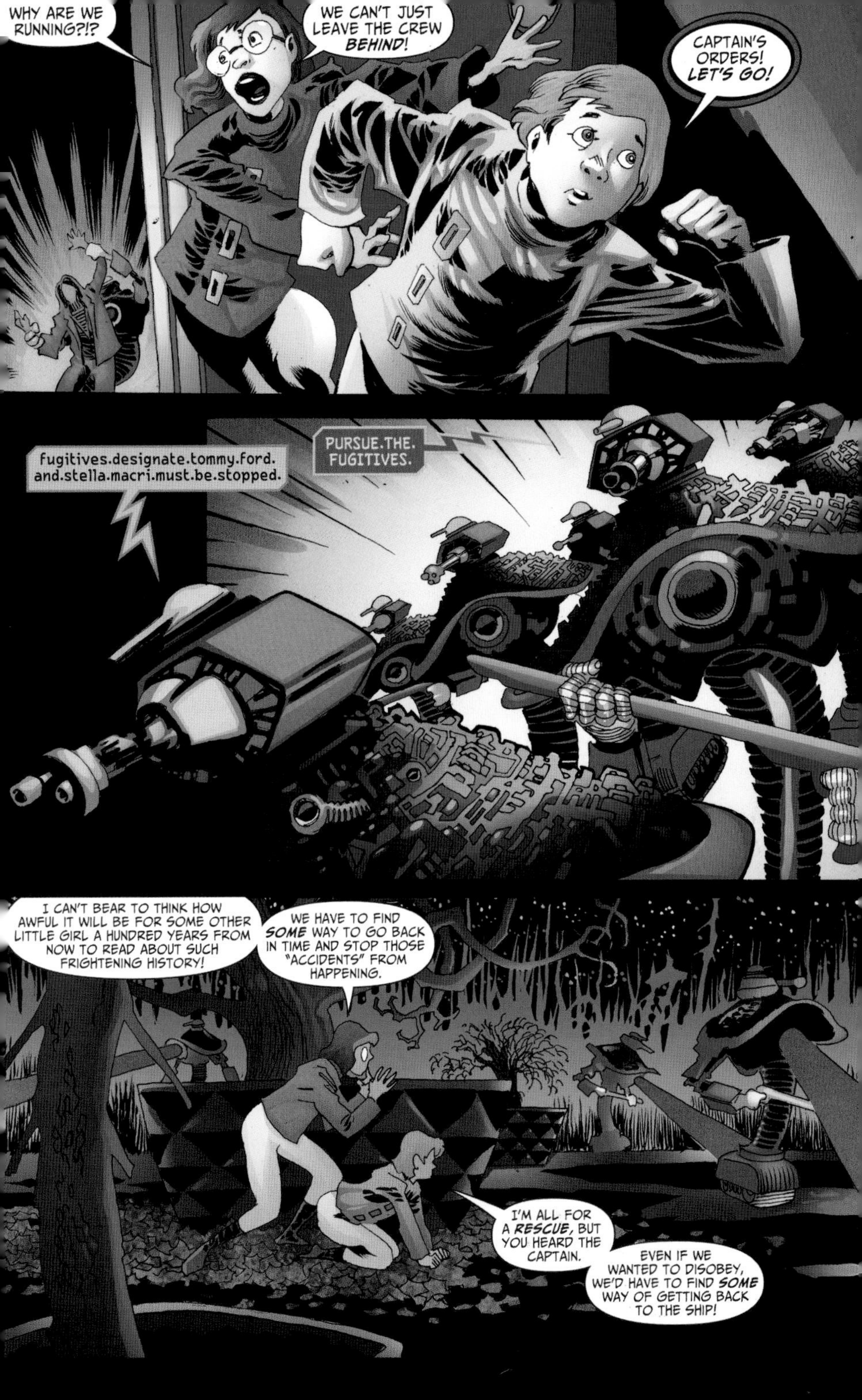
WHY ARE WE RUNNING?!?
WE CAN'T JUST LEAVE THE CREW *BEHIND*!
CAPTAIN'S ORDERS! *LET'S GO!*
fugitives.designate.tommy.ford. and.stella.macri.must.be.stopped.
PURSUE.THE. FUGITIVES.
I CAN'T BEAR TO THINK HOW AWFUL IT WILL BE FOR SOME OTHER LITTLE GIRL A HUNDRED YEARS FROM NOW TO READ ABOUT SUCH FRIGHTENING HISTORY!
WE HAVE TO FIND *SOME* WAY TO GO BACK IN TIME AND STOP THOSE "ACCIDENTS" FROM HAPPENING.
I'M ALL FOR A *RESCUE,* BUT YOU HEARD THE CAPTAIN.
EVEN IF WE WANTED TO DISOBEY, WE'D HAVE TO FIND *SOME* WAY OF GETTING BACK TO THE SHIP!

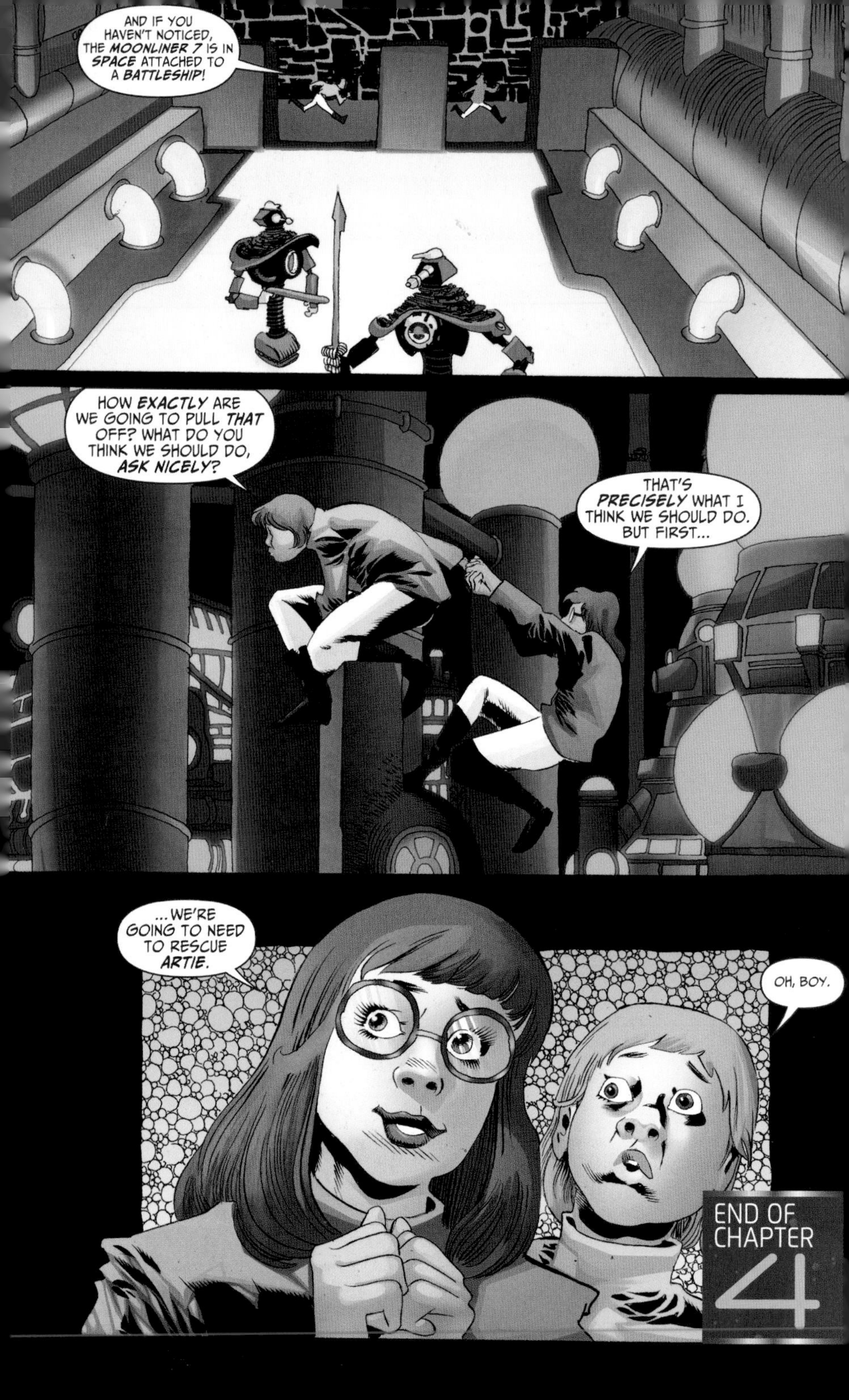
AND IF YOU HAVEN'T NOTICED, THE MOONLINER 7 IS IN SPACE ATTACHED TO A BATTLESHIP!
HOW EXACTLY ARE WE GOING TO PULL THAT OFF? WHAT DO YOU THINK WE SHOULD DO, ASK NICELY?
THAT'S PRECISELY WHAT I THINK WE SHOULD DO. BUT FIRST...
...WE'RE GOING TO NEED TO RESCUE ARTIE.
OH, BOY.
END OF CHAPTER 4

CHAPTER 5

IMPOSSIBLE RESCUE

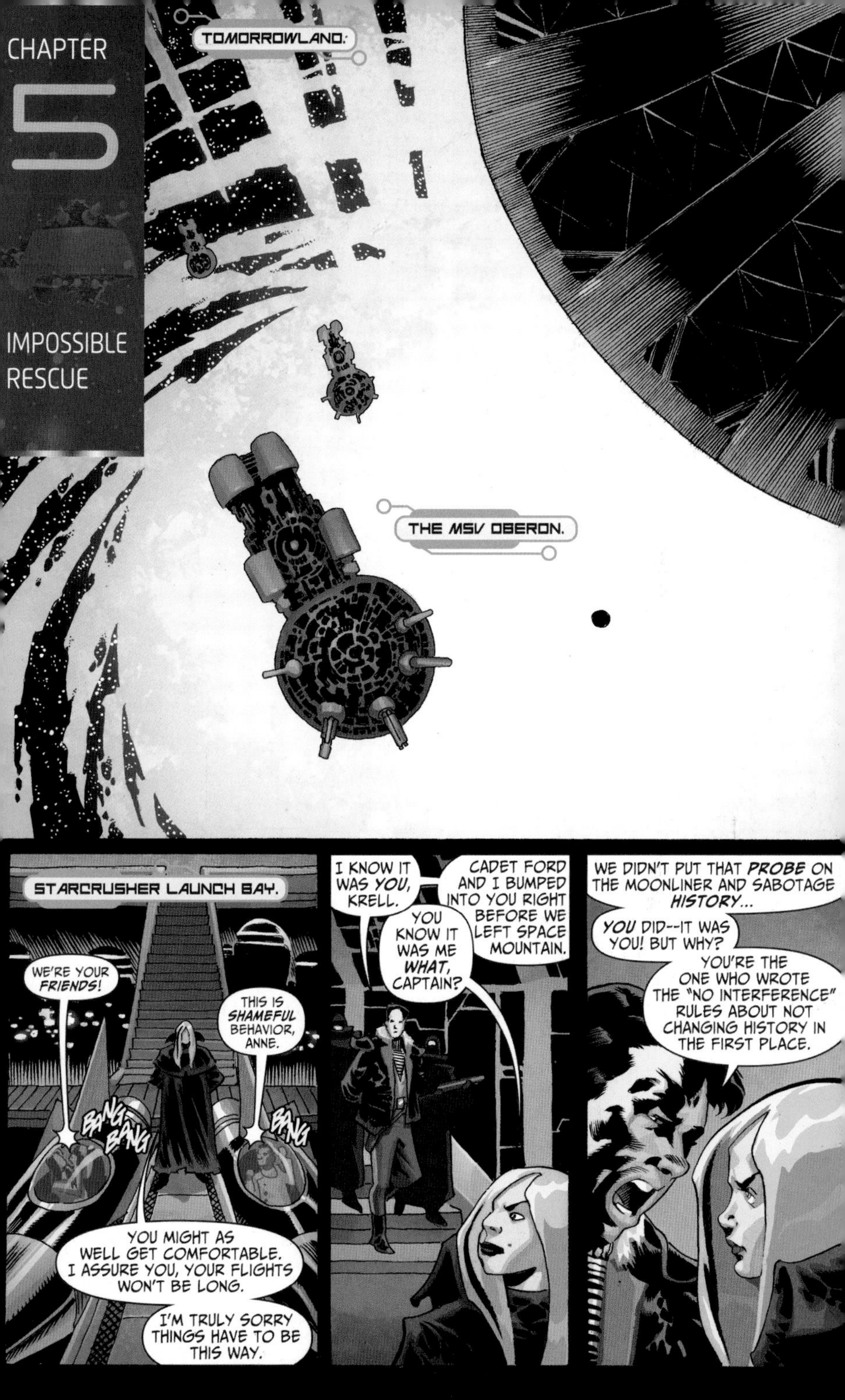
TOMORROWLAND.
THE MSV OBERON.
STARCRUSHER LAUNCH BAY.
WE'RE YOUR FRIENDS!
THIS IS SHAMEFUL BEHAVIOR, ANNE.
BANG BANG
BANG
YOU MIGHT AS WELL GET COMFORTABLE. I ASSURE YOU, YOUR FLIGHTS WON'T BE LONG.
I'M TRULY SORRY THINGS HAVE TO BE THIS WAY.
I KNOW IT WAS YOU, KRELL.
CADET FORD AND I BUMPED INTO YOU RIGHT BEFORE WE LEFT SPACE MOUNTAIN.
YOU KNOW IT WAS ME WHAT, CAPTAIN?
WE DIDN'T PUT THAT PROBE ON THE MOONLINER AND SABOTAGE HISTORY...
YOU DID--IT WAS YOU! BUT WHY?
YOU'RE THE ONE WHO WROTE THE "NO INTERFERENCE" RULES ABOUT NOT CHANGING HISTORY IN THE FIRST PLACE.

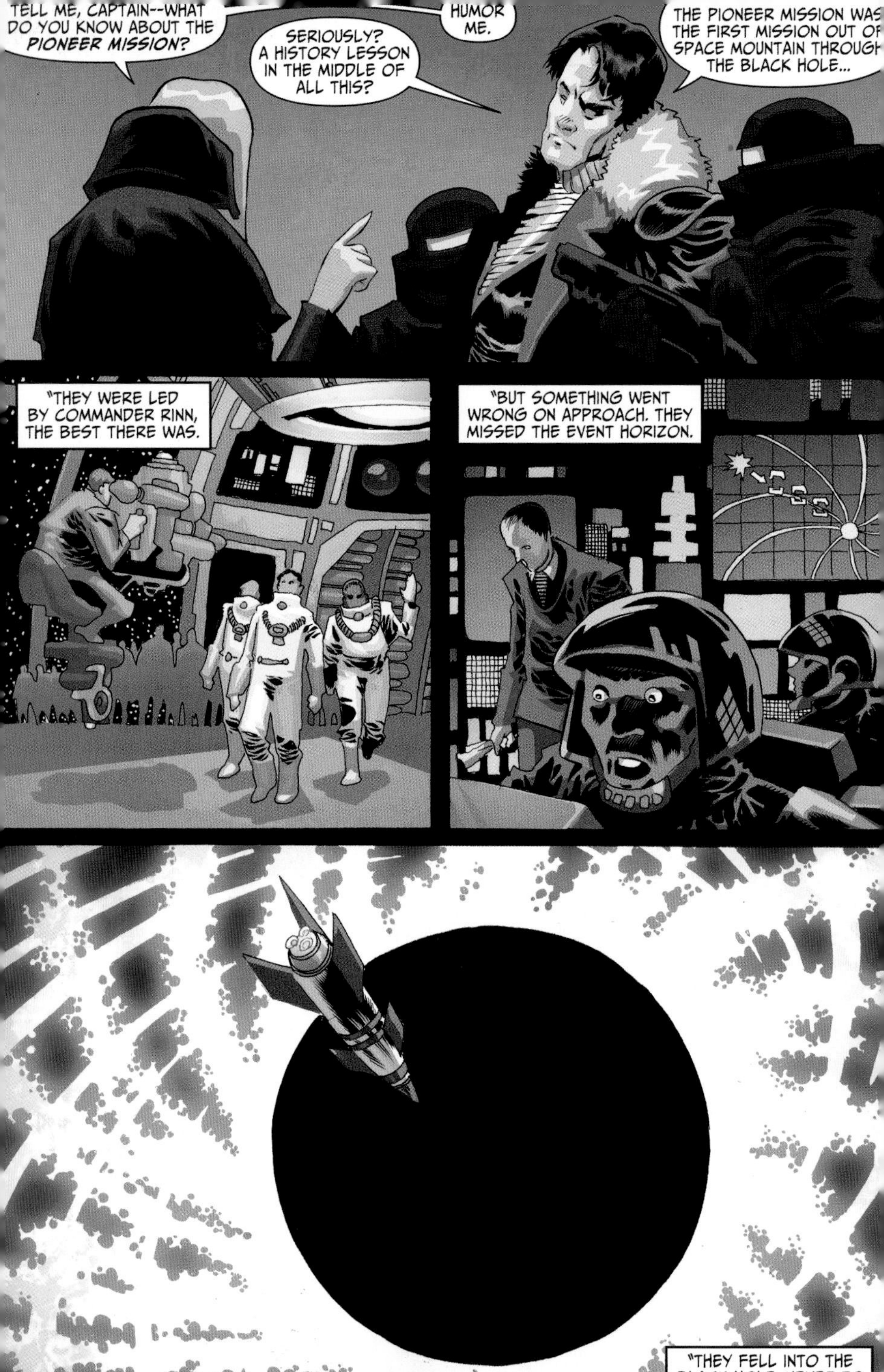
TELL ME, CAPTAIN--WHAT DO YOU KNOW ABOUT THE *PIONEER MISSION*?
SERIOUSLY? A HISTORY LESSON IN THE MIDDLE OF ALL THIS?
HUMOR ME.
THE PIONEER MISSION WAS THE FIRST MISSION OUT OF SPACE MOUNTAIN THROUGH THE BLACK HOLE...
"THEY WERE LED BY COMMANDER RINN, THE BEST THERE WAS.
"BUT SOMETHING WENT WRONG ON APPROACH. THEY MISSED THE EVENT HORIZON.
"THEY FELL INTO THE BLACK HOLE, NEVER TO BE HEARD FROM AGAIN."

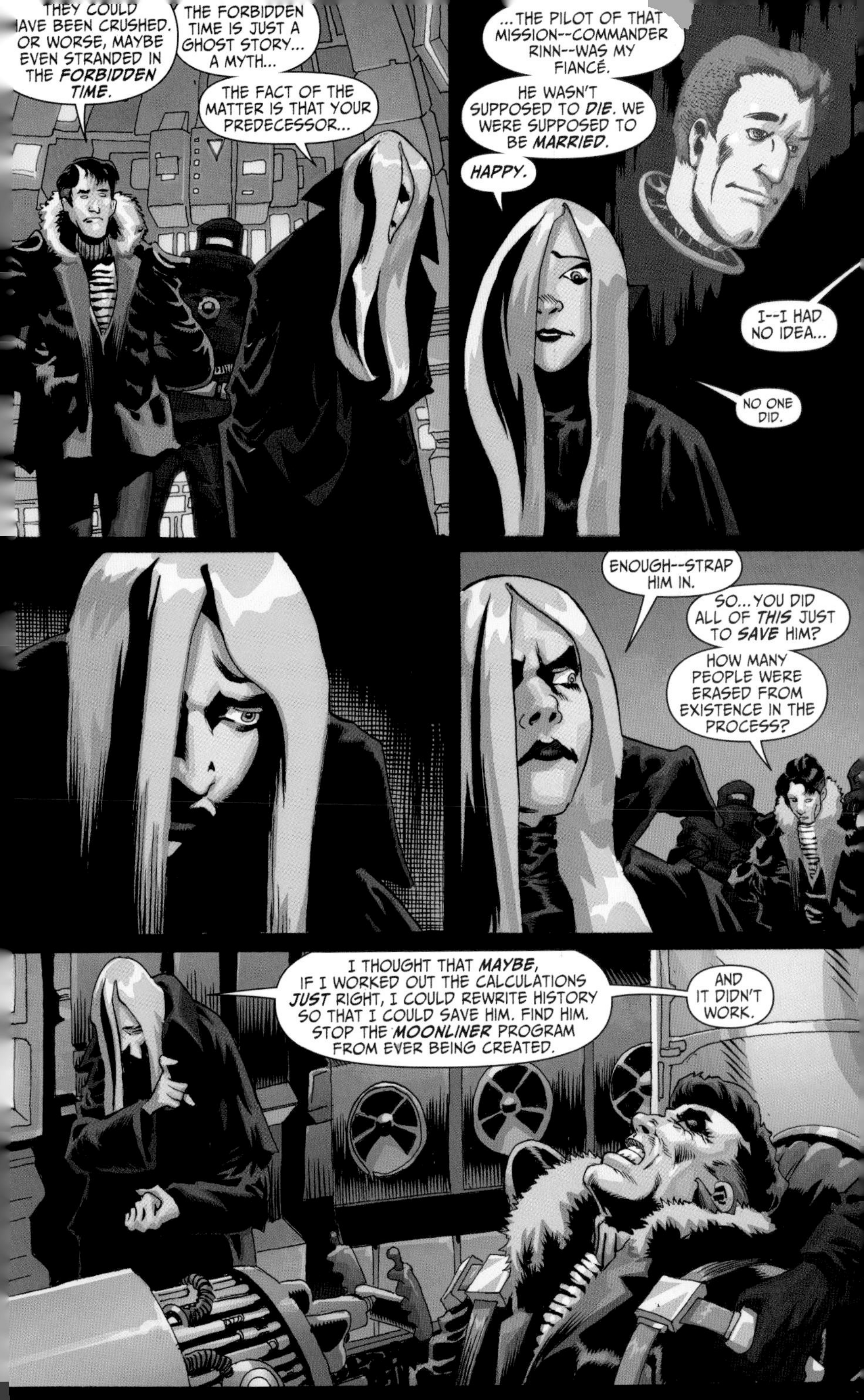

THEY COULD HAVE BEEN CRUSHED. OR WORSE, MAYBE EVEN STRANDED IN THE **FORBIDDEN TIME**.
THE FORBIDDEN TIME IS JUST A GHOST STORY... A MYTH...
THE FACT OF THE MATTER IS THAT YOUR PREDECESSOR...
...THE PILOT OF THAT MISSION--COMMANDER RINN--WAS MY FIANCÉ.
HE WASN'T SUPPOSED TO ***DIE***. WE WERE SUPPOSED TO BE ***MARRIED***.
HAPPY.
I--I HAD NO IDEA...
NO ONE DID.
ENOUGH--STRAP HIM IN.
SO...YOU DID ALL OF ***THIS*** JUST TO ***SAVE*** HIM?
HOW MANY PEOPLE WERE ERASED FROM EXISTENCE IN THE PROCESS?
I THOUGHT THAT ***MAYBE***, IF I WORKED OUT THE CALCULATIONS ***JUST*** RIGHT, I COULD REWRITE HISTORY SO THAT I COULD SAVE HIM. FIND HIM. STOP THE ***MOONLINER*** PROGRAM FROM EVER BEING CREATED.
AND IT DIDN'T WORK.

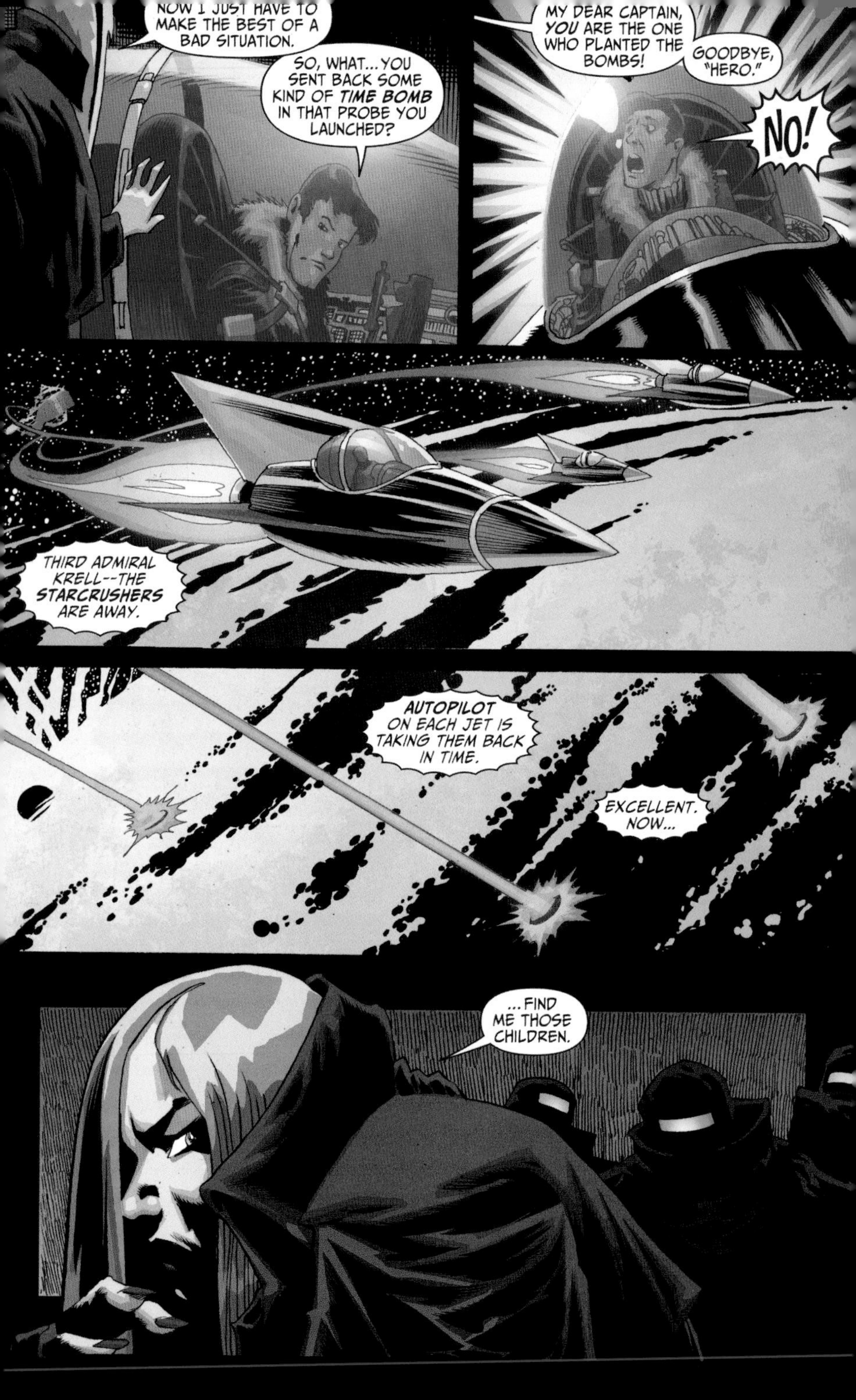

NOW I JUST HAVE TO MAKE THE BEST OF A BAD SITUATION.
SO, WHAT... YOU SENT BACK SOME KIND OF TIME BOMB IN THAT PROBE YOU LAUNCHED?
MY DEAR CAPTAIN, YOU ARE THE ONE WHO PLANTED THE BOMBS!
GOODBYE, "HERO."
NO!
THIRD ADMIRAL KRELL--THE STARCRUSHERS ARE AWAY.
AUTOPILOT ON EACH JET IS TAKING THEM BACK IN TIME.
EXCELLENT. NOW...
...FIND ME THOSE CHILDREN.

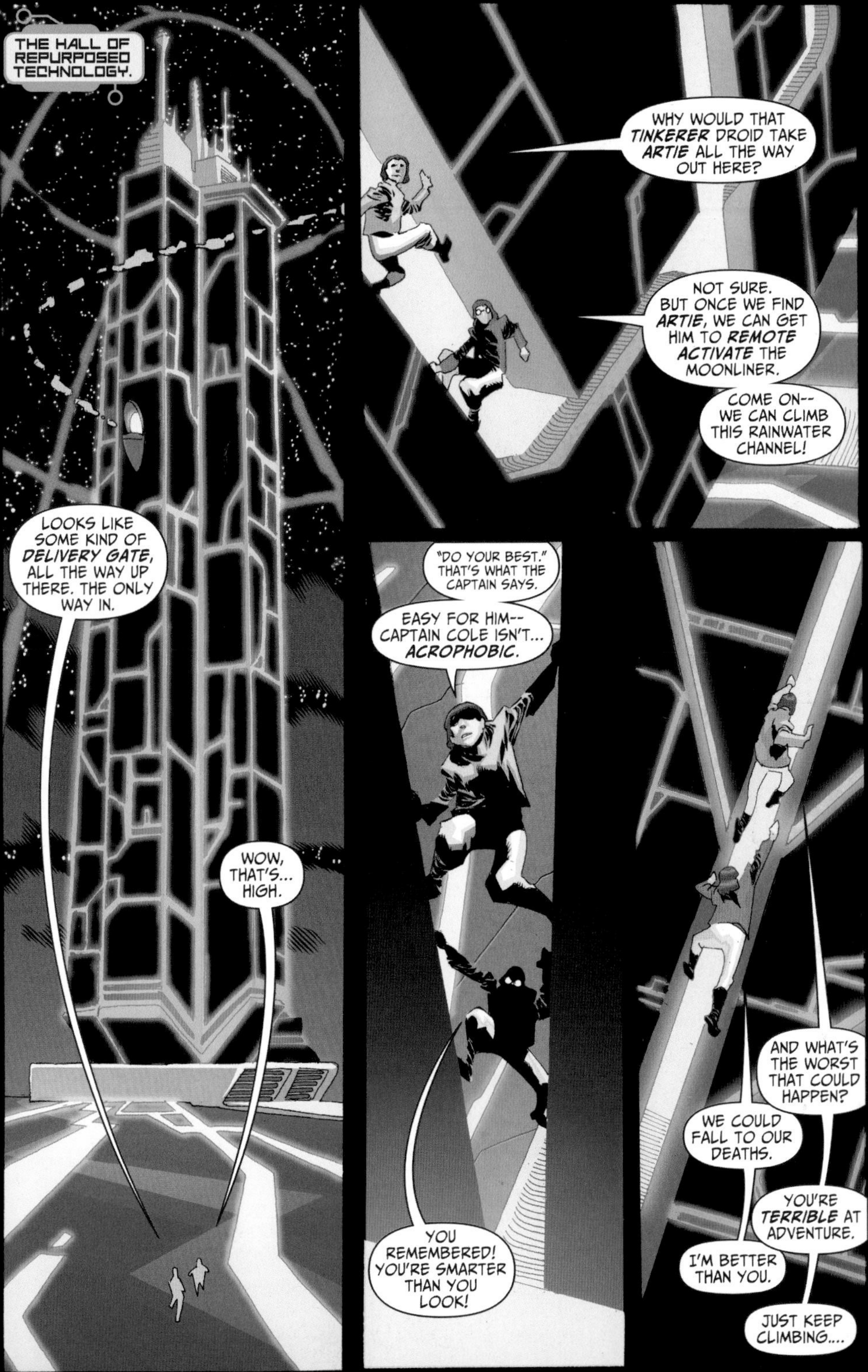
THE HALL OF REPURPOSED TECHNOLOGY.
LOOKS LIKE SOME KIND OF *DELIVERY GATE*, ALL THE WAY UP THERE. THE ONLY WAY IN.
WOW, THAT'S... HIGH.
WHY WOULD THAT *TINKERER* DROID TAKE *ARTIE* ALL THE WAY OUT HERE?
NOT SURE. BUT ONCE WE FIND *ARTIE*, WE CAN GET HIM TO *REMOTE ACTIVATE* THE MOONLINER.
COME ON-- WE CAN CLIMB THIS RAINWATER CHANNEL!
"DO YOUR BEST." THAT'S WHAT THE CAPTAIN SAYS.
EASY FOR HIM-- CAPTAIN COLE ISN'T... *ACROPHOBIC*.
YOU REMEMBERED! YOU'RE SMARTER THAN YOU LOOK!
AND WHAT'S THE WORST THAT COULD HAPPEN?
WE COULD FALL TO OUR DEATHS.
YOU'RE *TERRIBLE* AT ADVENTURE.
I'M BETTER THAN YOU.
JUST KEEP CLIMBING....

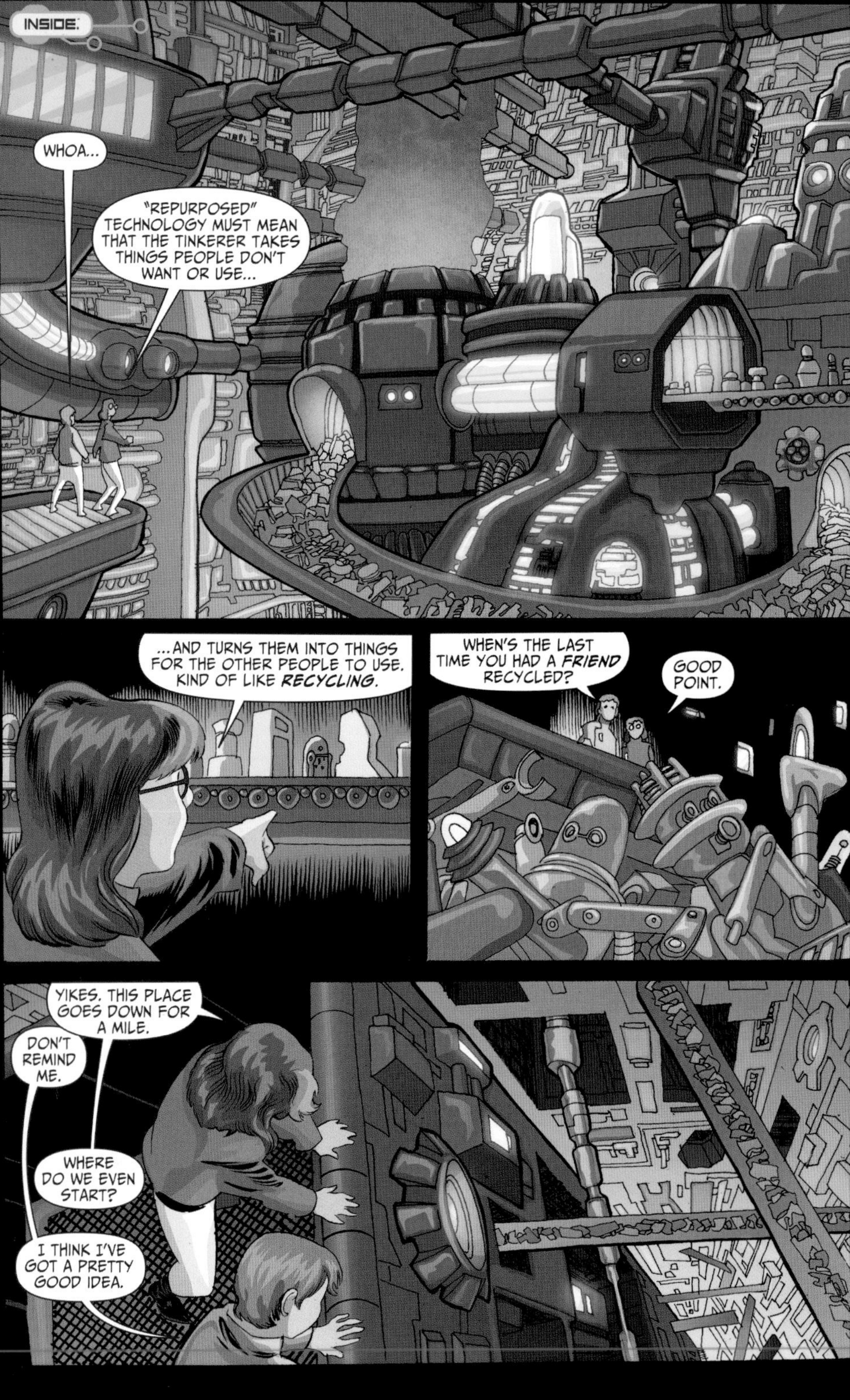
INSIDE:
WHOA...
"REPURPOSED" TECHNOLOGY MUST MEAN THAT THE TINKERER TAKES THINGS PEOPLE DON'T WANT OR USE...
...AND TURNS THEM INTO THINGS FOR THE OTHER PEOPLE TO USE. KIND OF LIKE RECYCLING.
WHEN'S THE LAST TIME YOU HAD A FRIEND RECYCLED?
GOOD POINT.
YIKES. THIS PLACE GOES DOWN FOR A MILE.
DON'T REMIND ME.
WHERE DO WE EVEN START?
I THINK I'VE GOT A PRETTY GOOD IDEA.

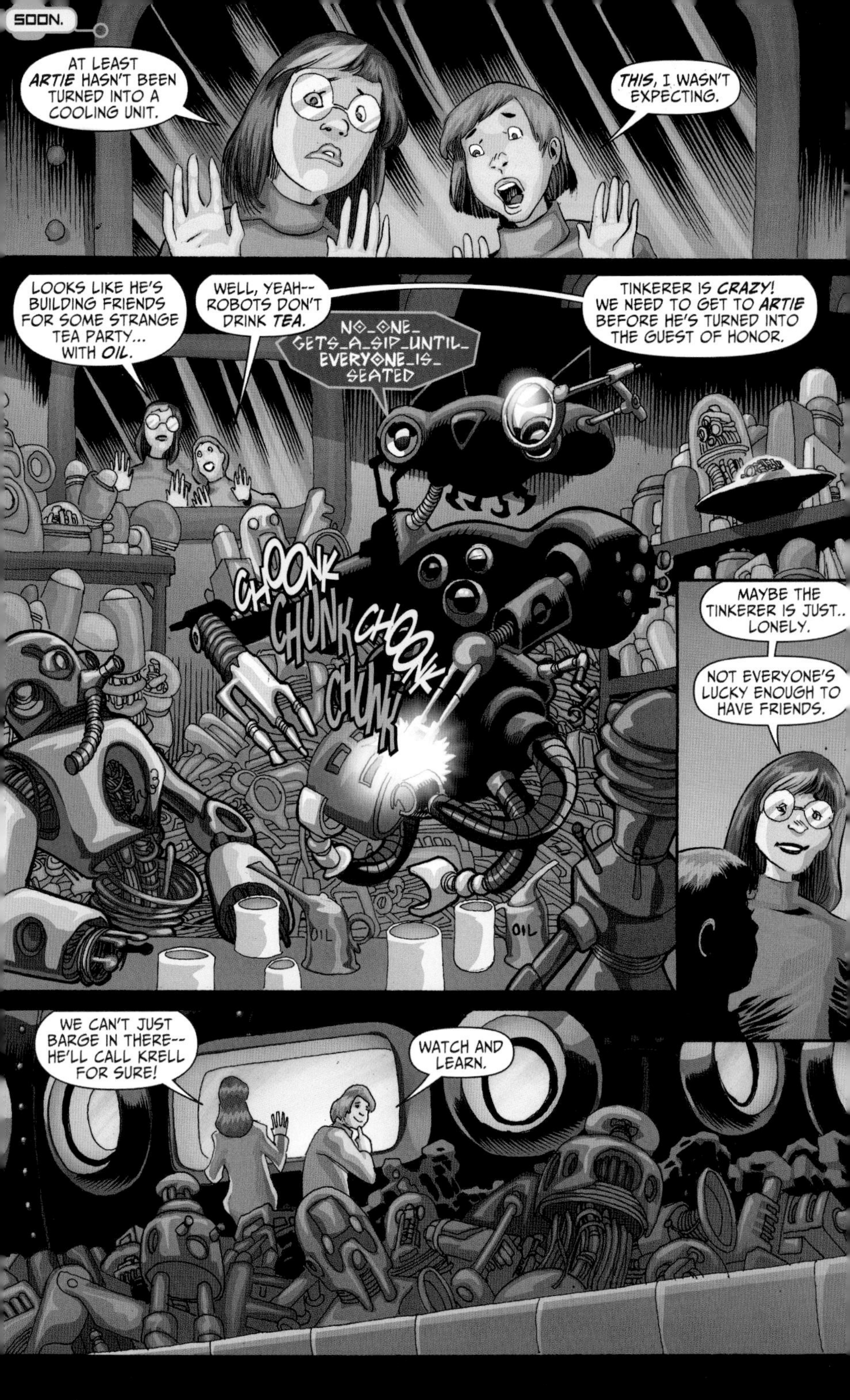
SOON.
AT LEAST ARTIE HASN'T BEEN TURNED INTO A COOLING UNIT.
THIS, I WASN'T EXPECTING.
LOOKS LIKE HE'S BUILDING FRIENDS FOR SOME STRANGE TEA PARTY... WITH OIL.
WELL, YEAH-- ROBOTS DON'T DRINK TEA.
TINKERER IS CRAZY! WE NEED TO GET TO ARTIE BEFORE HE'S TURNED INTO THE GUEST OF HONOR.
NO_ONE_ GETS_A_SIP_UNTIL_ EVERYONE_IS_ SEATED
CHOONK
CHUNK
CHOONK
CHUNK
OIL
OIL
MAYBE THE TINKERER IS JUST.. LONELY.
NOT EVERYONE'S LUCKY ENOUGH TO HAVE FRIENDS.
WE CAN'T JUST BARGE IN THERE-- HE'LL CALL KRELL FOR SURE!
WATCH AND LEARN.

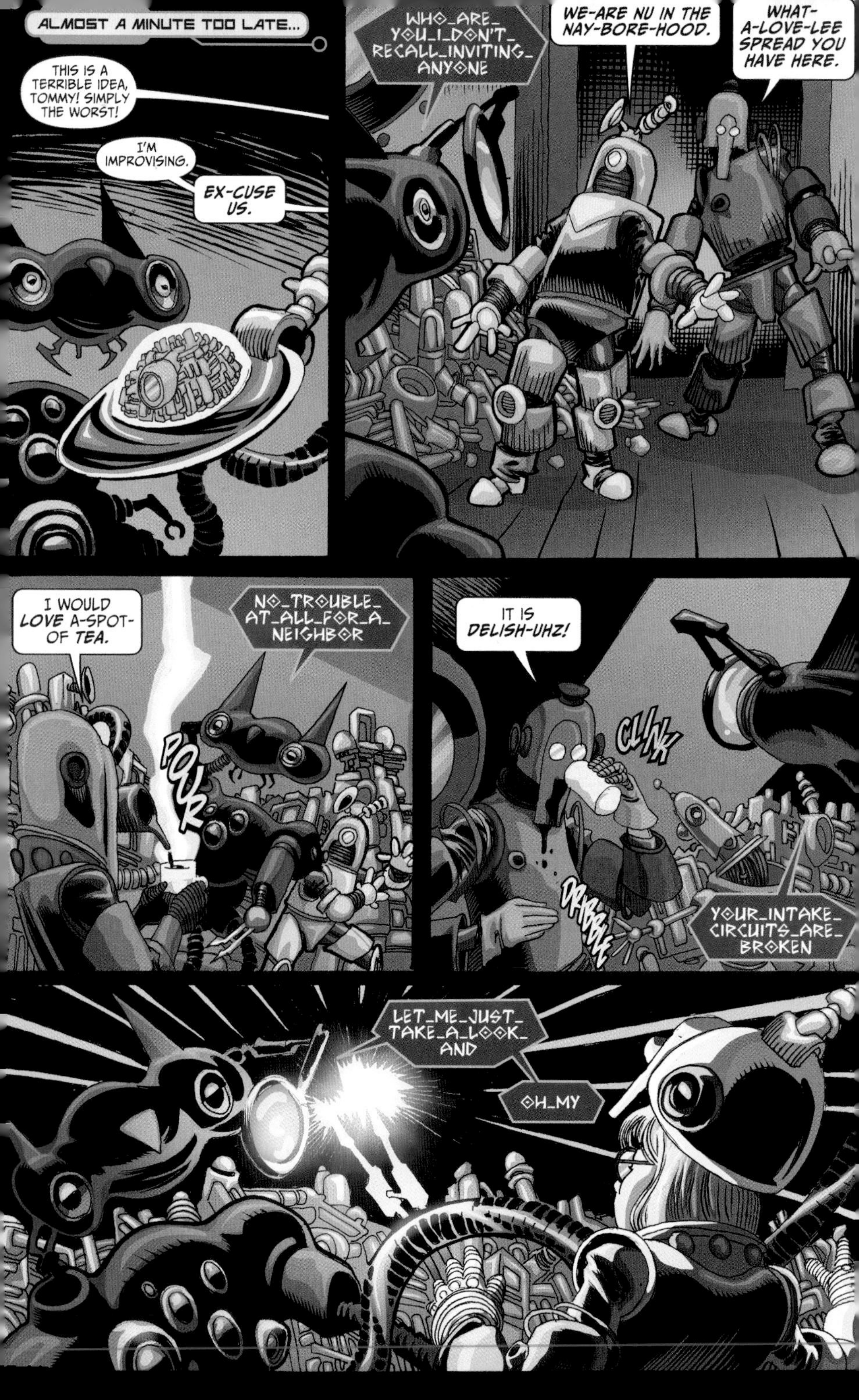

ALMOST A MINUTE TOO LATE...
THIS IS A TERRIBLE IDEA, TOMMY! SIMPLY THE WORST!
I'M IMPROVISING.
EX-CUSE US.
WHO_ARE_YOU_I_DON'T_RECALL_INVITING_ANYONE
WE-ARE NU IN THE NAY-BORE-HOOD.
WHAT-A-LOVE-LEE SPREAD YOU HAVE HERE.
I WOULD LOVE A-SPOT-OF TEA.
NO_TROUBLE_AT_ALL_FOR_A_NEIGHBOR
POUR
IT IS DELISH-UHZ!
CLINK
DRIBBLE
YOUR_INTAKE_CIRCUITS_ARE_BROKEN
LET_ME_JUST_TAKE_A_LOOK_AND
OH_MY

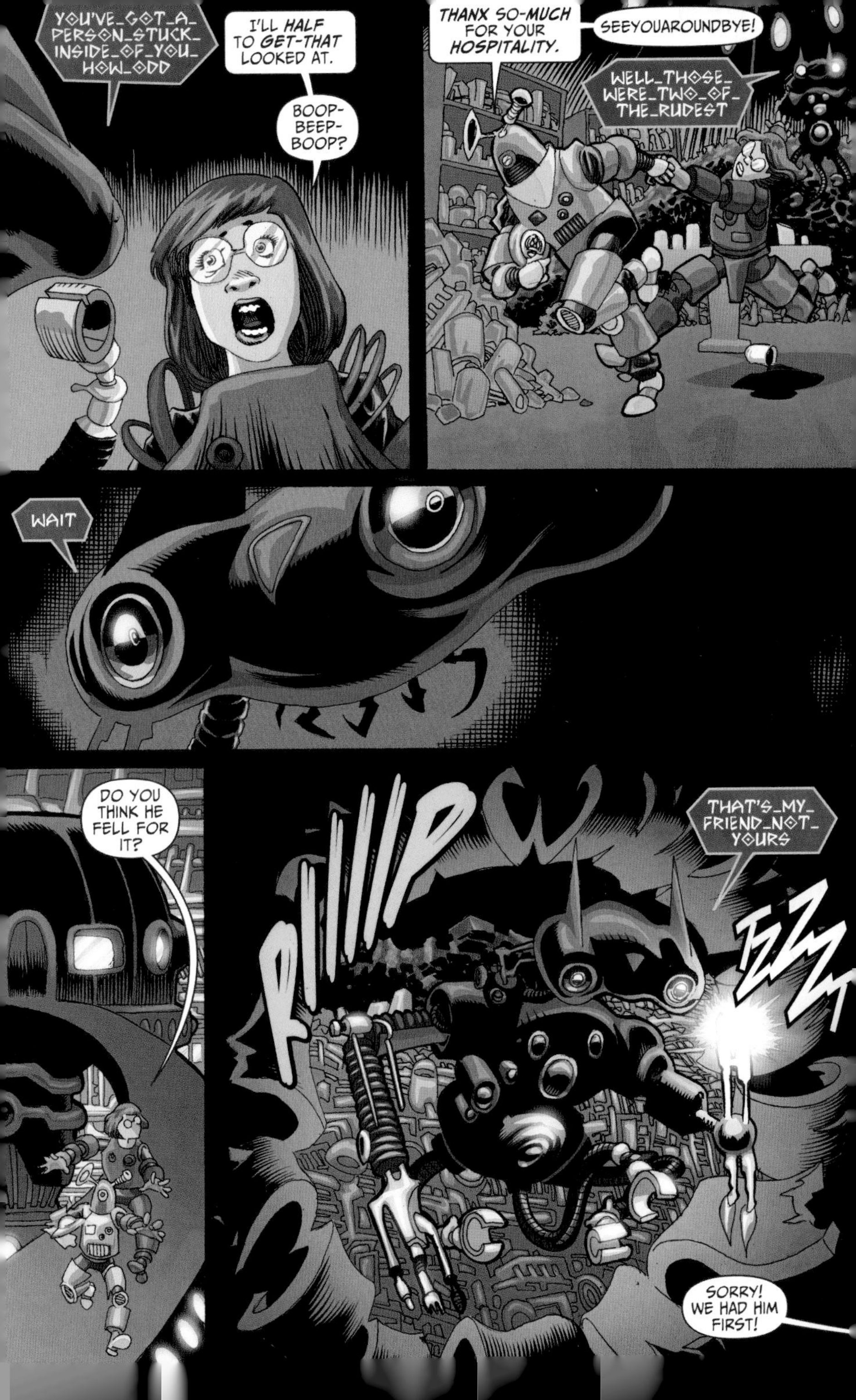
YOU'VE_GOT_A_PERSON_STUCK_INSIDE_OF_YOU_HOW_ODD
I'LL *HALF* TO *GET-THAT* LOOKED AT.
BOOP-BEEP-BOOP?
THANX SO-*MUCH* FOR YOUR *HOSPITALITY.*
SEEYOUAROUNDBYE!
WELL_THOSE_WERE_TWO_OF_THE_RUDEST
WAIT
DO YOU THINK HE FELL FOR IT?
THAT'S_MY_FRIEND_NOT_YOURS
SORRY! WE HAD HIM FIRST!

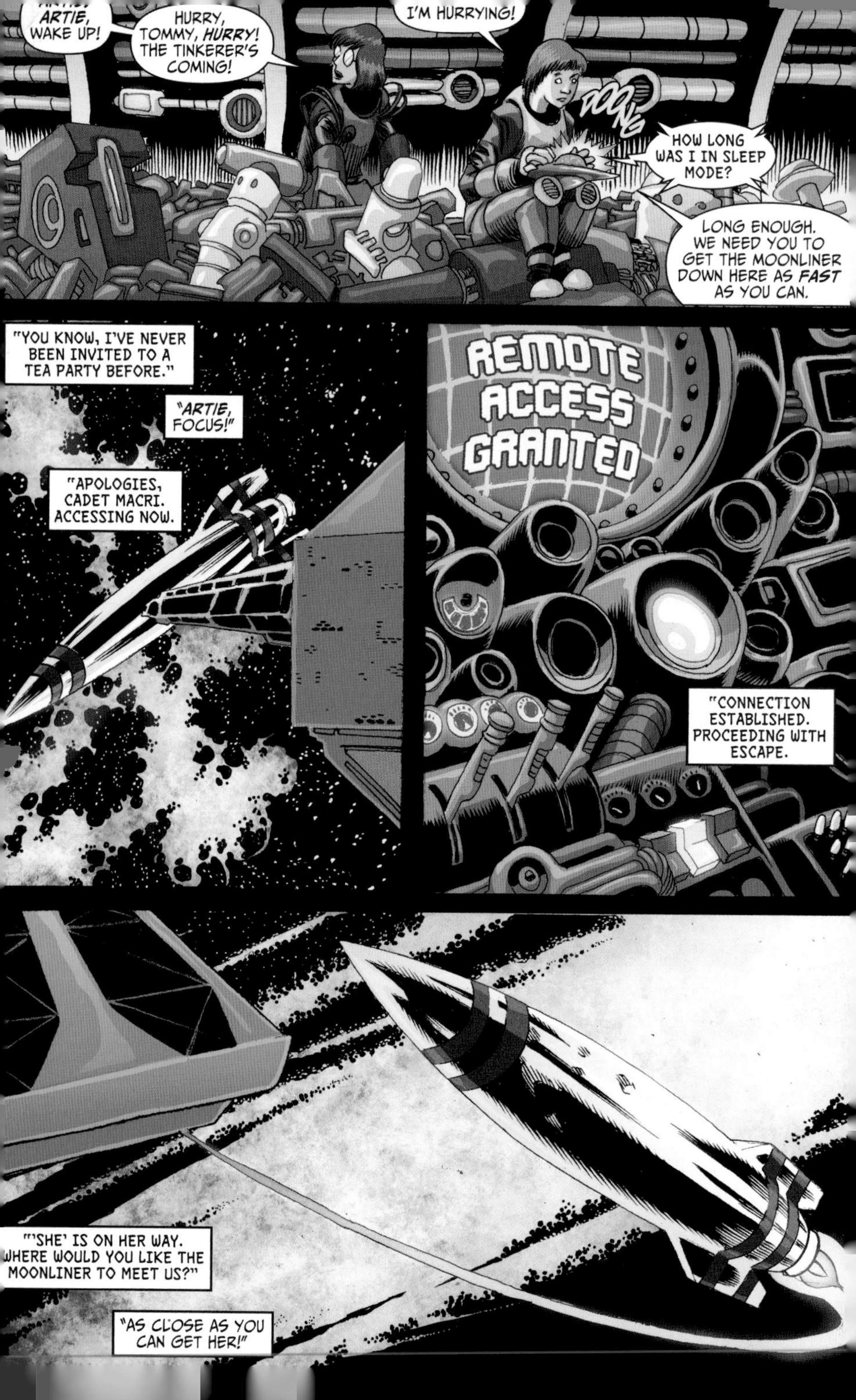
ARTIE, WAKE UP!
HURRY, TOMMY, HURRY! THE TINKERER'S COMING!
I'M HURRYING!
DOONG
HOW LONG WAS I IN SLEEP MODE?
LONG ENOUGH. WE NEED YOU TO GET THE MOONLINER DOWN HERE AS FAST AS YOU CAN.
"YOU KNOW, I'VE NEVER BEEN INVITED TO A TEA PARTY BEFORE."
"ARTIE, FOCUS!"
"APOLOGIES, CADET MACRI. ACCESSING NOW.
REMOTE ACCESS GRANTED
"CONNECTION ESTABLISHED. PROCEEDING WITH ESCAPE.
"'SHE' IS ON HER WAY. WHERE WOULD YOU LIKE THE MOONLINER TO MEET US?"
"AS CLOSE AS YOU CAN GET HER!"

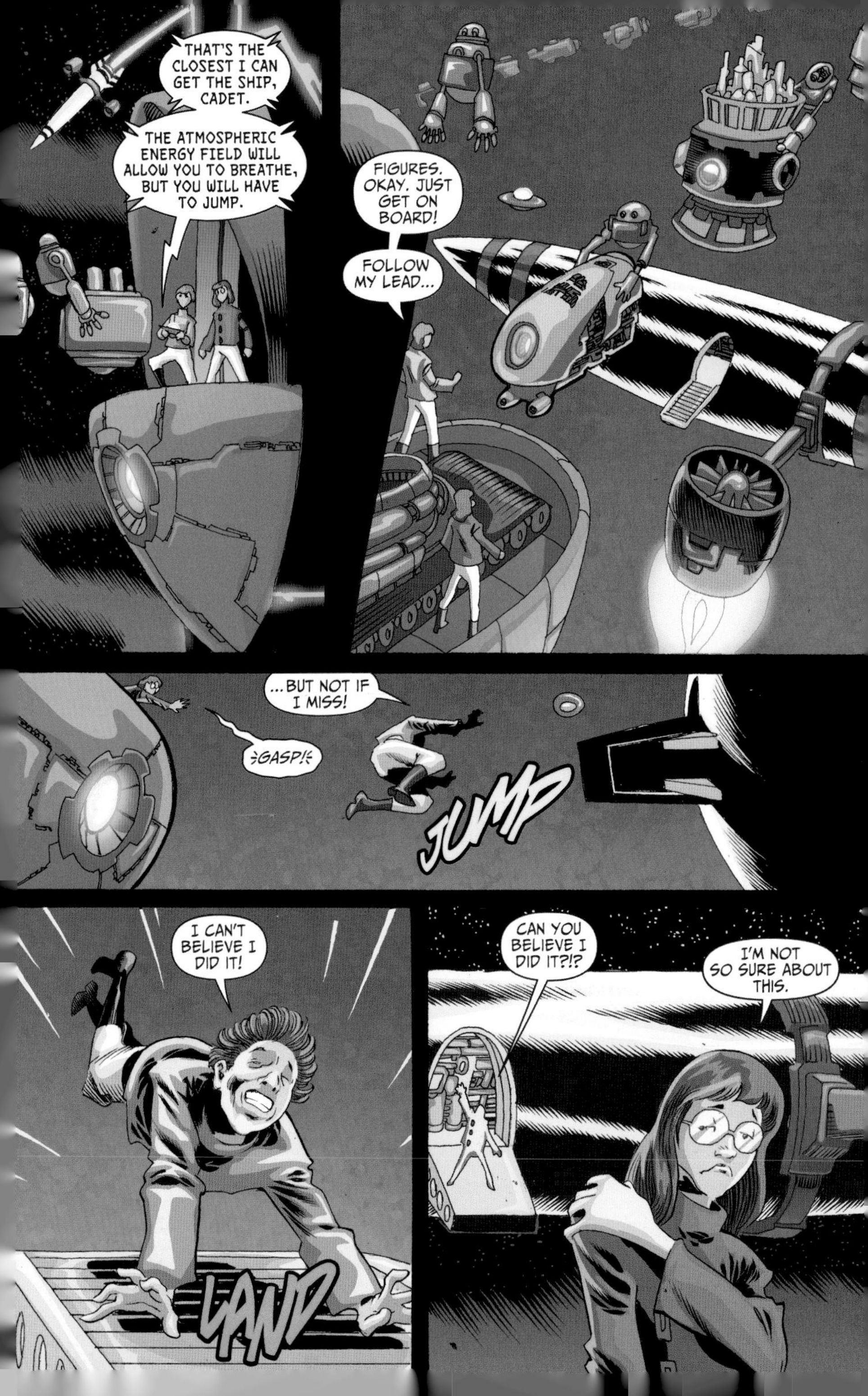
THAT'S THE CLOSEST I CAN GET THE SHIP, CADET.
THE ATMOSPHERIC ENERGY FIELD WILL ALLOW YOU TO BREATHE, BUT YOU WILL HAVE TO JUMP.
FIGURES. OKAY. JUST GET ON BOARD!
FOLLOW MY LEAD...
...BUT NOT IF I MISS!
GASP!
JUMP
I CAN'T BELIEVE I DID IT!
LAND
CAN YOU BELIEVE I DID IT?!?
I'M NOT SO SURE ABOUT THIS.

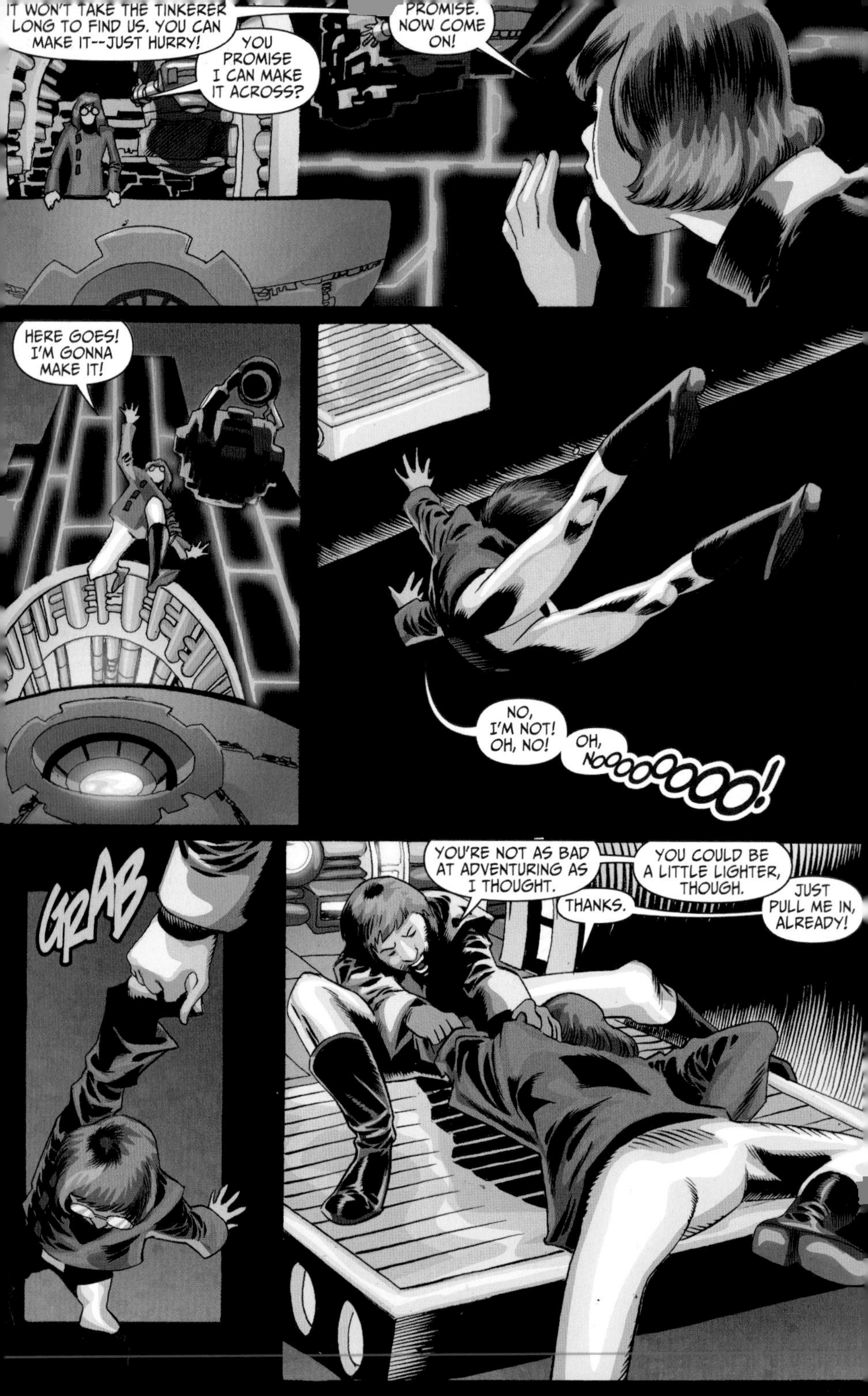
IT WON'T TAKE THE TINKERER LONG TO FIND US. YOU CAN MAKE IT--JUST HURRY!
YOU PROMISE I CAN MAKE IT ACROSS?
PROMISE. NOW COME ON!
HERE GOES! I'M GONNA MAKE IT!
NO, I'M NOT! OH, NO!
OH, NOOOOOOOOO!
GRAB
YOU'RE NOT AS BAD AT ADVENTURING AS I THOUGHT.
THANKS.
YOU COULD BE A LITTLE LIGHTER, THOUGH.
JUST PULL ME IN, ALREADY!

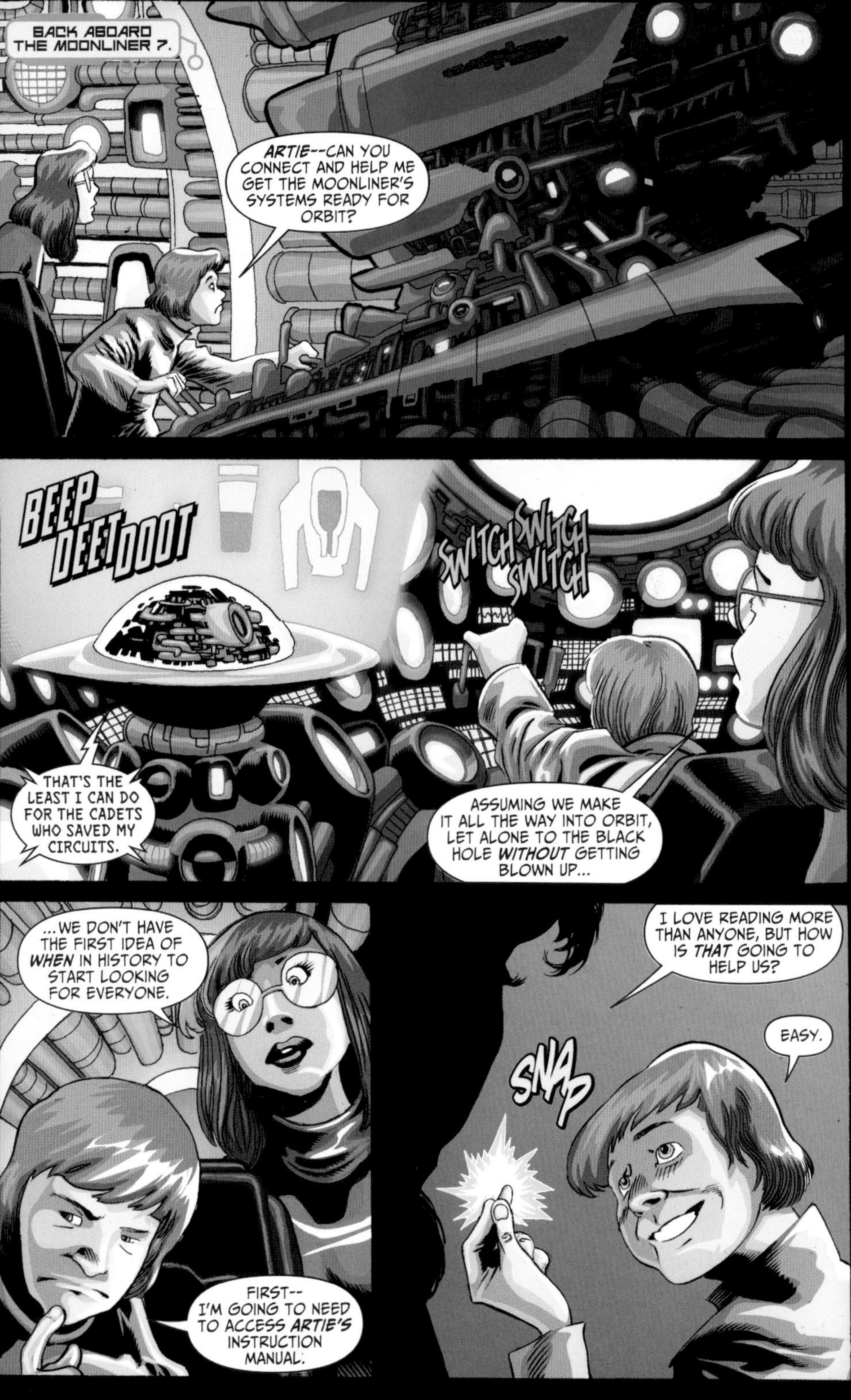
BACK ABOARD THE MOONLINER 7.
ARTIE--CAN YOU CONNECT AND HELP ME GET THE MOONLINER'S SYSTEMS READY FOR ORBIT?
BEEP DEET DOOT
SWITCH SWITCH SWITCH
THAT'S THE LEAST I CAN DO FOR THE CADETS WHO SAVED MY CIRCUITS.
ASSUMING WE MAKE IT ALL THE WAY INTO ORBIT, LET ALONE TO THE BLACK HOLE WITHOUT GETTING BLOWN UP...
...WE DON'T HAVE THE FIRST IDEA OF WHEN IN HISTORY TO START LOOKING FOR EVERYONE.
FIRST-- I'M GOING TO NEED TO ACCESS ARTIE'S INSTRUCTION MANUAL.
I LOVE READING MORE THAN ANYONE, BUT HOW IS THAT GOING TO HELP US?
EASY.
SNAP

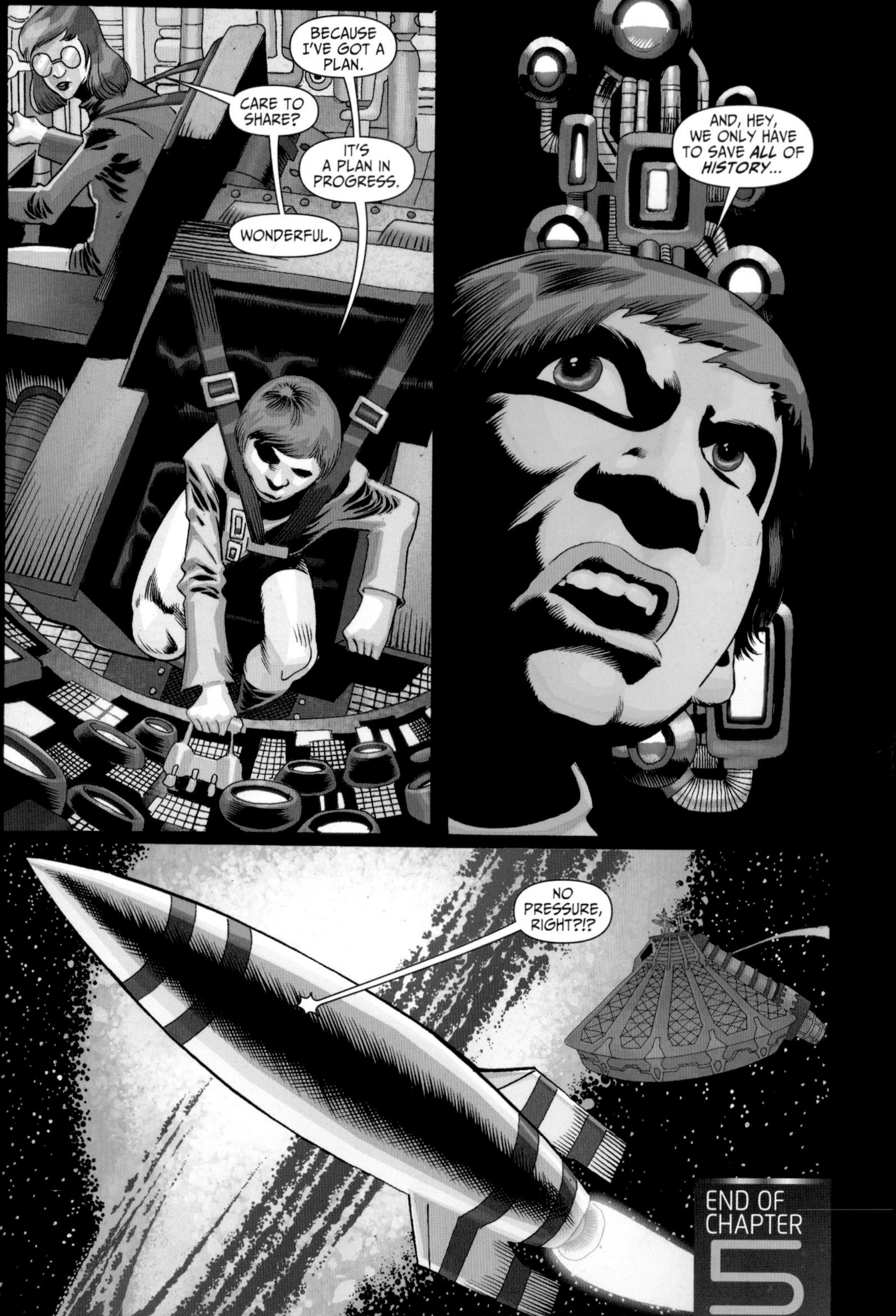
BECAUSE I'VE GOT A PLAN.
CARE TO SHARE?
IT'S A PLAN IN PROGRESS.
WONDERFUL.
AND, HEY, WE ONLY HAVE TO SAVE ALL OF HISTORY...
NO PRESSURE, RIGHT?!?
END OF CHAPTER 5

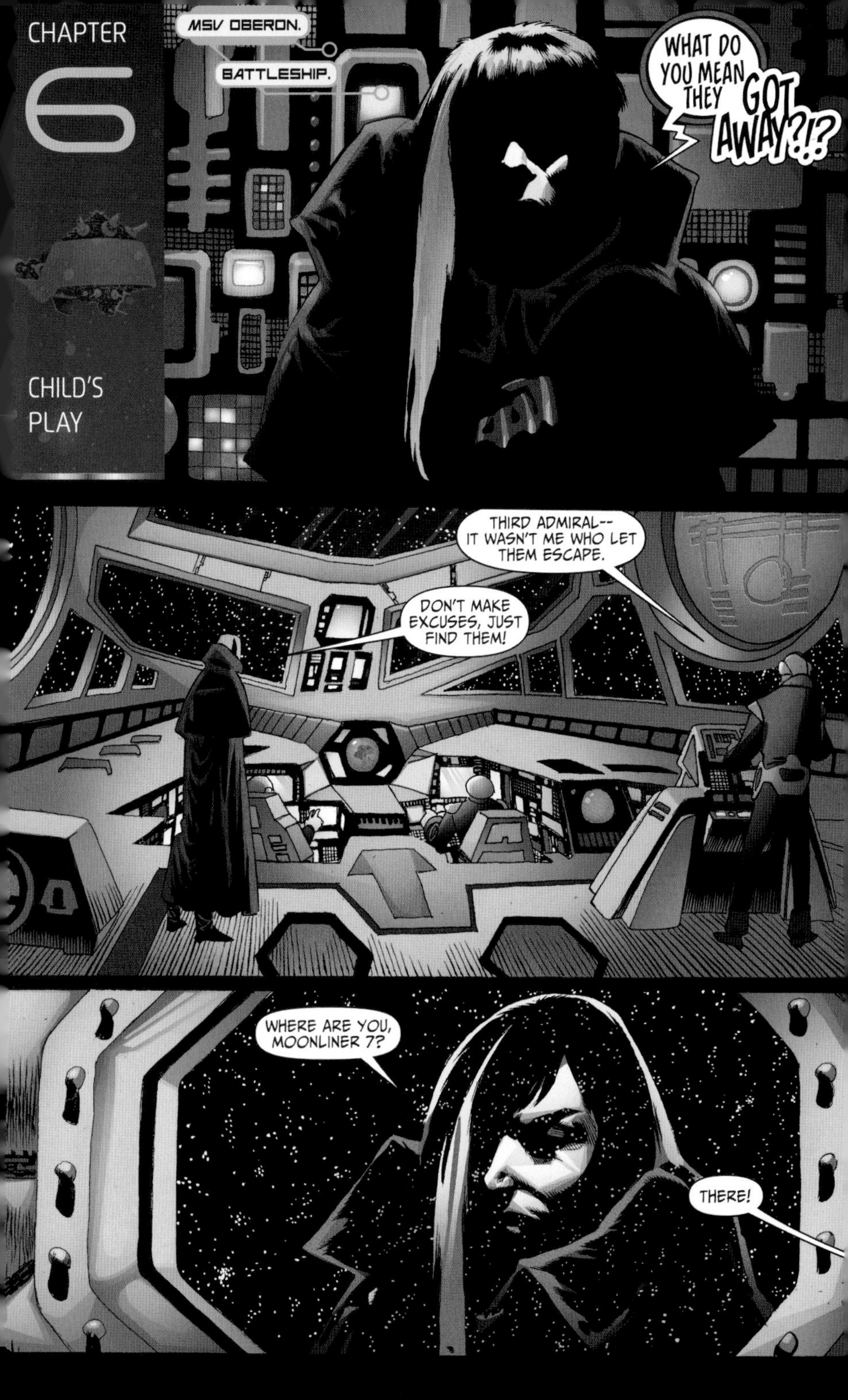

CHAPTER
6
CHILD'S PLAY
MSV OBERON.
BATTLESHIP.
WHAT DO YOU MEAN THEY GOT AWAY?!?
THIRD ADMIRAL-- IT WASN'T ME WHO LET THEM ESCAPE.
DON'T MAKE EXCUSES, JUST FIND THEM!
WHERE ARE YOU, MOONLINER 7?
THERE!

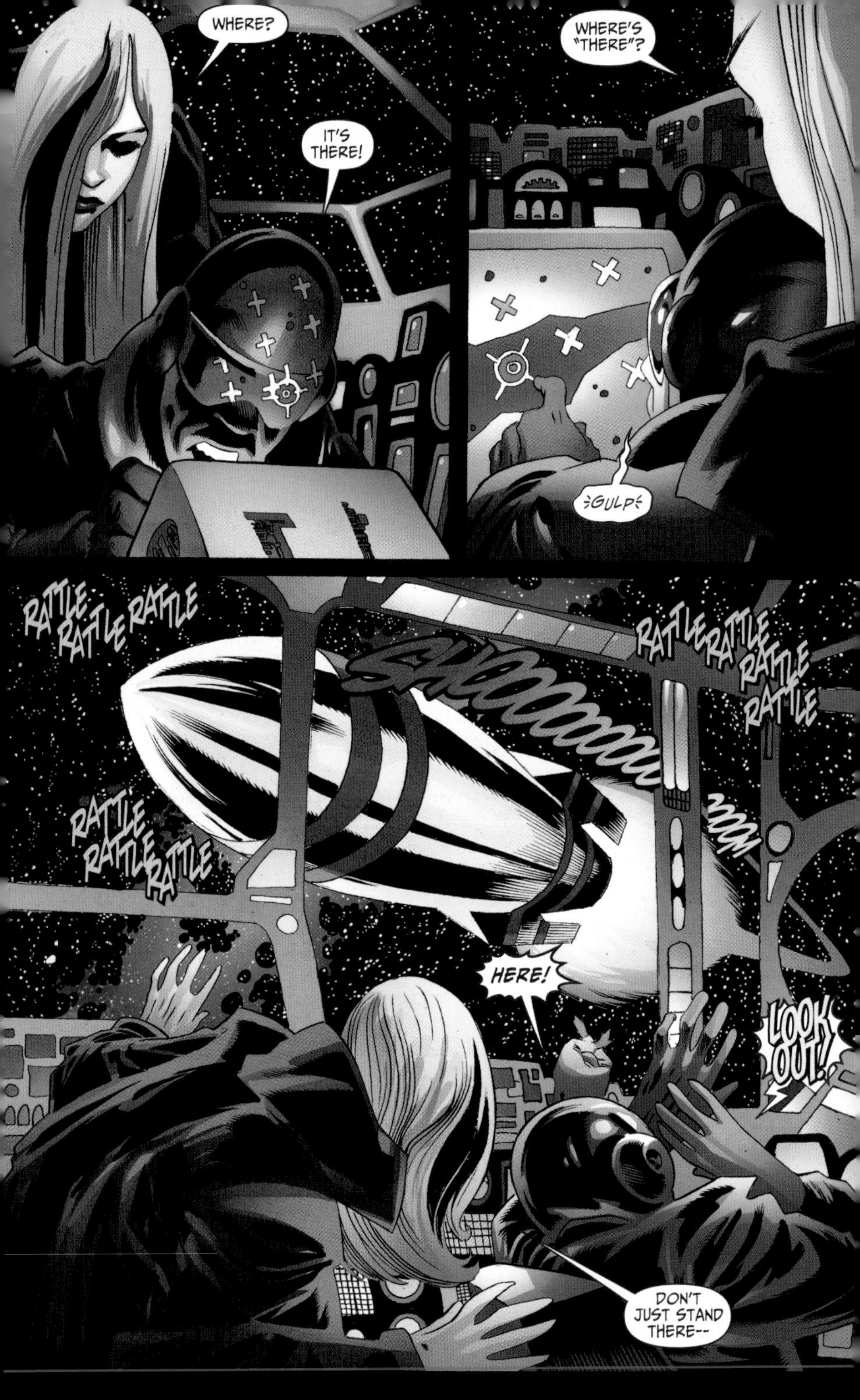
WHERE?
IT'S THERE!
WHERE'S "THERE"?
GULP
RATTLE RATTLE RATTLE RATTLE
RATTLE RATTLE RATTLE RATTLE
RATTLE RATTLE RATTLE
SHOOOOOOOM
HERE!
LOOK OUT!
DON'T JUST STAND THERE--

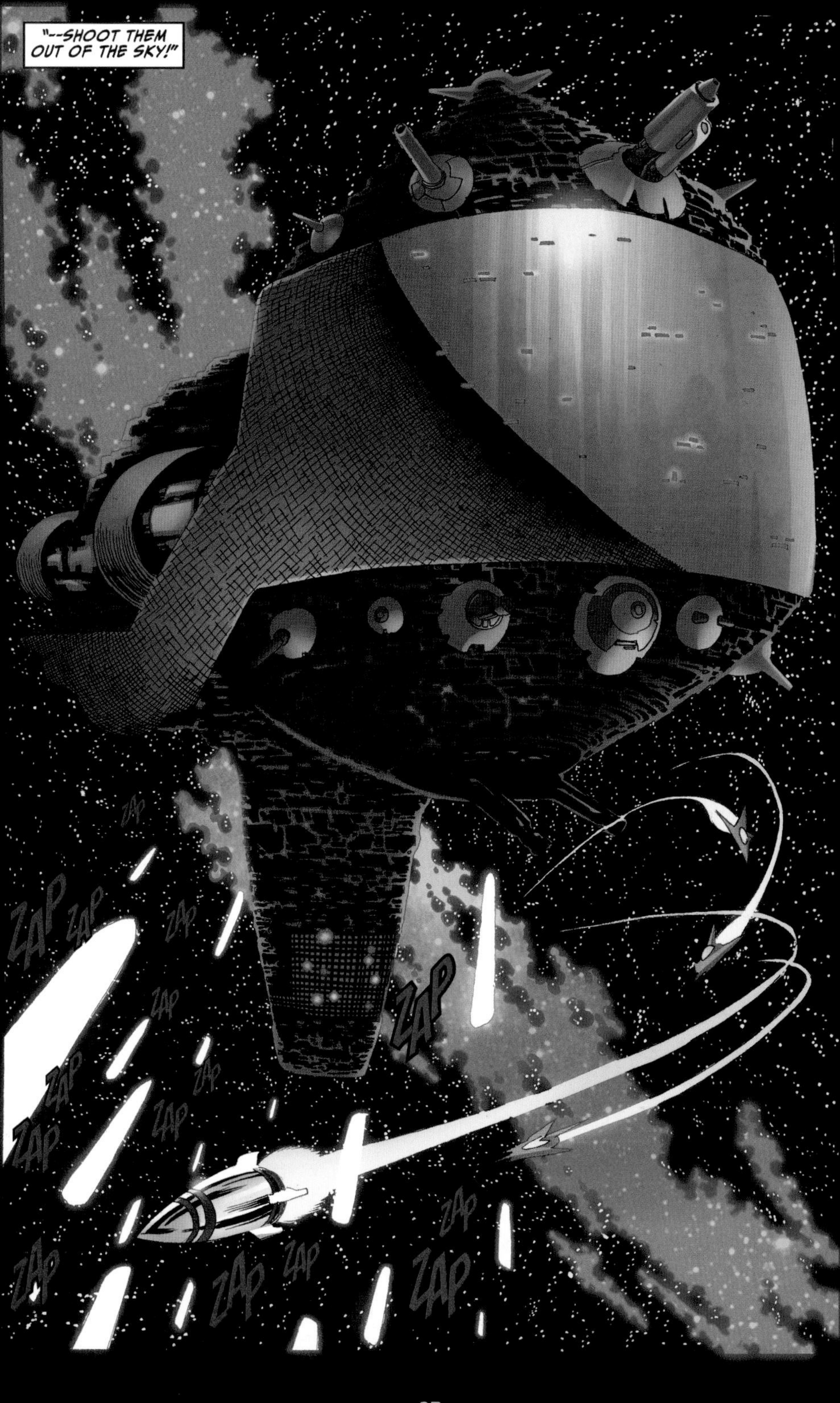
"--SHOOT THEM OUT OF THE SKY!"
ZAP
ZAP
ZAP
ZAP
ZAP
ZAP
ZAP
ZAP
ZAP
ZAP
ZAP
ZAP
ZAP
ZAP
ZAP

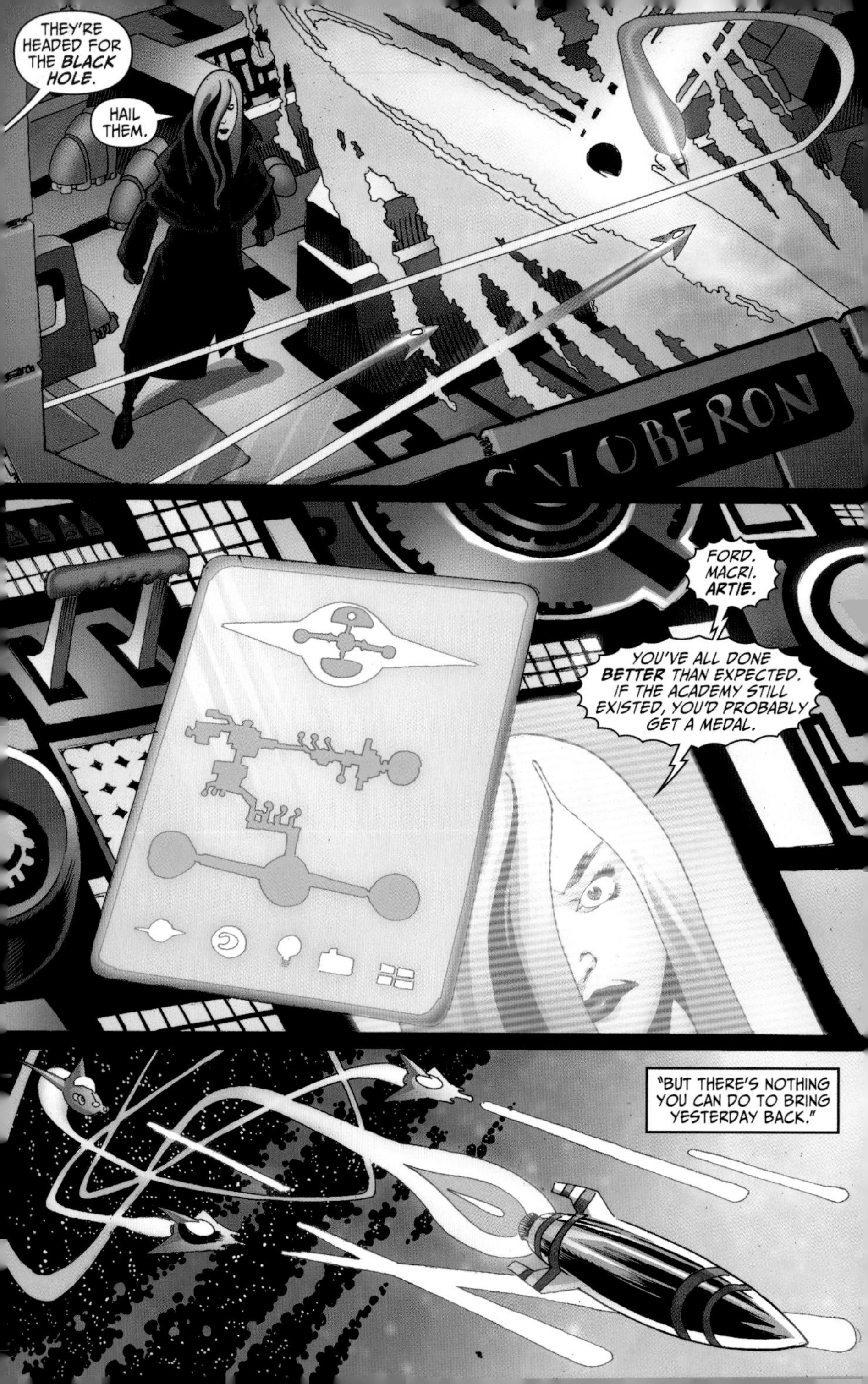
THEY'RE HEADED FOR THE BLACK HOLE.
HAIL THEM.
OBERON
FORD. MACRI. ARTIE.
YOU'VE ALL DONE BETTER THAN EXPECTED. IF THE ACADEMY STILL EXISTED, YOU'D PROBABLY GET A MEDAL.
"BUT THERE'S NOTHING YOU CAN DO TO BRING YESTERDAY BACK."

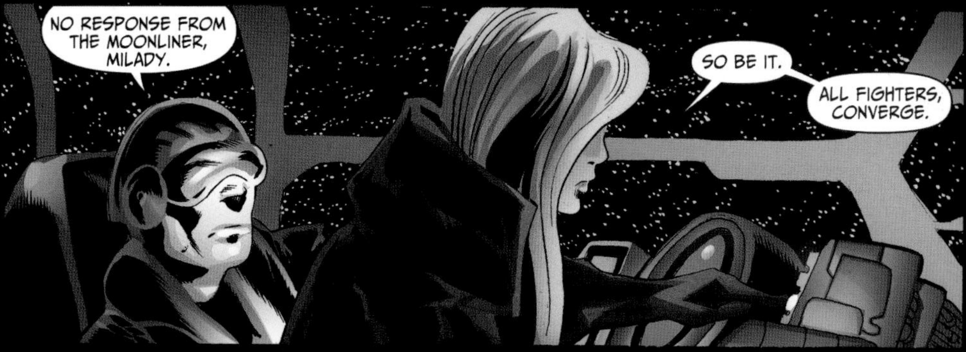
NO RESPONSE FROM THE MOONLINER, MILADY.
SO BE IT.
ALL FIGHTERS, CONVERGE.

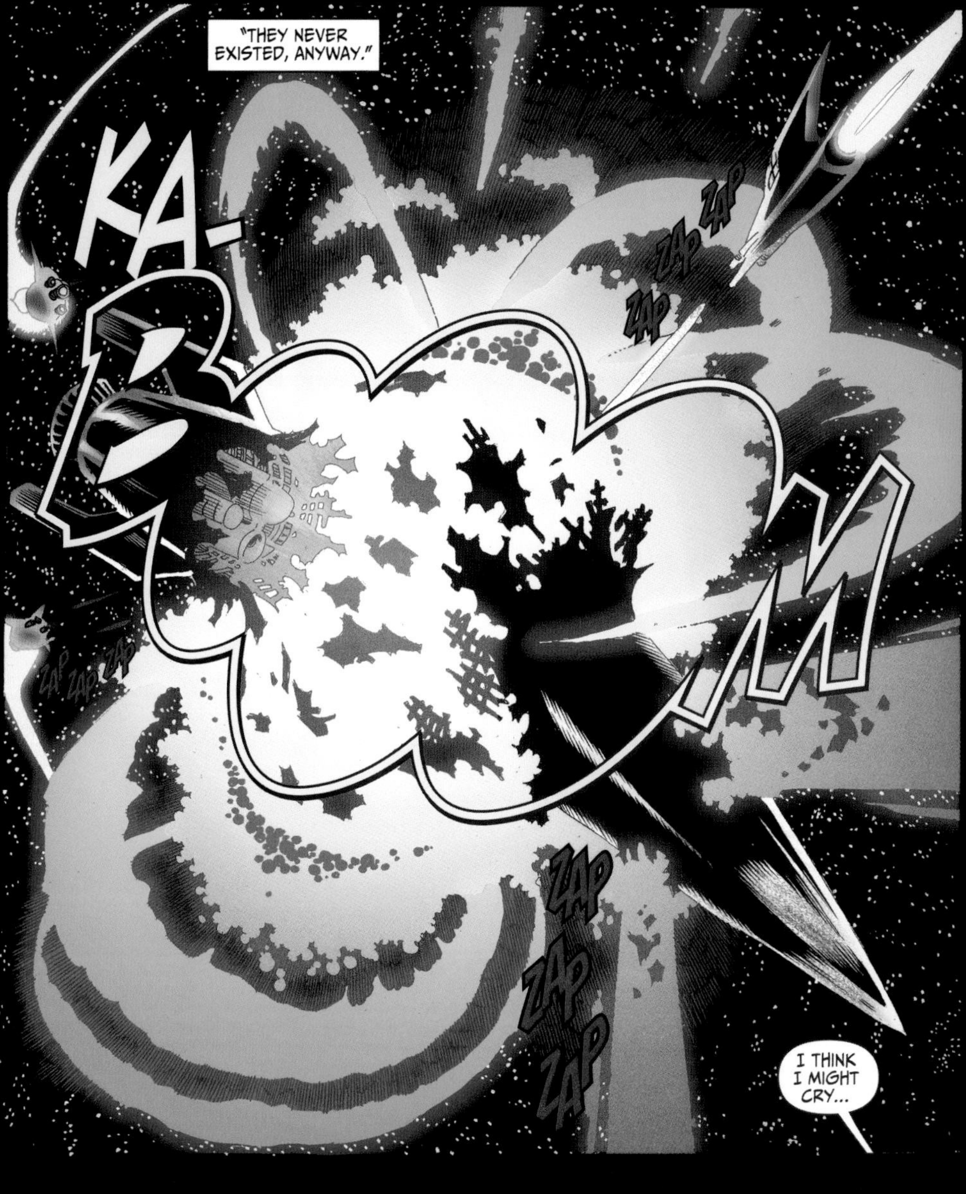
"THEY NEVER EXISTED, ANYWAY."
KA-BOOM
ZAP ZAP ZAP ZAP
ZAP ZAP ZAP
ZAP ZAP ZAP
I THINK I MIGHT CRY...

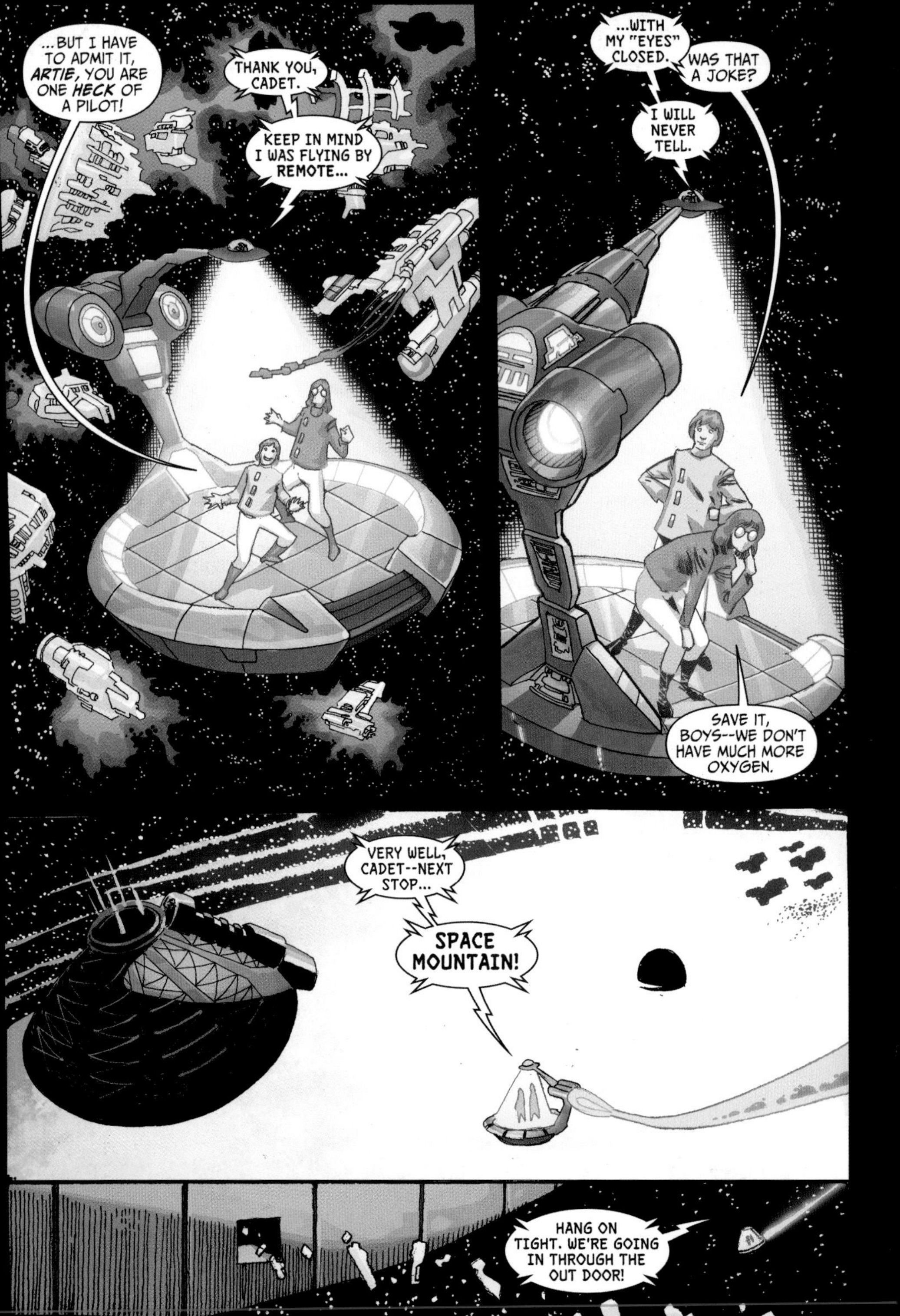
...BUT I HAVE TO ADMIT IT, ARTIE, YOU ARE ONE HECK OF A PILOT!
THANK YOU, CADET.
KEEP IN MIND I WAS FLYING BY REMOTE...
...WITH MY "EYES" CLOSED.
WAS THAT A JOKE?
I WILL NEVER TELL.
SAVE IT, BOYS--WE DON'T HAVE MUCH MORE OXYGEN.
VERY WELL, CADET--NEXT STOP...
SPACE MOUNTAIN!
HANG ON TIGHT. WE'RE GOING IN THROUGH THE OUT DOOR!

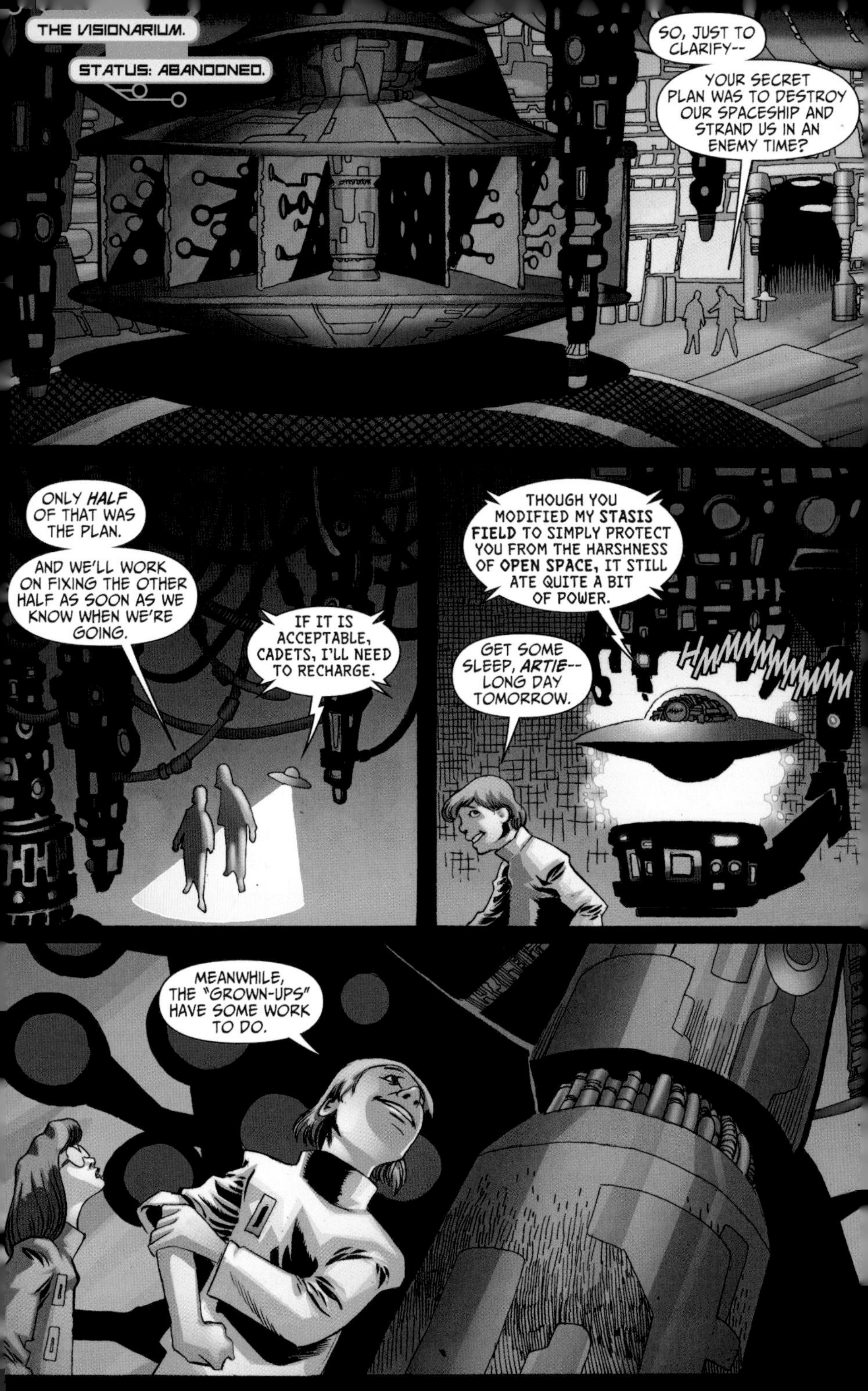
THE VISIONARIUM.
STATUS: ABANDONED.
SO, JUST TO CLARIFY--
YOUR SECRET PLAN WAS TO DESTROY OUR SPACESHIP AND STRAND US IN AN ENEMY TIME?
ONLY HALF OF THAT WAS THE PLAN.
AND WE'LL WORK ON FIXING THE OTHER HALF AS SOON AS WE KNOW WHEN WE'RE GOING.
IF IT IS ACCEPTABLE, CADETS, I'LL NEED TO RECHARGE.
THOUGH YOU MODIFIED MY STASIS FIELD TO SIMPLY PROTECT YOU FROM THE HARSHNESS OF OPEN SPACE, IT STILL ATE QUITE A BIT OF POWER.
GET SOME SLEEP, ARTIE-- LONG DAY TOMORROW.
HMMMMMMMMMMMMM
MEANWHILE, THE "GROWN-UPS" HAVE SOME WORK TO DO.

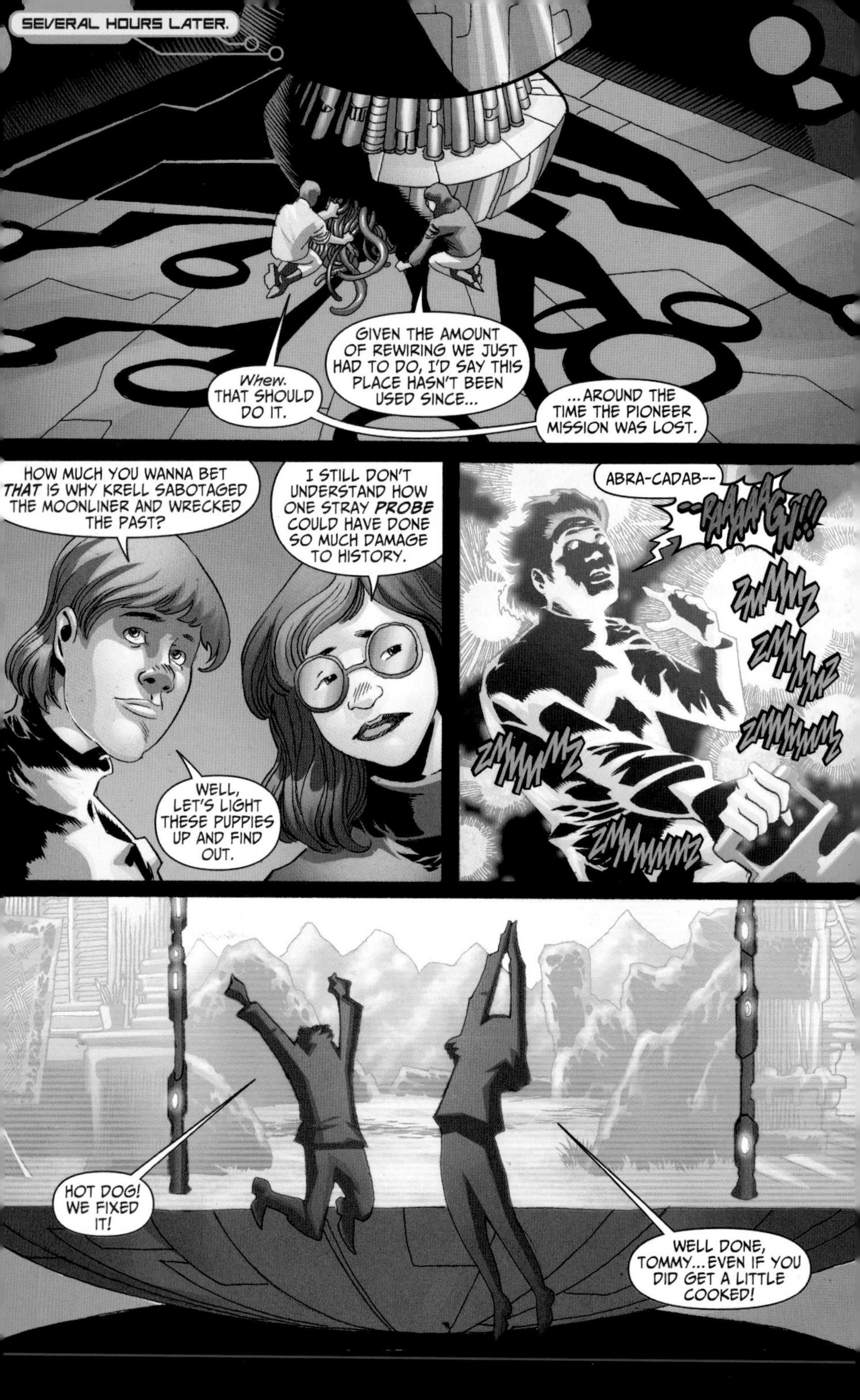
SEVERAL HOURS LATER.
Whew. THAT SHOULD DO IT.
GIVEN THE AMOUNT OF REWIRING WE JUST HAD TO DO, I'D SAY THIS PLACE HASN'T BEEN USED SINCE...
...AROUND THE TIME THE PIONEER MISSION WAS LOST.
HOW MUCH YOU WANNA BET ***THAT*** IS WHY KRELL SABOTAGED THE MOONLINER AND WRECKED THE PAST?
I STILL DON'T UNDERSTAND HOW ONE STRAY ***PROBE*** COULD HAVE DONE SO MUCH DAMAGE TO HISTORY.
WELL, LET'S LIGHT THESE PUPPIES UP AND FIND OUT.
ABRA-CADAB--
--RAAAAAGH!!!
ZMMMZ
ZMMMMZ
ZMMMMMZ
ZMMMMMZ
ZMMMMMMZ
HOT DOG! WE FIXED IT!
WELL DONE, TOMMY...EVEN IF YOU DID GET A LITTLE COOKED!

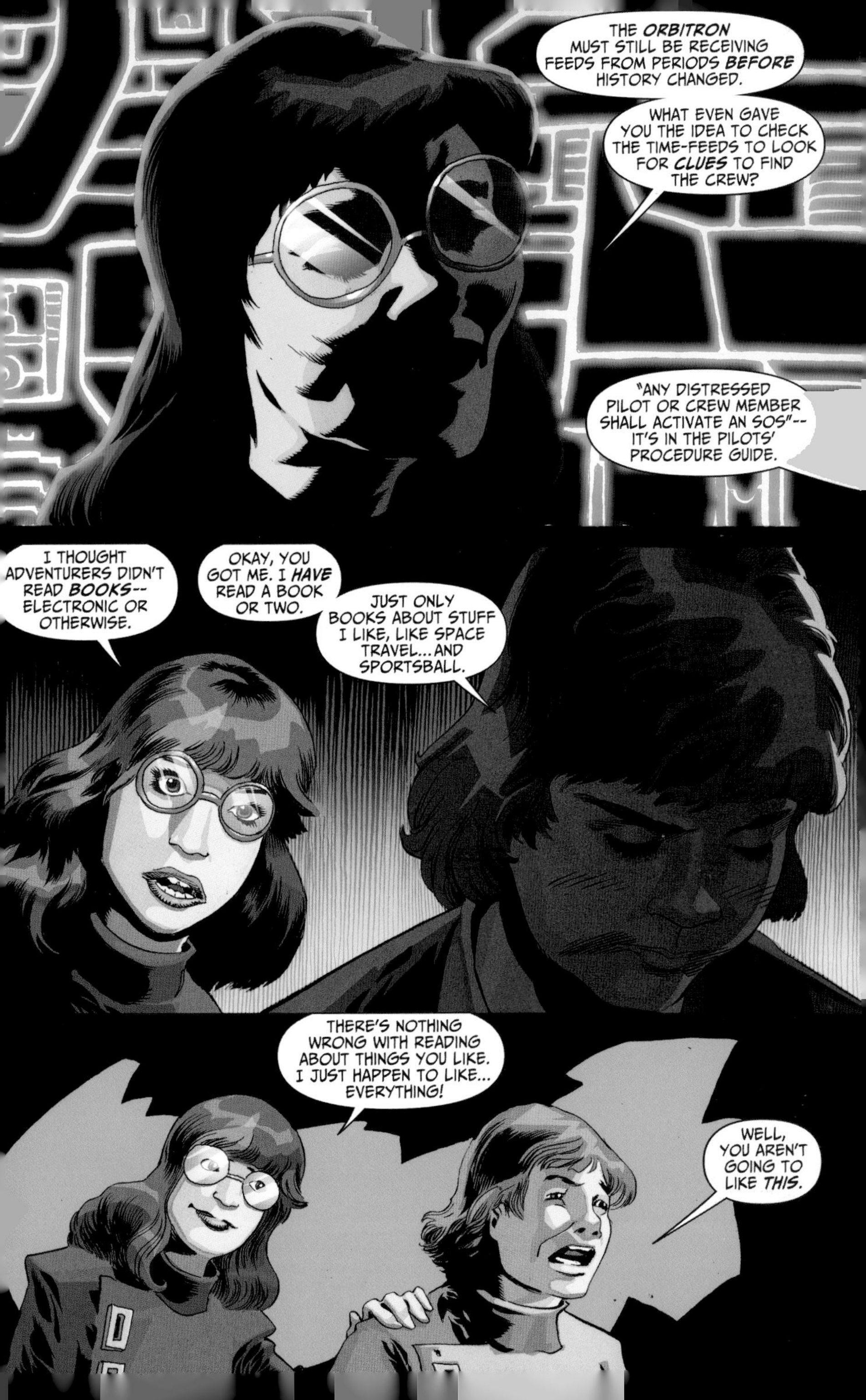
THE *ORBITRON* MUST STILL BE RECEIVING FEEDS FROM PERIODS *BEFORE* HISTORY CHANGED.
WHAT EVEN GAVE YOU THE IDEA TO CHECK THE TIME-FEEDS TO LOOK FOR *CLUES* TO FIND THE CREW?
"ANY DISTRESSED PILOT OR CREW MEMBER SHALL ACTIVATE AN SOS"-- IT'S IN THE PILOTS' PROCEDURE GUIDE.
I THOUGHT ADVENTURERS DIDN'T READ *BOOKS*-- ELECTRONIC OR OTHERWISE.
OKAY, YOU GOT ME. I *HAVE* READ A BOOK OR TWO.
JUST ONLY BOOKS ABOUT STUFF I LIKE, LIKE SPACE TRAVEL... AND SPORTSBALL.
THERE'S NOTHING WRONG WITH READING ABOUT THINGS YOU LIKE. I JUST HAPPEN TO LIKE... EVERYTHING!
WELL, YOU AREN'T GOING TO LIKE *THIS*.

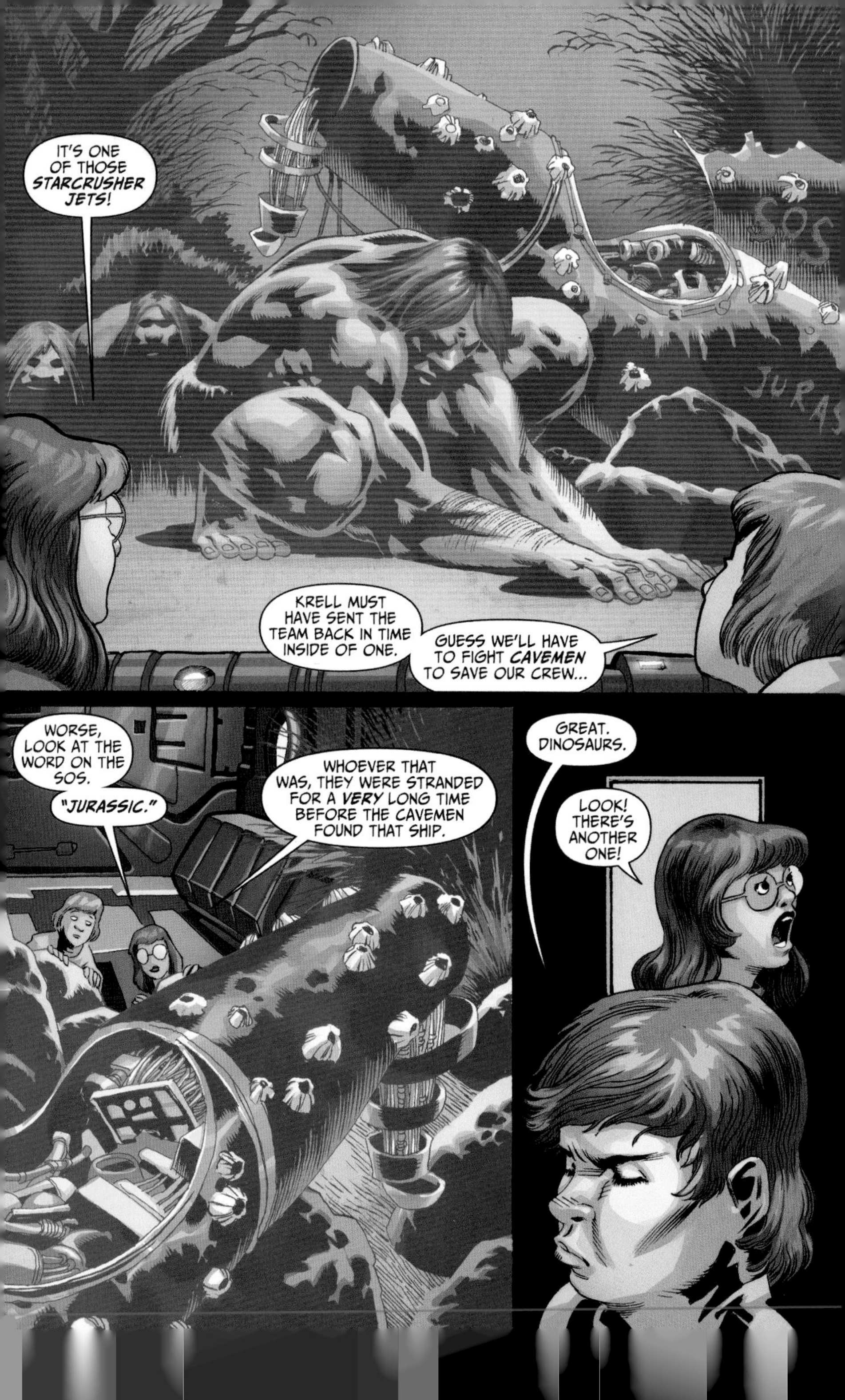
IT'S ONE OF THOSE STARCRUSHER JETS!
SOS
JURAS
KRELL MUST HAVE SENT THE TEAM BACK IN TIME INSIDE OF ONE.
GUESS WE'LL HAVE TO FIGHT CAVEMEN TO SAVE OUR CREW...
WORSE, LOOK AT THE WORD ON THE SOS.
"JURASSIC."
WHOEVER THAT WAS, THEY WERE STRANDED FOR A VERY LONG TIME BEFORE THE CAVEMEN FOUND THAT SHIP.
GREAT. DINOSAURS.
LOOK! THERE'S ANOTHER ONE!

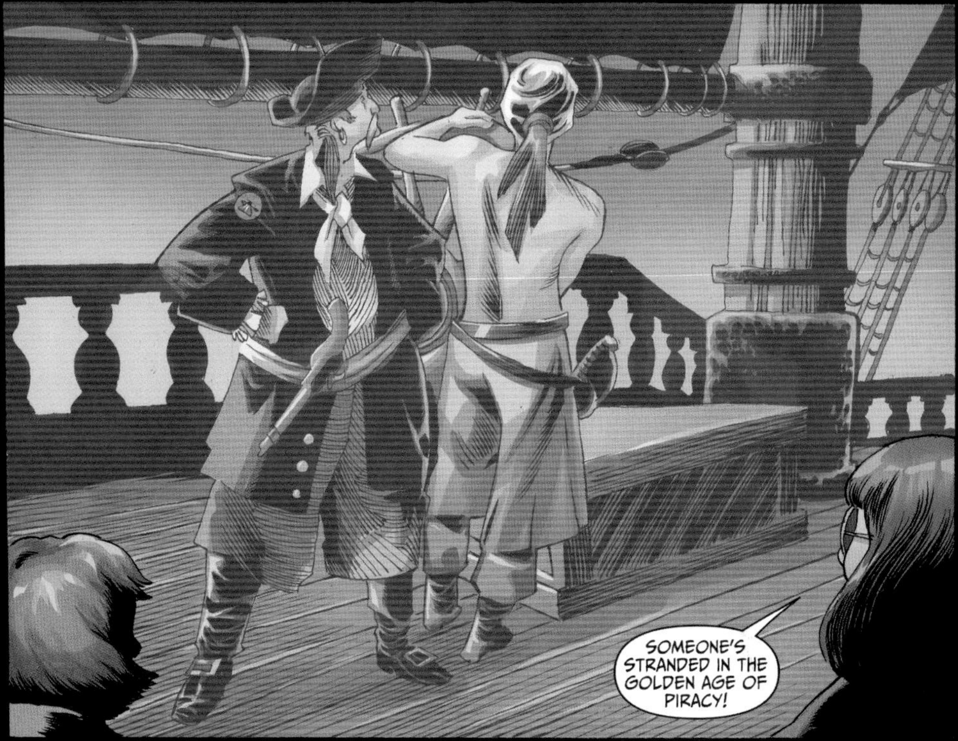
SOMEONE'S STRANDED IN THE GOLDEN AGE OF PIRACY!

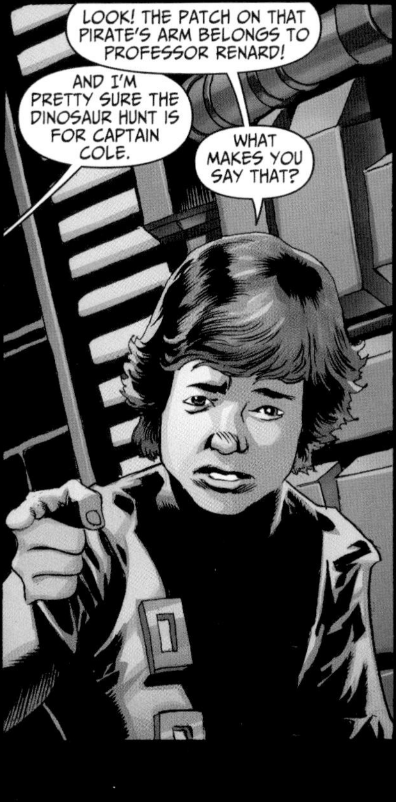
LOOK! THE PATCH ON THAT PIRATE'S ARM BELONGS TO PROFESSOR RENARD!
AND I'M PRETTY SURE THE DINOSAUR HUNT IS FOR CAPTAIN COLE.
WHAT MAKES YOU SAY THAT?

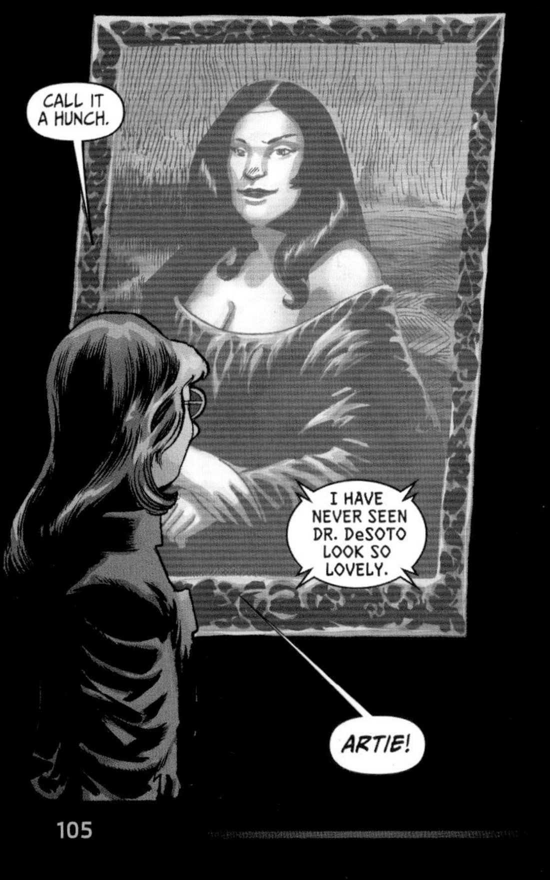
CALL IT A HUNCH.
I HAVE NEVER SEEN DR. DeSOTO LOOK SO LOVELY.
ARTIE!

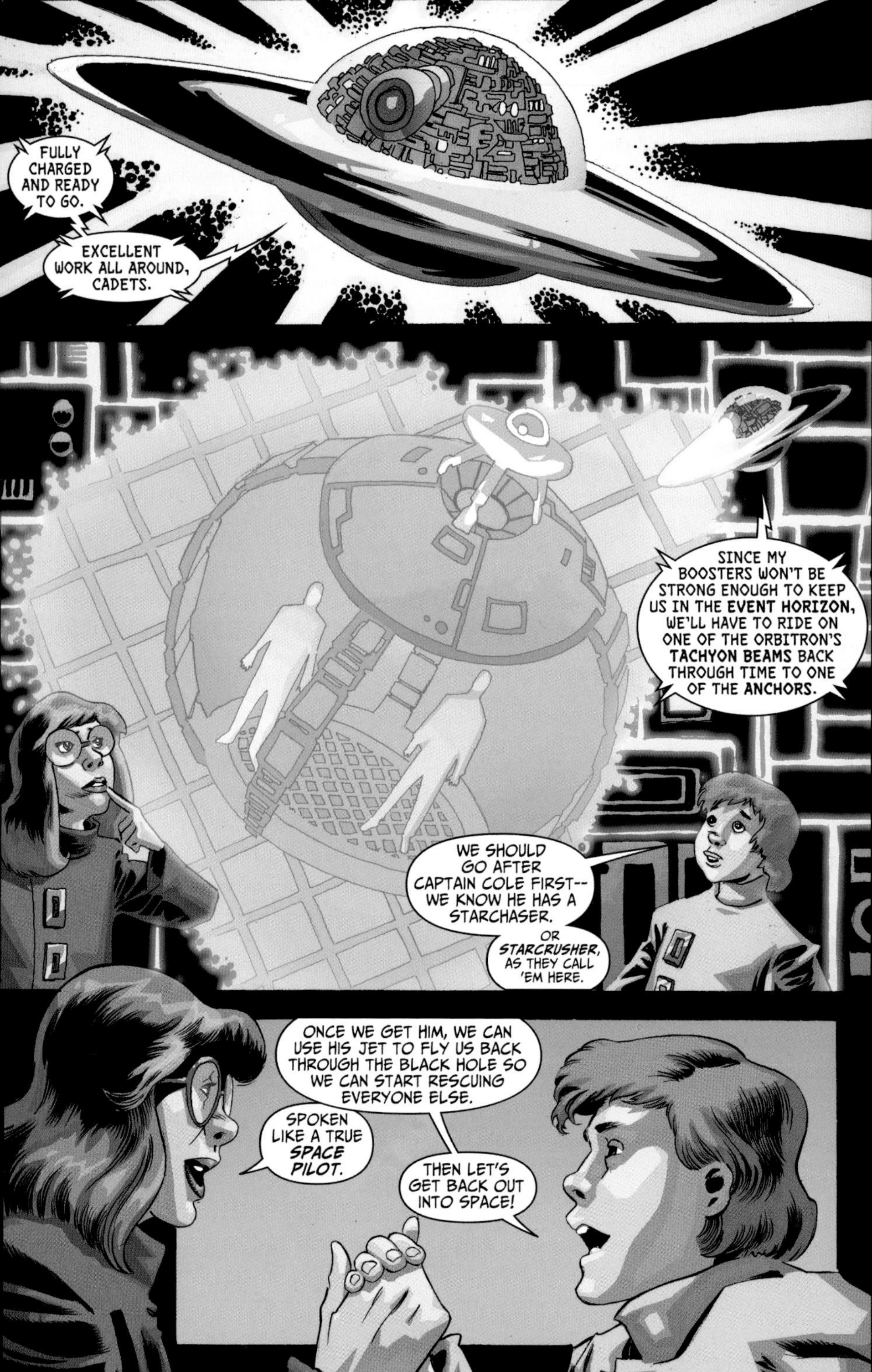
FULLY CHARGED AND READY TO GO.
EXCELLENT WORK ALL AROUND, CADETS.
SINCE MY BOOSTERS WON'T BE STRONG ENOUGH TO KEEP US IN THE EVENT HORIZON, WE'LL HAVE TO RIDE ON ONE OF THE ORBITRON'S TACHYON BEAMS BACK THROUGH TIME TO ONE OF THE ANCHORS.
WE SHOULD GO AFTER CAPTAIN COLE FIRST-- WE KNOW HE HAS A STARCHASER.
OR STARCRUSHER, AS THEY CALL 'EM HERE.
ONCE WE GET HIM, WE CAN USE HIS JET TO FLY US BACK THROUGH THE BLACK HOLE SO WE CAN START RESCUING EVERYONE ELSE.
SPOKEN LIKE A TRUE SPACE PILOT.
THEN LET'S GET BACK OUT INTO SPACE!

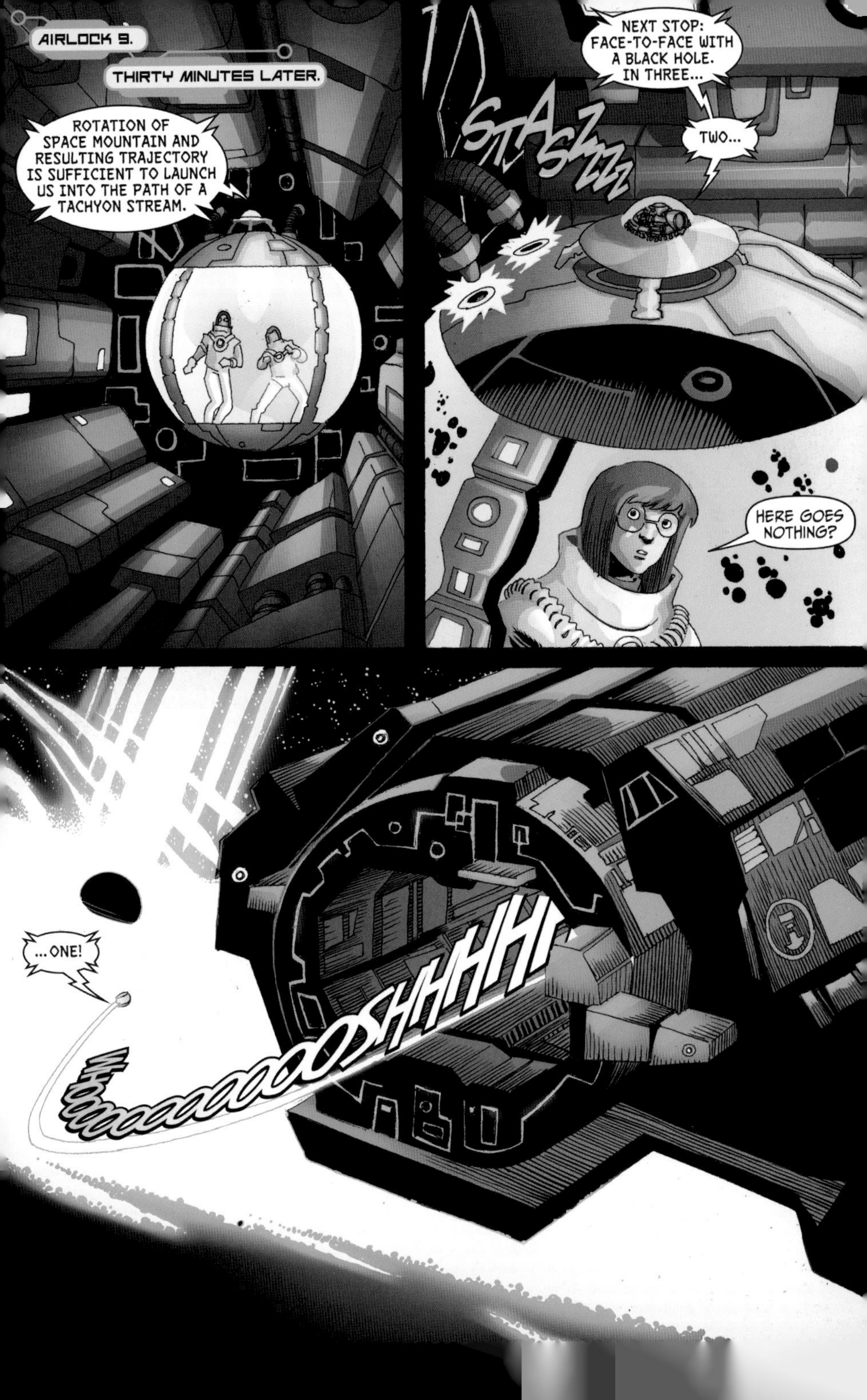
AIRLOCK 9.
THIRTY MINUTES LATER.
ROTATION OF SPACE MOUNTAIN AND RESULTING TRAJECTORY IS SUFFICIENT TO LAUNCH US INTO THE PATH OF A TACHYON STREAM.
NEXT STOP: FACE-TO-FACE WITH A BLACK HOLE. IN THREE...
STASZZZZ
TWO...
HERE GOES NOTHING?
...ONE!
WHOOOOOOOOOOOOSHHHHH

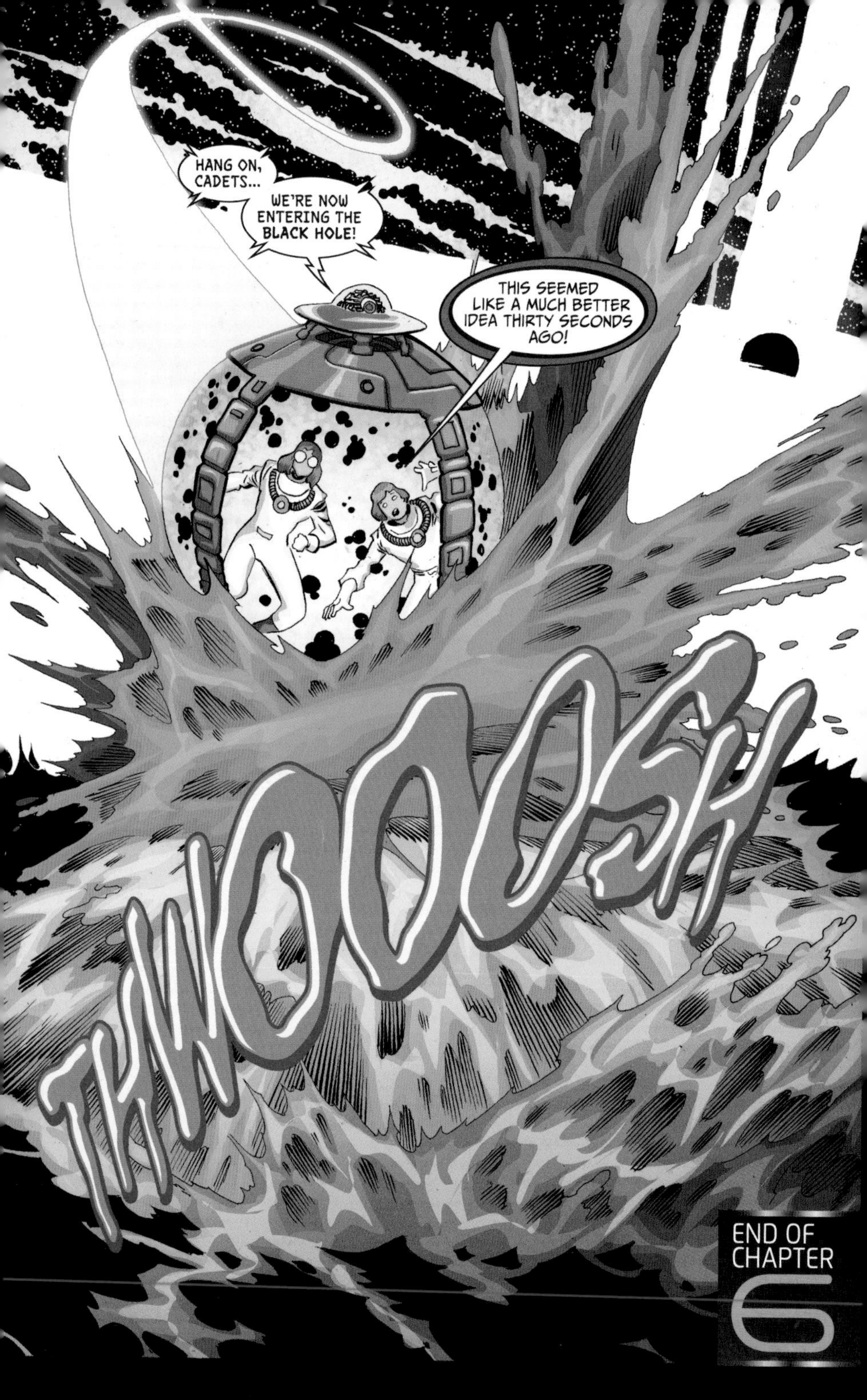
HANG ON, CADETS...
WE'RE NOW ENTERING THE BLACK HOLE!
THIS SEEMED LIKE A MUCH BETTER IDEA THIRTY SECONDS AGO!
THWOOOSH
END OF CHAPTER 6

PART THREE

BACK TO THE FUTURE

WHO CONTROLS THE PAST
CONTROLS THE FUTURE:
WHO CONTROLS THE PRESENT
CONTROLS THE PAST.

—GEORGE ORWELL

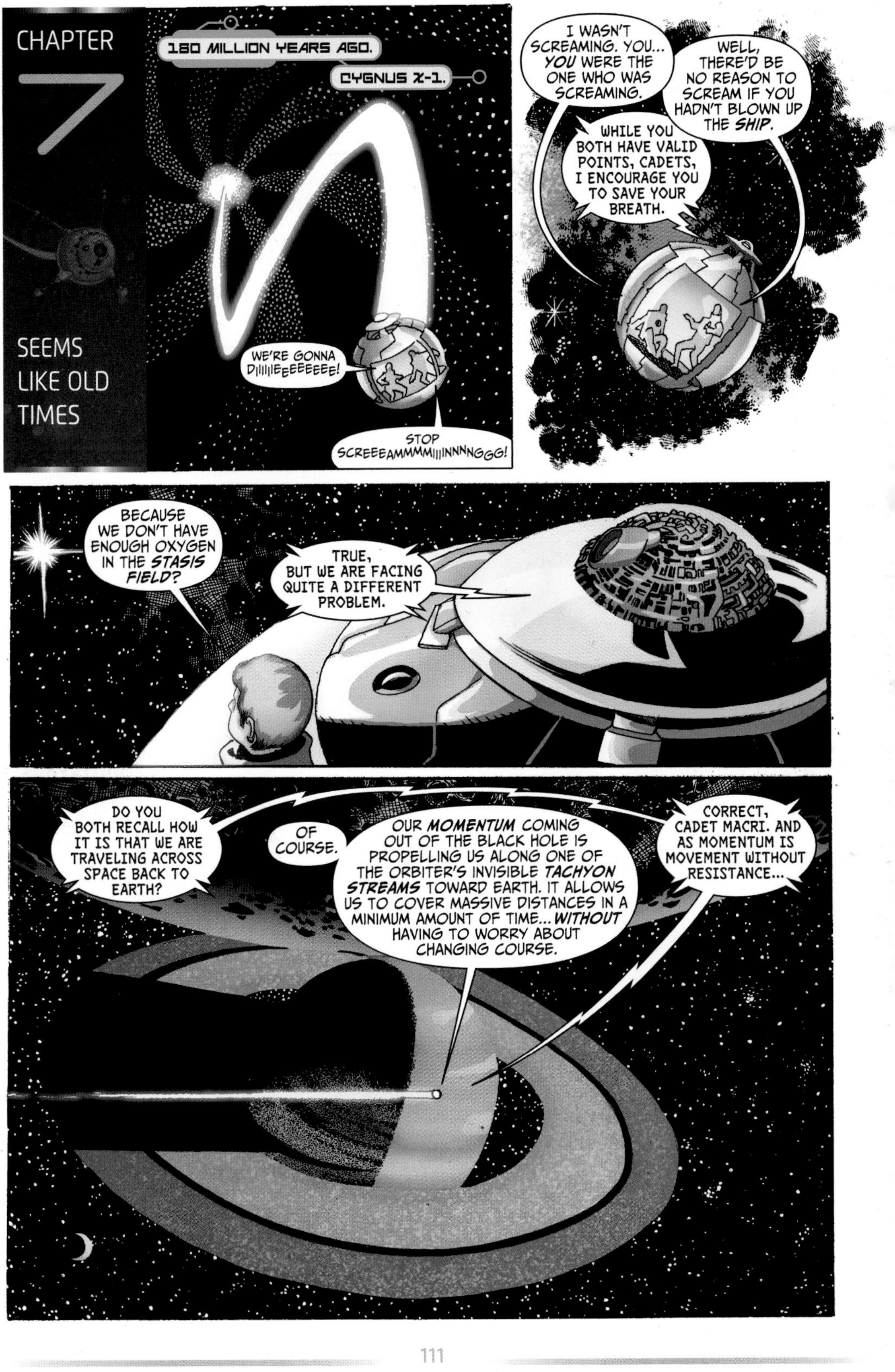
CHAPTER 7
SEEMS LIKE OLD TIMES
180 MILLION YEARS AGO.
CYGNUS X-1.
WE'RE GONNA DIIIIIEEEEEEEE!
STOP SCREEEAMMMMIIIINNNNGGG!
I WASN'T SCREAMING. YOU... YOU WERE THE ONE WHO WAS SCREAMING.
WELL, THERE'D BE NO REASON TO SCREAM IF YOU HADN'T BLOWN UP THE SHIP.
WHILE YOU BOTH HAVE VALID POINTS, CADETS, I ENCOURAGE YOU TO SAVE YOUR BREATH.
BECAUSE WE DON'T HAVE ENOUGH OXYGEN IN THE STASIS FIELD?
TRUE, BUT WE ARE FACING QUITE A DIFFERENT PROBLEM.
DO YOU BOTH RECALL HOW IT IS THAT WE ARE TRAVELING ACROSS SPACE BACK TO EARTH?
OF COURSE.
OUR MOMENTUM COMING OUT OF THE BLACK HOLE IS PROPELLING US ALONG ONE OF THE ORBITER'S INVISIBLE TACHYON STREAMS TOWARD EARTH. IT ALLOWS US TO COVER MASSIVE DISTANCES IN A MINIMUM AMOUNT OF TIME... WITHOUT HAVING TO WORRY ABOUT CHANGING COURSE.
CORRECT, CADET MACRI. AND AS MOMENTUM IS MOVEMENT WITHOUT RESISTANCE...

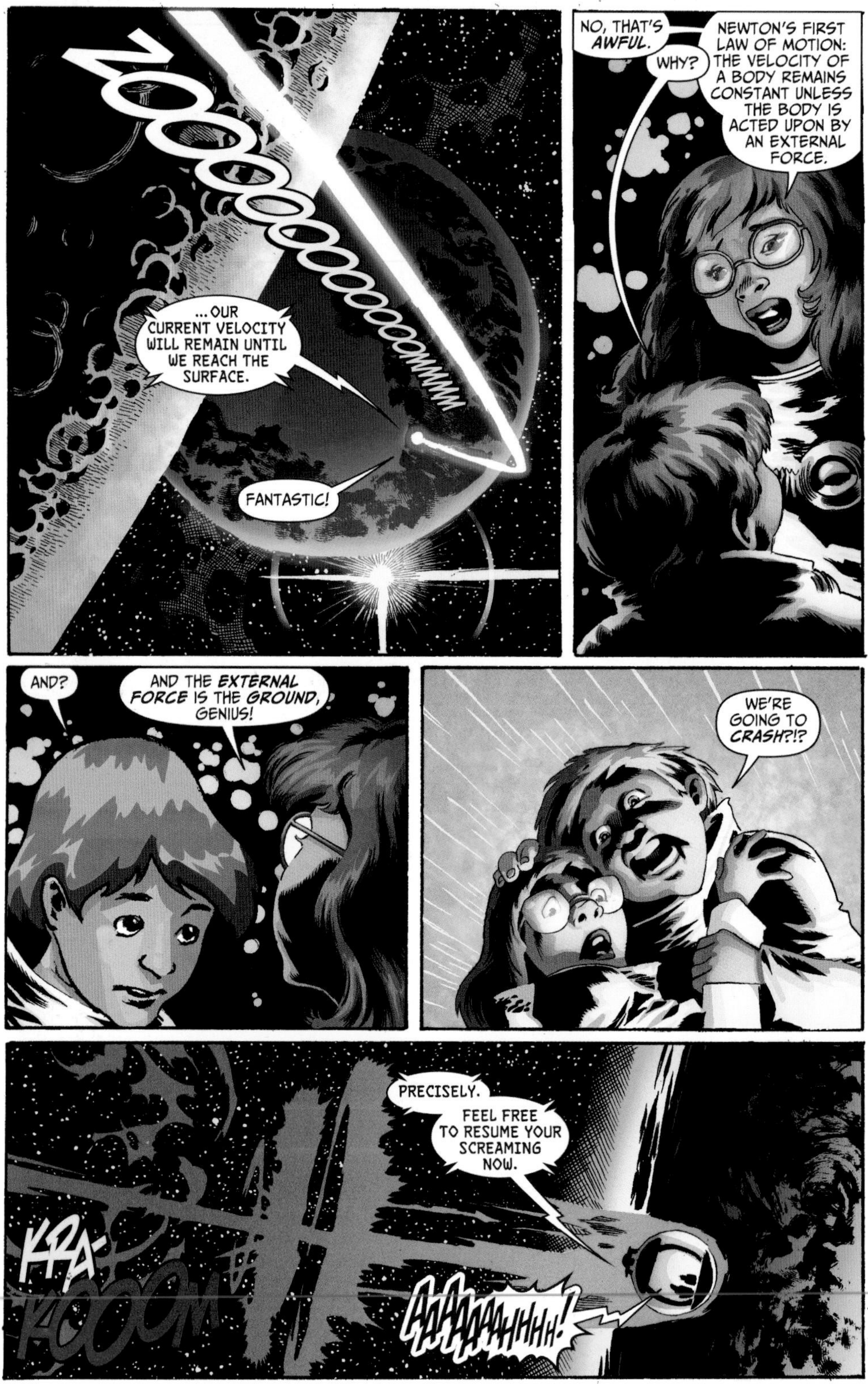
ZOOOOOOOOOOOOOOOMMMM
...OUR CURRENT VELOCITY WILL REMAIN UNTIL WE REACH THE SURFACE.
FANTASTIC!
NO, THAT'S AWFUL.
WHY?
NEWTON'S FIRST LAW OF MOTION: THE VELOCITY OF A BODY REMAINS CONSTANT UNLESS THE BODY IS ACTED UPON BY AN EXTERNAL FORCE.
AND?
AND THE EXTERNAL FORCE IS THE GROUND, GENIUS!
WE'RE GOING TO CRASH?!?
PRECISELY.
FEEL FREE TO RESUME YOUR SCREAMING NOW.
KRA-KOOOM
AAAAAAAHHHH!

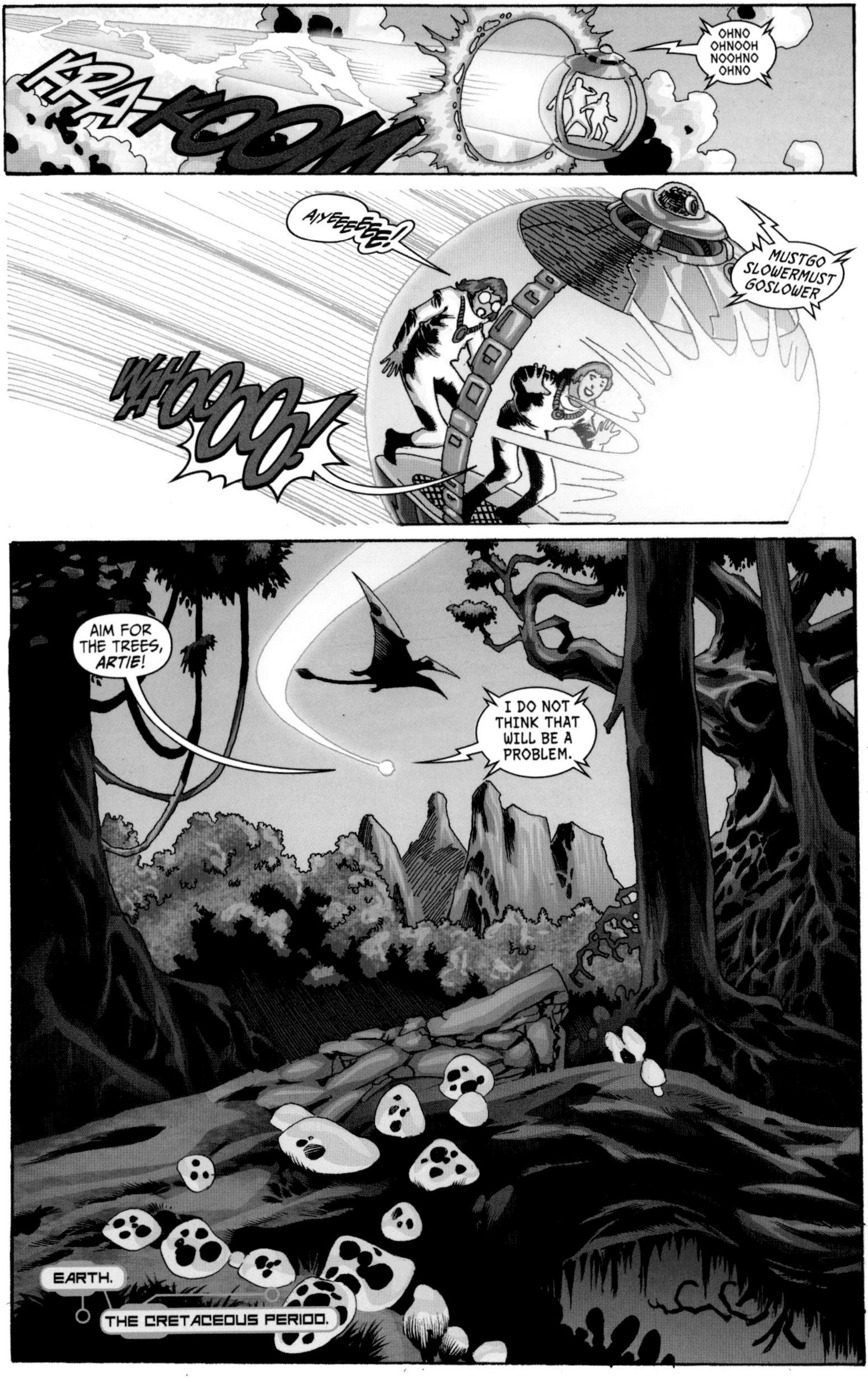
KRA-KOOM
OHNO OHNOOH NOOHNO OHNO
AIYEEEEEEE!
MUSTGO SLOWERMUST GOSLOWER
WHOOOOOO!
AIM FOR THE TREES, ARTIE!
I DO NOT THINK THAT WILL BE A PROBLEM.
EARTH.
THE CRETACEOUS PERIOD.

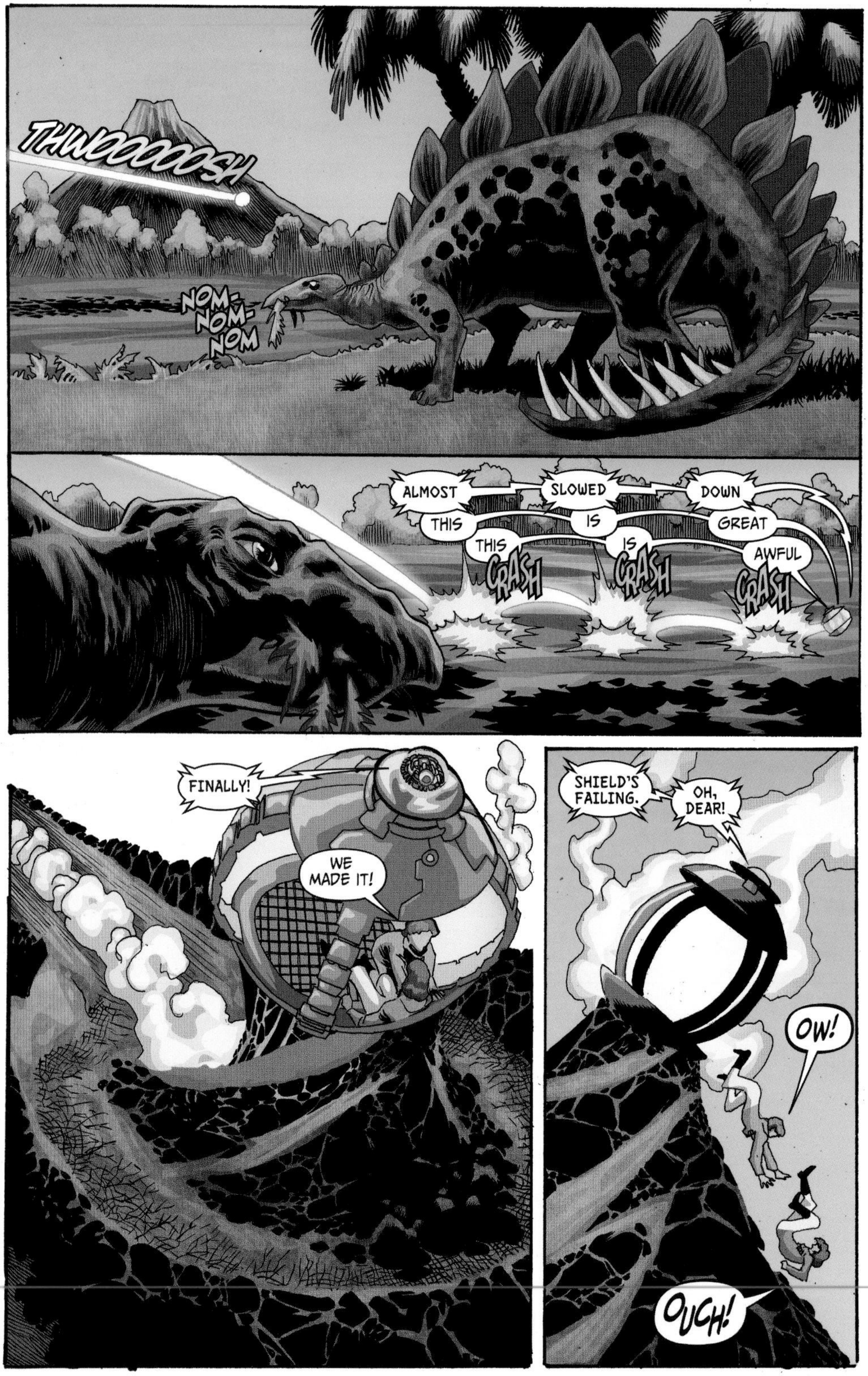
THWOOOOOOSH
NOM-NOM-NOM
ALMOST
SLOWED
DOWN
THIS
IS
GREAT
THIS
CRASH
IS
CRASH
AWFUL
CRASH
FINALLY!
WE MADE IT!
SHIELD'S FAILING.
OH, DEAR!
OW!
OUCH!

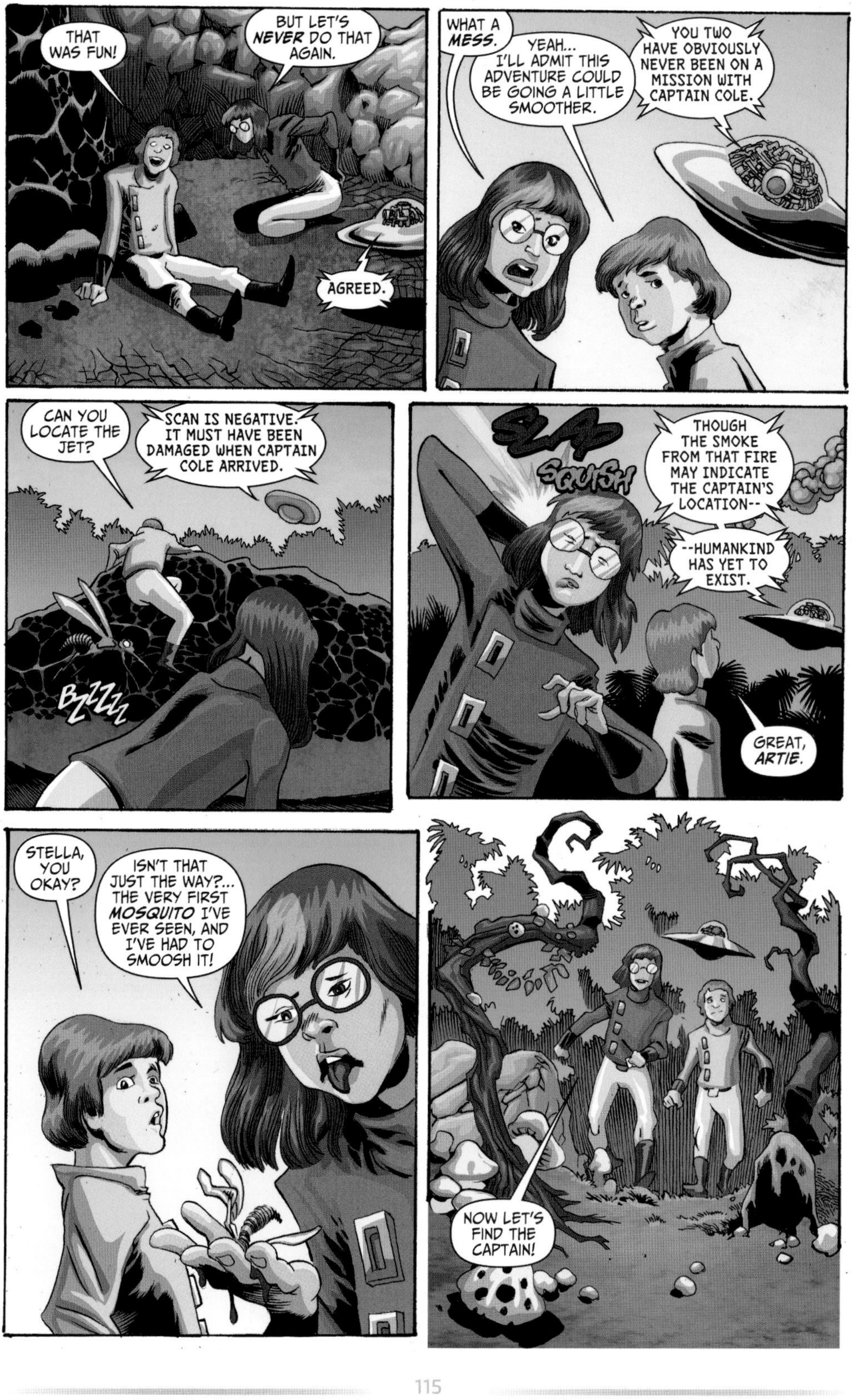
THAT WAS FUN!
BUT LET'S *NEVER* DO THAT AGAIN.
AGREED.
WHAT A *MESS*.
YEAH... I'LL ADMIT THIS ADVENTURE COULD BE GOING A LITTLE SMOOTHER.
YOU TWO HAVE OBVIOUSLY NEVER BEEN ON A MISSION WITH CAPTAIN COLE.
CAN YOU LOCATE THE JET?
SCAN IS NEGATIVE. IT MUST HAVE BEEN DAMAGED WHEN CAPTAIN COLE ARRIVED.
BZZZZZ
SLAP
SQUISH
THOUGH THE SMOKE FROM THAT FIRE MAY INDICATE THE CAPTAIN'S LOCATION--
--HUMANKIND HAS YET TO EXIST.
GREAT, *ARTIE*.
STELLA, YOU OKAY?
ISN'T THAT JUST THE WAY?... THE VERY FIRST *MOSQUITO* I'VE EVER SEEN, AND I'VE HAD TO SMOOSH IT!
NOW LET'S FIND THE CAPTAIN!

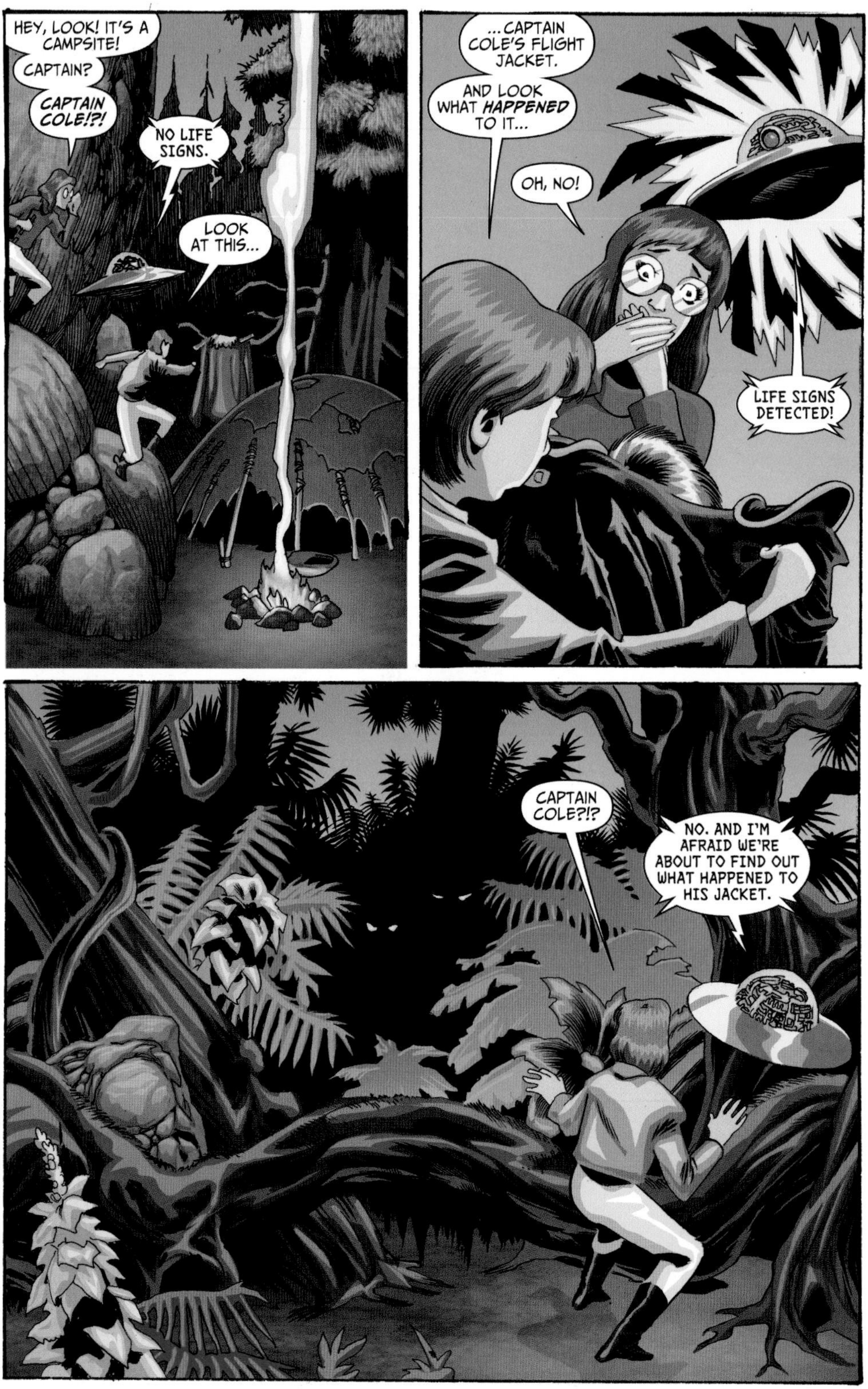

HEY, LOOK! IT'S A CAMPSITE!
CAPTAIN?
CAPTAIN COLE!?!
NO LIFE SIGNS.
LOOK AT THIS...
...CAPTAIN COLE'S FLIGHT JACKET.
AND LOOK WHAT HAPPENED TO IT...
OH, NO!
LIFE SIGNS DETECTED!
CAPTAIN COLE?!?
NO. AND I'M AFRAID WE'RE ABOUT TO FIND OUT WHAT HAPPENED TO HIS JACKET.

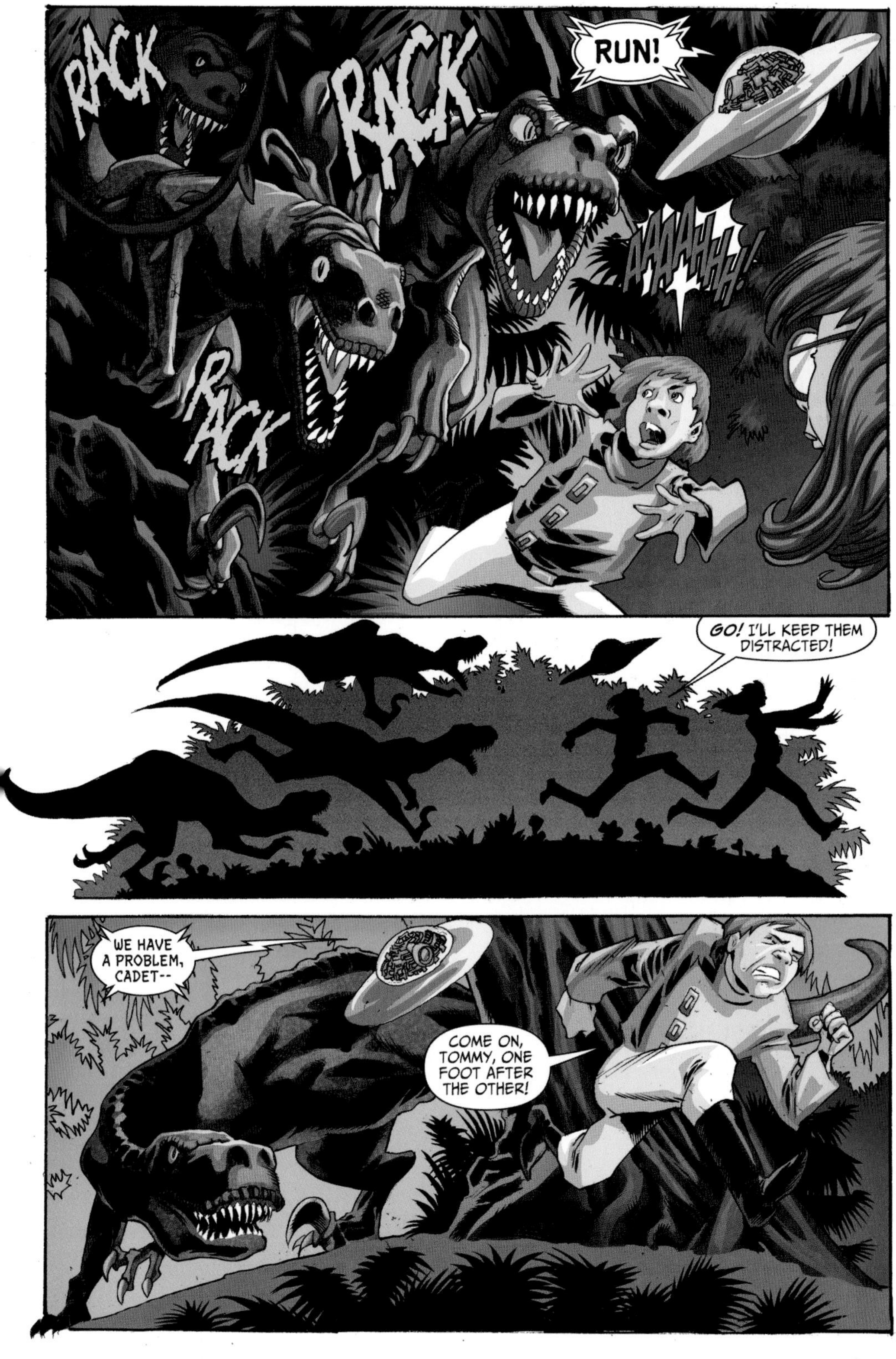
RACK
RACK
RACK
RUN!
AAAAHHH!
GO! I'LL KEEP THEM DISTRACTED!
WE HAVE A PROBLEM, CADET--
COME ON, TOMMY, ONE FOOT AFTER THE OTHER!

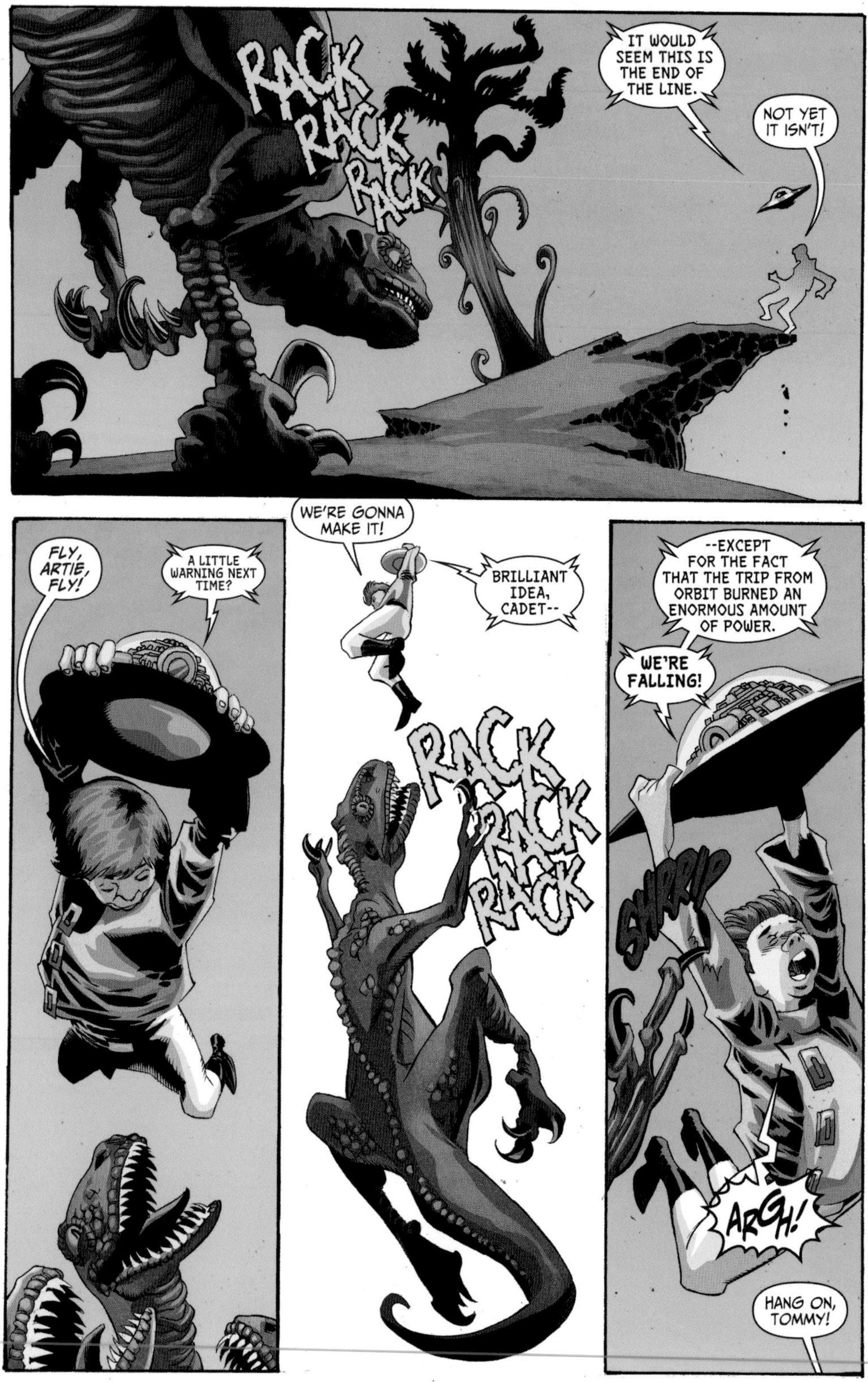
RACK
RACK
RACK
IT WOULD SEEM THIS IS THE END OF THE LINE.
NOT YET IT ISN'T!
FLY, ARTIE, FLY!
A LITTLE WARNING NEXT TIME?
WE'RE GONNA MAKE IT!
BRILLIANT IDEA, CADET--
RACK
RACK
RACK
--EXCEPT FOR THE FACT THAT THE TRIP FROM ORBIT BURNED AN ENORMOUS AMOUNT OF POWER.
WE'RE FALLING!
SHRRIP
ARGH!
HANG ON, TOMMY!

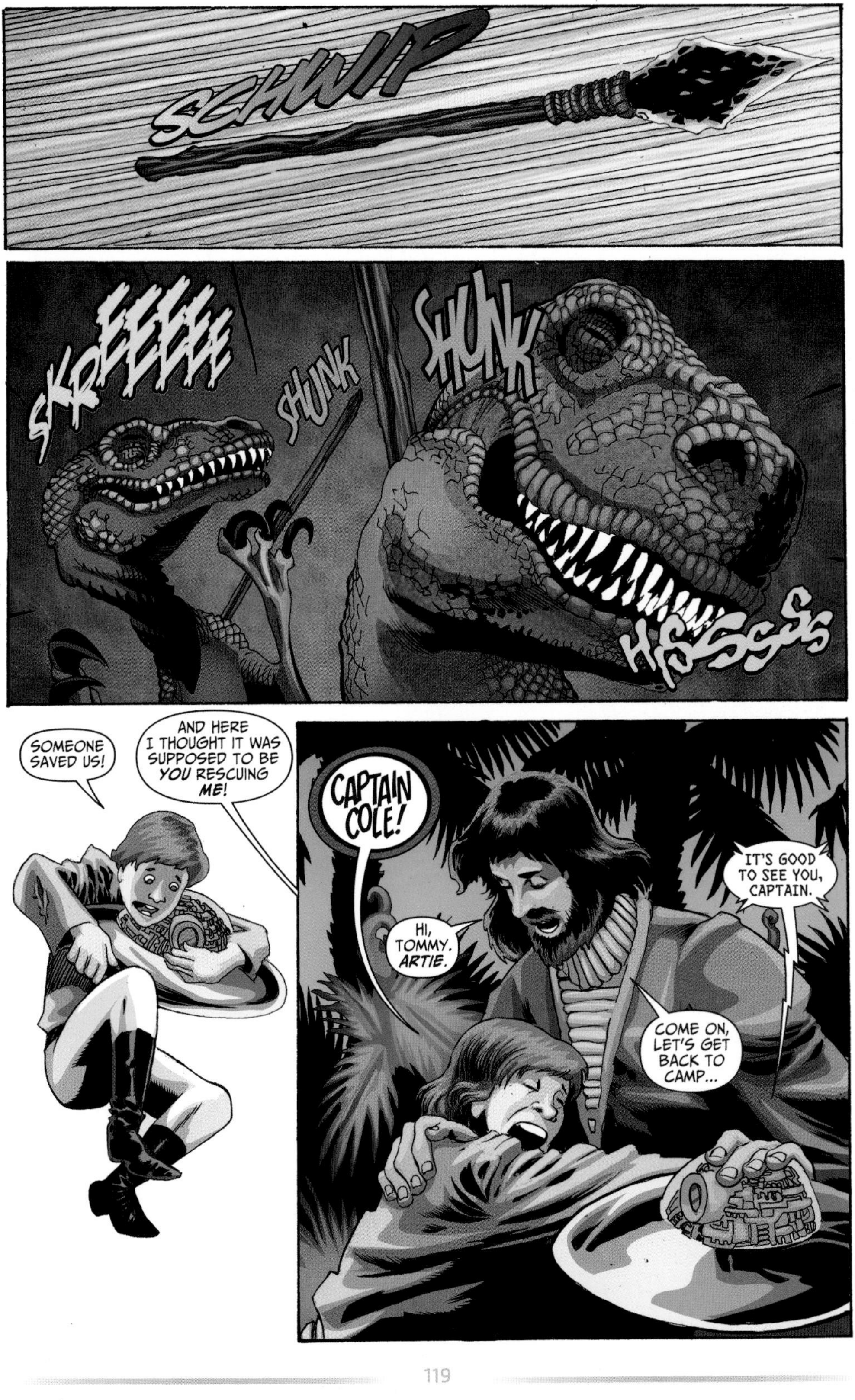
SCHWIP
SKREEEEEE
SHUNK
SHUNK
HSSSSS
SOMEONE SAVED US!
AND HERE I THOUGHT IT WAS SUPPOSED TO BE *YOU* RESCUING *ME*!
CAPTAIN COLE!
HI, TOMMY. *ARTIE*.
IT'S GOOD TO SEE YOU, CAPTAIN.
COME ON, LET'S GET BACK TO CAMP...

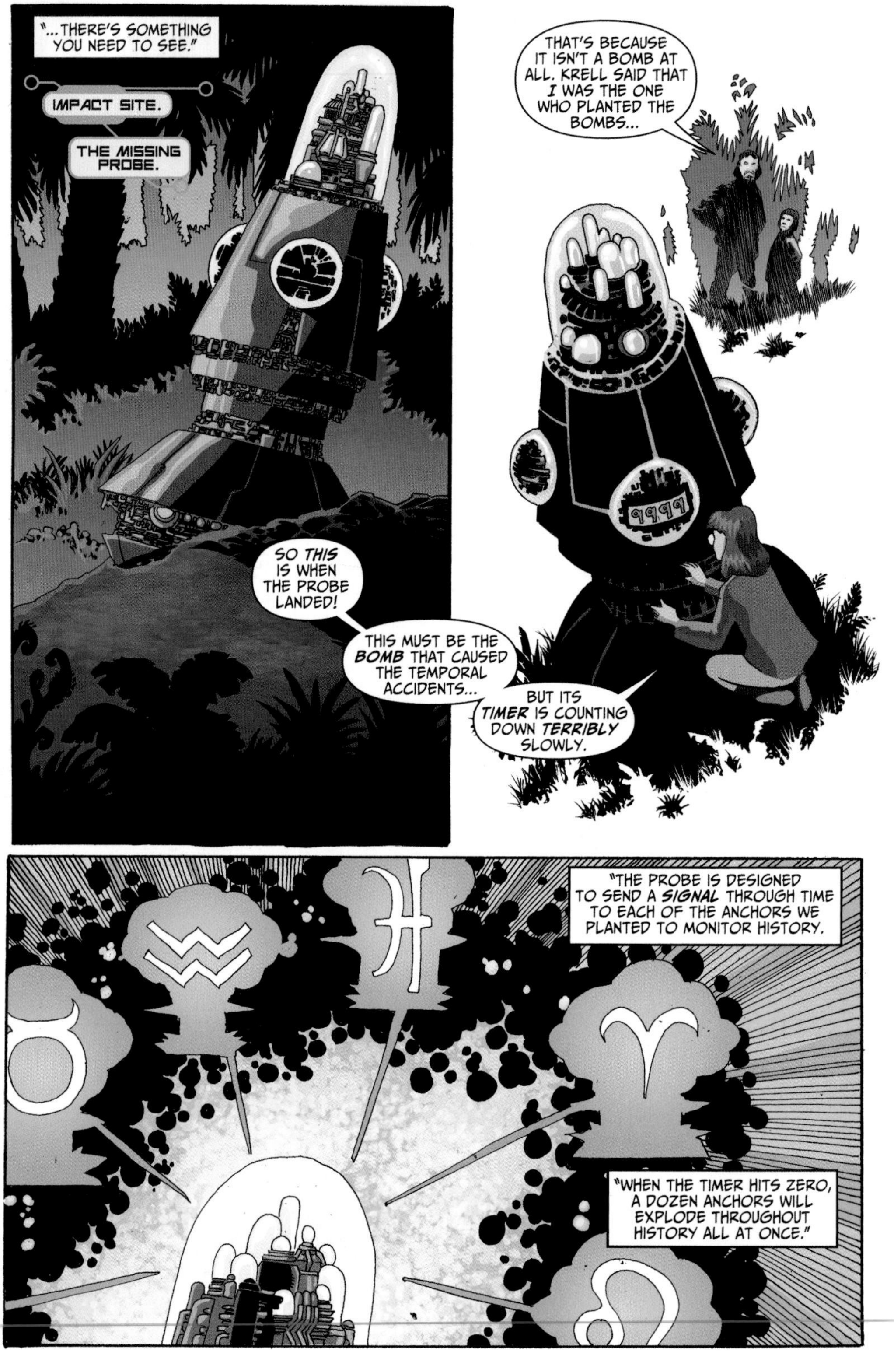
"...THERE'S SOMETHING YOU NEED TO SEE."
IMPACT SITE.
THE MISSING PROBE.
THAT'S BECAUSE IT ISN'T A BOMB AT ALL. KRELL SAID THAT I WAS THE ONE WHO PLANTED THE BOMBS...
SO THIS IS WHEN THE PROBE LANDED!
THIS MUST BE THE BOMB THAT CAUSED THE TEMPORAL ACCIDENTS...
BUT ITS TIMER IS COUNTING DOWN TERRIBLY SLOWLY.
"THE PROBE IS DESIGNED TO SEND A SIGNAL THROUGH TIME TO EACH OF THE ANCHORS WE PLANTED TO MONITOR HISTORY.
"WHEN THE TIMER HITS ZERO, A DOZEN ANCHORS WILL EXPLODE THROUGHOUT HISTORY ALL AT ONCE."

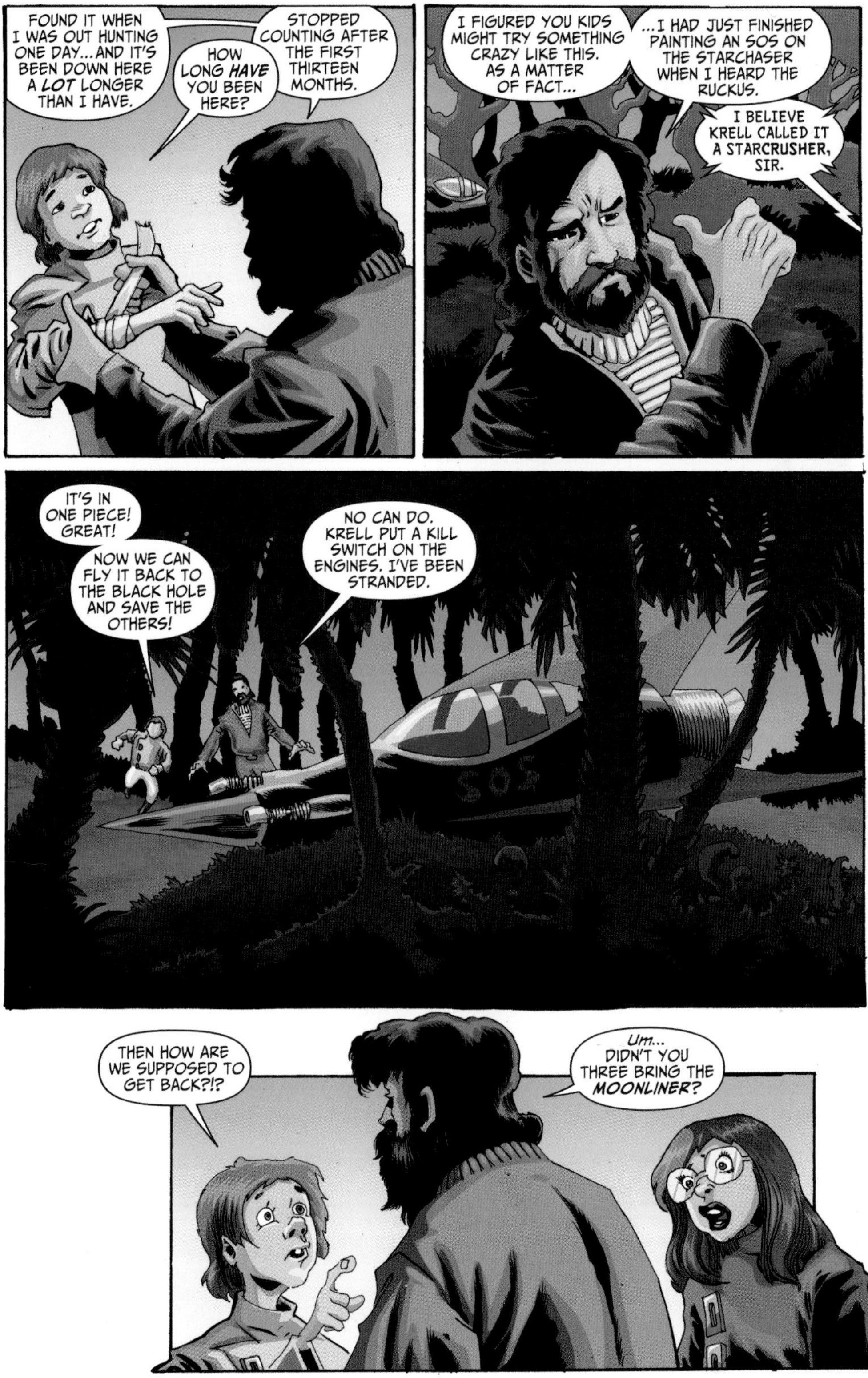
FOUND IT WHEN I WAS OUT HUNTING ONE DAY... AND IT'S BEEN DOWN HERE A *LOT* LONGER THAN I HAVE.
HOW LONG *HAVE* YOU BEEN HERE?
STOPPED COUNTING AFTER THE FIRST THIRTEEN MONTHS.
I FIGURED YOU KIDS MIGHT TRY SOMETHING CRAZY LIKE THIS. AS A MATTER OF FACT...
...I HAD JUST FINISHED PAINTING AN SOS ON THE STARCHASER WHEN I HEARD THE RUCKUS.
I BELIEVE KRELL CALLED IT A STARCRUSHER, SIR.
IT'S IN ONE PIECE! GREAT!
NOW WE CAN FLY IT BACK TO THE BLACK HOLE AND SAVE THE OTHERS!
NO CAN DO. KRELL PUT A KILL SWITCH ON THE ENGINES. I'VE BEEN STRANDED.
SOS
THEN HOW ARE WE SUPPOSED TO GET BACK?!?
Um... DIDN'T YOU THREE BRING THE *MOONLINER*?

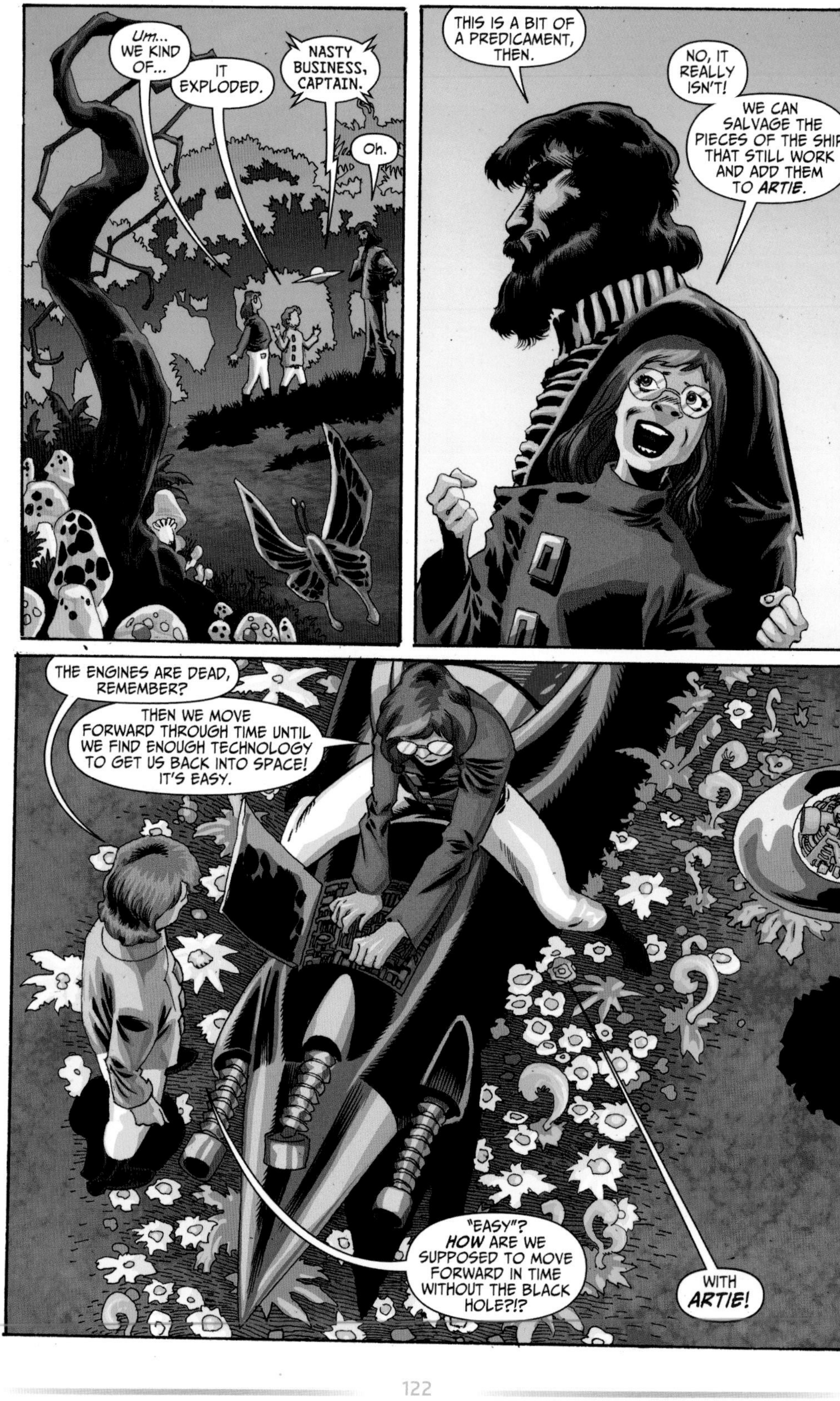
Um... WE KIND OF...
IT EXPLODED.
NASTY BUSINESS, CAPTAIN.
Oh.
THIS IS A BIT OF A PREDICAMENT, THEN.
NO, IT REALLY ISN'T!
WE CAN SALVAGE THE PIECES OF THE SHIP THAT STILL WORK AND ADD THEM TO ARTIE.
THE ENGINES ARE DEAD, REMEMBER?
THEN WE MOVE FORWARD THROUGH TIME UNTIL WE FIND ENOUGH TECHNOLOGY TO GET US BACK INTO SPACE! IT'S EASY.
"EASY"? HOW ARE WE SUPPOSED TO MOVE FORWARD IN TIME WITHOUT THE BLACK HOLE?!?
WITH ARTIE!

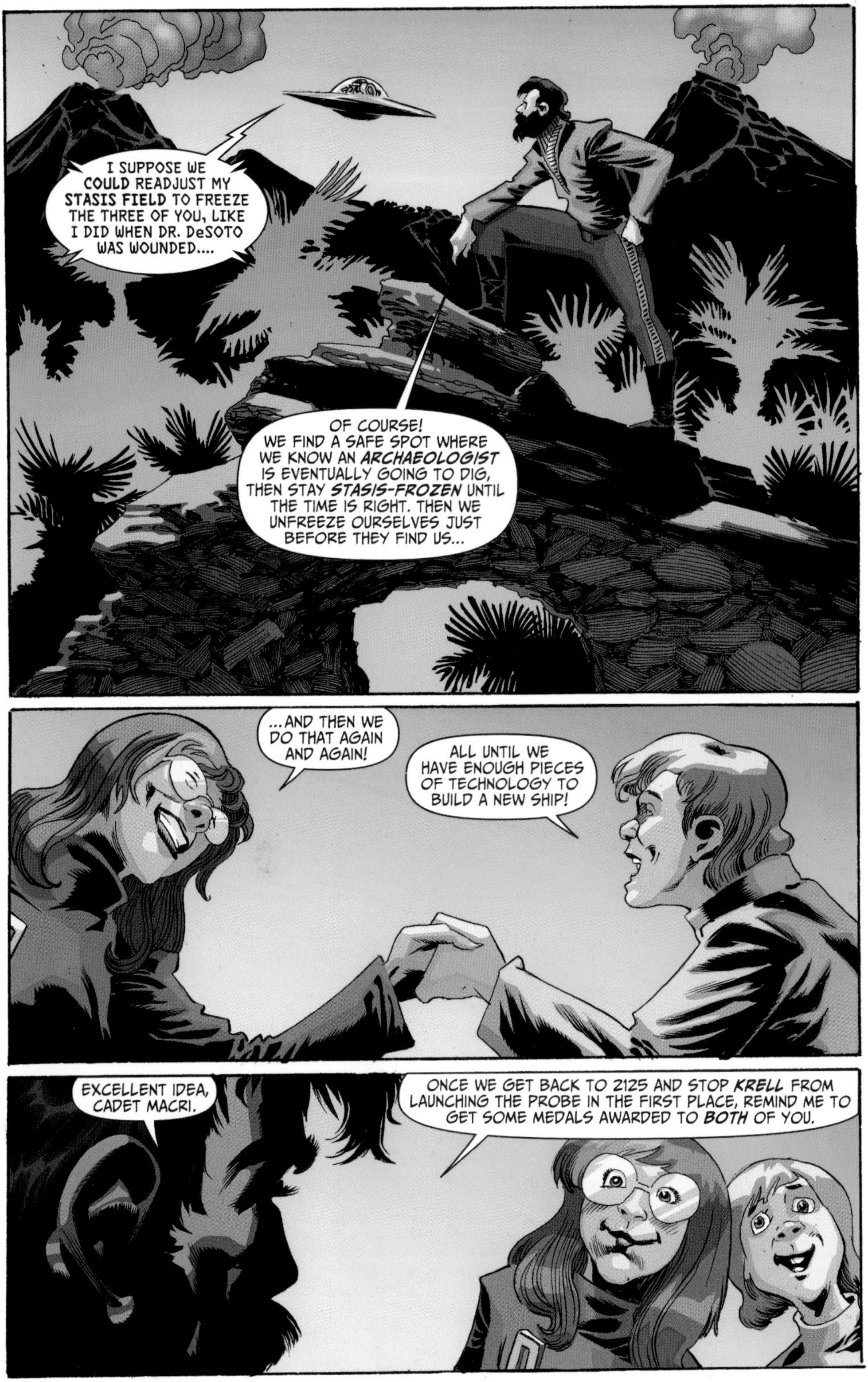
I SUPPOSE WE COULD READJUST MY STASIS FIELD TO FREEZE THE THREE OF YOU, LIKE I DID WHEN DR. DeSOTO WAS WOUNDED....
OF COURSE! WE FIND A SAFE SPOT WHERE WE KNOW AN ARCHAEOLOGIST IS EVENTUALLY GOING TO DIG, THEN STAY STASIS-FROZEN UNTIL THE TIME IS RIGHT. THEN WE UNFREEZE OURSELVES JUST BEFORE THEY FIND US...
...AND THEN WE DO THAT AGAIN AND AGAIN!
ALL UNTIL WE HAVE ENOUGH PIECES OF TECHNOLOGY TO BUILD A NEW SHIP!
EXCELLENT IDEA, CADET MACRI.
ONCE WE GET BACK TO 2125 AND STOP KRELL FROM LAUNCHING THE PROBE IN THE FIRST PLACE, REMIND ME TO GET SOME MEDALS AWARDED TO BOTH OF YOU.

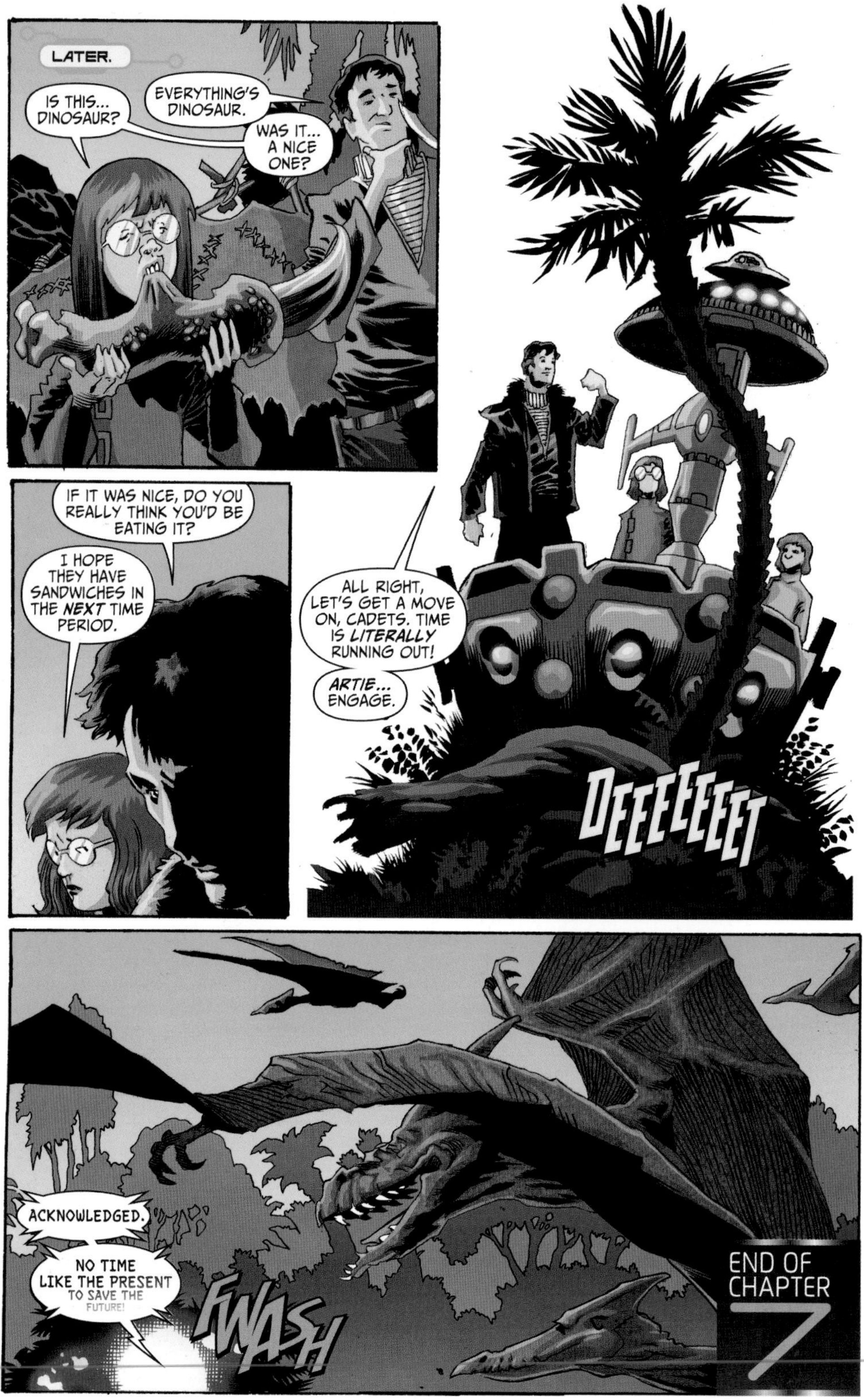
LATER.
IS THIS... DINOSAUR?
EVERYTHING'S DINOSAUR.
WAS IT... A NICE ONE?
IF IT WAS NICE, DO YOU REALLY THINK YOU'D BE EATING IT?
I HOPE THEY HAVE SANDWICHES IN THE *NEXT* TIME PERIOD.
ALL RIGHT, LET'S GET A MOVE ON, CADETS. TIME IS *LITERALLY* RUNNING OUT!
ARTIE... ENGAGE.
DEEEEEEET
ACKNOWLEDGED.
NO TIME LIKE THE PRESENT TO SAVE THE FUTURE!
FWASH
END OF CHAPTER 7

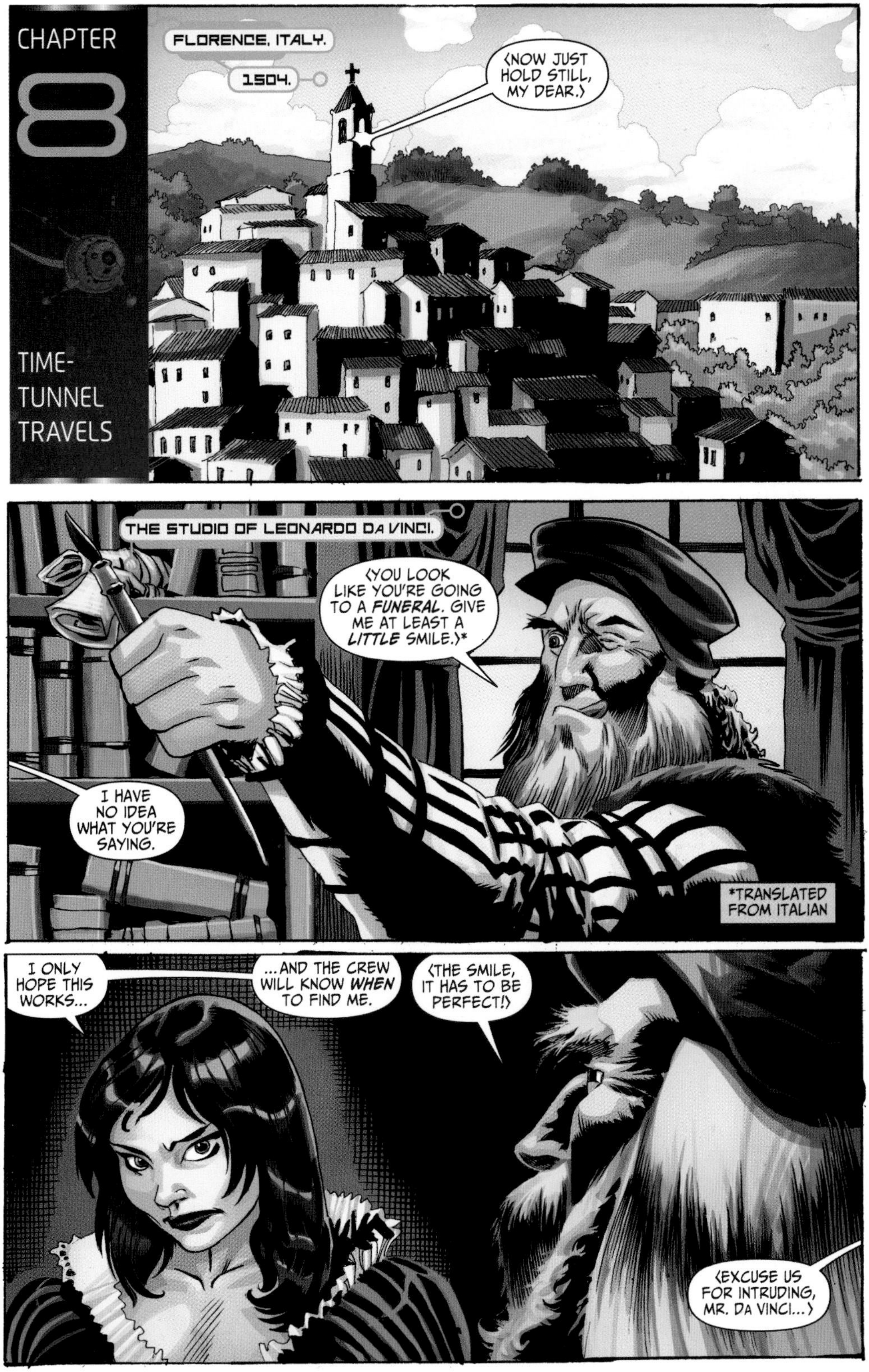
CHAPTER 8
TIME-TUNNEL TRAVELS
FLORENCE, ITALY.
1504.
‹NOW JUST HOLD STILL, MY DEAR.›
THE STUDIO OF LEONARDO DA VINCI.
‹YOU LOOK LIKE YOU'RE GOING TO A FUNERAL. GIVE ME AT LEAST A LITTLE SMILE.›*
I HAVE NO IDEA WHAT YOU'RE SAYING.
*TRANSLATED FROM ITALIAN
I ONLY HOPE THIS WORKS...
...AND THE CREW WILL KNOW WHEN TO FIND ME.
‹THE SMILE, IT HAS TO BE PERFECT!›
‹EXCUSE US FOR INTRUDING, MR. DA VINCI...›

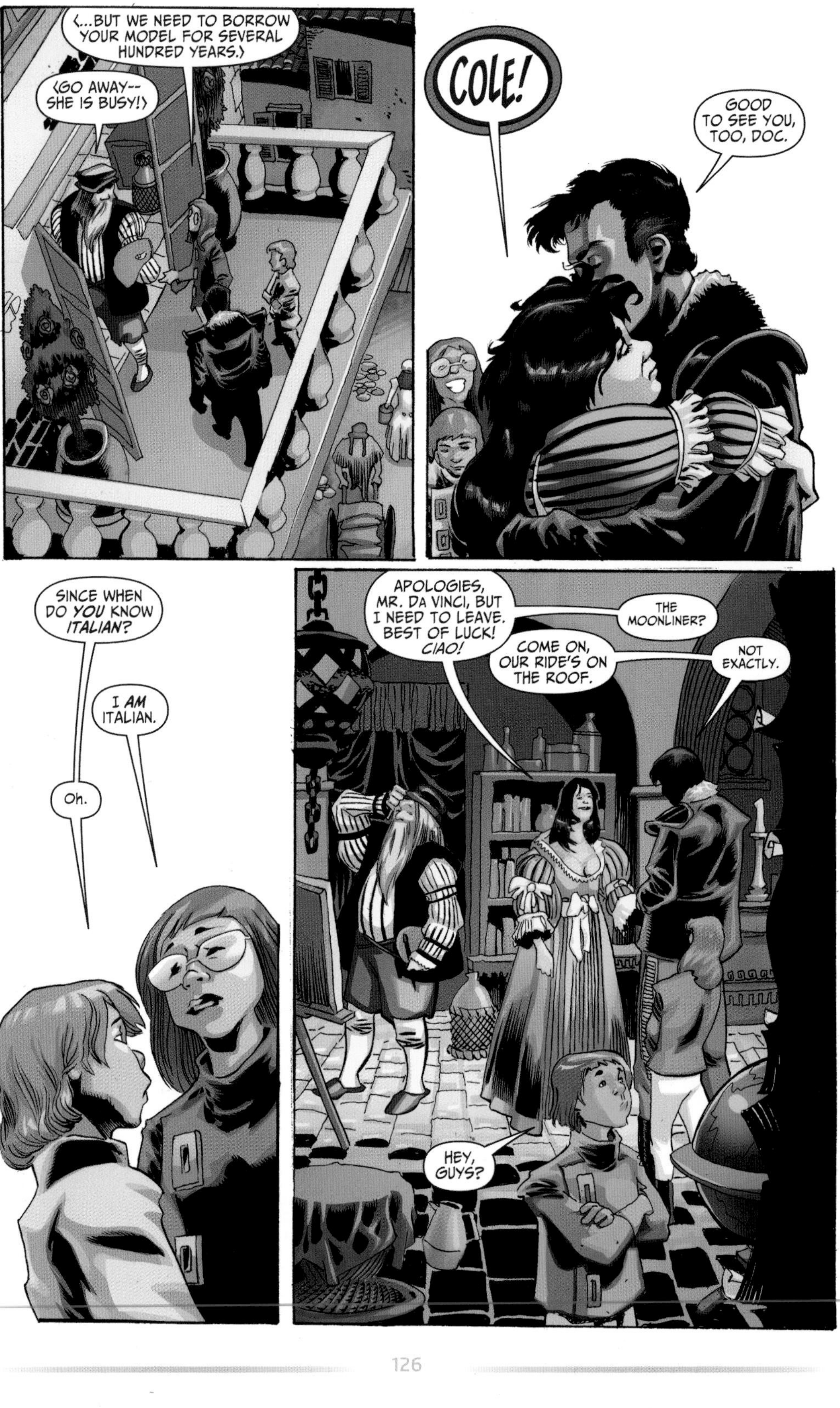
<...BUT WE NEED TO BORROW YOUR MODEL FOR SEVERAL HUNDRED YEARS.>
<GO AWAY-- SHE IS BUSY!>
COLE!
GOOD TO SEE YOU, TOO, DOC.
SINCE WHEN DO *YOU* KNOW *ITALIAN?*
I *AM* ITALIAN.
Oh.
APOLOGIES, MR. DA VINCI, BUT I NEED TO LEAVE. BEST OF LUCK! *CIAO!*
THE MOONLINER?
COME ON, OUR RIDE'S ON THE ROOF.
NOT EXACTLY.
HEY, GUYS?

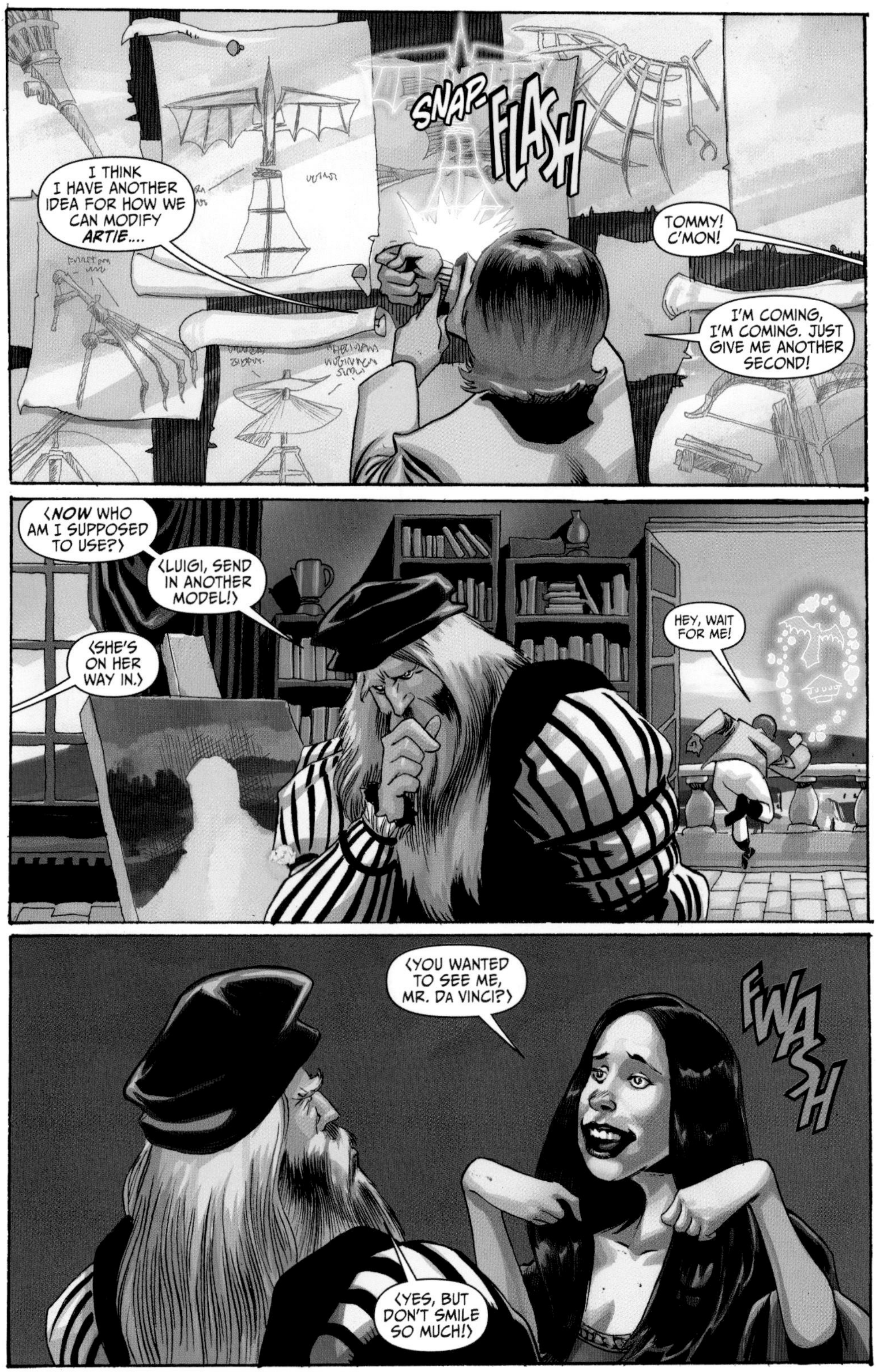
SNAP
FLASH
I THINK I HAVE ANOTHER IDEA FOR HOW WE CAN MODIFY ARTIE....
TOMMY! C'MON!
I'M COMING, I'M COMING. JUST GIVE ME ANOTHER SECOND!
‹NOW WHO AM I SUPPOSED TO USE?›
‹LUIGI, SEND IN ANOTHER MODEL!›
‹SHE'S ON HER WAY IN.›
HEY, WAIT FOR ME!
‹YOU WANTED TO SEE ME, MR. DA VINCI?›
FWASH
‹YES, BUT DON'T SMILE SO MUCH!›

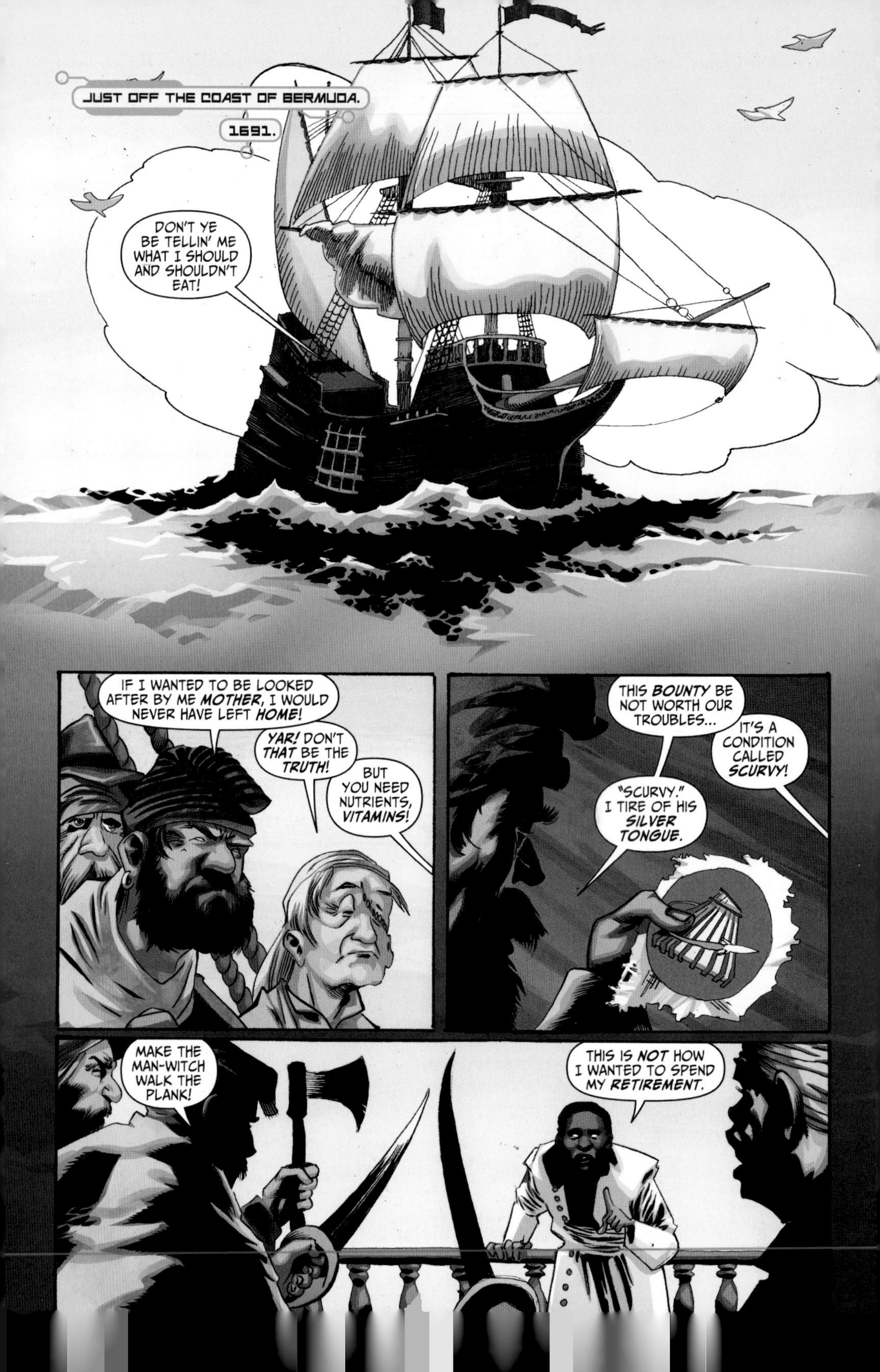

JUST OFF THE COAST OF BERMUDA.
1691.
DON'T YE BE TELLIN' ME WHAT I SHOULD AND SHOULDN'T EAT!
IF I WANTED TO BE LOOKED AFTER BY ME MOTHER, I WOULD NEVER HAVE LEFT HOME!
YAR! DON'T THAT BE THE TRUTH!
BUT YOU NEED NUTRIENTS, VITAMINS!
THIS BOUNTY BE NOT WORTH OUR TROUBLES...
IT'S A CONDITION CALLED SCURVY!
"SCURVY." I TIRE OF HIS SILVER TONGUE.
MAKE THE MAN-WITCH WALK THE PLANK!
THIS IS NOT HOW I WANTED TO SPEND MY RETIREMENT.

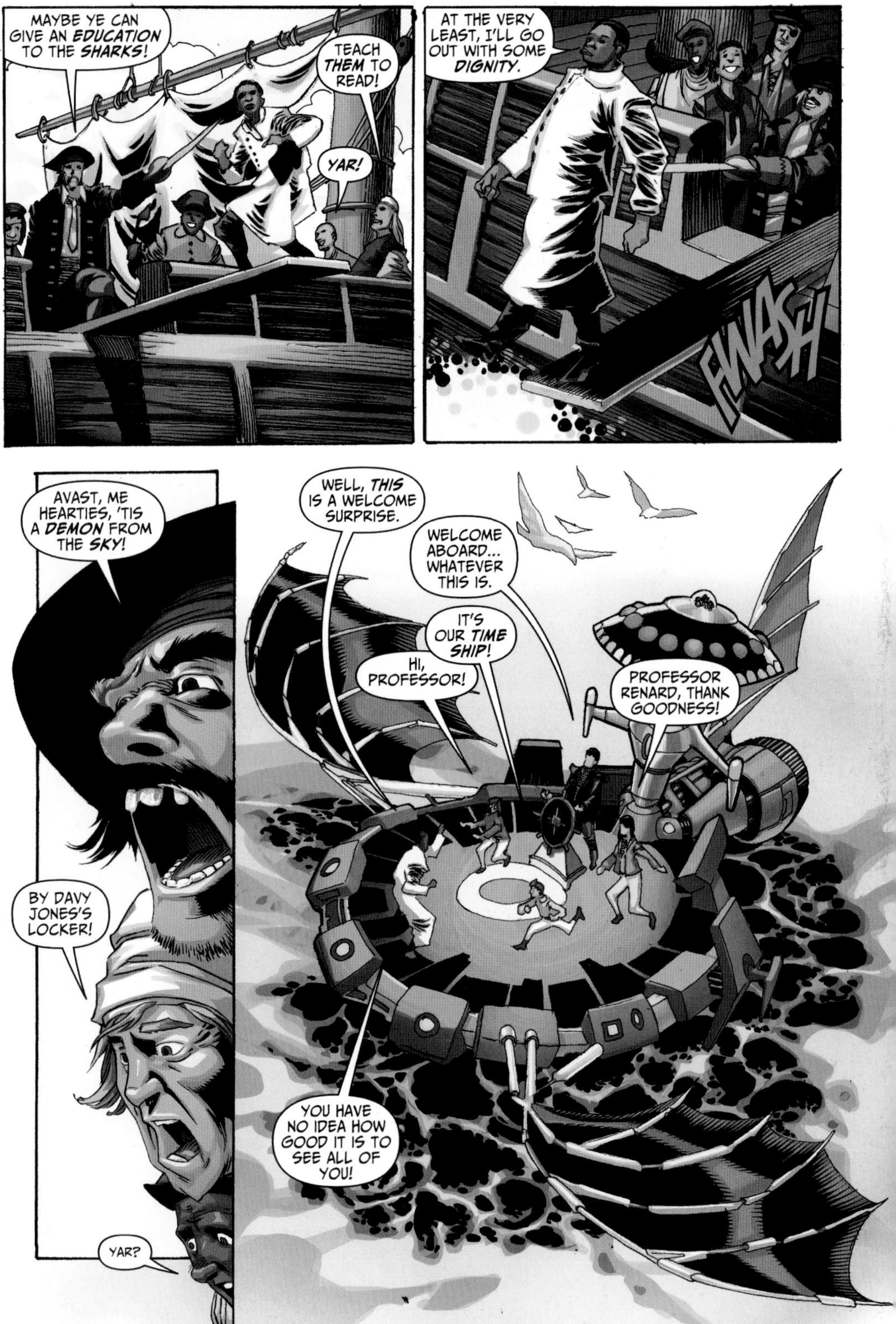
MAYBE YE CAN GIVE AN *EDUCATION* TO THE *SHARKS*!
TEACH *THEM* TO READ!
YAR!
AT THE VERY LEAST, I'LL GO OUT WITH SOME *DIGNITY*.
FWASH
AVAST, ME HEARTIES, 'TIS A *DEMON* FROM THE *SKY*!
BY DAVY JONES'S LOCKER!
YAR?
WELL, *THIS* IS A WELCOME SURPRISE.
WELCOME ABOARD... WHATEVER THIS IS.
IT'S OUR *TIME SHIP*!
HI, PROFESSOR!
PROFESSOR RENARD, THANK GOODNESS!
YOU HAVE NO IDEA HOW GOOD IT IS TO SEE ALL OF YOU!

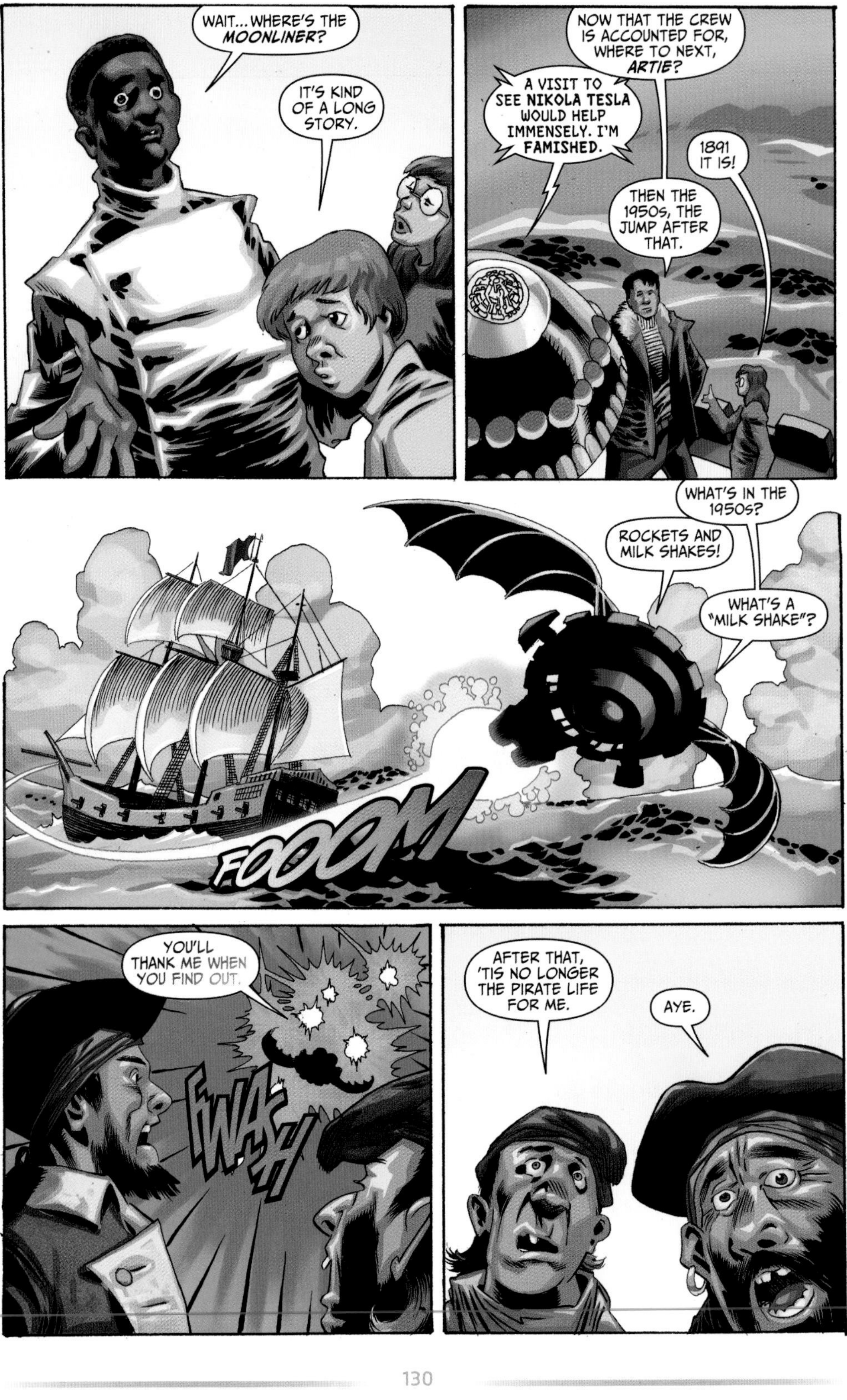
WAIT... WHERE'S THE MOONLINER?
IT'S KIND OF A LONG STORY.
NOW THAT THE CREW IS ACCOUNTED FOR, WHERE TO NEXT, ARTIE?
A VISIT TO SEE NIKOLA TESLA WOULD HELP IMMENSELY. I'M FAMISHED.
THEN THE 1950s, THE JUMP AFTER THAT.
1891 IT IS!
WHAT'S IN THE 1950s?
ROCKETS AND MILK SHAKES!
WHAT'S A "MILK SHAKE"?
FOOOM
YOU'LL THANK ME WHEN YOU FIND OUT.
FWAK!
AFTER THAT, 'TIS NO LONGER THE PIRATE LIFE FOR ME.
AYE.

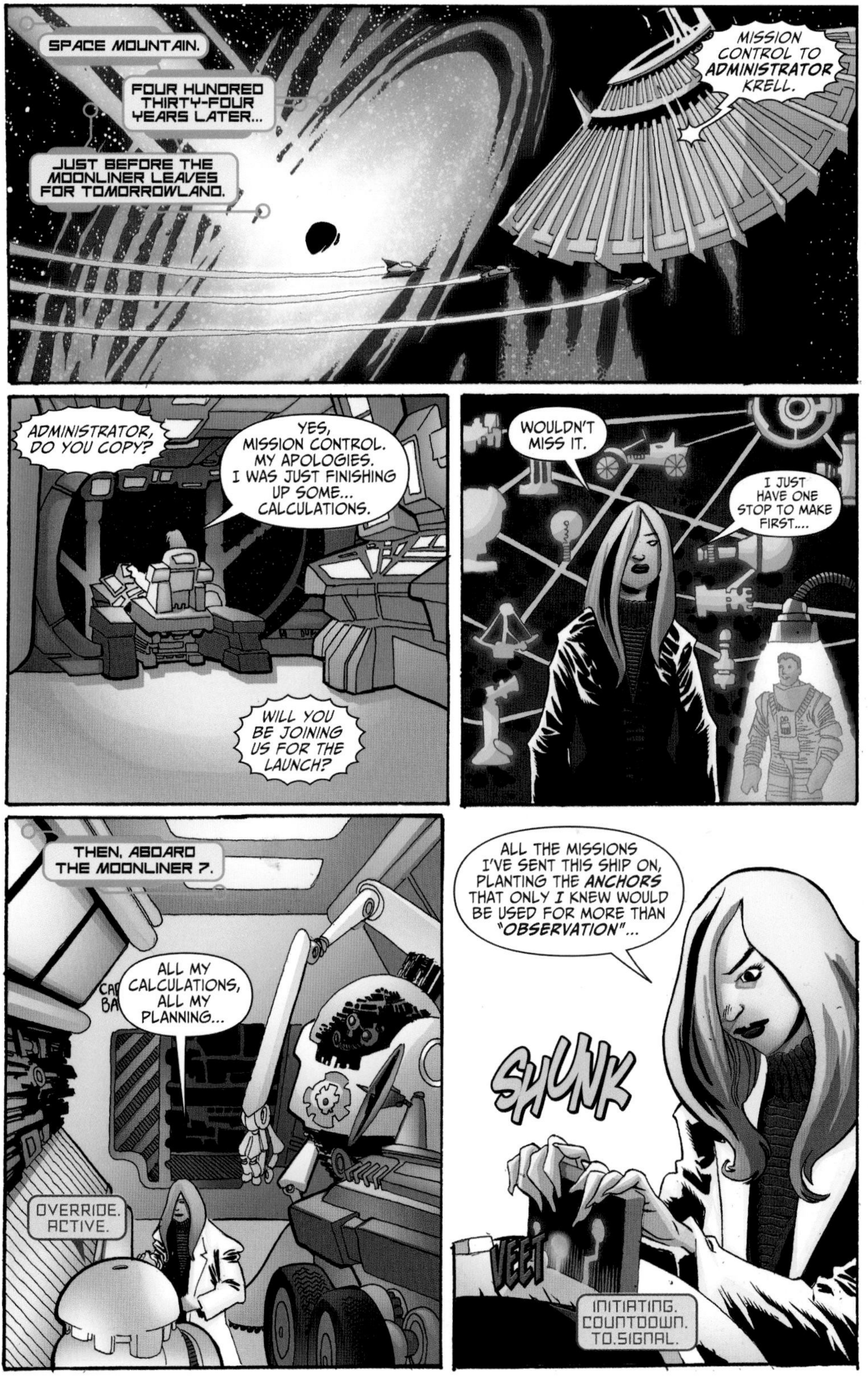
SPACE MOUNTAIN.
FOUR HUNDRED THIRTY-FOUR YEARS LATER...
JUST BEFORE THE MOONLINER LEAVES FOR TOMORROWLAND.
MISSION CONTROL TO ADMINISTRATOR KRELL.
ADMINISTRATOR, DO YOU COPY?
YES, MISSION CONTROL. MY APOLOGIES. I WAS JUST FINISHING UP SOME... CALCULATIONS.
WILL YOU BE JOINING US FOR THE LAUNCH?
WOULDN'T MISS IT.
I JUST HAVE ONE STOP TO MAKE FIRST....
THEN, ABOARD THE MOONLINER 7.
ALL MY CALCULATIONS, ALL MY PLANNING...
OVERRIDE. ACTIVE.
ALL THE MISSIONS I'VE SENT THIS SHIP ON, PLANTING THE ANCHORS THAT ONLY I KNEW WOULD BE USED FOR MORE THAN "OBSERVATION"...
SHUNK
VEET
INITIATING. COUNTDOWN. TO.SIGNAL.

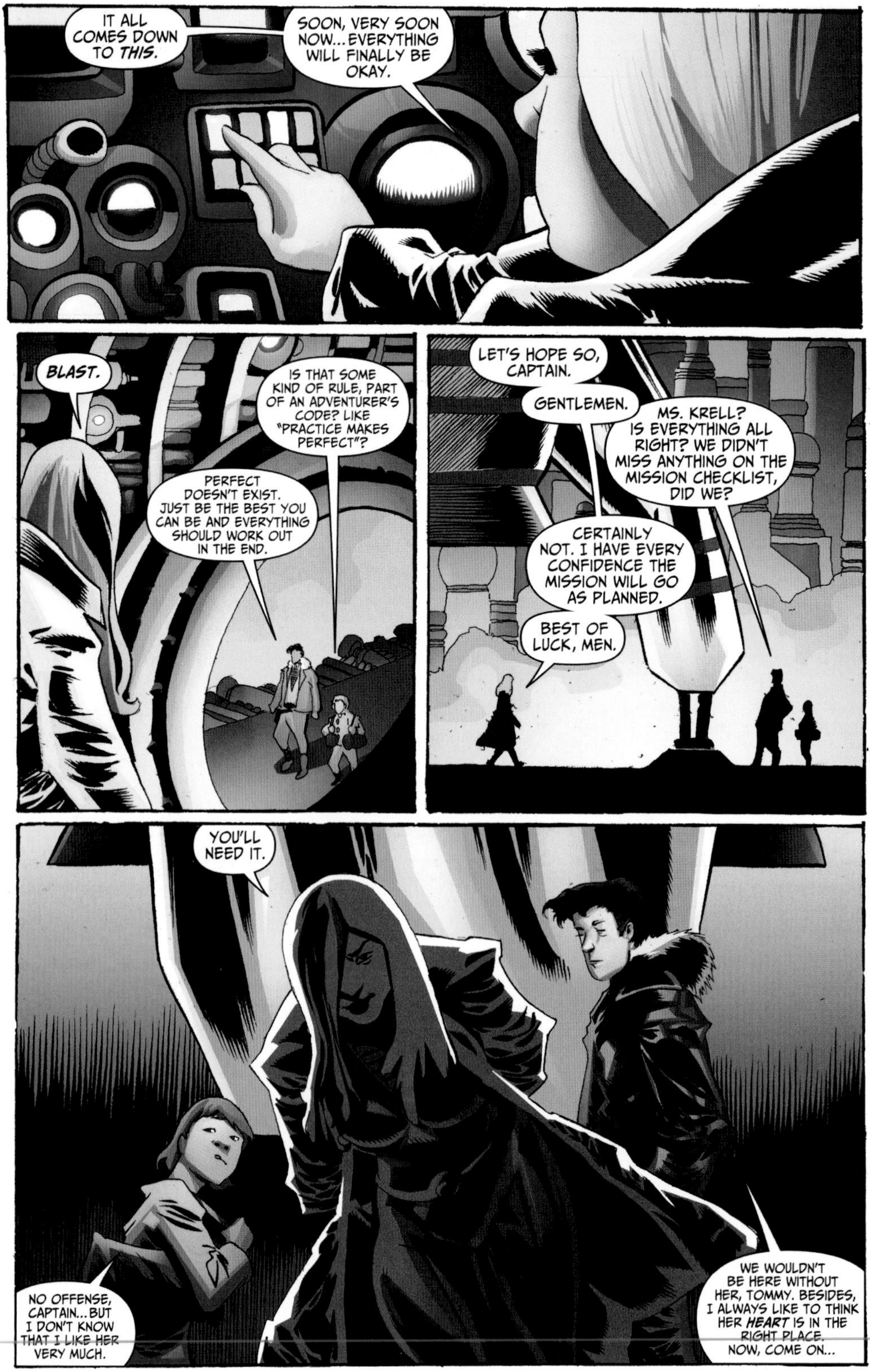
IT ALL COMES DOWN TO *THIS*.
SOON, VERY SOON NOW... EVERYTHING WILL FINALLY BE OKAY.
BLAST.
IS THAT SOME KIND OF RULE, PART OF AN ADVENTURER'S CODE? LIKE "PRACTICE MAKES PERFECT"?
PERFECT DOESN'T EXIST. JUST BE THE BEST YOU CAN BE AND EVERYTHING SHOULD WORK OUT IN THE END.
LET'S HOPE SO, CAPTAIN.
GENTLEMEN.
MS. KRELL? IS EVERYTHING ALL RIGHT? WE DIDN'T MISS ANYTHING ON THE MISSION CHECKLIST, DID WE?
CERTAINLY NOT. I HAVE EVERY CONFIDENCE THE MISSION WILL GO AS PLANNED.
BEST OF LUCK, MEN.
YOU'LL NEED IT.
NO OFFENSE, CAPTAIN... BUT I DON'T KNOW THAT I LIKE HER VERY MUCH.
WE WOULDN'T BE HERE WITHOUT HER, TOMMY. BESIDES, I ALWAYS LIKE TO THINK HER *HEART* IS IN THE RIGHT PLACE. NOW, COME ON...

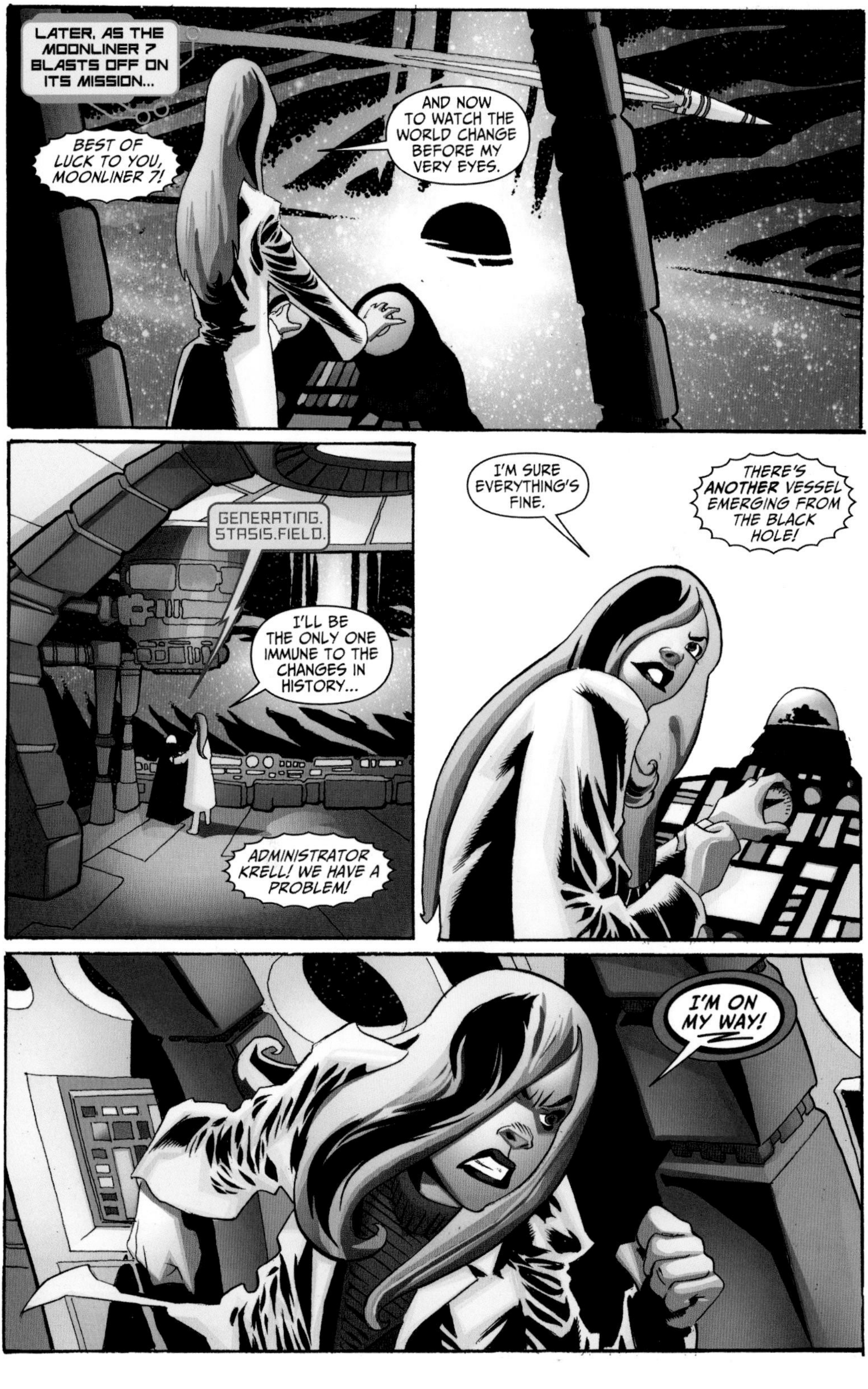
LATER, AS THE MOONLINER 7 BLASTS OFF ON ITS MISSION...
BEST OF LUCK TO YOU, MOONLINER 7!
AND NOW TO WATCH THE WORLD CHANGE BEFORE MY VERY EYES.
GENERATING. STASIS.FIELD.
I'LL BE THE ONLY ONE IMMUNE TO THE CHANGES IN HISTORY...
ADMINISTRATOR KRELL! WE HAVE A PROBLEM!
I'M SURE EVERYTHING'S FINE.
THERE'S ANOTHER VESSEL EMERGING FROM THE BLACK HOLE!
I'M ON MY WAY!

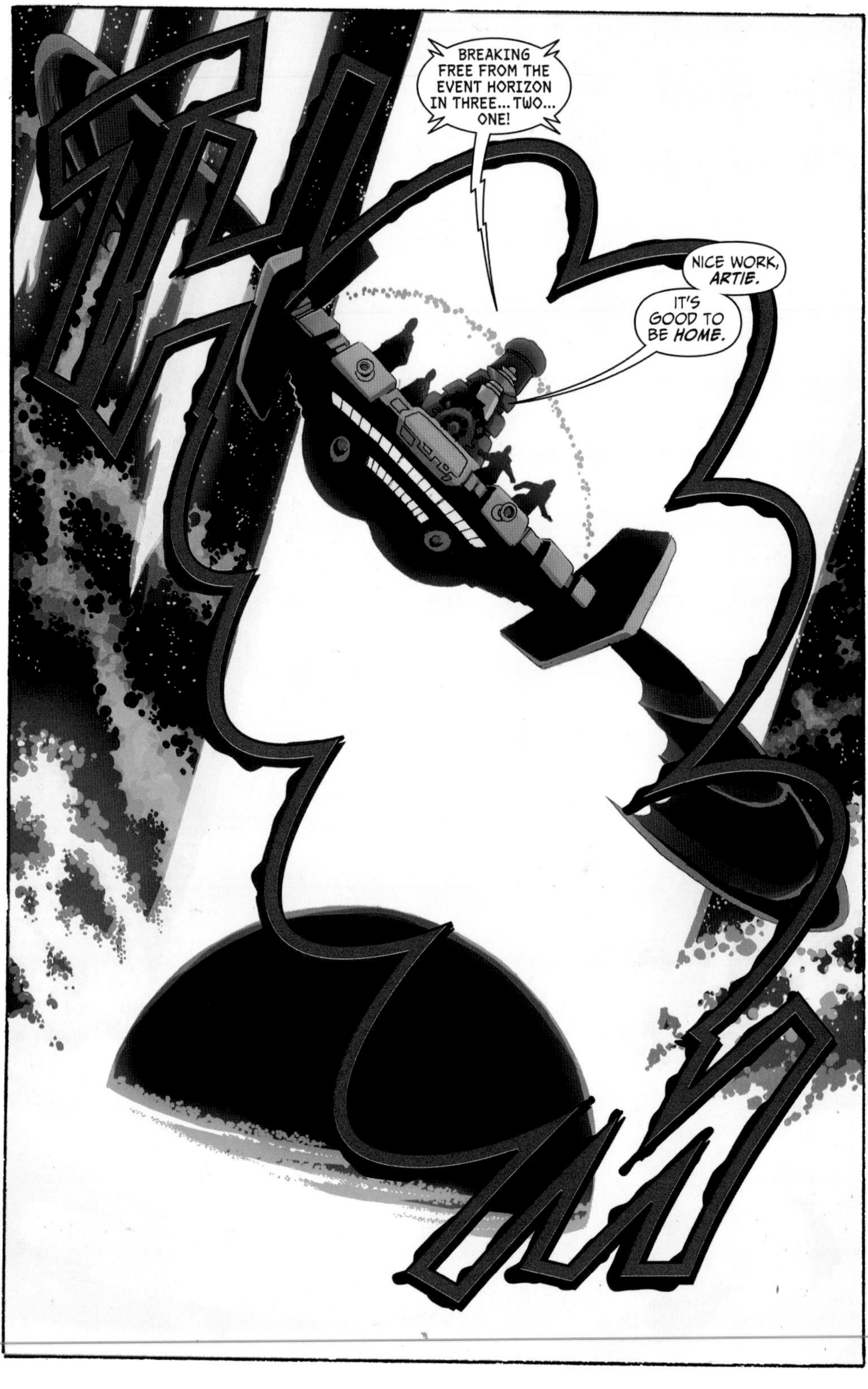
BREAKING FREE FROM THE EVENT HORIZON IN THREE... TWO... ONE!
NICE WORK, ARTIE.
IT'S GOOD TO BE HOME.

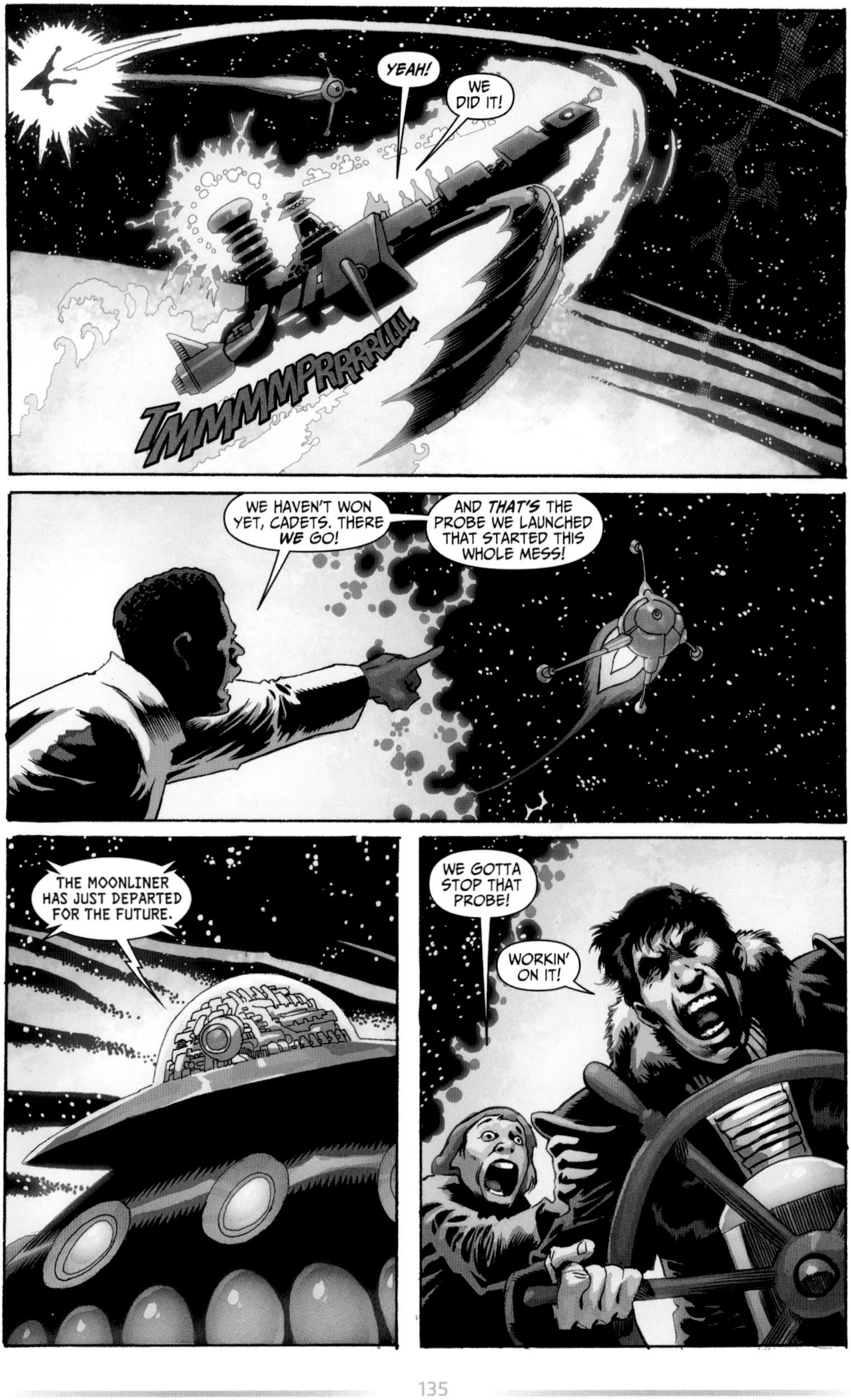
YEAH!
WE DID IT!
TMMMMPRRRRLLLL!
WE HAVEN'T WON YET, CADETS. THERE *WE* GO!
AND *THAT'S* THE PROBE WE LAUNCHED THAT STARTED THIS WHOLE MESS!
THE MOONLINER HAS JUST DEPARTED FOR THE FUTURE.
WE GOTTA STOP THAT PROBE!
WORKIN' ON IT!

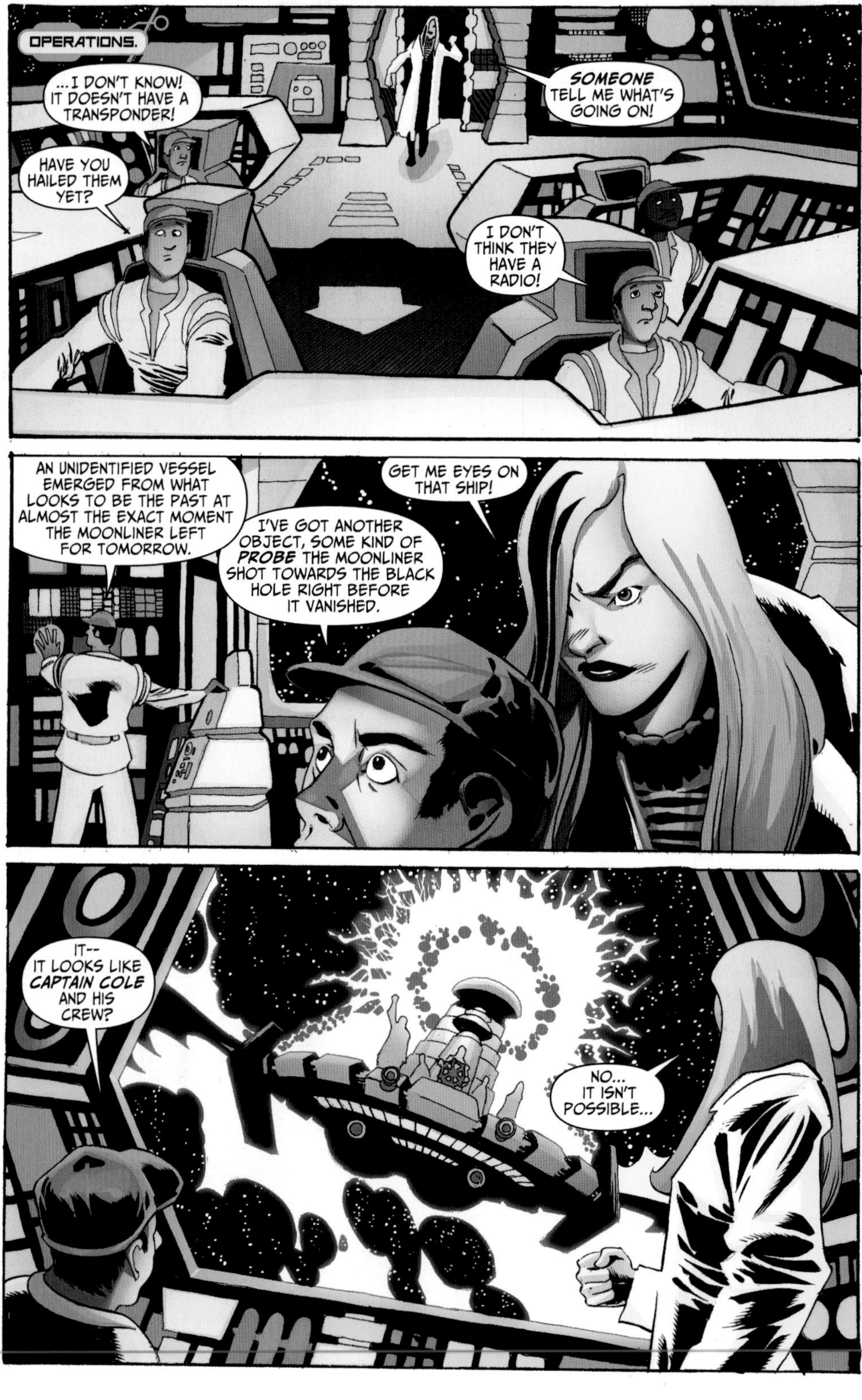
OPERATIONS.
...I DON'T KNOW! IT DOESN'T HAVE A TRANSPONDER!
HAVE YOU HAILED THEM YET?
SOMEONE TELL ME WHAT'S GOING ON!
I DON'T THINK THEY HAVE A RADIO!
AN UNIDENTIFIED VESSEL EMERGED FROM WHAT LOOKS TO BE THE PAST AT ALMOST THE EXACT MOMENT THE MOONLINER LEFT FOR TOMORROW.
I'VE GOT ANOTHER OBJECT, SOME KIND OF PROBE THE MOONLINER SHOT TOWARDS THE BLACK HOLE RIGHT BEFORE IT VANISHED.
GET ME EYES ON THAT SHIP!
IT-- IT LOOKS LIKE CAPTAIN COLE AND HIS CREW?
NO... IT ISN'T POSSIBLE...

IT LOOKS LIKE THEY'RE GOING AFTER THE PROBE!

SHOOT THEM DOWN!

WHY WOULD WE SHOOT DOWN THE MOONLINER CREW?

I CAN'T LET THIS HAPPEN...

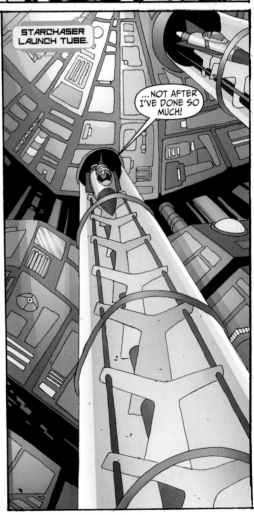

STARCHASER LAUNCH TUBE.

...NOT AFTER I'VE DONE SO MUCH!

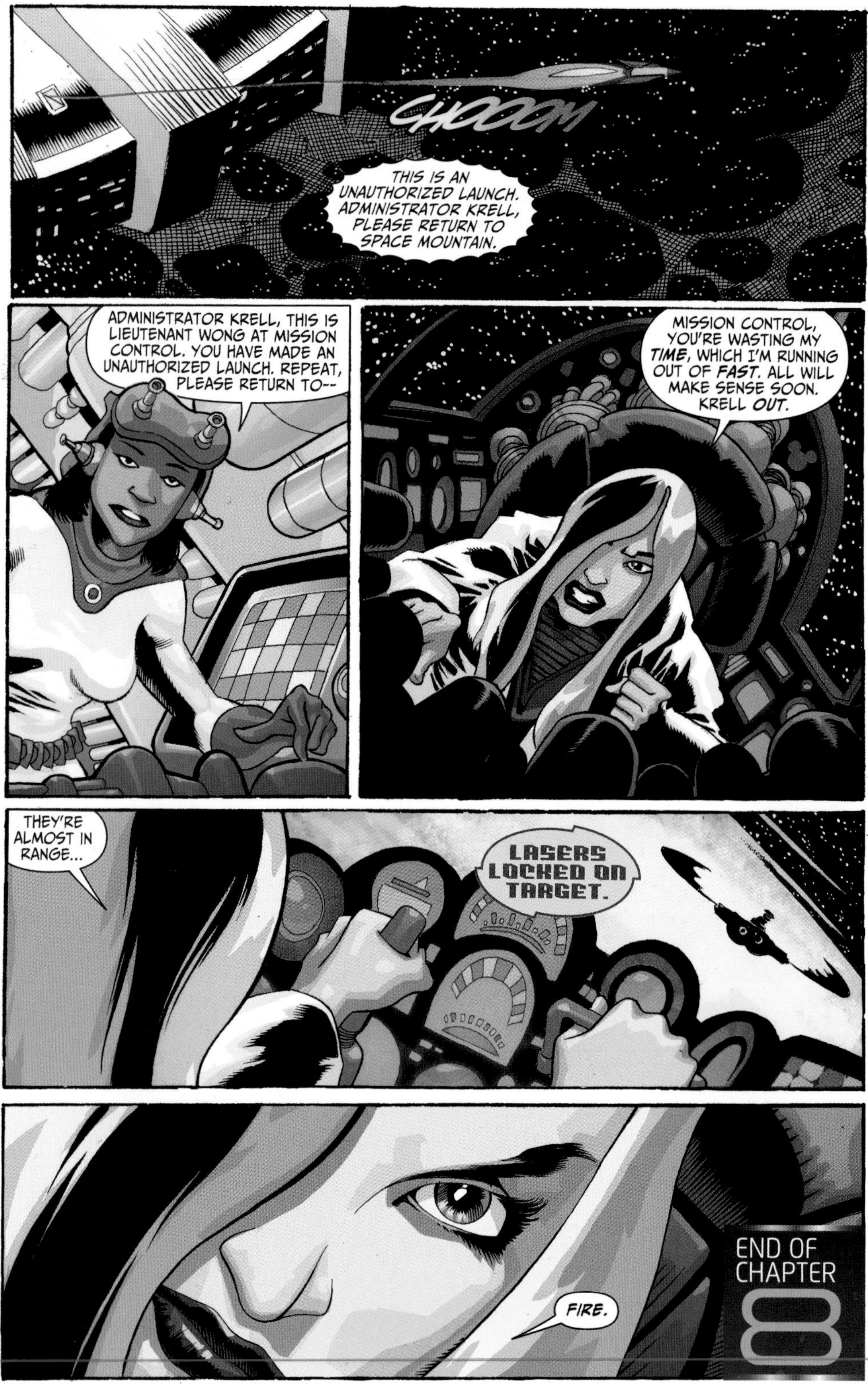
CHOOOM
THIS IS AN UNAUTHORIZED LAUNCH. ADMINISTRATOR KRELL, PLEASE RETURN TO SPACE MOUNTAIN.
ADMINISTRATOR KRELL, THIS IS LIEUTENANT WONG AT MISSION CONTROL. YOU HAVE MADE AN UNAUTHORIZED LAUNCH. REPEAT, PLEASE RETURN TO--
MISSION CONTROL, YOU'RE WASTING MY *TIME*, WHICH I'M RUNNING OUT OF *FAST*. ALL WILL MAKE SENSE SOON. KRELL *OUT*.
THEY'RE ALMOST IN RANGE...
LASERS LOCKED ON TARGET.
FIRE.
END OF CHAPTER 8

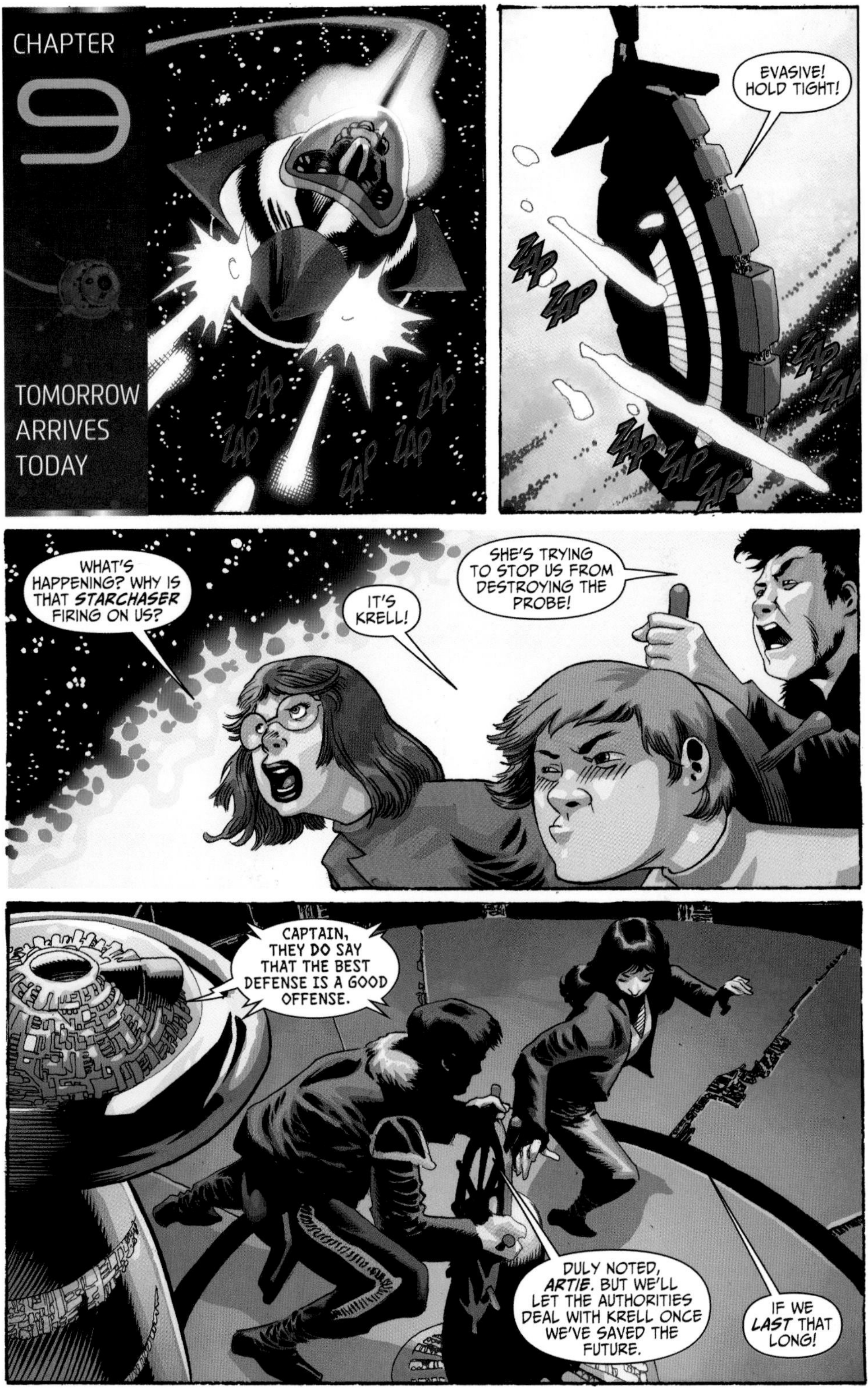
CHAPTER
9
TOMORROW ARRIVES TODAY
ZAP
ZAP
ZAP
ZAP
ZAP
EVASIVE! HOLD TIGHT!
ZAP
ZAP
ZAP
ZAP
ZAP
ZAP
ZAP
WHAT'S HAPPENING? WHY IS THAT STARCHASER FIRING ON US?
IT'S KRELL!
SHE'S TRYING TO STOP US FROM DESTROYING THE PROBE!
CAPTAIN, THEY DO SAY THAT THE BEST DEFENSE IS A GOOD OFFENSE.
DULY NOTED, ARTIE. BUT WE'LL LET THE AUTHORITIES DEAL WITH KRELL ONCE WE'VE SAVED THE FUTURE.
IF WE LAST THAT LONG!

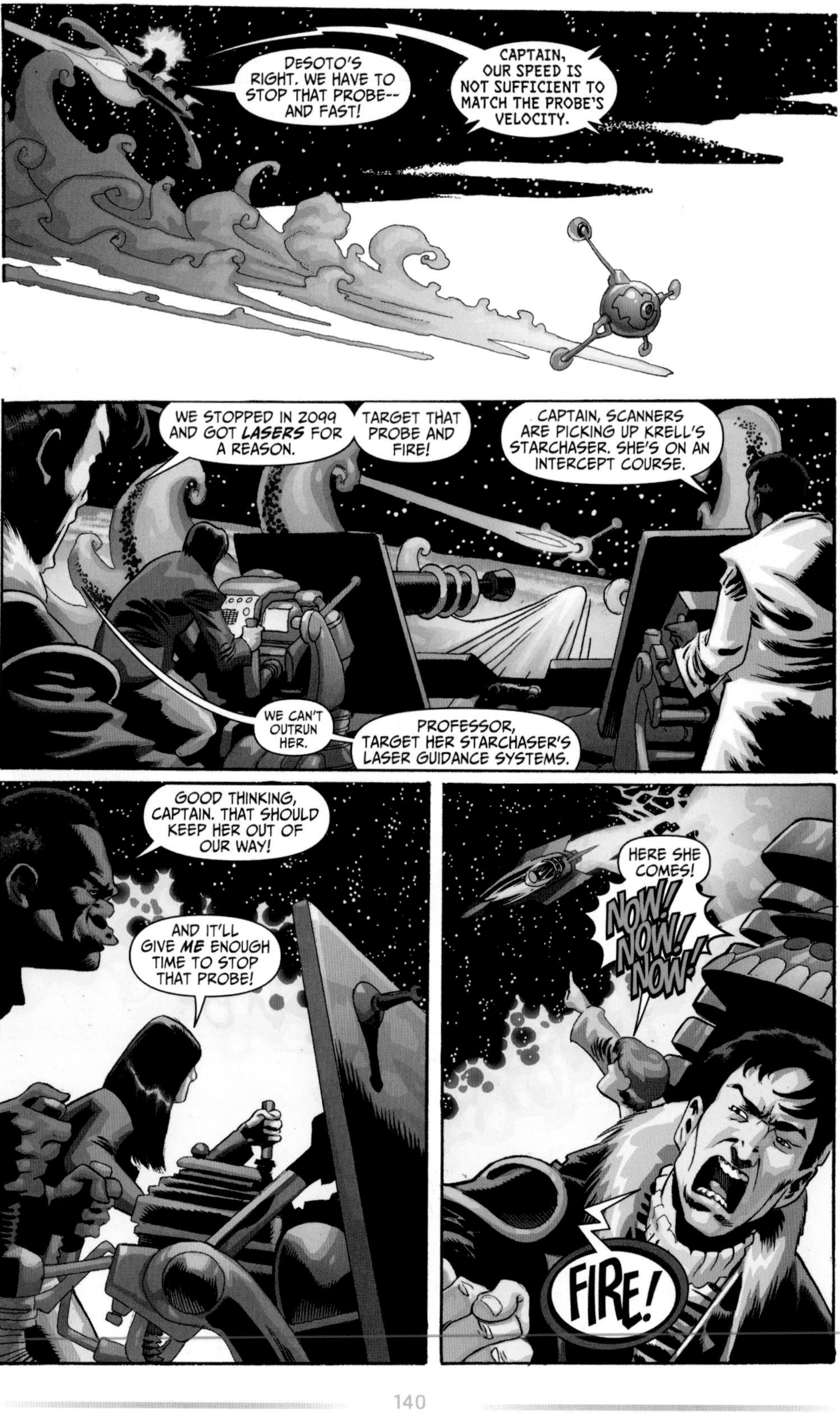
DESOTO'S RIGHT. WE HAVE TO STOP THAT PROBE-- AND FAST!
CAPTAIN, OUR SPEED IS NOT SUFFICIENT TO MATCH THE PROBE'S VELOCITY.
WE STOPPED IN 2099 AND GOT LASERS FOR A REASON.
TARGET THAT PROBE AND FIRE!
CAPTAIN, SCANNERS ARE PICKING UP KRELL'S STARCHASER. SHE'S ON AN INTERCEPT COURSE.
WE CAN'T OUTRUN HER.
PROFESSOR, TARGET HER STARCHASER'S LASER GUIDANCE SYSTEMS.
GOOD THINKING, CAPTAIN. THAT SHOULD KEEP HER OUT OF OUR WAY!
AND IT'LL GIVE ME ENOUGH TIME TO STOP THAT PROBE!
HERE SHE COMES!
NOW! NOW! NOW!
FIRE!

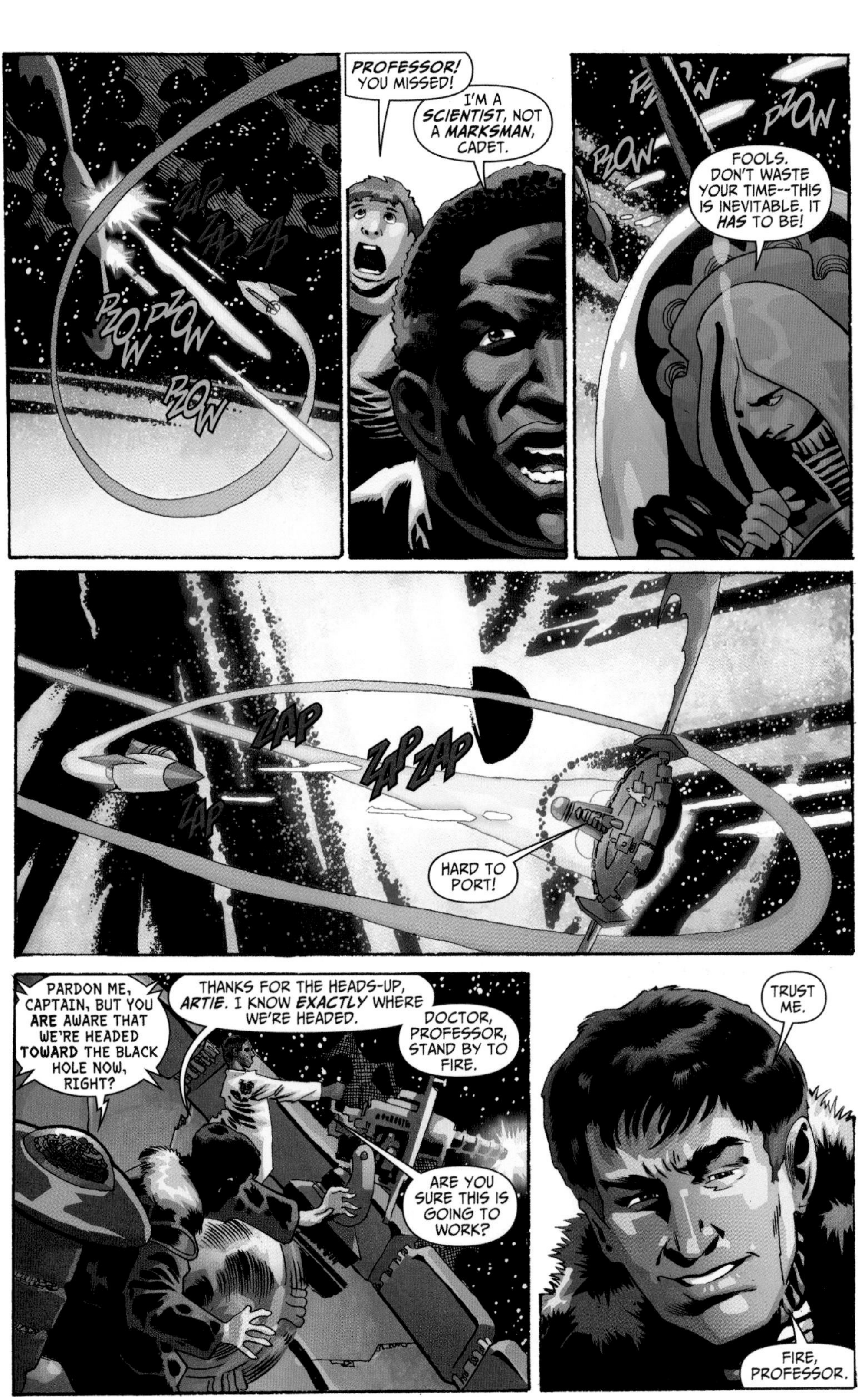
ZAP ZAP ZAP
PZOW PZOW
PZOW
PROFESSOR! YOU MISSED!
I'M A SCIENTIST, NOT A MARKSMAN, CADET.
PZOW PZOW
PZOW
FOOLS. DON'T WASTE YOUR TIME--THIS IS INEVITABLE. IT HAS TO BE!
ZAP
ZAP ZAP
ZAP
HARD TO PORT!
PARDON ME, CAPTAIN, BUT YOU ARE AWARE THAT WE'RE HEADED TOWARD THE BLACK HOLE NOW, RIGHT?
THANKS FOR THE HEADS-UP, ARTIE. I KNOW EXACTLY WHERE WE'RE HEADED.
DOCTOR, PROFESSOR, STAND BY TO FIRE.
ARE YOU SURE THIS IS GOING TO WORK?
TRUST ME.
FIRE, PROFESSOR.

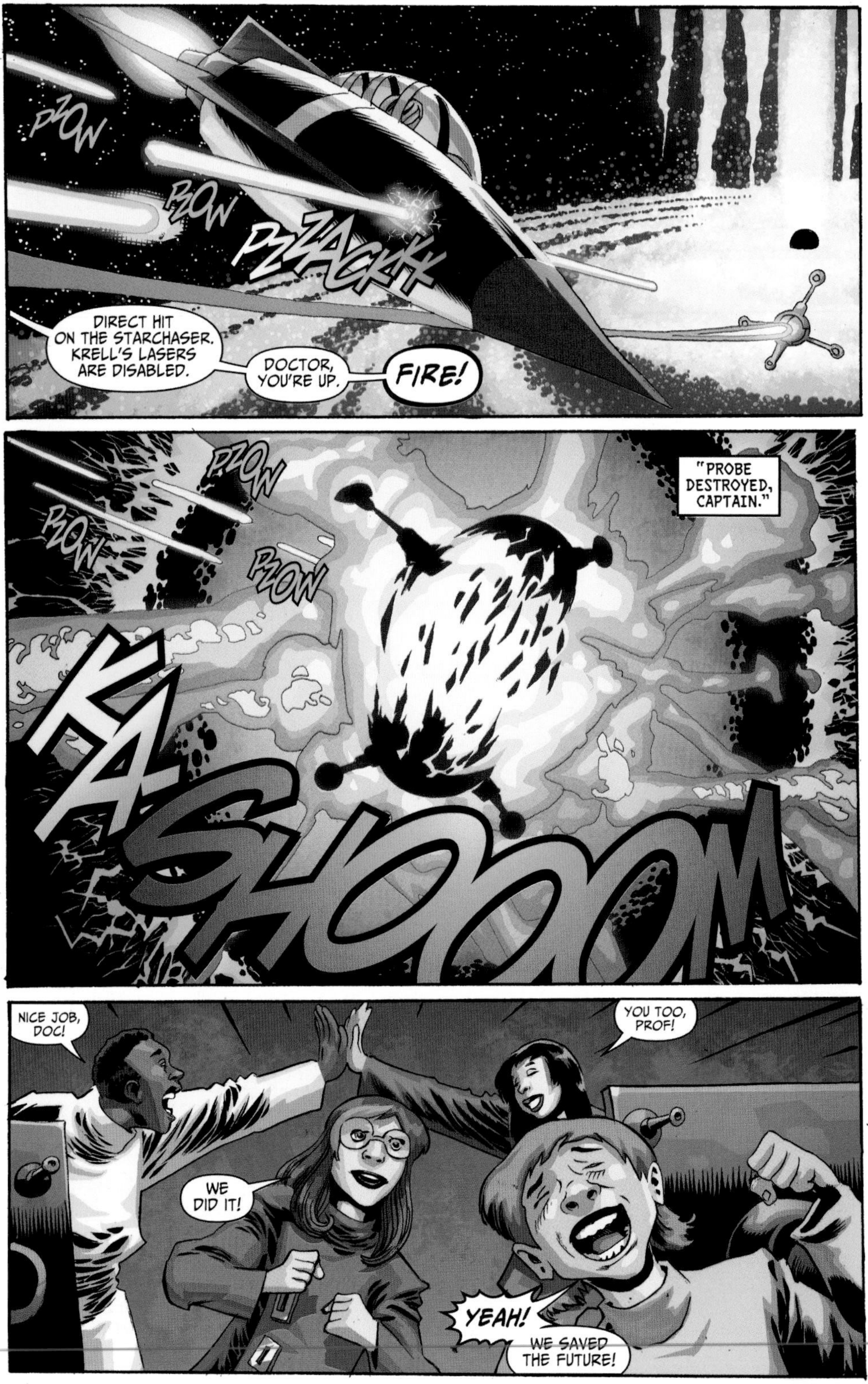
PZOW
PZOW
PZZACKKK
DIRECT HIT ON THE STARCHASER. KRELL'S LASERS ARE DISABLED.
DOCTOR, YOU'RE UP.
FIRE!
"PROBE DESTROYED, CAPTAIN."
PZOW
PZOW
PZOW
KA-SHOOOM
NICE JOB, DOC!
YOU TOO, PROF!
WE DID IT!
YEAH!
WE SAVED THE FUTURE!

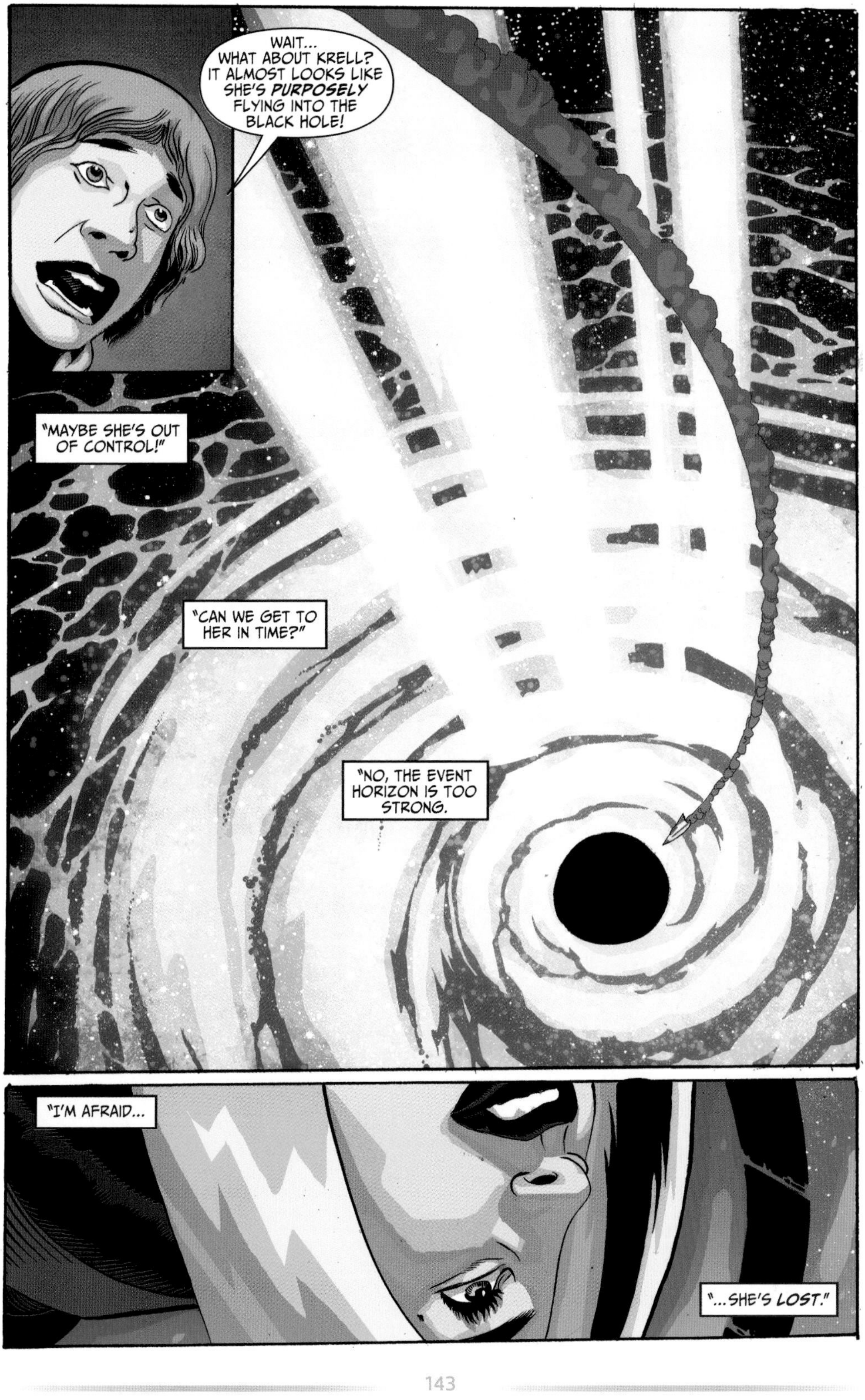
WAIT... WHAT ABOUT KRELL? IT ALMOST LOOKS LIKE SHE'S PURPOSELY FLYING INTO THE BLACK HOLE!
"MAYBE SHE'S OUT OF CONTROL!"
"CAN WE GET TO HER IN TIME?"
"NO, THE EVENT HORIZON IS TOO STRONG.
"I'M AFRAID...
"...SHE'S LOST."

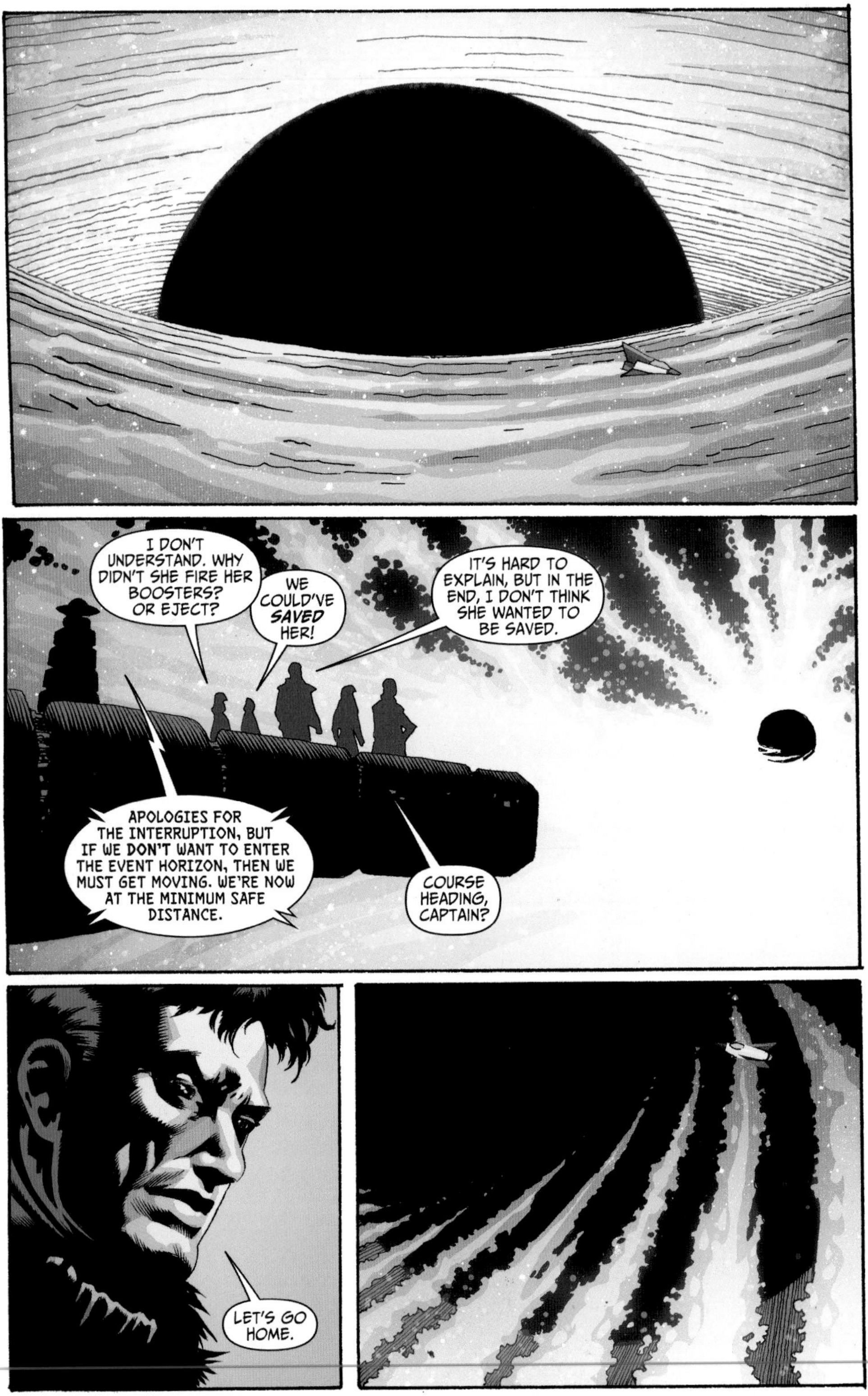
I DON'T UNDERSTAND. WHY DIDN'T SHE FIRE HER BOOSTERS? OR EJECT?
WE COULD'VE **SAVED** HER!
IT'S HARD TO EXPLAIN, BUT IN THE END, I DON'T THINK SHE WANTED TO BE SAVED.
APOLOGIES FOR THE INTERRUPTION, BUT IF WE **DON'T** WANT TO ENTER THE EVENT HORIZON, THEN WE MUST GET MOVING. WE'RE NOW AT THE MINIMUM SAFE DISTANCE.
COURSE HEADING, CAPTAIN?
LET'S GO HOME.

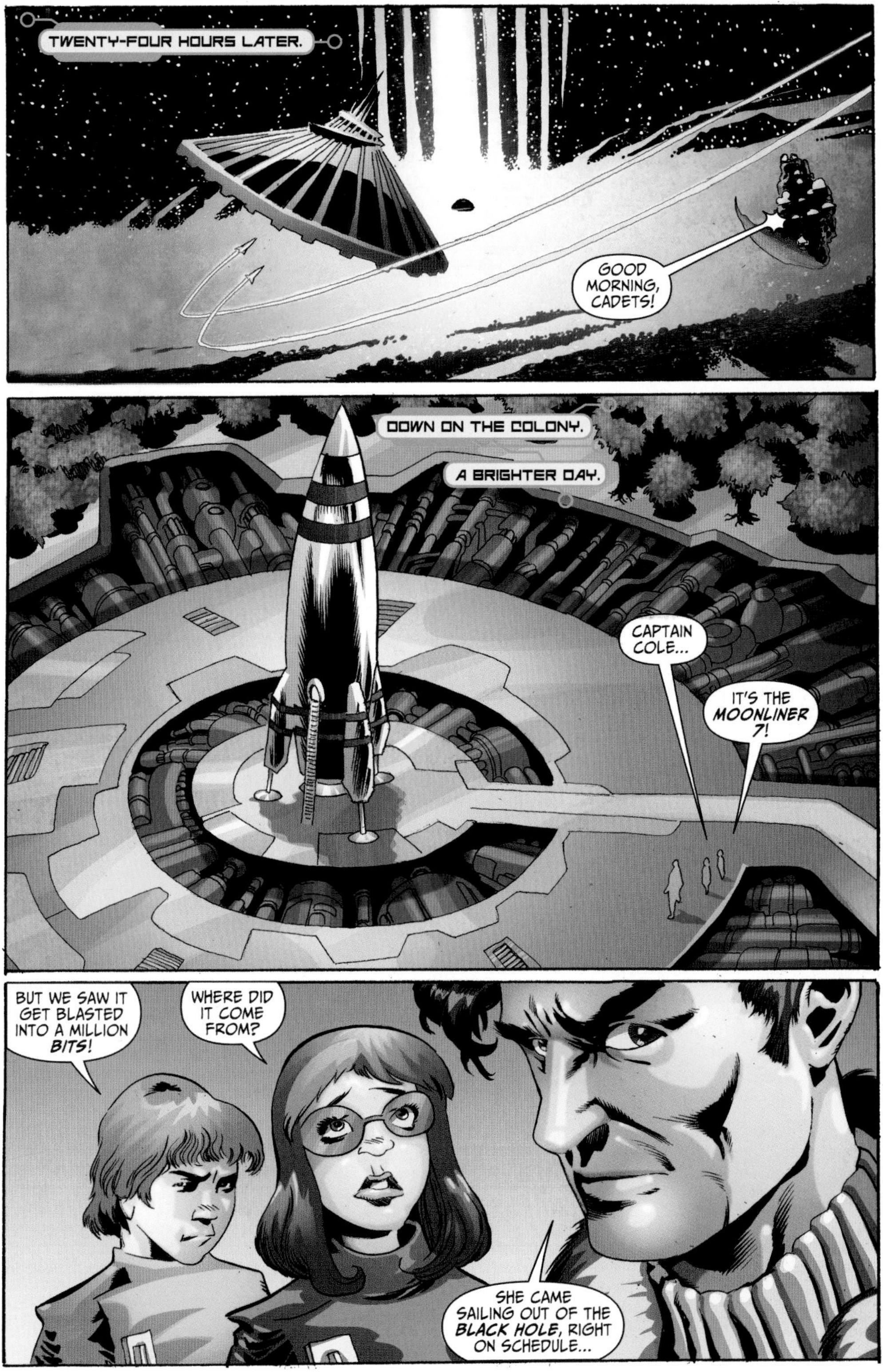
TWENTY-FOUR HOURS LATER.
GOOD MORNING, CADETS!
DOWN ON THE COLONY.
A BRIGHTER DAY.
CAPTAIN COLE...
IT'S THE MOONLINER 7!
BUT WE SAW IT GET BLASTED INTO A MILLION BITS!
WHERE DID IT COME FROM?
SHE CAME SAILING OUT OF THE BLACK HOLE, RIGHT ON SCHEDULE...

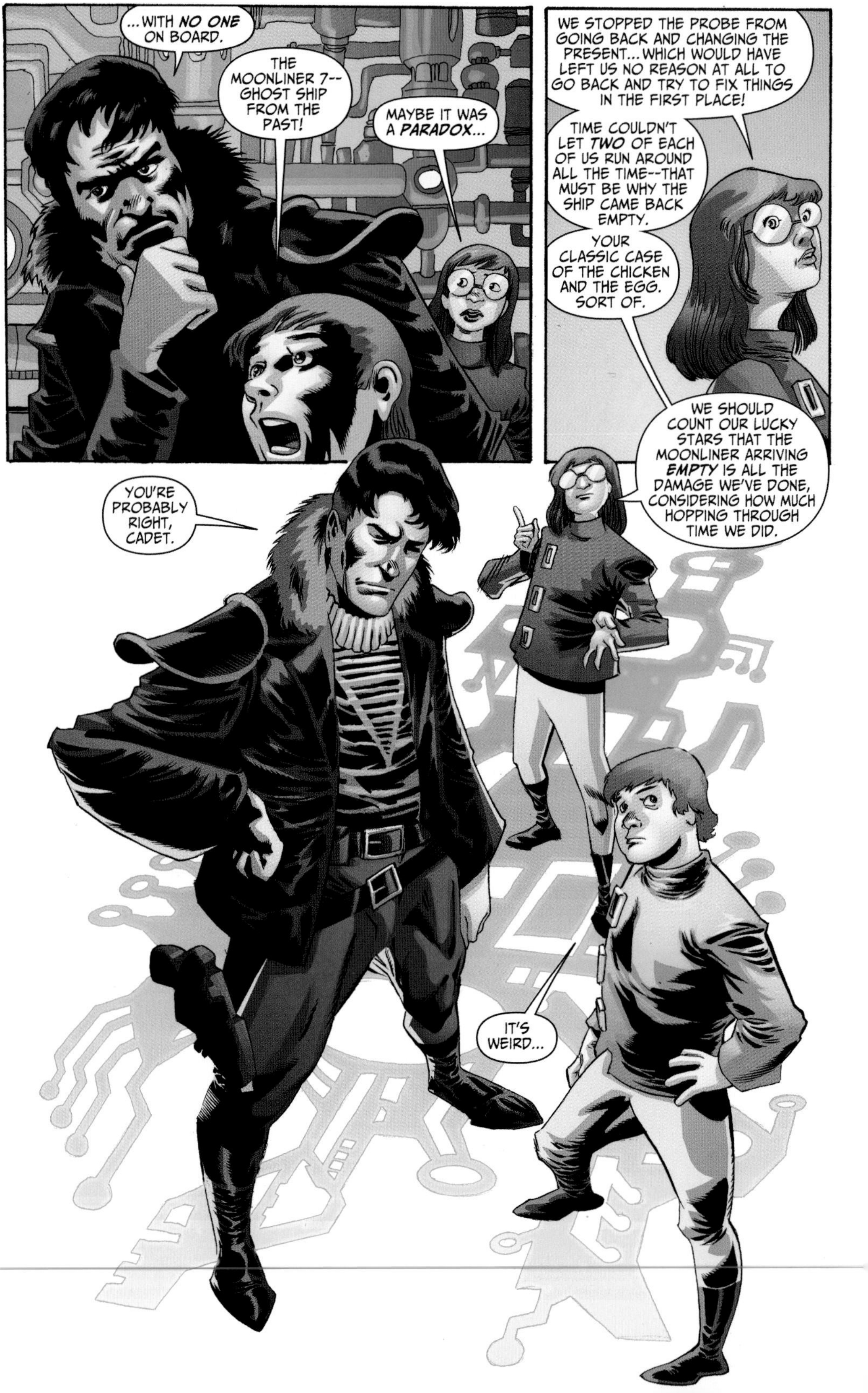
...WITH NO ONE ON BOARD.
THE MOONLINER 7-- GHOST SHIP FROM THE PAST!
MAYBE IT WAS A PARADOX...
WE STOPPED THE PROBE FROM GOING BACK AND CHANGING THE PRESENT... WHICH WOULD HAVE LEFT US NO REASON AT ALL TO GO BACK AND TRY TO FIX THINGS IN THE FIRST PLACE!
TIME COULDN'T LET TWO OF EACH OF US RUN AROUND ALL THE TIME--THAT MUST BE WHY THE SHIP CAME BACK EMPTY.
YOUR CLASSIC CASE OF THE CHICKEN AND THE EGG. SORT OF.
WE SHOULD COUNT OUR LUCKY STARS THAT THE MOONLINER ARRIVING EMPTY IS ALL THE DAMAGE WE'VE DONE, CONSIDERING HOW MUCH HOPPING THROUGH TIME WE DID.
YOU'RE PROBABLY RIGHT, CADET.
IT'S WEIRD...

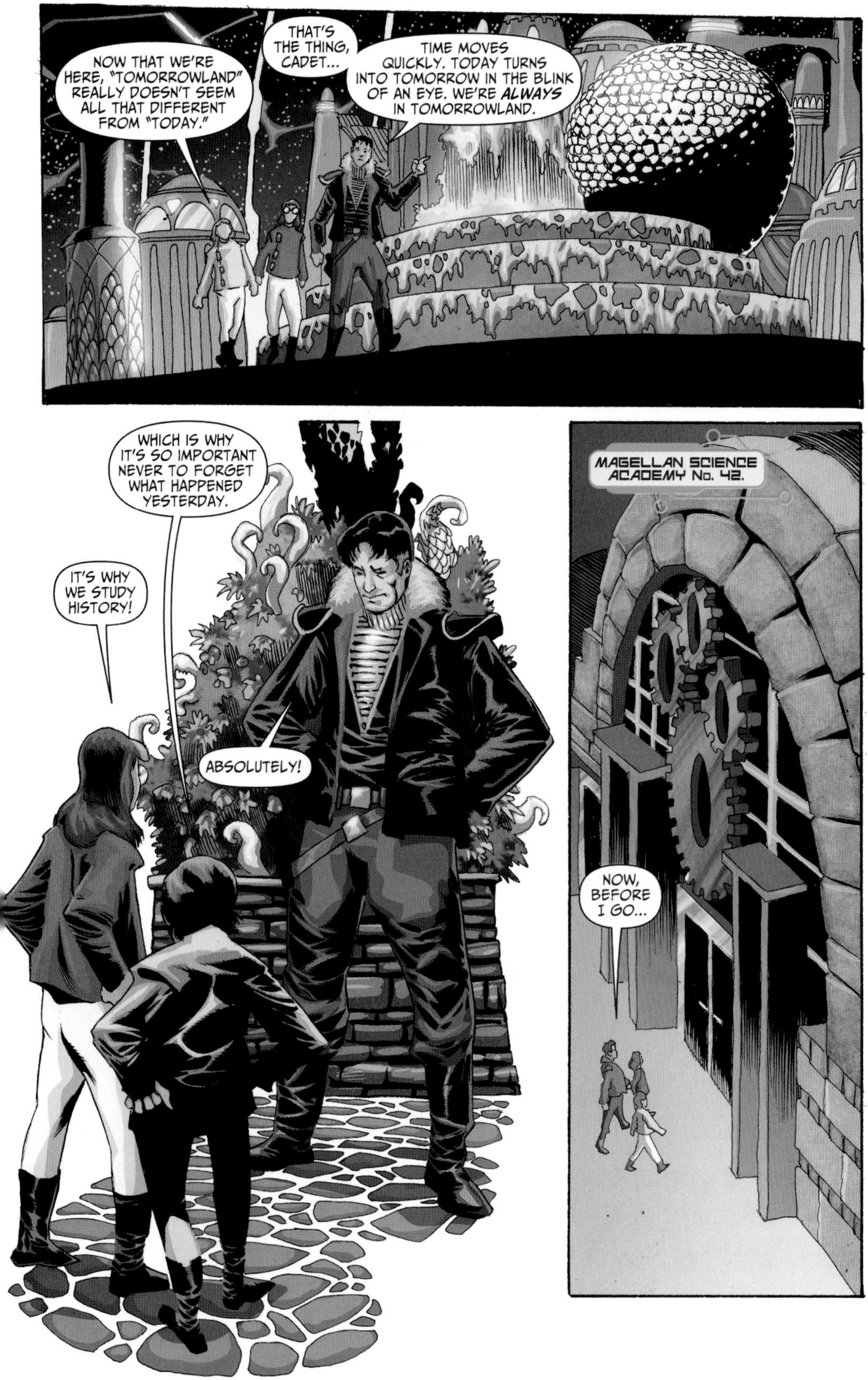
NOW THAT WE'RE HERE, "TOMORROWLAND" REALLY DOESN'T SEEM ALL THAT DIFFERENT FROM "TODAY."
THAT'S THE THING, CADET...
TIME MOVES QUICKLY. TODAY TURNS INTO TOMORROW IN THE BLINK OF AN EYE. WE'RE *ALWAYS* IN TOMORROWLAND.
WHICH IS WHY IT'S SO IMPORTANT NEVER TO FORGET WHAT HAPPENED YESTERDAY.
IT'S WHY WE STUDY HISTORY!
ABSOLUTELY!
MAGELLAN SCIENCE ACADEMY No. 42.
NOW, BEFORE I GO...

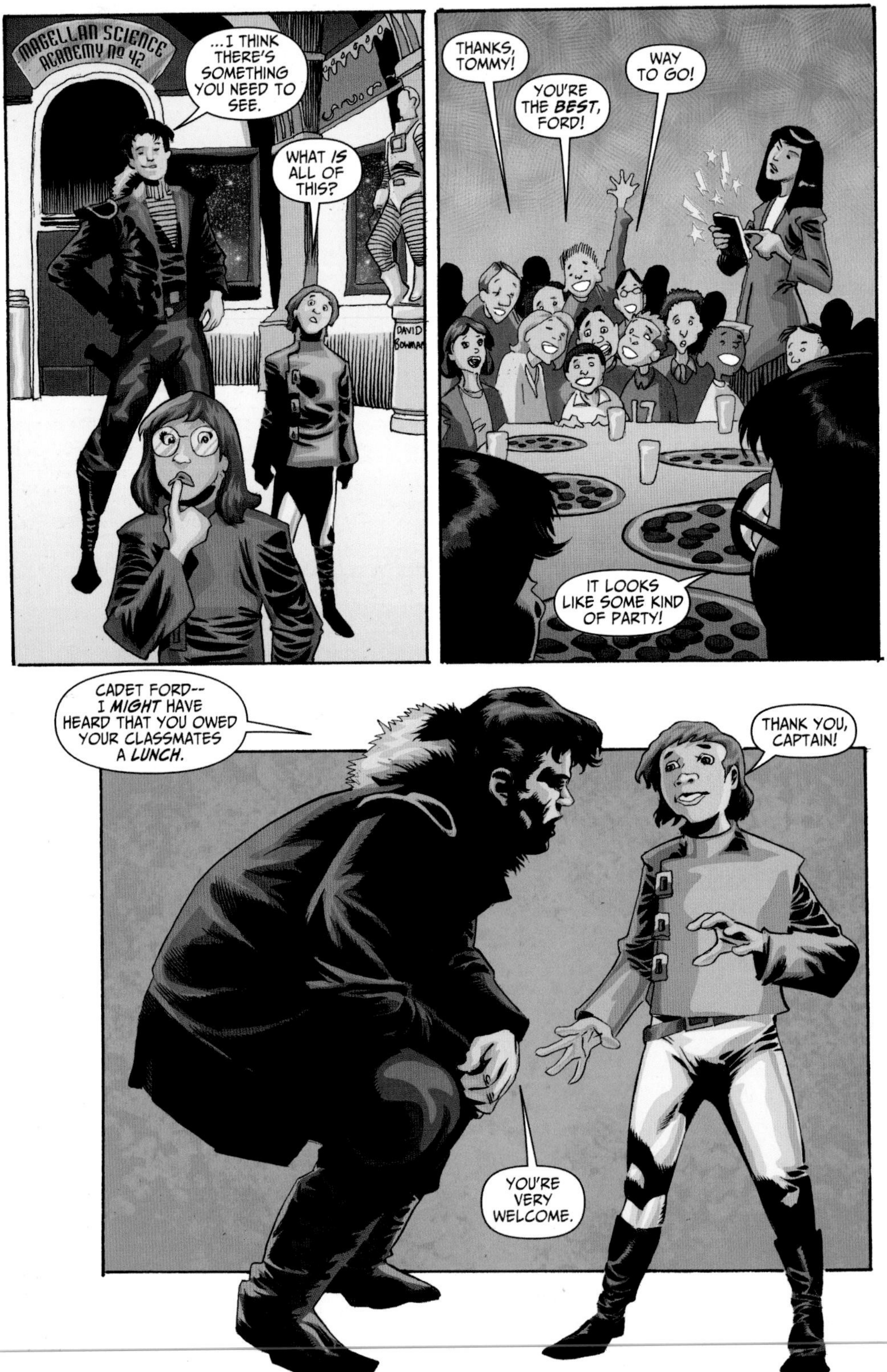
MAGELLAN SCIENCE ACADEMY No 42
...I THINK THERE'S SOMETHING YOU NEED TO SEE.
WHAT IS ALL OF THIS?
DAVID BOWMAN
THANKS, TOMMY!
YOU'RE THE BEST, FORD!
WAY TO GO!
IT LOOKS LIKE SOME KIND OF PARTY!
CADET FORD-- I MIGHT HAVE HEARD THAT YOU OWED YOUR CLASSMATES A LUNCH.
THANK YOU, CAPTAIN!
YOU'RE VERY WELCOME.

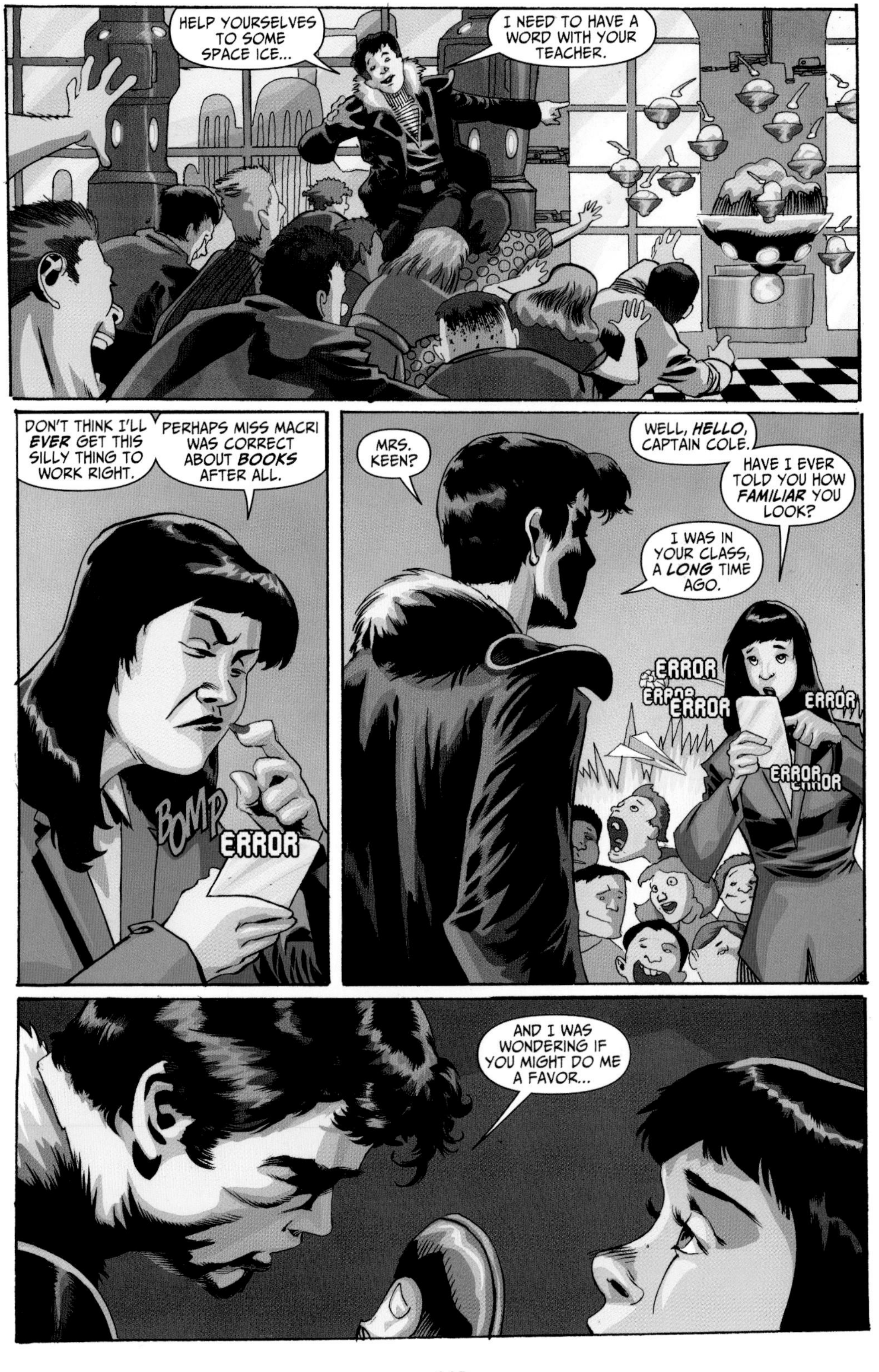
HELP YOURSELVES TO SOME SPACE ICE...
I NEED TO HAVE A WORD WITH YOUR TEACHER.
DON'T THINK I'LL EVER GET THIS SILLY THING TO WORK RIGHT.
PERHAPS MISS MACRI WAS CORRECT ABOUT BOOKS AFTER ALL.
BOMP
ERROR
MRS. KEEN?
WELL, HELLO, CAPTAIN COLE.
HAVE I EVER TOLD YOU HOW FAMILIAR YOU LOOK?
I WAS IN YOUR CLASS, A LONG TIME AGO.
ERROR
ERROR
ERROR
ERROR
AND I WAS WONDERING IF YOU MIGHT DO ME A FAVOR...

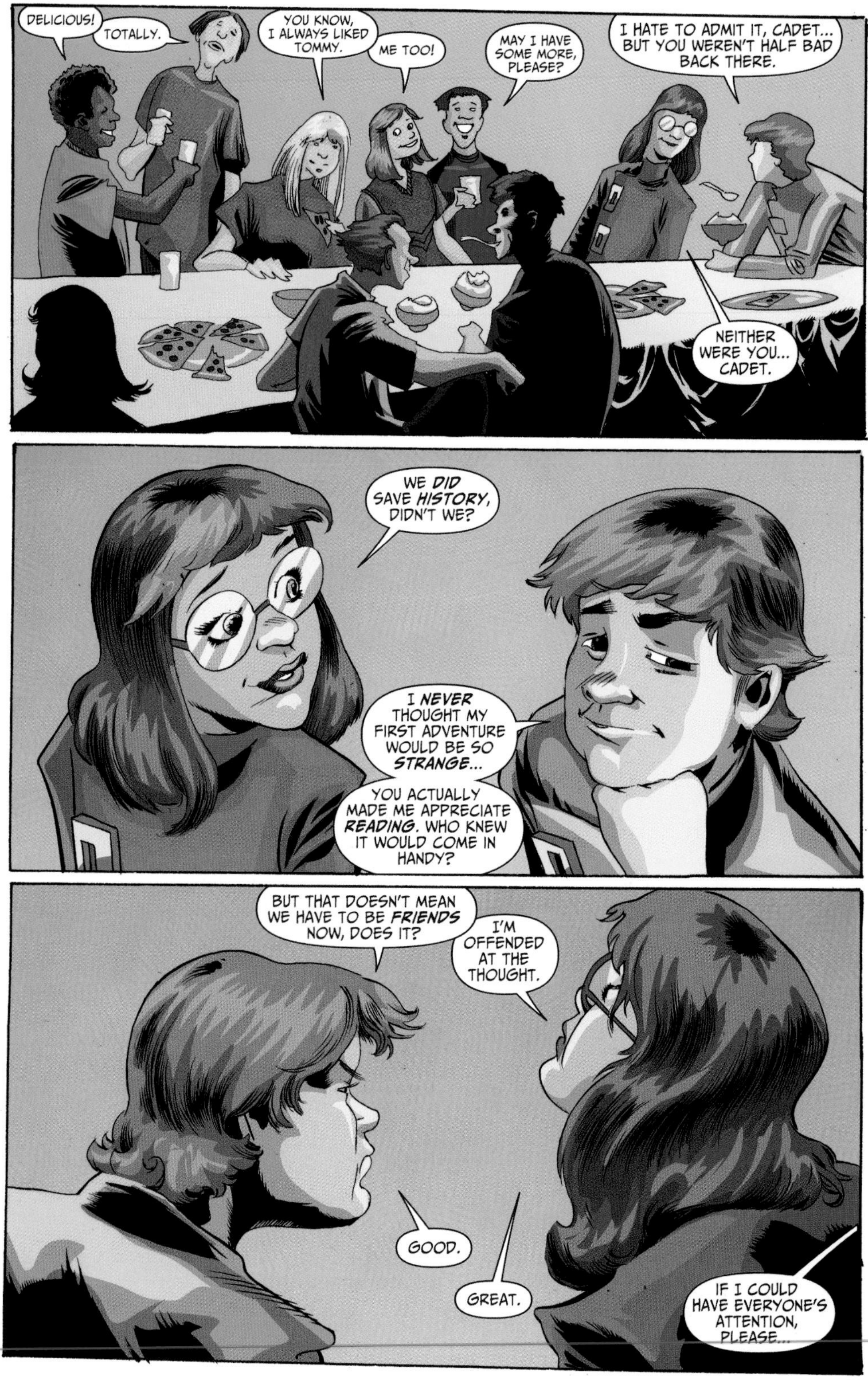
DELICIOUS!
TOTALLY.
YOU KNOW, I ALWAYS LIKED TOMMY.
ME TOO!
MAY I HAVE SOME MORE, PLEASE?
I HATE TO ADMIT IT, CADET... BUT YOU WEREN'T HALF BAD BACK THERE.
NEITHER WERE YOU... CADET.
WE DID SAVE HISTORY, DIDN'T WE?
I NEVER THOUGHT MY FIRST ADVENTURE WOULD BE SO STRANGE...
YOU ACTUALLY MADE ME APPRECIATE READING. WHO KNEW IT WOULD COME IN HANDY?
BUT THAT DOESN'T MEAN WE HAVE TO BE FRIENDS NOW, DOES IT?
I'M OFFENDED AT THE THOUGHT.
GOOD.
GREAT.
IF I COULD HAVE EVERYONE'S ATTENTION, PLEASE...

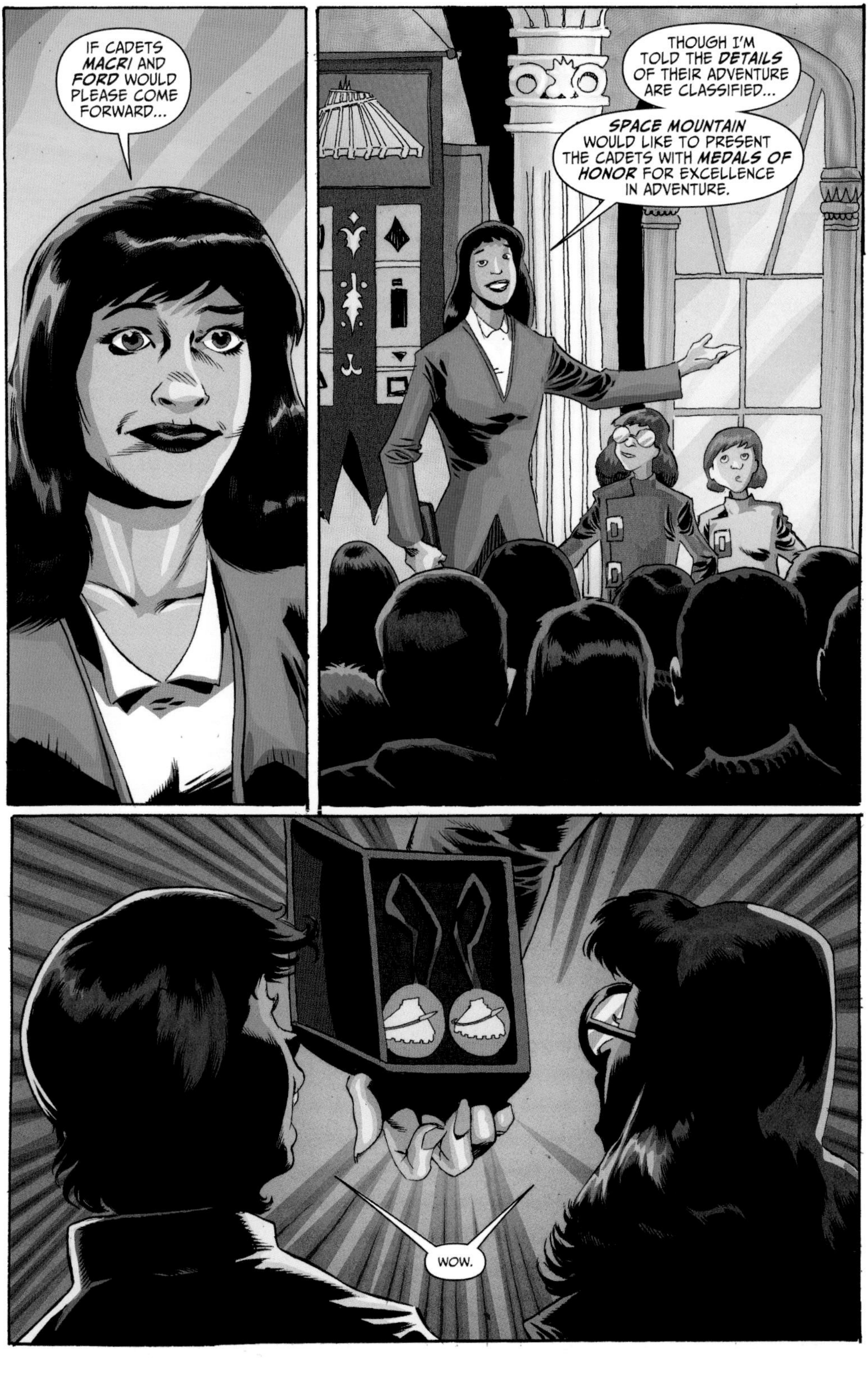
IF CADETS MACRI AND FORD WOULD PLEASE COME FORWARD...
THOUGH I'M TOLD THE DETAILS OF THEIR ADVENTURE ARE CLASSIFIED...
SPACE MOUNTAIN WOULD LIKE TO PRESENT THE CADETS WITH MEDALS OF HONOR FOR EXCELLENCE IN ADVENTURE.
WOW.

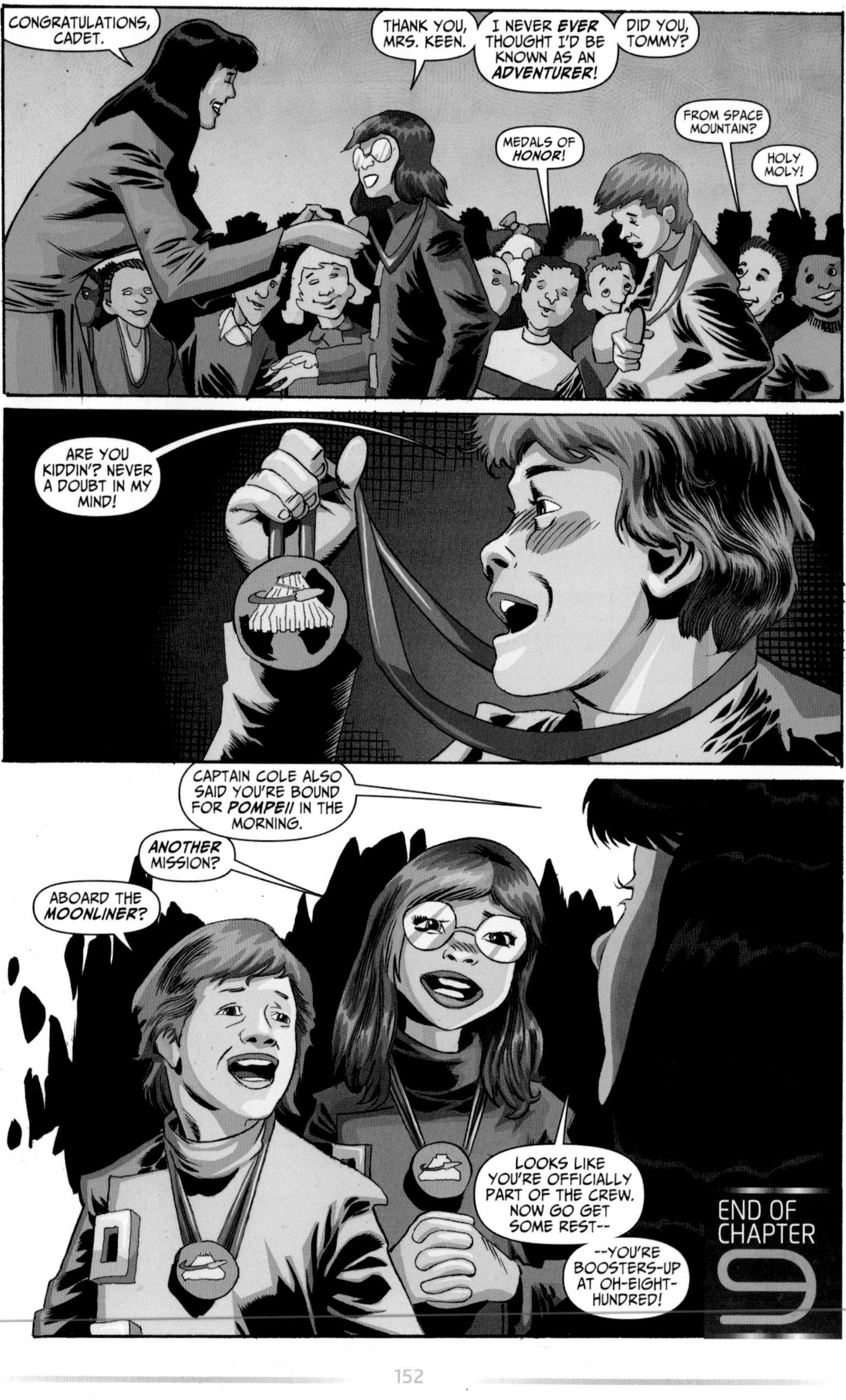
CONGRATULATIONS, CADET.
THANK YOU, MRS. KEEN.
I NEVER EVER THOUGHT I'D BE KNOWN AS AN ADVENTURER!
DID YOU, TOMMY?
FROM SPACE MOUNTAIN?
MEDALS OF HONOR!
HOLY MOLY!
ARE YOU KIDDIN'? NEVER A DOUBT IN MY MIND!
CAPTAIN COLE ALSO SAID YOU'RE BOUND FOR POMPEII IN THE MORNING.
ANOTHER MISSION?
ABOARD THE MOONLINER?
LOOKS LIKE YOU'RE OFFICIALLY PART OF THE CREW. NOW GO GET SOME REST--
--YOU'RE BOOSTERS-UP AT OH-EIGHT-HUNDRED!
END OF CHAPTER 9

EPILOGUE

PAST IMPERFECT

LOST TIME IS NEVER
FOUND AGAIN.
—BENJAMIN FRANKLIN

EPILOGUE: PAST IMPERFECT

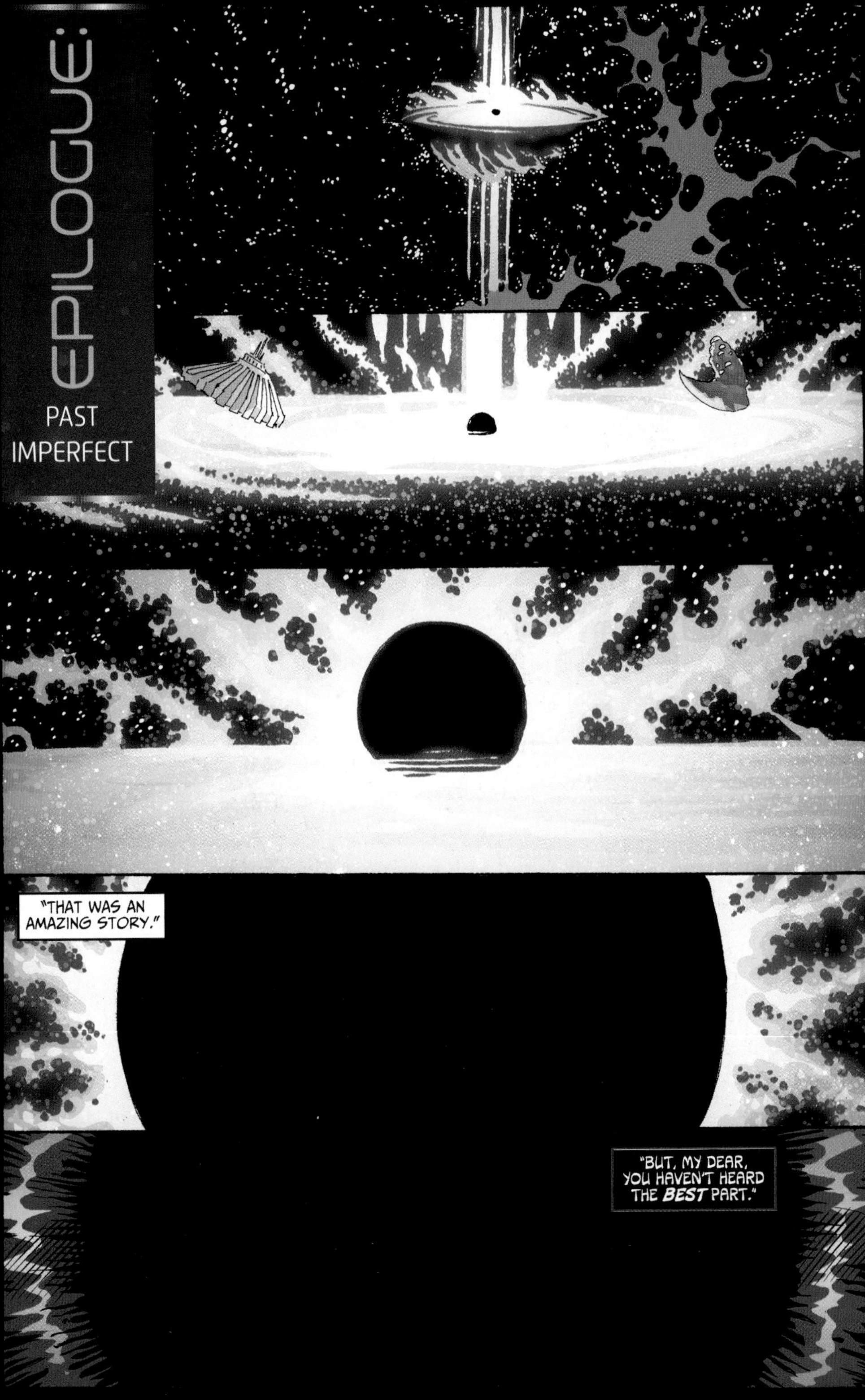
"THAT WAS AN AMAZING STORY."
"BUT, MY DEAR, YOU HAVEN'T HEARD THE BEST PART."

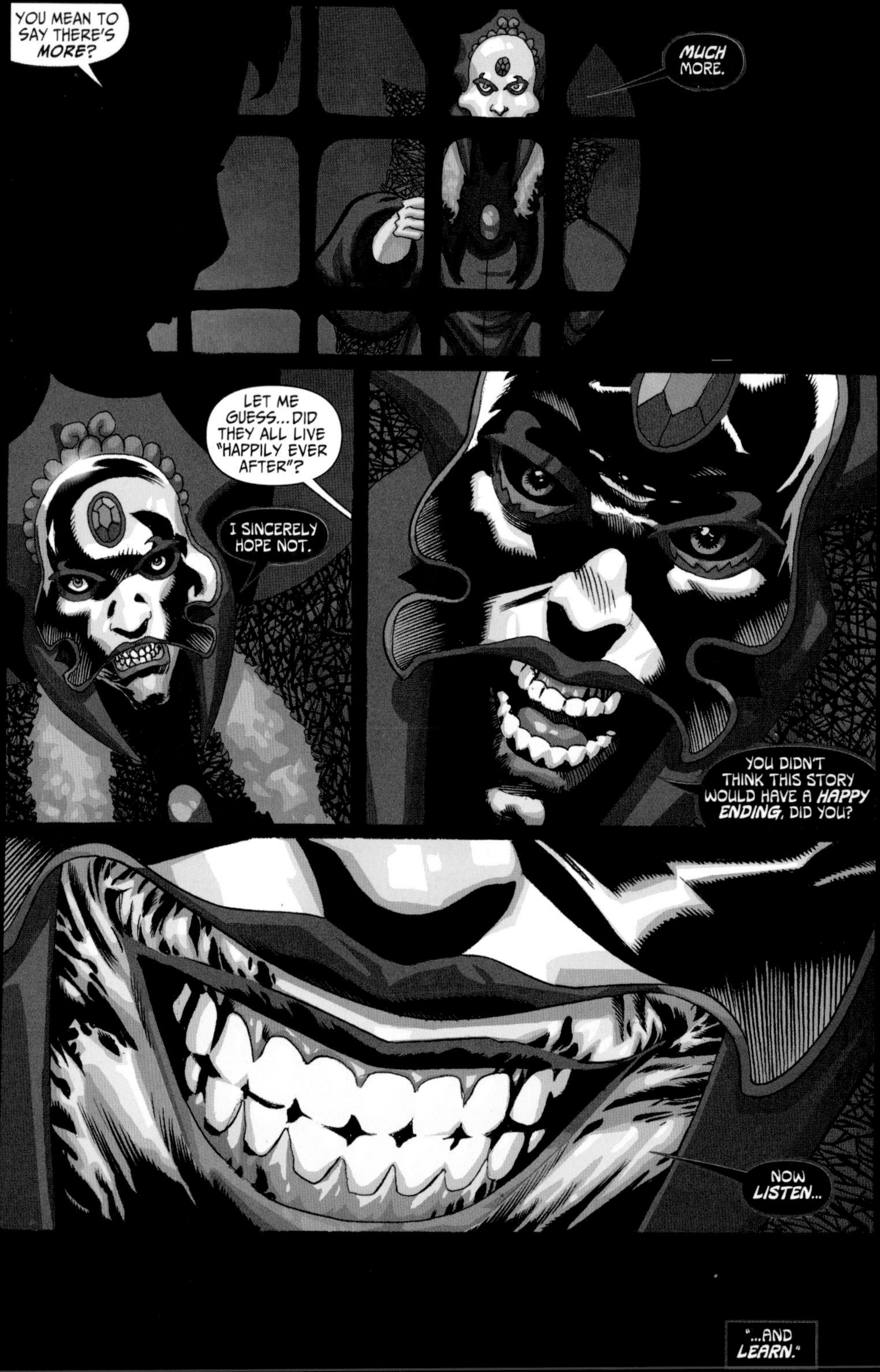

YOU MEAN TO SAY THERE'S MORE?
MUCH MORE.
LET ME GUESS...DID THEY ALL LIVE "HAPPILY EVER AFTER"?
I SINCERELY HOPE NOT.
YOU DIDN'T THINK THIS STORY WOULD HAVE A HAPPY ENDING, DID YOU?
NOW LISTEN...
"...AND LEARN."

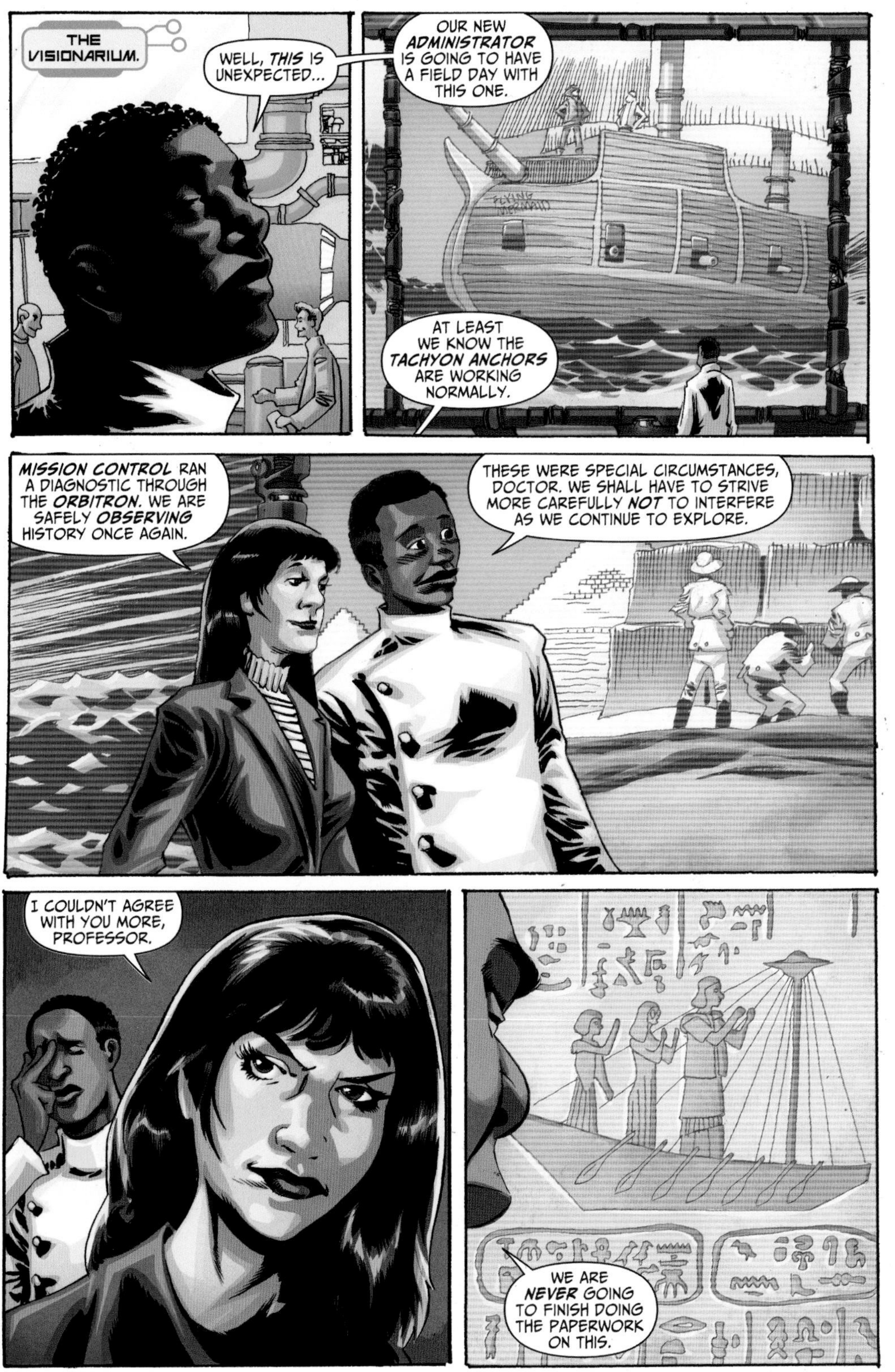
THE VISIONARIUM.
WELL, THIS IS UNEXPECTED...
OUR NEW ADMINISTRATOR IS GOING TO HAVE A FIELD DAY WITH THIS ONE.
AT LEAST WE KNOW THE TACHYON ANCHORS ARE WORKING NORMALLY.
MISSION CONTROL RAN A DIAGNOSTIC THROUGH THE ORBITRON. WE ARE SAFELY OBSERVING HISTORY ONCE AGAIN.
THESE WERE SPECIAL CIRCUMSTANCES, DOCTOR. WE SHALL HAVE TO STRIVE MORE CAREFULLY NOT TO INTERFERE AS WE CONTINUE TO EXPLORE.
I COULDN'T AGREE WITH YOU MORE, PROFESSOR.
WE ARE NEVER GOING TO FINISH DOING THE PAPERWORK ON THIS.

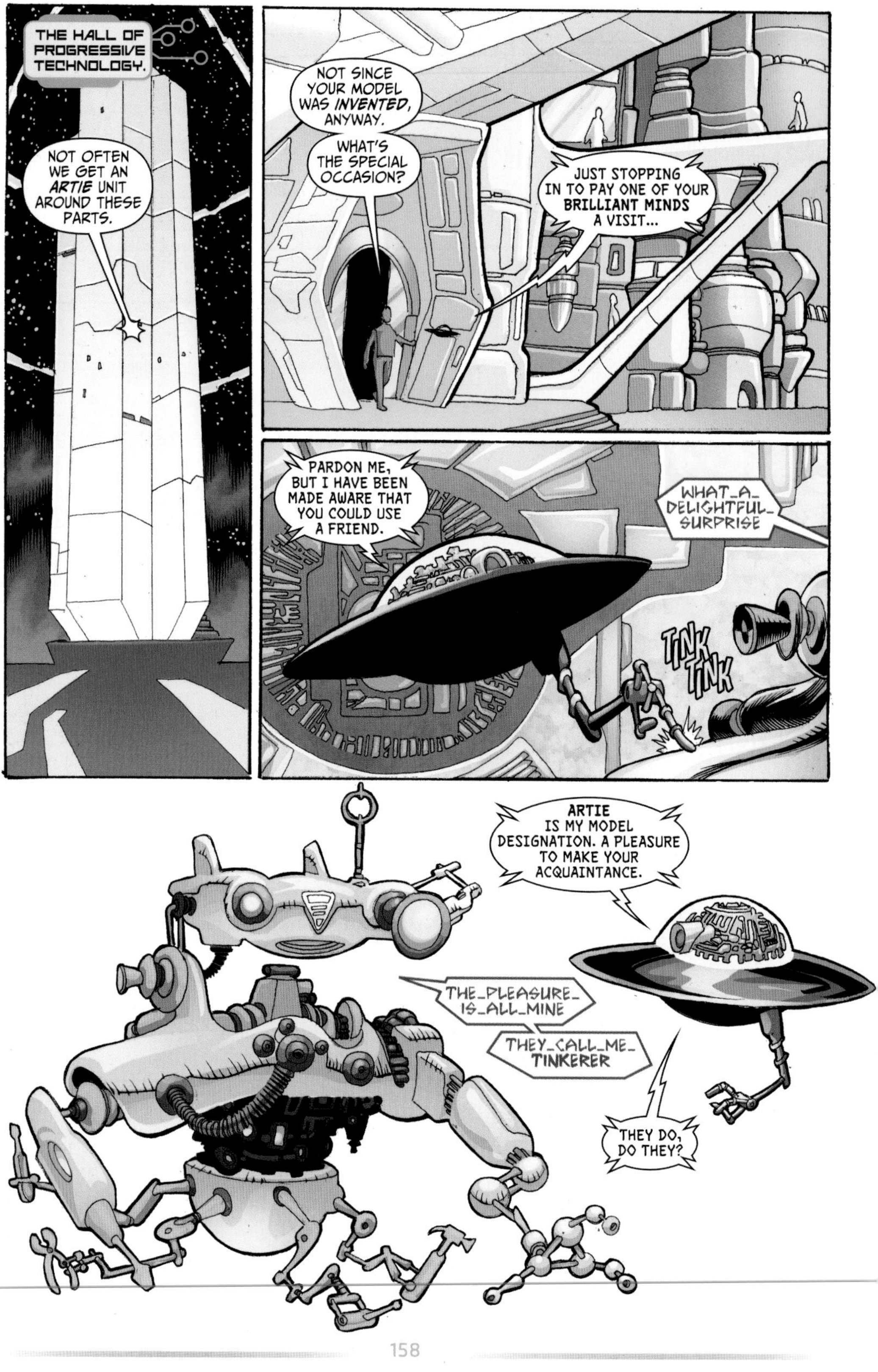
THE HALL OF PROGRESSIVE TECHNOLOGY.
NOT OFTEN WE GET AN *ARTIE* UNIT AROUND THESE PARTS.
NOT SINCE YOUR MODEL WAS *INVENTED*, ANYWAY.
WHAT'S THE SPECIAL OCCASION?
JUST STOPPING IN TO PAY ONE OF YOUR **BRILLIANT MINDS** A VISIT...
PARDON ME, BUT I HAVE BEEN MADE AWARE THAT YOU COULD USE A FRIEND.
WHAT_A_ DELIGHTFUL_ SURPRISE
TINK TINK
ARTIE IS MY MODEL DESIGNATION. A PLEASURE TO MAKE YOUR ACQUAINTANCE.
THE_PLEASURE_ IS_ALL_MINE
THEY_CALL_ME_ **TINKERER**
THEY DO, DO THEY?

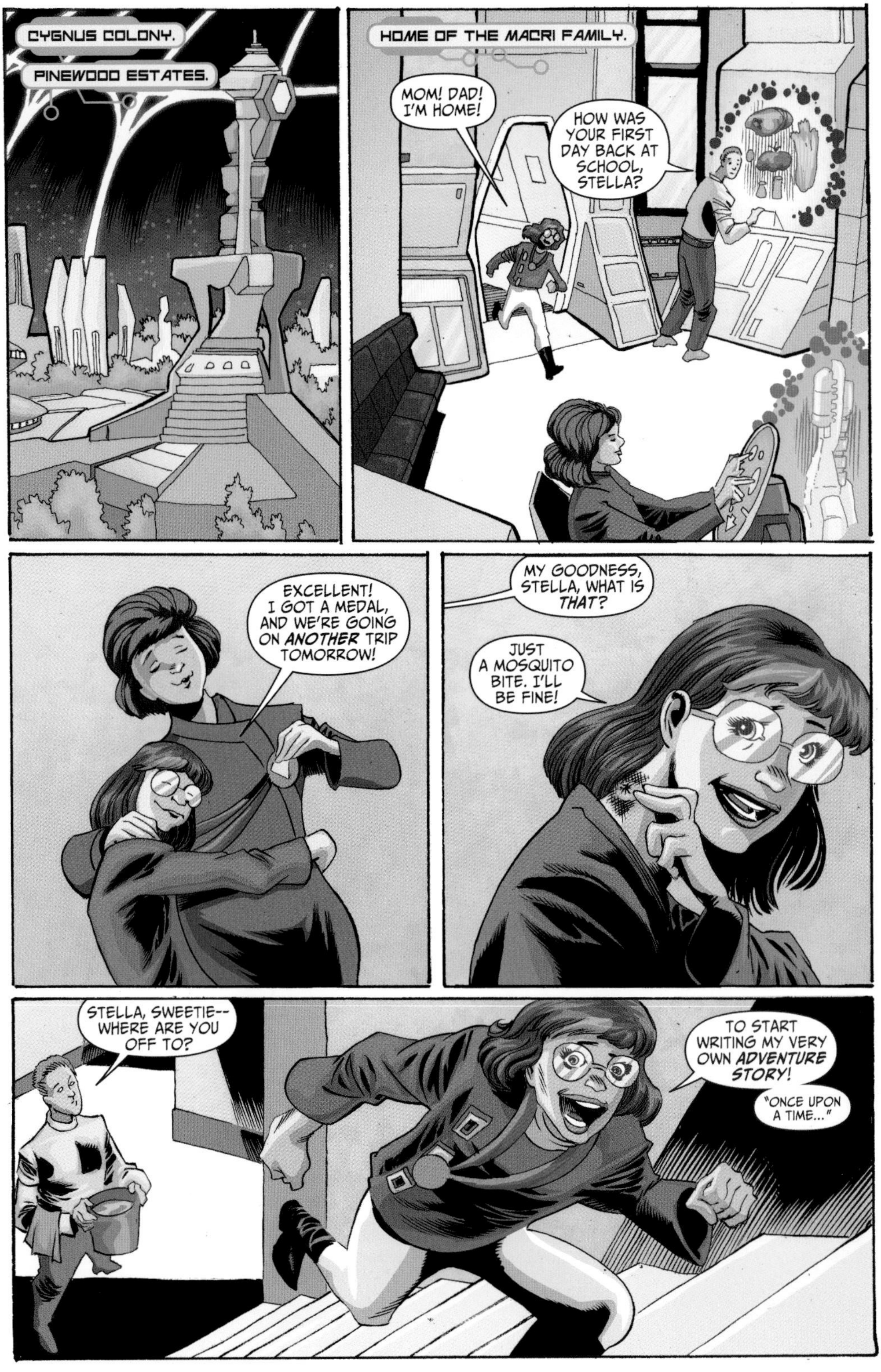
CYGNUS COLONY.
PINEWOOD ESTATES.
HOME OF THE MACRI FAMILY.
MOM! DAD! I'M HOME!
HOW WAS YOUR FIRST DAY BACK AT SCHOOL, STELLA?
EXCELLENT! I GOT A MEDAL, AND WE'RE GOING ON ANOTHER TRIP TOMORROW!
MY GOODNESS, STELLA, WHAT IS THAT?
JUST A MOSQUITO BITE. I'LL BE FINE!
STELLA, SWEETIE-- WHERE ARE YOU OFF TO?
TO START WRITING MY VERY OWN ADVENTURE STORY!
"ONCE UPON A TIME..."

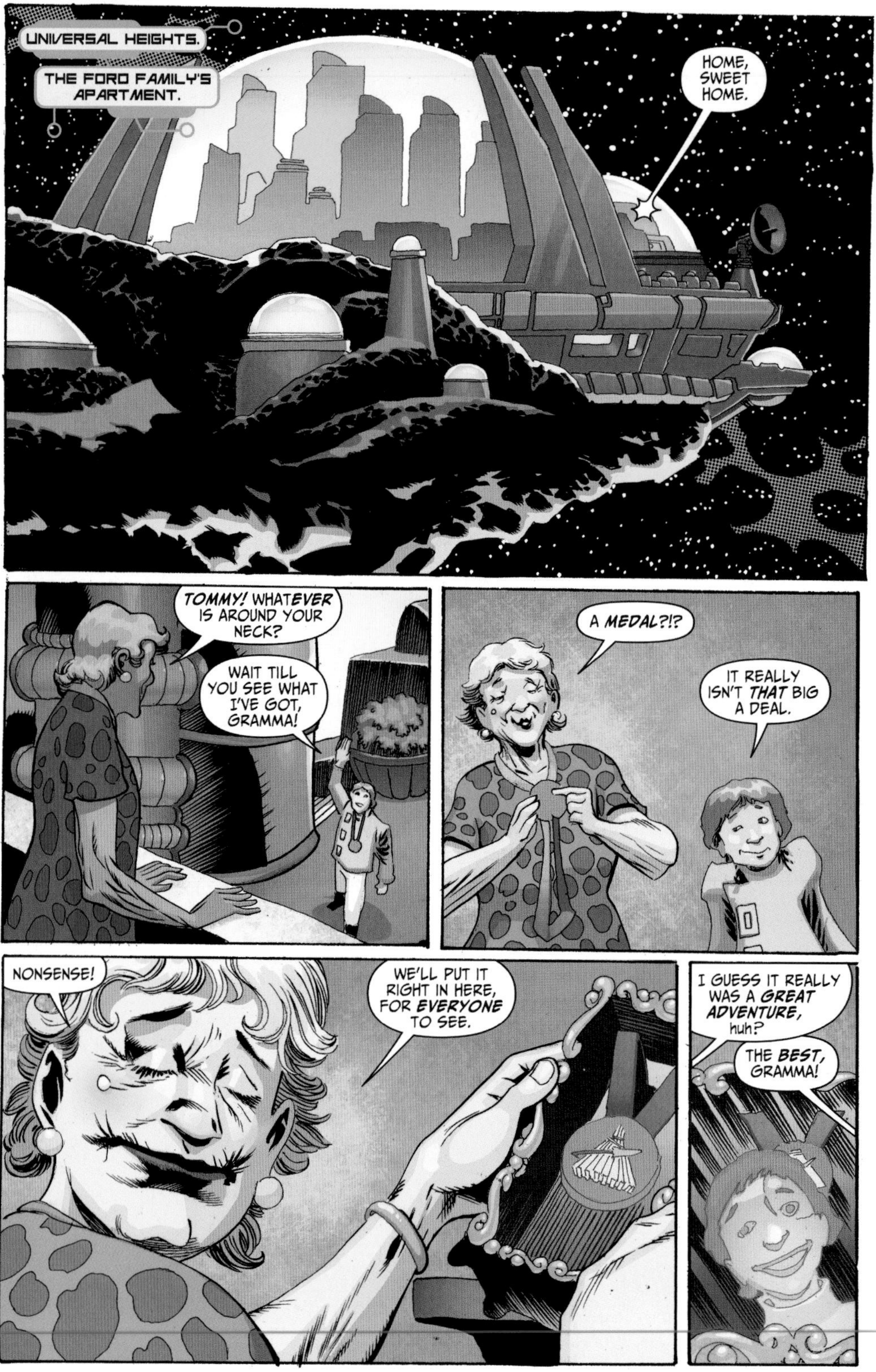
UNIVERSAL HEIGHTS.
THE FORD FAMILY'S APARTMENT.
HOME, SWEET HOME.
TOMMY! WHATEVER IS AROUND YOUR NECK?
WAIT TILL YOU SEE WHAT I'VE GOT, GRAMMA!
A MEDAL?!?
IT REALLY ISN'T THAT BIG A DEAL.
NONSENSE!
WE'LL PUT IT RIGHT IN HERE, FOR EVERYONE TO SEE.
I GUESS IT REALLY WAS A GREAT ADVENTURE, huh?
THE BEST, GRAMMA!

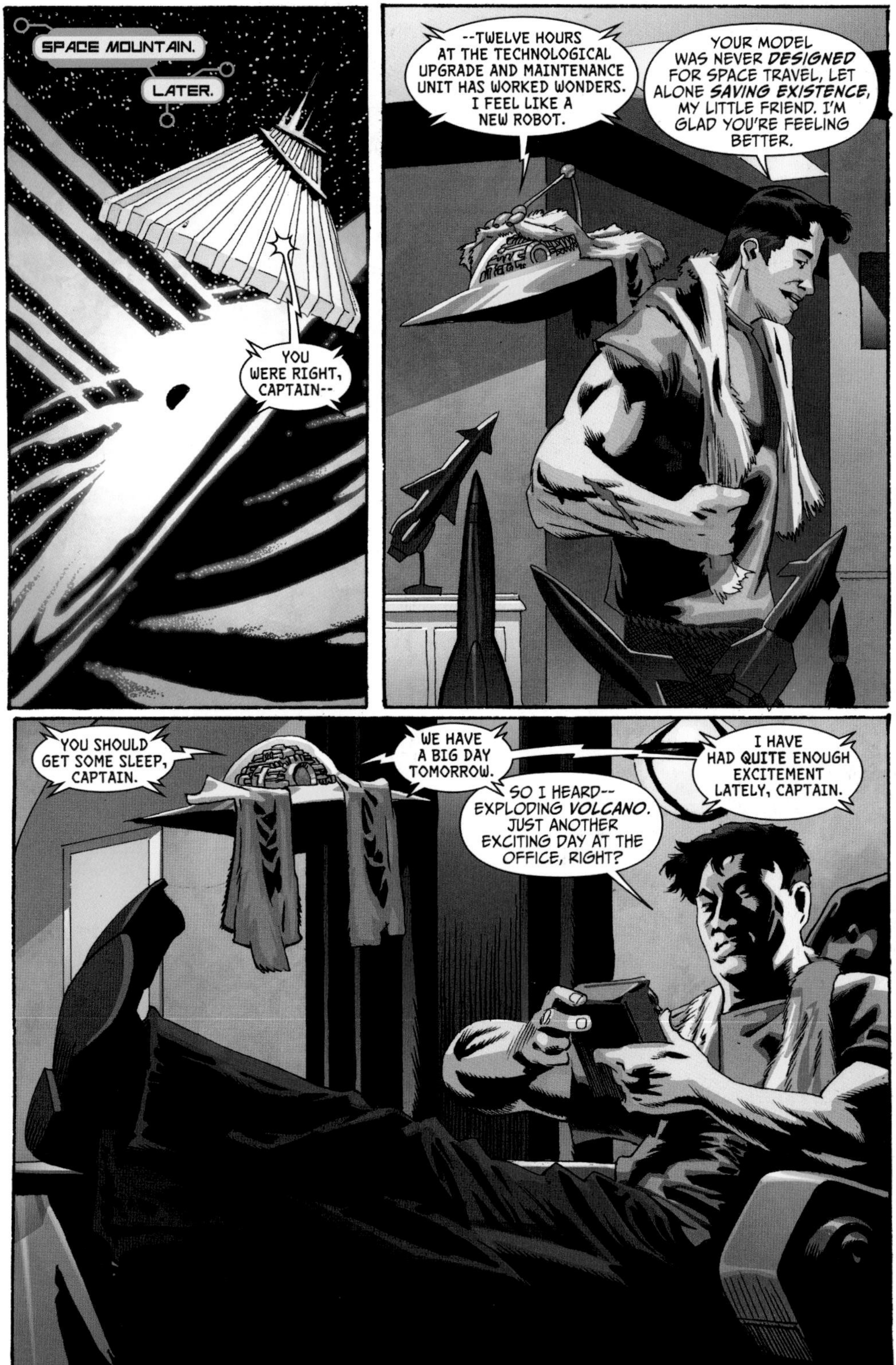
SPACE MOUNTAIN.
LATER.
YOU WERE RIGHT, CAPTAIN--
--TWELVE HOURS AT THE TECHNOLOGICAL UPGRADE AND MAINTENANCE UNIT HAS WORKED WONDERS. I FEEL LIKE A NEW ROBOT.
YOUR MODEL WAS NEVER DESIGNED FOR SPACE TRAVEL, LET ALONE SAVING EXISTENCE, MY LITTLE FRIEND. I'M GLAD YOU'RE FEELING BETTER.
YOU SHOULD GET SOME SLEEP, CAPTAIN.
WE HAVE A BIG DAY TOMORROW.
SO I HEARD-- EXPLODING VOLCANO. JUST ANOTHER EXCITING DAY AT THE OFFICE, RIGHT?
I HAVE HAD QUITE ENOUGH EXCITEMENT LATELY, CAPTAIN.

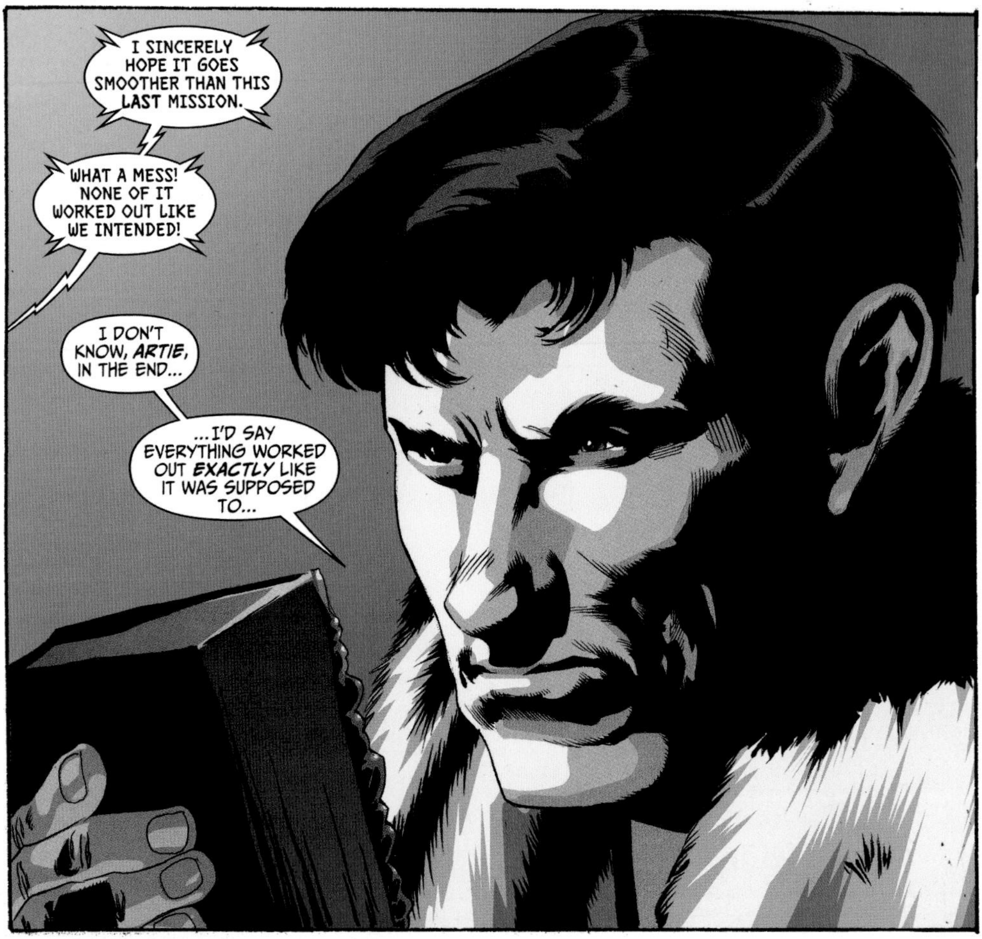
I SINCERELY HOPE IT GOES SMOOTHER THAN THIS LAST MISSION.
WHAT A MESS! NONE OF IT WORKED OUT LIKE WE INTENDED!
I DON'T KNOW, ARTIE, IN THE END...
...I'D SAY EVERYTHING WORKED OUT EXACTLY LIKE IT WAS SUPPOSED TO...

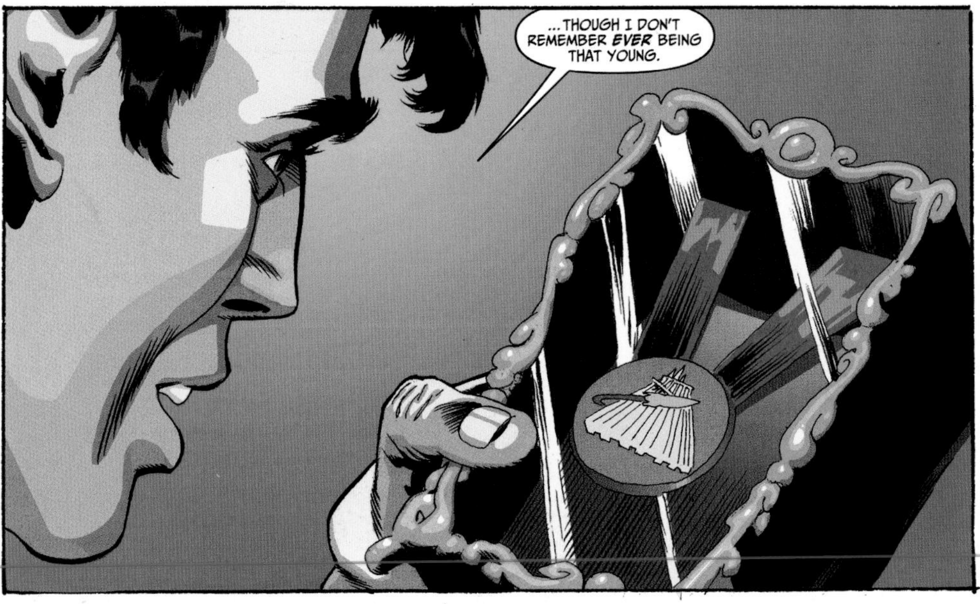
...THOUGH I DON'T REMEMBER EVER BEING THAT YOUNG.

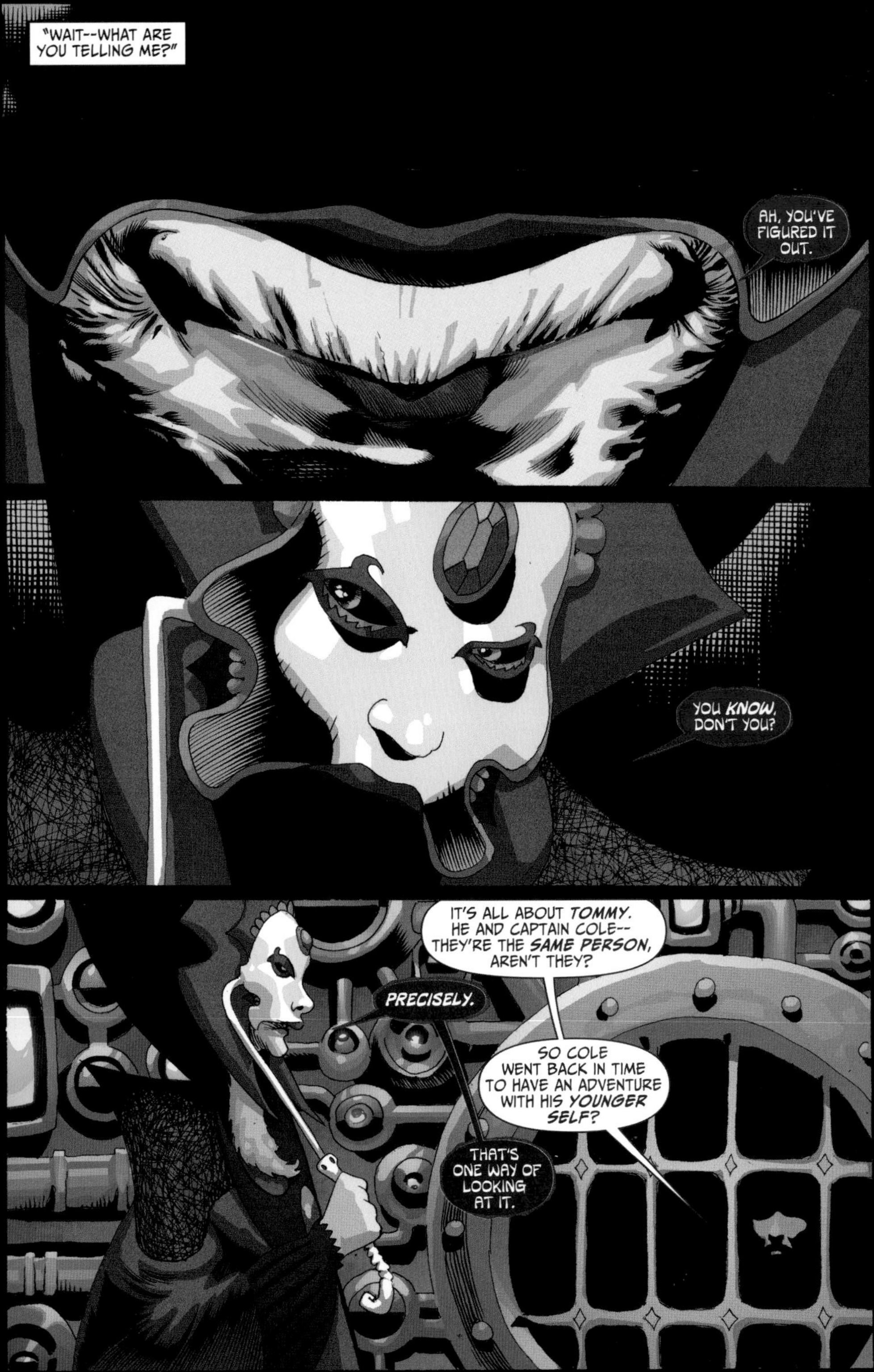
"WAIT--WHAT ARE YOU TELLING ME?"
AH, YOU'VE FIGURED IT OUT.
YOU KNOW, DON'T YOU?
IT'S ALL ABOUT TOMMY. HE AND CAPTAIN COLE-- THEY'RE THE SAME PERSON, AREN'T THEY?
PRECISELY.
SO COLE WENT BACK IN TIME TO HAVE AN ADVENTURE WITH HIS YOUNGER SELF?
THAT'S ONE WAY OF LOOKING AT IT.

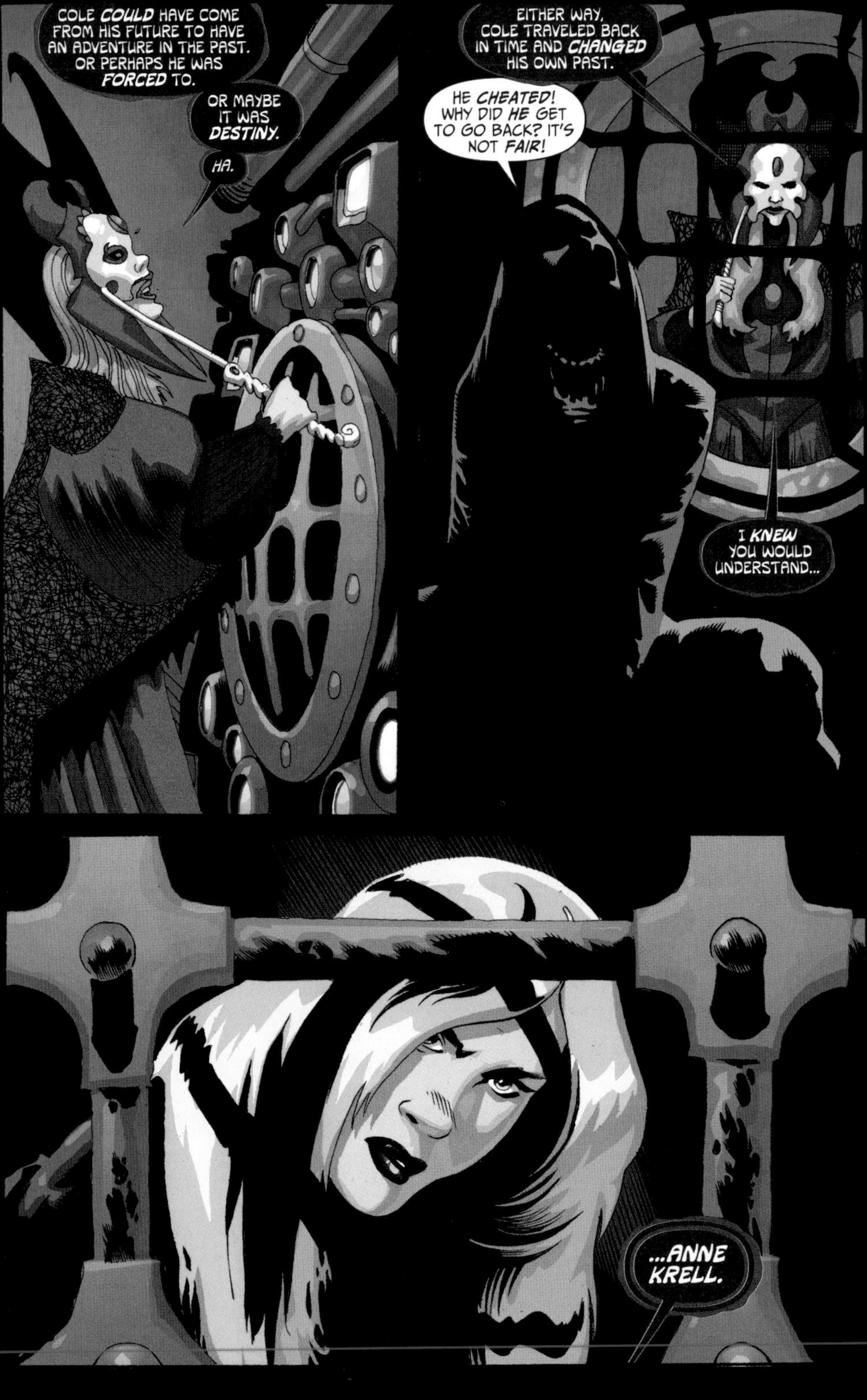
COLE COULD HAVE COME FROM HIS FUTURE TO HAVE AN ADVENTURE IN THE PAST. OR PERHAPS HE WAS FORCED TO.
OR MAYBE IT WAS DESTINY.
HA.
EITHER WAY, COLE TRAVELED BACK IN TIME AND CHANGED HIS OWN PAST.
HE CHEATED! WHY DID HE GET TO GO BACK? IT'S NOT FAIR!
I KNEW YOU WOULD UNDERSTAND...
...ANNE KRELL.

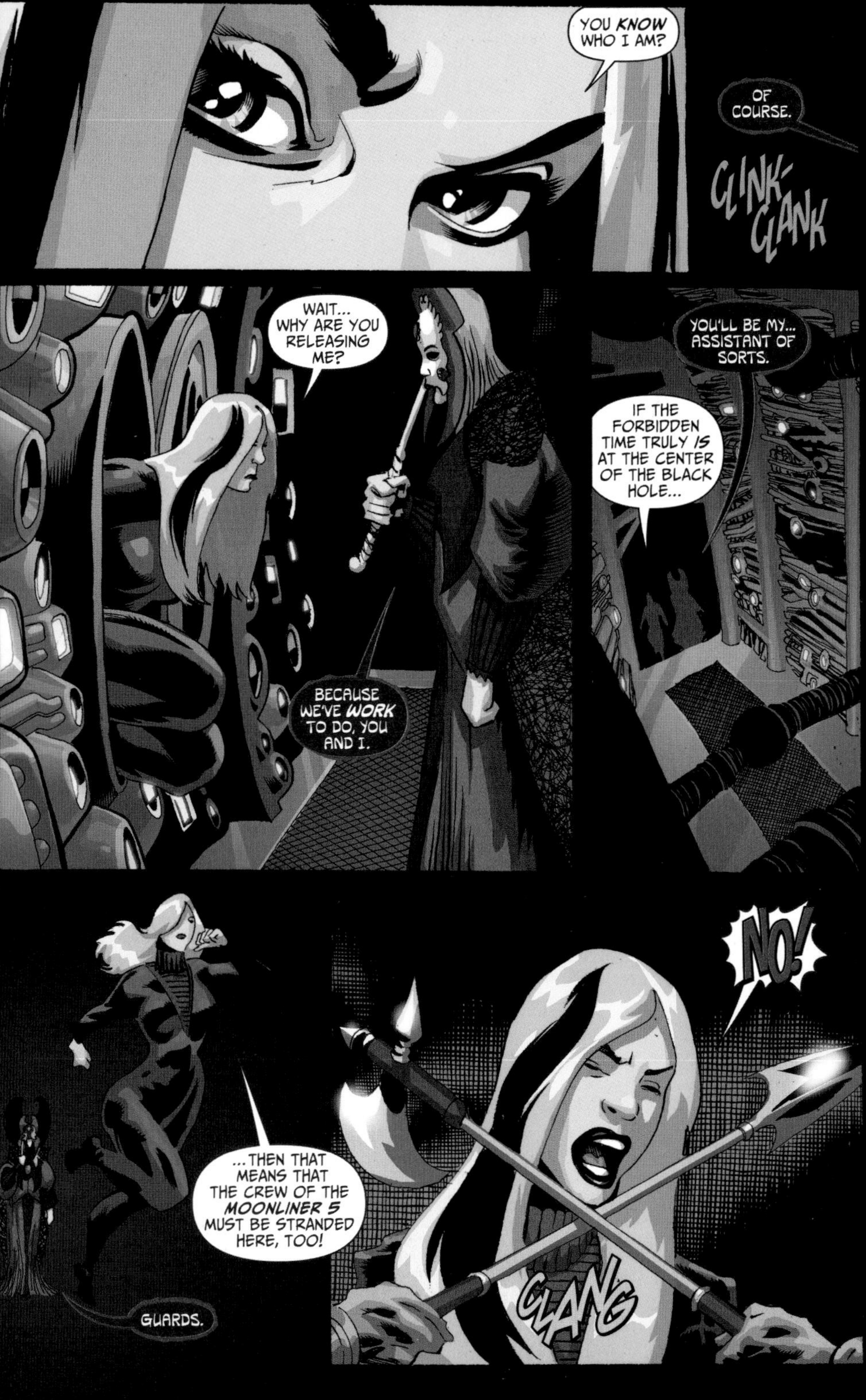
YOU KNOW WHO I AM?
OF COURSE.
CLINK-CLANK
WAIT... WHY ARE YOU RELEASING ME?
BECAUSE WE'VE WORK TO DO, YOU AND I.
YOU'LL BE MY... ASSISTANT OF SORTS.
IF THE FORBIDDEN TIME TRULY IS AT THE CENTER OF THE BLACK HOLE...
...THEN THAT MEANS THAT THE CREW OF THE MOONLINER 5 MUST BE STRANDED HERE, TOO!
GUARDS.
NO!
CLANG

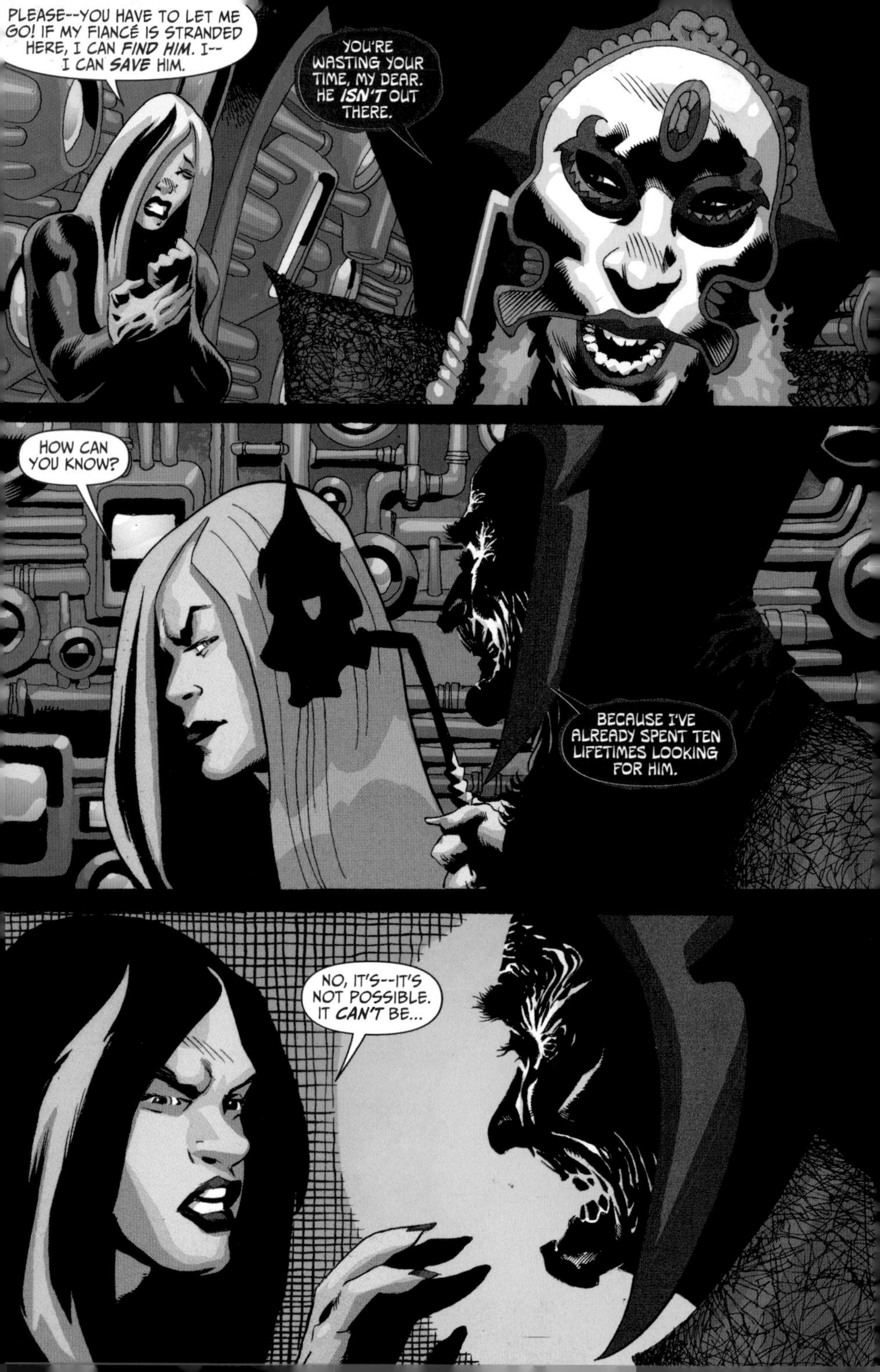
PLEASE--YOU HAVE TO LET ME GO! IF MY FIANCÉ IS STRANDED HERE, I CAN FIND HIM. I-- I CAN SAVE HIM.
YOU'RE WASTING YOUR TIME, MY DEAR. HE ISN'T OUT THERE.
HOW CAN YOU KNOW?
BECAUSE I'VE ALREADY SPENT TEN LIFETIMES LOOKING FOR HIM.
NO, IT'S--IT'S NOT POSSIBLE. IT CAN'T BE...

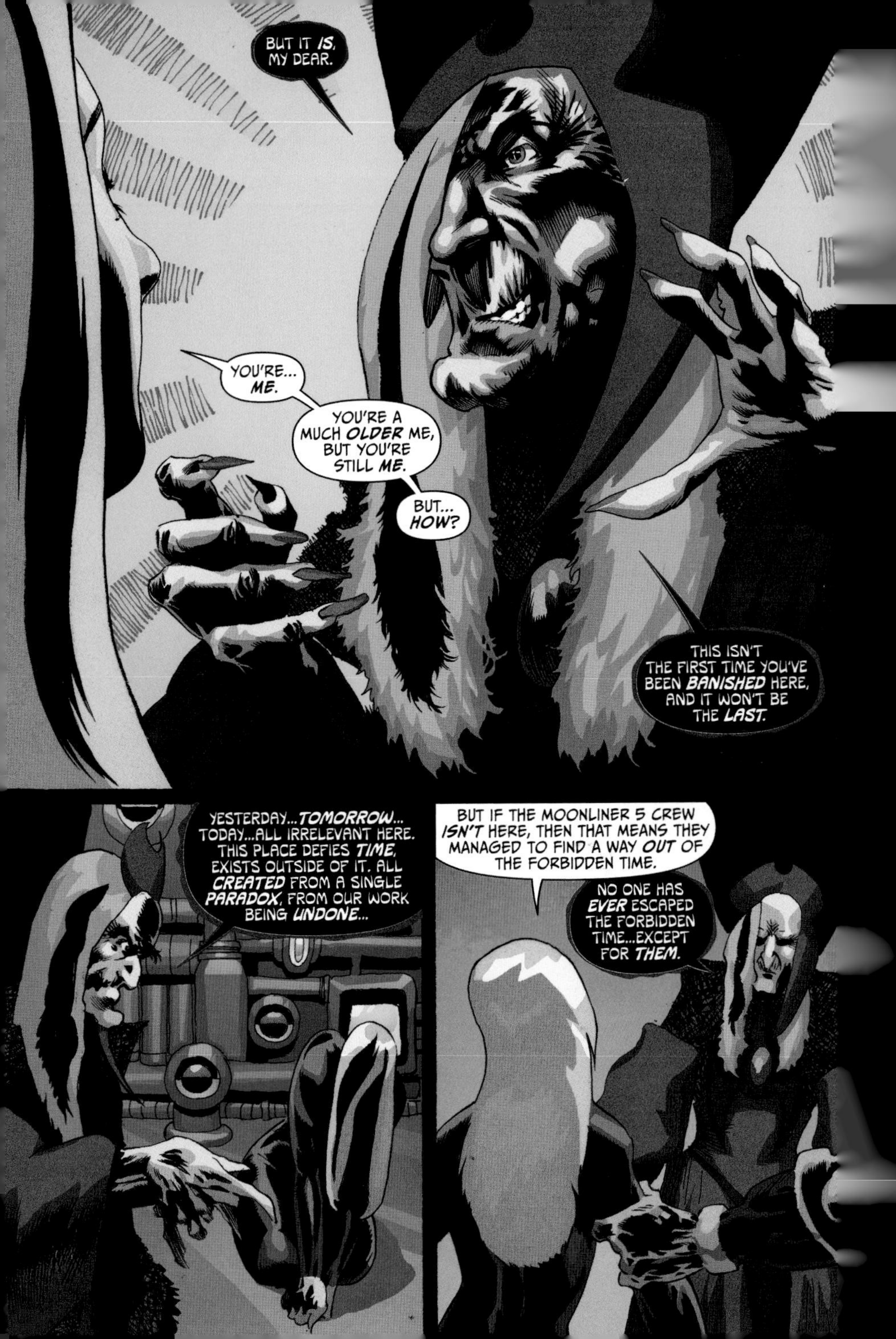

BUT IT IS, MY DEAR.
YOU'RE... ME.
YOU'RE A MUCH OLDER ME, BUT YOU'RE STILL ME.
BUT... HOW?
THIS ISN'T THE FIRST TIME YOU'VE BEEN BANISHED HERE, AND IT WON'T BE THE LAST.
YESTERDAY...TOMORROW... TODAY...ALL IRRELEVANT HERE. THIS PLACE DEFIES TIME, EXISTS OUTSIDE OF IT. ALL CREATED FROM A SINGLE PARADOX, FROM OUR WORK BEING UNDONE...
BUT IF THE MOONLINER 5 CREW ISN'T HERE, THEN THAT MEANS THEY MANAGED TO FIND A WAY OUT OF THE FORBIDDEN TIME.
NO ONE HAS EVER ESCAPED THE FORBIDDEN TIME...EXCEPT FOR THEM.

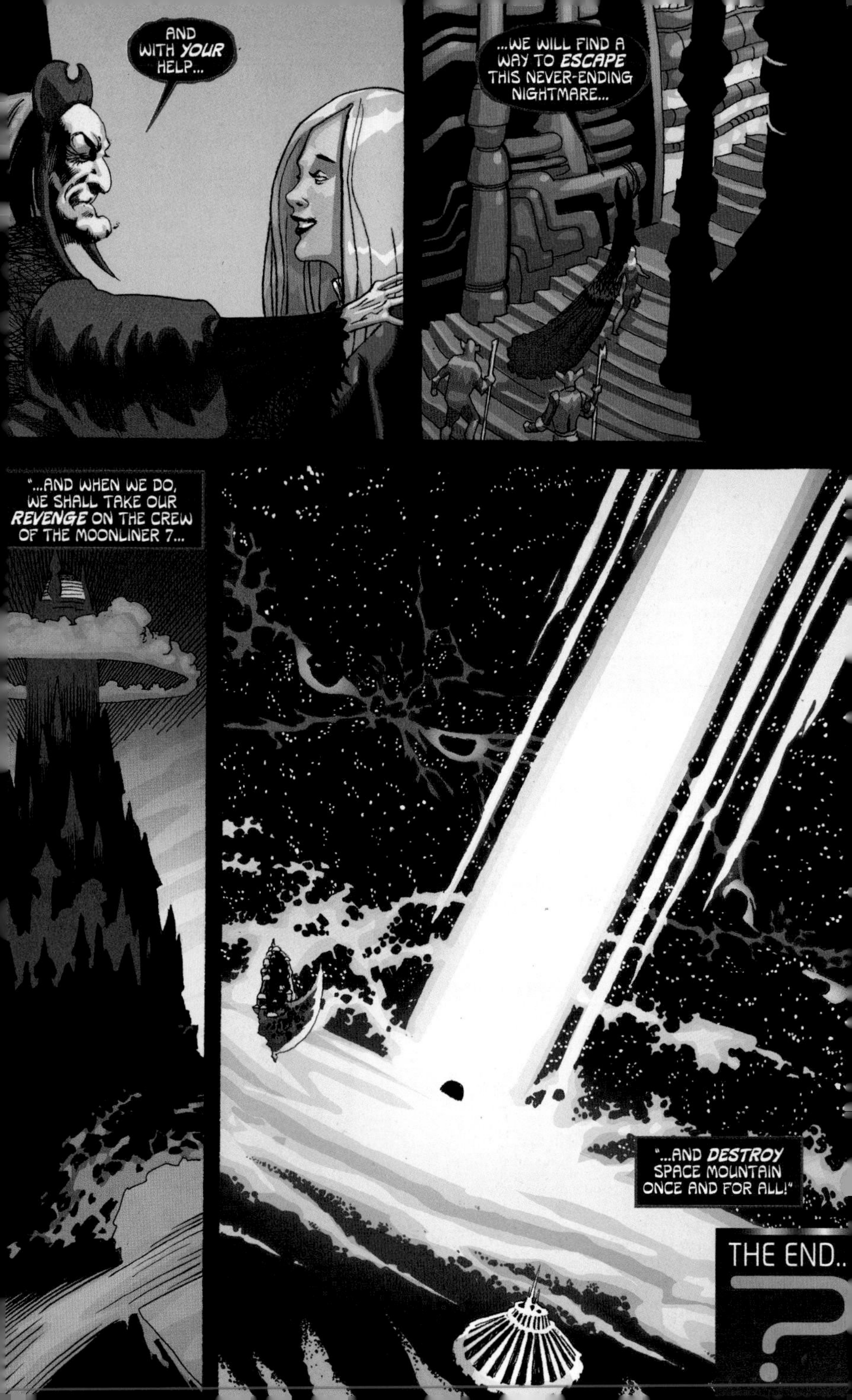
AND WITH YOUR HELP...
...WE WILL FIND A WAY TO ESCAPE THIS NEVER-ENDING NIGHTMARE...
"...AND WHEN WE DO, WE SHALL TAKE OUR REVENGE ON THE CREW OF THE MOONLINER 7...
"...AND DESTROY SPACE MOUNTAIN ONCE AND FOR ALL!"
THE END..?

THE END

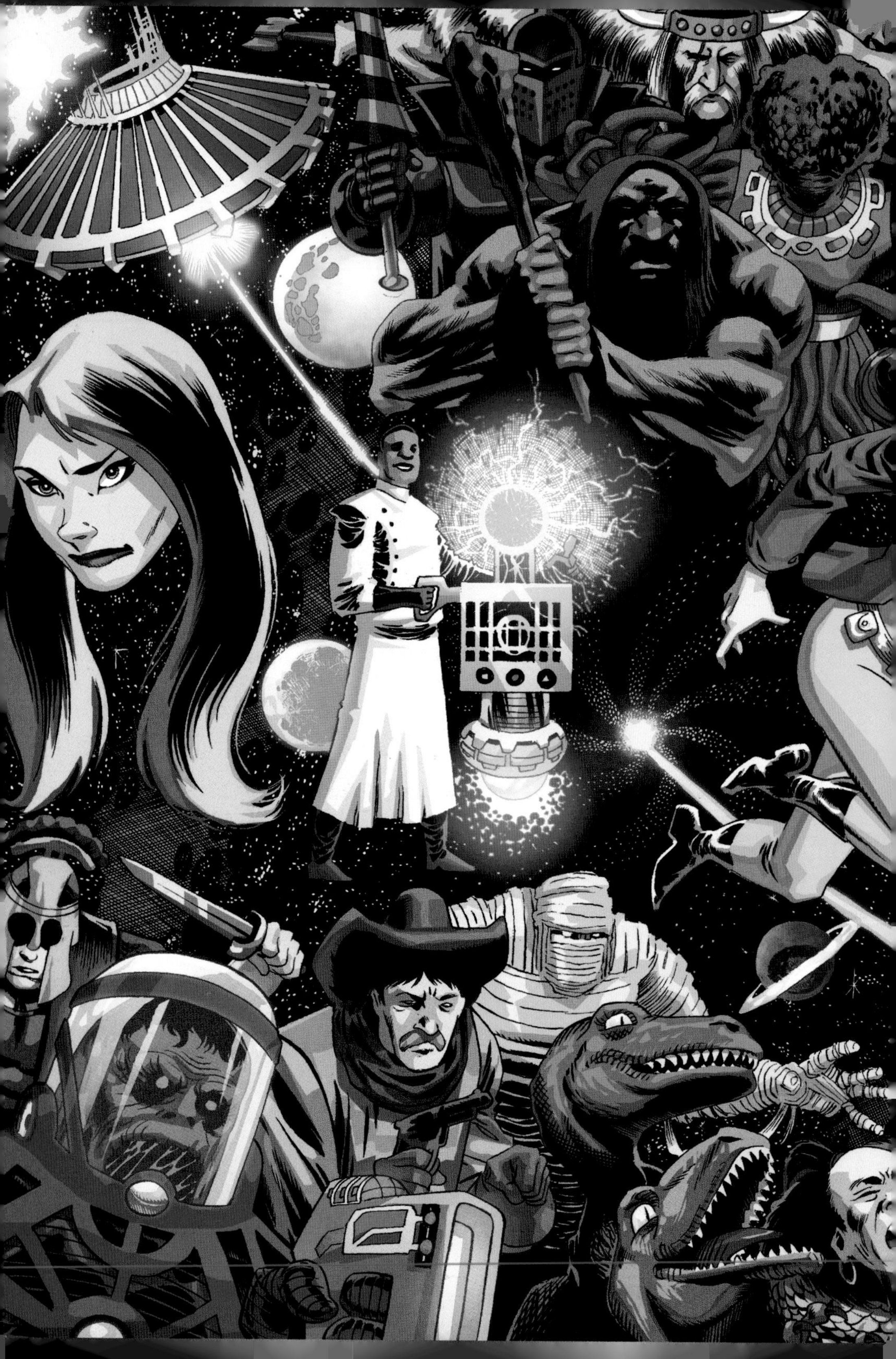

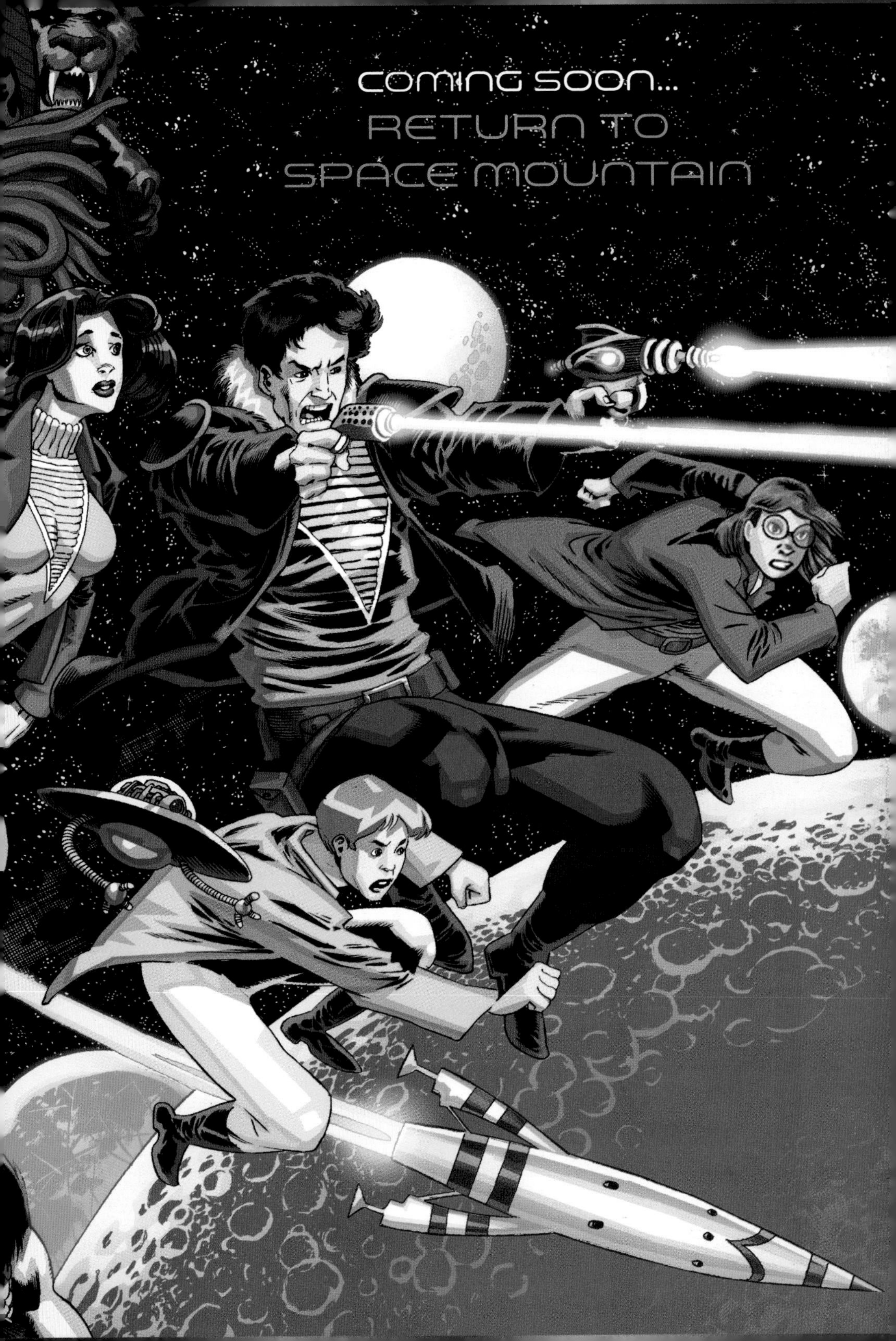
COMING SOON...
RETURN TO
SPACE MOUNTAIN

BEHIND THE SCENES OF *SPACE MOUNTAIN*: SCRIPT PAGE

Here's a look at the how this comic book was made, from the script page to the finished page. We start with Bryan Q. Miller's sensational script, which, at this point in the story, focuses on the crew of the Moonliner 7 as they travel toward the black hole...and have some fun along the way.

BRYAN Q. MILLER / SPACE MOUNTAIN / CHAPTER 3

PAGE FOUR

INT. COCKPIT - MOONLINER 7
PANEL ONE
ON TOMMY, smiling ARTIE's way, taking in the mess he's made.

1. TOMMY: Hey ARTIE, would you mind helping get this cleaned up?

2. ARTIE: Acknowledged, Cadet.

PANEL TWO
ARTIE zips around the cabin, vacuuming up the spheres. Tommy's drifting back down by Stella "p-shaw!" expression. Stella's arms are folded and she's rolling her eyes.

3. SFX (on ARTIE): sip!

4. STELLA: I'm SHOCKED, Tommy - you didn't read ARTIE's manual, DID you?

5. TOMMY: With as much as I know about machines, are you kidding me?

6. TOMMY: ARTIE's model is state of the art! I've got blueprints of his assembly run on my wall at home.

7. ARTIE: Well, now I'm just uncomfortable.

PANEL THREE
ON COLE, strapping himself back in - behind him, everyone starts to climb back down into their seats. He's about to hit a green-lit switch.

8. COLE: Okay, okay - enough fun, folks. Gravity coming back on in three, two...

PANEL FOUR
Cole hits the switch, turning it red, and they all flop back down into their seats.

9. SFX (on floor): GRVVVVVVVV

10. ALL: woop / ow / oof / okay

BEHIND THE SCENES OF *SPACE MOUNTAIN*: *PENCILS PAGE*

Bryan's superb script then went to the great Kelley Jones to pencil. Check out all the detail (and emotion) Kelley put into these impressive pencils. Also notice how the storytelling evolves from one stage to the other, but how the main point of the scene always stays the same.

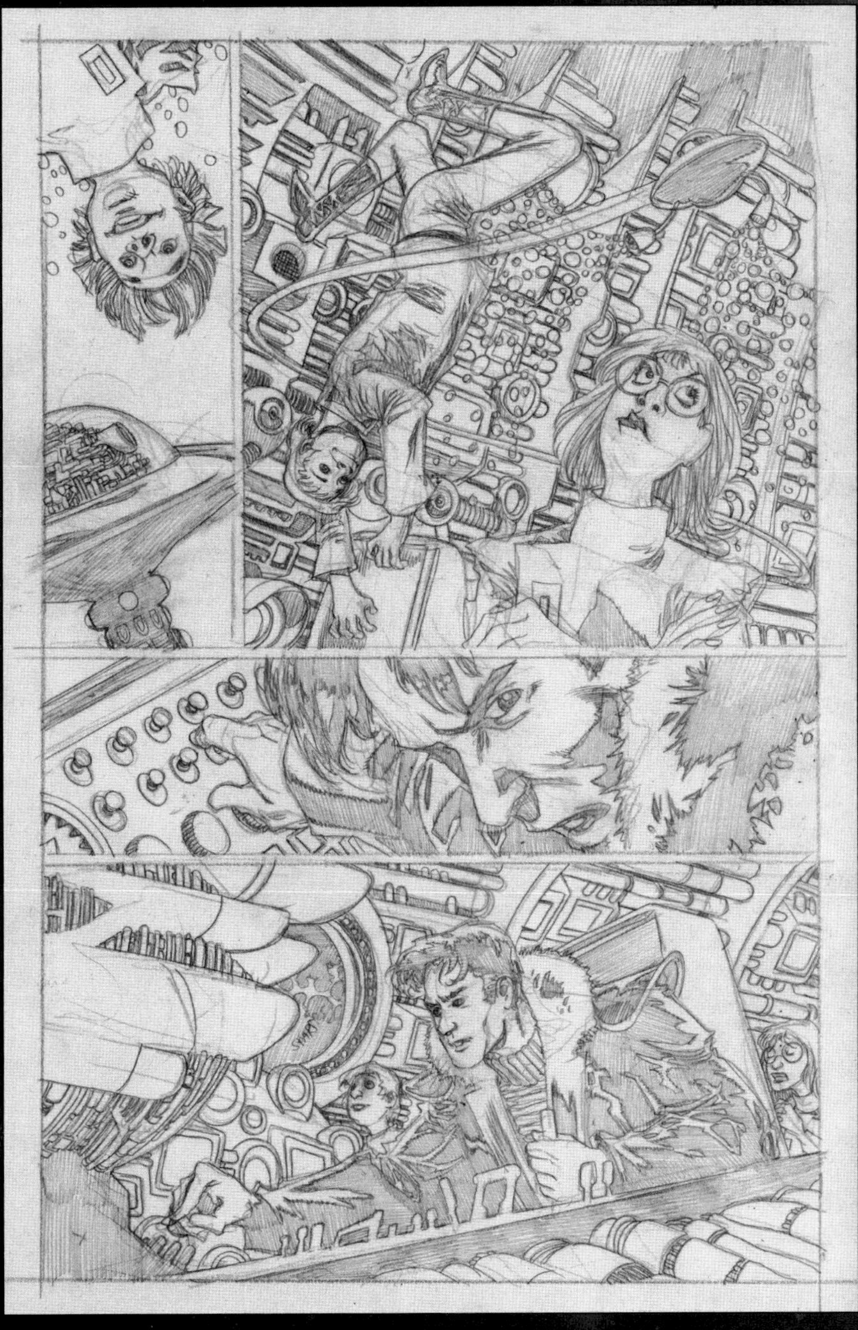

BEHIND THE SCENES OF *SPACE MOUNTAIN*: *INKS PAGE*

Kelley then put down his pencil and picked up a brush and a bottle of ink. He very meticulously went over every pencil line, adding depth, shadow, and weight with every thin and thick black line. Man, this guy is good!

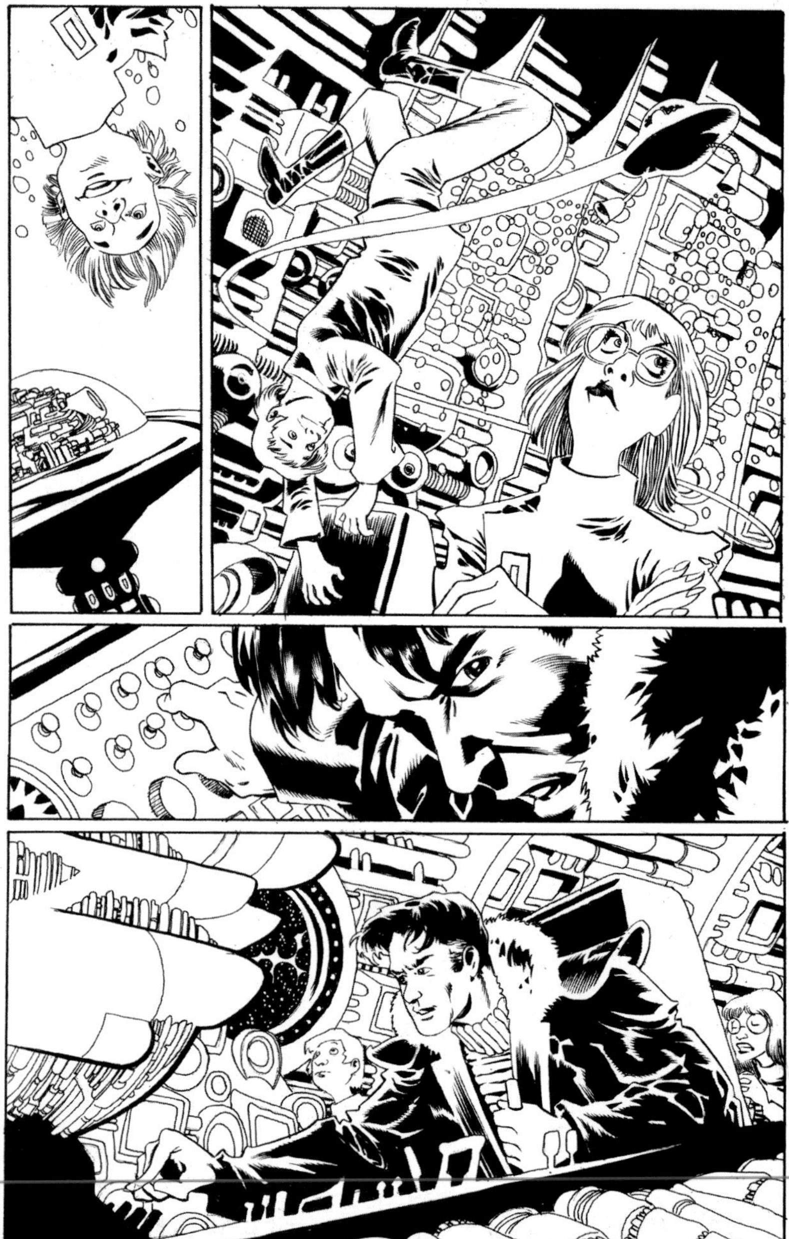

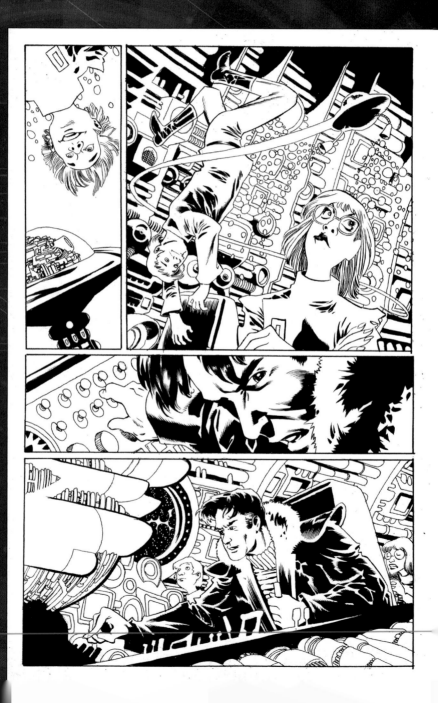

BEHIND THE SCENES OF *SPACE MOUNTAIN*: *COLORS PAGE*

From there, the always-amazing Rob Leigh added the lettering, sound effects, and the word balloons, and Brian Miller, the colorist—not to be confused with Bryan Q. Miller, the writer—added various combinations of red, yellow, and blue to bring the page to life in startling and vibrant color. Great work from a great team!

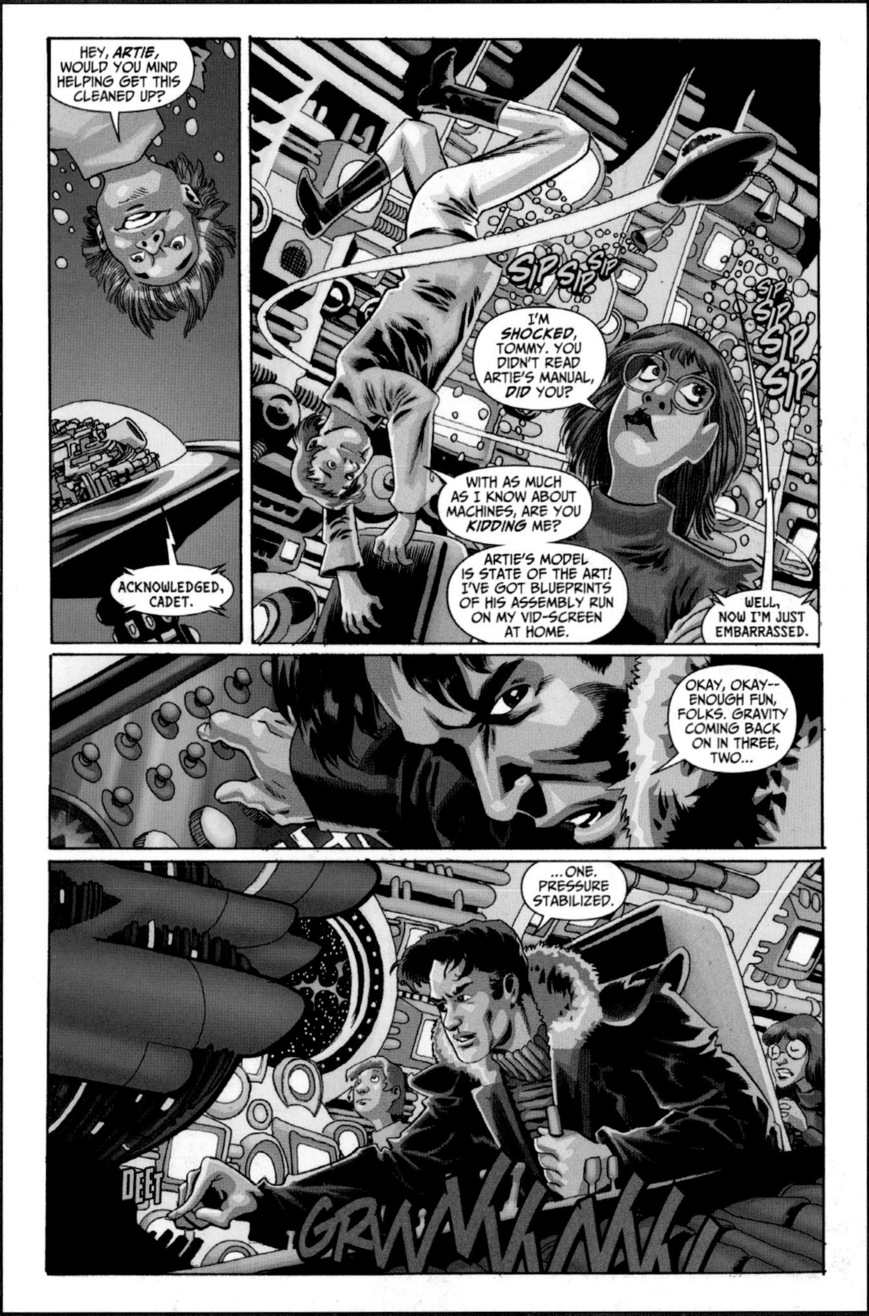

HEY, *ARTIE*, WOULD YOU MIND HELPING GET THIS CLEANED UP?
ACKNOWLEDGED, CADET.
SIP SIP SIP SIP
SIP SIP SIP SIP
I'M *SHOCKED*, TOMMY. YOU DIDN'T READ ARTIE'S MANUAL, *DID* YOU?
WITH AS MUCH AS I KNOW ABOUT MACHINES, ARE YOU *KIDDING* ME?
ARTIE'S MODEL IS STATE OF THE ART! I'VE GOT BLUEPRINTS OF HIS ASSEMBLY RUN ON MY VID-SCREEN AT HOME.
WELL, NOW I'M JUST EMBARRASSED.
OKAY, OKAY-- ENOUGH FUN, FOLKS. GRAVITY COMING BACK ON IN THREE, TWO...
...ONE. PRESSURE STABILIZED.
DEET
GRWKKKKK

SPACE MOUNTAIN

BIOS

BRYAN Q. MILLER

Wondernaut and fair-weather Fictionary, Bryan Q. Miller has written television (most notably Syfy's *Defiance* and the CW's *Arrow* and *Smallville*), features, and the printed page (*Teen Titans*; *Batgirl*, Vol. 3; *Smallville*, season 11). He lives in Los Angeles, doesn't eat meat, and will always love astronauts, no matter how hard the march of time would like us to forget. He has also never seen a Frankenstein.

KELLEY JONES

Kelley Jones has been drawing comics for almost thirty years. While he is known for working with Neil Gaiman on *Sandman* and bringing life to DC's *Deadman*, he is most known for being one of the definitive artists on *Batman*. Kelley lives in Northern California with his wife, Lynn, and his two sons, Sam and Carter, along with a bunch of cats, dogs, lizards, fish, and a big spider named Hairy Kong.

HI-FI COLOUR DESIGN, BRIAN & KRISTY MILLER

In 1998, Brian walked away from an art director's position to start Hi-Fi Colour Design with Kristy and a group of talented creators. Kristy handles the day-to-day, nonartistic side of Hi-Fi, while Brian continues to color, paint, and art direct. Hi-Fi Colour Design currently works for many major toy and game manufacturers, as well as comic and book publishers, and has worked on every character from Amethyst to Zatanna, so you could say Hi-Fi has colored it all from A to Z.

ROB LEIGH

Rob Leigh has been in the comics biz for over twenty years as a letterer and inker. A graduate of the Kubert School, he resides in the northeast with his wife, Vaughan, and his cat/studiomate, Barley. On the rare occasions his editors unchain him from his computer, he escapes to the sanctuary of woods and water.

MICHAEL SIGLAIN

Before joining Disney Publishing, Mike was lucky enough to work in film and television production, and at DC Comics, where, among other things, he edited their flagship title *Detective Comics*. While at Disney, Mike has worked on live-action film tie-in books and Marvel Press Super Hero books, and is excited to start work on a few upcoming Lucasfilm titles. Mike lives on Long Island with his wife and two young daughters, and knows just how lucky he is.